Roms, Bombs & Zoms

Edited by
Monique Snyman

EVIL GIRLFRIEND MEDIA

Published by Evil Girlfriend Media, P.O. BOX 3856, Federal Way, WA 98063
Copyright © 2013

All rights reserved. Any reproduction or distribution of this book, in part or in whole, or transmission in any form, or by any means, electronic, mechanical, photocopying, recording or otherwise, without the written permission of the publisher or author is theft.
Any similarity to persons living or dead is purely coincidental.

Cover photo by Christy Varonfakis Johnson.
Cover design by Matt Youngmark.

"I'll Come Back," copyright © 2013 by Michelle Kilmer.
"Nathan's Promise," copyright © 2013 by Ken MacGregor.
"Your Cheatin' Heart," copyright © 2013 by Katie Cord, reprinted from *He Left Her at the Altar, She Left Him to the Zombies*
"Needs of a Half-Dead Heart," copyright © 2013 by Randy Henderson.
"When the Last War Ended," copyright © 2013 Paul S. Huggins.
"What I Was There For," copyright © 2013 by Matt Youngmark and Dawn Marie Pares.
"The Second Battle of Gettysburg," copyright © 2013 by Kriscinda Lee Everitt.
"Though She Be Little, She Is Fierce," copyright © 2013 by Michele Roger.
"Church of the Risen Dead," copyright © 2013 by Tom D. Wright.
"Post Bomb Zombie Romland," copyright © 2013 by Dana Wright.
"Mama," copyright © 2013 by Jay Wilburn.
"Soul Ties," copyright © 2013 by Katie Jones.
"Until the End," copyright © 2013 by Patrick D'Orazio.
"From Safety to Where," copyright © 2013 by Kris Freestone.
"The Tower," copyright © 2013 by Joshua Brown.
"Till Death We Do Not Part," copyright © 2013 by Killion Slade.
"An Undying Love," copyright © 2013 by John Edward Betancourt.
"I've Got You Under My Skin," copyright © 2013 by Anthony J. Rapino and Monique Snyman.

ISBN-13: 978-0615910833
ISBN-10: 0615910831

Dedicated to all those who are clueless in romance,

dropping bombs without intent,

and for those brave zombies of heartache,

who rise and love again.

Table of Contents

Foreward, *Monique Snyman* **7**

I'll Come Back, *Michelle Kilmer* **9**

Nathan's Promise, *Ken MacGregor* **25**

Your Cheatin' Heart, *Katie Cord* **31**

Needs of a Half-Dead Heart, *Randy Henderson* **45**

When the Last War Ended, *Paul S. Huggins* **57**

What I Was There For, *Matt Youngmark and Dawn Marie Pares* **69**

The Second Battle of Gettysburg, *Kriscinda Lee Everitt* **89**

Though She Be Little, She Is Fierce, *Michele Roger* **113**

Church of the Risen Dead, *Tom D. Wright* **125**

Post Bomb Zombie Romland, *Dana Wright* **143**

Mama, *Jay Wilburn* **159**

Soul Ties, *Katie Jones* **175**

Until the End, *Patrick D'Orazio* **189**

From Safety to Where, *Kris Freestone* **219**

The Tower, *Joshua Brown* **237**

Till Death We Do Not Part, *Killion Slade* **249**

An Undying Love, *John Edward Betancourt* **263**

I've Got You Under My Skin, *Anthony J. Rapino and Monique Snyman* **275**

Biographies **291**

Introduction

What makes us human? Many philosophers have tried to provide an answer, which generally leans toward our ability to think logically, but many people may not concur with that train of thought. What's more is the question as to whether the undead—*if* such a catastrophe ever occurs—will still have remnants of their humanity left, after they have died... Now, personally I can't answer the latter, but I can give my opinion on the question of what makes us human. For one, I believe that our compassion differentiates us from everything else. Granted, sometimes it's difficult to find compassion in the modern world, but it is out there, and *Roms, Bombs & Zoms* has incorporated that theme into the anthology.

Every story that has been selected has three very distinctive things present. Romance, bombs, and zombies. Each of these three characteristics can be interpreted in various ways. Romance, generally used to show love towards someone/something else, brings out the humanity in the stories. Bombs, interpreted in a number of ways—from literal to metaphorical—is used to showcase the calamity that these characters have to go through—living, dead, or undead. And lastly we have the zombies, which can be interpreted as the traditional, ripping your face off with their teeth kind of zombies or the kind where everyone is transfixed with updating their Facebook status, but is generally used just to make things extra awesome for the reader.

Roms, Bombs & Zoms features new writers, as well as a few distinguished authors, each with their own unique story and twist. We have traditional zombies, modern zombies and we even have a bit of necromancy here and there to keep things interesting. Love is present in various forms, and bombs... boy do we have some great bombs in this anthology! But there is so much more to offer than just that.

Every story was selected to entertain the reader, while keeping in mind the question of what makes us human, as well as touching on the subject of what happens to our humanity when we turn into flesh-eating monsters that would devour our own mothers when we rise from the dead. We also have superheroes, wizards, necromancers, viruses, scientists and even some B-movie interpretations featured in this book. Frankly, it's just one big joyride through the valley of death, but hey, you be the judge.

Monique Snyman, Editor
Pretoria, South Africa
April 17, 2013

I'LL COME BACK
By Michelle Kilmer

In a small farm community—still untouched by a spreading plague—in a back room of a cottage, a young man gently pulled a wooden chair away from a desk, trying to keep its legs from scraping on the floor and waking his lover. The candlelight flickered, creating moving shadows over her strong form. He pulled a single sheet of paper to the middle of the tabletop and began his first letter to her.

Anne,

We promised to write each other during the war, but I have started my first letter early. I'm so happy that you came to my cottage this evening. You look so soft and warm and that is how I want to remember you. Not wearing fatigues, not carrying a sniper rifle. You are too delicate to be covered in all those layers of drab greens and browns and too kind to be covered in blood.

It's a backwards world we live in where the government would send our child-bearers and caregivers to the front lines. I'm a better shot than you, but the army didn't want to hear it. You are smaller and more agile. You have a heart that tells you the world is worth fighting for.

I can't believe you ship out tomorrow, and I cannot fathom this place without you. Please promise me that you'll come back.

Always,
Matthew

He folded the stiff paper, stuck it in an envelope and into a pocket of her army-issued duffel bag. Rejoining her under the blankets, he pressed his body close to hers and relished the feeling until he fell asleep too.

The next morning Anne was bursting with excitement and pacing the tiny kitchen. She was barely able to finish her breakfast.

"Do you think I'll get to kill any of them?" she asked Matthew as she stared dreamily out the kitchen window and across the farmland beyond.

"Your enthusiasm is frightening, Anne." Matthew sipped his steaming coffee and patted the table with his hand. "Sit down and eat. You won't be here again for a long time."

Anne did as he asked, but her legs bounced furiously under the table and she tapped her fork on the edge of the ceramic plate in front of her. "I can't stop thinking about what it will be like."

"The time will come when you are out there wishing you were back here eating your breakfast with me," Matthew said.

"Okay, okay. I'm eating!" Anne took a bite of eggs and finished them shortly after. Matthew cleared the table and picked up the overstuffed duffel bag that Anne had dragged to the door.

"It's time to go," he said sadly.

She followed him to his rusting pickup truck. They drove for a half hour to a makeshift army base in the nearest large city. The camp was a bustle of activity. Women of every imaginable shape, age and color were walking with purpose in all directions. Anne felt anxious to be dropped into the chaos, but she knew it was a relatively serene place when compared to the front lines of the war she was about to join.

Matthew turned to her in the cab of the truck. "Remember to keep your boots laced tight and your hair short." He tried to think of more survival tactics, but those were the only two that surfaced in his worried brain.

"Those are funny parting words, Matt," Anne laughed as she kissed him goodbye. She hopped from the truck and pulled her pack and duffel from the truck bed. The weight of the supplies forced her boots deeper into the muddy ground.

"I love you, Anne. And… aim for the head!" he yelled as she trudged off toward the check-in line.

A few weeks passed. He forced himself to wait for a letter from her before writing another one himself. One morning, after coming home from helping at his father's farm, a mailman brought him the envelope he'd been waiting for. His hands trembled as he ripped it open and read.

Dearest Matthew,

We've traveled so much it is becoming difficult to keep track of where I am. I guess wherever the dead are rising, that's where they'll send us next. You thought I was excited but the other women in my platoon, some of them scare me with their readiness to kill.

I found your letter in my duffel bag. Thankfully it didn't get wet in the poor weather we've had. I opened it at breakfast, a terrible slop they call rehydrated eggs. It tastes entirely manufactured; nothing like the eggs from our farms. I already wish I was back there eating breakfast with you.

Training was easy enough. In fact, it was almost the same as army basic training, except for a few additional courses that I will describe below.

Temporary Treatment of Bite Wounds—we had to bite one another so we could learn to recognize the feeling and they showed us several tourniquet techniques to reduce blood flow. We also practiced using sharp weapons to cut through animal bones. It felt wrong, but I know it will be much harder in the field if we have to do an amputation on the fly. The plague spreads so quickly once it gets inside of you. We have to move fast.

The Psychology of Killing Your Friends—you get the point. We were forced to describe an imaginary death of a partner. I chose my ex-boyfriend, because I simply could not imagine you in such a way. He was so dumb he may have already contracted the infection from one of these things.

Tracking the Infected—turns out this is very similar to tracking large game, broken twigs, footprints and the like. But we also learned how to recognize the smell of their rotting flesh. The worst part about this class was the recordings they played of their moaning. We could hear screams on the tape. Those people are probably dead.

Thinking of you,
Anne

Goosebumps grew on his arms every time he thought of the monsters she would have to battle. Matthew re-read the letter several times, even though half of its content grossed him out. He imagined her soft voice reading the words to him and he immediately sat down at his desk to write a letter back.

Anne,

I was so happy to receive your first correspondence but upon opening it, I became rather ill. You are a peculiar girl. Perhaps in later letters you can be less descriptive or talk on other subjects instead of the work you are doing. Tell me about the weather or more about the bad food. I don't want to know about the infected or the twisted things the army is drilling into your brain.

I was at my father's farm today. One of the pregnant cows had her calf after much difficulty. My father had to tie a rope around the calf's legs to pull it out. It was messy and I nearly lost my lunch. If you were here you would have been right in there helping, I know.

I've been thinking that it wouldn't take much for us to get a bigger place of our own. By the time you return home my savings will have doubled and my mother offered to give us the calf and some chickens to start a farm.

Please stay well,
Matthew

He took the freshly sealed envelope and ran from the cottage and down the road to catch up with the postal worker.

To pass time and in preparation for Anne's return, Matthew began looking for land that was both suitable for tillage and fair in price.

Across the ocean, the war against the plague raged on. Anne and her battalion were shipped away to Europe to bolster the troops of affected countries. Now that training had ended and the real fighting was on the horizon, she had little time to write home. It was a month and a half before she found a moment of downtime to pen another letter to her lover.

Matthew,

You can blame my father for making me so strange! I grew up killing the chickens for dinner by his request. None of it bothers me as it should, but they need people like me. Someone has to kill the infected.

I'm sorry this letter is so short; please don't think I am mad at you. We are moving towns once again and one step closer to battle.

-Anne

He looked the paper over for more words. The letter was too short and loveless. For weeks he waited for another letter, but one didn't come. Time passed painfully slowly, and he feared for Anne's safety as the news reported ever growing numbers of the infected. With a mailbag empty of letters for him, the postal worker avoided Matthew's gaze. His heart was saddened further when the new calf was found dead in his parents' barn. It was one less reason for Anne to protect herself and return home to him.

Anne,

I wish you would write more. I'm worried sick about you and my loneliness is unbearable at times. The calf that was promised to us has passed away and the farm doctor has no answers, my parents are torn up about it. The calf's mother wails mournfully at all hours.

I haven't given up on the search for our farm. I found a place with a home already built, but the cost is more than we'll ever have. Maybe if I tell them you are fighting in the war they'll lower the price?

Have you seen anything beautiful where they've shipped you? The world is so large and you've only ever seen here. It must be an incredible experience, beyond the killing.

With all of my love,
Matthew

―◆―

Just after Anne read the latest letter from Matthew, her battalion leader gave the women terrifying news. They would reach the front lines the next day and meet their undead adversaries head on. That night she lay awake in her tent, her body coursing with fear. In a tent somewhere nearby, another sleepless woman was reciting their training motto: *"In the head if they're dead,"* over and over again.

Before the sun rose, Anne fell into a fitful sleep and dreamed of a farm with a once beautiful house now wrecked by time and the elements. She lived there with Matthew and they were building a life together, but there was something off about the place. In the dream, Anne walked into the chicken coop and was hit with the smell of decay. She looked high and low, counting the chickens and searching for the one that had died, but she couldn't find a body. It was only when one of the chickens pecked a hole in one of her feet that she realized the living birds smelled like death. Once the chickens saw the blood, and smelled it, they all began to attack her. Anne ran from the coop, but her feet sank in the mud. She struggled to get free but her sharp movements only made the mud cling tighter around her legs. Across the field, the dead calf from Matthew's parents' farm walked slowly toward her, its eyes milky and its skin sloughing off.

She woke covered in sweat. When she emerged from her tent, she saw that all the other women were packed and ready to fight.

With fear still heavy in her body, she changed her clothes, packed her belongings and made sure her gun was clean.

Her first battle was reminiscent of one from the Civil War. Two sides met in the middle of a field and spilled each other's blood until a winner was declared. Luckily for the battalion, the infected had little strategy and hardly ever got creative. Not one of the women fell that day, but what they witnessed could never be unseen.

Matthew,

I know you don't want to hear about this, but I have to tell you. The infected are horrible. I've never seen anything like them; bodies covered in rotting wounds, their faces wearing evil, snarling grins. The fear I feel when I fight them is not something they can train us to ignore. After our first encounter, many of us are having nightmares. Screams erupt from tents as women wake terrified of these monsters that we can't escape. We could use a few men here to tell us 'everything will be all right'.

I'm trying to fall asleep, but I'm scared of what I'll see.

-Anne

Anne,

Do they have therapists with you? The government must be doing something to help minimize the mental and emotional scarring. I want our life to start together when you get home.

I have some good news!

I found a plot of land that we can afford and there's a small creek running through the backyard. There is just enough space for some chickens and my father has offered us the next calf born. I should know within the week if my offer is accepted.

Think good thoughts for us please,

Matthew

dangling eye swaying in counterpoint. Harley showed Nathan his fingertip on her tongue.

She had always been an incorrigible flirt.

Harley leaned in toward Nathan, still balancing the piece of meat on her tongue. He watched it wobble a bit as she moved closer to him. When she was inches away, stretching up on her toes to reach him, Nathan opened his mouth, inviting her to kiss him. She passed the fingertip from her tongue to Nathan's, and he took it and swallowed it.

Their tongues played a little during the exchange and Harley savored the sharp, sweet, slightly spoiled flavor of Nathan's mouth. Every time she kissed him, it was different. It was if she was tracking his death with her tongue. She was becoming a connoisseur of his changing taste, a gourmet of his decay.

Nathan moaned into her mouth and she could feel the sound all the way to her toes. It was the only noise he could make these days, but somehow he managed to make it sound sexy. Harley slid her body against her lover's, wrapped her arms around his back and laid her head on Nathan's chest.

He hugged her tightly against him, her loose flesh sliding across her ribs, and they stood this way for a long time, as though nothing else in the world mattered. If Harley still had breath in her lungs, she would have sighed, content.

When they were alive, Harley and Nathan had such wonderful plans. They had talked about the future all the time, what they would do when they grew up, what they would achieve, where they would live… the works! They were crazy in love, planning out their lives in great detail with the certainty that is unique to the young.

The two kids dreamed of a house in the suburbs, a heap of children, and a dog.

Harley was a jock, pretty and popular, all lean muscle and attitude; Nathan was the class clown, over-tall and skinny, knees and elbows jutting in all directions. Harley's friends were appalled when she started dating Nathan, but he made her laugh, and he was cute, in a rough, clumsy, boyish way. To her he was perfect, and to him, she was even more so.

They were both high school seniors when Harley got bitten.

She was walking home from school, her book/gym-bag slung over one shoulder, putting off thinking about the dreaded geometry test. Harley was already fantasizing about meeting Nathan after dinner, the way they usually did, so her mind was dwelling and her focus was off. They had a special place in the woods behind his house. They called it a tree-house, but it was just five one-by-fours nailed to the trunk of an ancient maple tree to make a ladder. Long ago, the wood had been painted green, a ghost of color still visible on the edges. It was dirty, uncomfortable and far from stable, but to Harley it was the most romantic place she'd ever seen. She had made up her mind: it had been long enough; tonight, she was jumping Nathan's bones… Harley forgot all about the impending geometry test.

Harley was about three blocks away from home when the ugly, smelly man staggered into her. She gave him a wide berth, but she refused to look at him, so she was unprepared when he lurched into her. She yelled, "Hey!", but he grabbed her and bit her, breaking the skin with his jagged teeth. Harley slammed her bag into him, knocking the man to the ground, and she ran. She skipped going home and went straight to the tree-house, texting Nathan when she got there:

At tree-house. I was attacked!

He showed up ten minutes later, near panic. She showed him the bite on her shoulder. He tried not to let it show, but Harley could tell Nathan was scared and a little disgusted by what he saw. Then again, the bite didn't look good. Red lines radiated out from it, infection almost visibly crawling through her veins.

"Jesus, babe," Nathan had said. Harley had smiled at him; she loved it when he called her babe. "We need to get you to a hospital."

By way of response, Harley passed out. Nathan wasn't able to get Harley down from the tree-house, so he had to wait for her to wake up.

She never did, but when she opened her eyes, the first thing she did was bite Nathan. She took a chunk from his left arm, and sat chewing it, scrutinizing her boyfriend as she tasted his warm flesh in her mouth.

Nathan didn't scream, even though it hurt like hell. He held his wounded arm and rocked back and forth, staring at Harley as if she was some wild animal.

She was still hungry, but something kept Harley from eating any more of Nathan. She watched him, too.

"I love you," Nathan told her. "Now and forever, no matter what happens." Harley smiled at him, tried to tell him she loved him too, but her voice wouldn't work. He saw the look in her eyes, though, and he knew. Together, they watched as the tiny red lines spread out from Nathan's bite. The infection took hold and killed Harley's lover, then remade him.

"No matter what," Nathan repeated. It was the last thing he ever said, and Harley would never forget it.

Nathan passed out, and then he died. He got back up a while later as a different being, but Harley was still there, and that's all that mattered to him. The newly-deads made their way down the ladder, clumsily. Harley fell and tore her cheek on the bark, but was otherwise undamaged. Nathan only contracted a few scrapes, but he hardly felt them.

Nathan touched her teeth through the wound, fascinated. Harley playfully snapped at him, making him smile.

Together, they set out into the world, often holding hands and sharing meals. One of their early meals had hit Nathan with a tire iron, knocking loose that one eye, but Harley tore out the man's throat with her teeth, and together they devoured his succulent flesh. After that, they were careful to watch each other's backs.

Now she looked up at Nathan's face from within the hug. He looked down at her, eye hanging out a bit from his face. Some parts of Harley's memory were long gone, but things relating to Nathan seemed to stick. For a moment, she felt the tiniest regret they would never grow old together. They would never have kids. Her womb might as well be a tomb, her ovaries useless, and her eggs all dead. Nathan was not much better off: there was no blood to pump to his sex and his sperm had long since stopped swimming.

However, there were other ways. Harley leaned back in her lover's arms and looked around her. She grinned at all the undead children she and Nathan had made since they died. They were surrounded by the shuffling horde she and her lover had created. Hundreds upon hundreds of them surrounded them as their children begat more.

It was biblical in scope.

It was so simple, too. You feed, your food comes back as your child, and your child feeds again. It was beautiful, really: a circle of unlife.

Harley heard a massive thump. The sound was followed by a light so bright it ruined her eyes. Frantic, she felt out with her hands and found Nathan, pulling him close, afraid. Seconds later, the city was engulfed in a flame so hot it melted steel, before they seared away into nothingness.

The undead around them were obliterated, and Harley and Nathan's shadows were burned onto the wall.

It was all that was left of the lovers. They would still be there, holding one another, thousands of years later, when the radiation cleared out.

Harley and Nathan together, now and forever, no matter what happens.

YOUR CHEATIN' HEART

By Katie Cord

The screen door burst open like a meth lab gone bad. Joelynn Smythe stepped out onto her old weathered porch and screamed at the top of her lungs, "God damn you, Jerry! When I get to hell, I'm gonna kill you again!" Being a widow shouldn't feel like this. She'd always thought when Jerry died, she'd be devastated with grief. Instead, she wanted to run down to the graveyard, shovel him up, and beat his cold limp body until there was nothing left. How could her high school sweetheart, the man who'd made her prom night magic, and the father to her two children abandon her like this? Their life had been good and now he was gone.

She surveyed the old porch. Drab grey cracks lined the wood. *Who am I kiddin'?* she thought. She was fifty-eight years old, living in a rundown trailer. One day she was going to walk out on that porch and meet her death in a crash of rotted wood, but she wasn't ready today.

Joelynn tiptoed over to her rusted green porch swing, her cigarette pack weighing heavy in her snug pants pocket. She fished out a Pall Mall unfiltered and lit it. The red tip glowed as she sucked in the toxins that kept her anxiety at bay. There'd be no more worry over the raspy cough that'd plagued her for years, or the results of it in the sink every morning. She had about six months to live and would fall apart one piece at a time, unless she ended it herself. She closed her eyes, listening to the competing creaks of the porch and swing.

She didn't want to deal with all the problems Jerry had caused. She wanted to remember their lives as being happily ever after, but the only memories that ran through her head were the drinking, the crystal meth, the pills, and him running off their kids. She wanted to remember 1974, a boy with a wicked smile who'd told her she was pretty and didn't ever have to worry. But he'd turned into a drug-dealing two-timing son of bitch who'd dragged her down for years.

Now this, she thought as she inhaled deeply. There was time to hide her decay, but not much. The trick was making what time her body had left matter.

As she swayed in the swing she thought of her two beautiful daughters, somewhere out in the world. The bastard had run them off before they were even of age. She hoped they were safe, with loving men that treated them well. Hell, she didn't care if they were loving women, just as long as they were happy.

She'd tried her hardest to be the kind of woman she thought she should be—one that went to college and made their family proud. But fear crept up on her and put her in a choke hold. She'd been an artist, painting anything she laid her eyes on. Her work had been displayed at the community center, and she was awarded a scholarship to Loyola. She went—for one semester. The first time a professor told her that her work was shit, she ran straight back to this little town and shoved herself into a role she never wanted. That trip home had been nothing but a death sentence.

She looked down at her flip-flopped feet. The doctor had warned her to protect them, but this was southern Mississippi; who the hell wore covered shoes in the summer? She stared at the smooth blackened edge where her pinky toe had been just a week earlier. Funny thing was, once the tissue died, you didn't feel it anymore. It was just there. It went from pale, to grey, to blue, to black. She originally thought it was a bruise, but then it continued to grow. The doctor had been the least of her concerns as money exchanged hands on her polyester couch, never reaching hers. Jerry just *had* to have his cigs and Mountain Dew with Jack. Joelynn's health was never a priority for him, and if she admitted it to herself, it wasn't really for her either. Everything had always been about Jerry.

She remembered the look on the doctor's face when she showed him the toe. His lips had formed a thick grim line. She wasn't sure how he had managed to speak through it. "Mrs. Smythe, anybody else in your family got this problem?" His dark eyes held accusations more than questions.

She paused cautiously before answering. "What you mean, Doc? Anybody else stub their toe? *No.* My husband Jerry died four days ago, but they said he died 'cause he's an old drunk." Come to think of it, no one had told Joelynn exactly how Jerry died. They found him on the side of the road; she imagined he'd tumbled over in a drunken stupor and died of exposure.

The doctor leaned away from her foot. "You and Jerry do any zubbing?"

"What the hell is zubbing?"

The doctor pushed himself away from the examination table, the small wheels on his stool scratching at the linoleum. He folded his fingers together and took a deep breath. "Mrs. Smythe, it looks like you've contracted Virus Z-38. People can only contract this strain through sexual contact with zombies."

Joelynn felt the blood rush from her head to her stomach. She had to brace herself before speaking. "You're telling me Jerry was having sex with zombies?"

The doctor, his lips still a tight line, leaned against the wall and nodded solemnly.

She pounded her fist into the red vinyl exam table. "Damn Viagra! This is all you people's faults! If that man couldn't have gotten it up, I wouldn't have this."

The doctor walked over to her and gently placed his hand on her arm. The cool soft palm felt comforting, but it didn't soothe her anger. The doctor continued, "I hear there's a zubbing joint around here. People go to these clubs, get high and drunk, and have sex with these bodies. I'm seeing it a lot in your age group and in the young kids. You probably got six months to live. If you want, I can refer you to someone who can help ease the process."

Joelynn shook her head. "No. I got unfinished business."

She looked down at the foot and turned away. "Just get rid of the evidence." The doctor complied. He didn't need to numb it; the toe was dead. The doctor clipped it off with a tool that reminded her of the pruning shears she'd used to harvest Mary Jane back in the eighties, except these were shiny and clean. As she walked out of the exam room, she scanned the lobby, looking at the faces of people she'd known her whole life. She wondered if anyone could tell she had the virus. Were they looking at her limp, or were they worried about their own problems? Did everyone in their small community know about this zubbing thing? The zombies were all supposed to be gone, but people must have been hiding them. Apparently, it wasn't even folks that loved their family members too much to let them go. It was sick, twisted, perverted people putting them in places and doing dirty things with their bodies—people like Jerry.

She'd paced her little trailer for days, trying to accept her fate. The porch swing had been somewhat soothing, but today there was unrest in her soul as she sat recalling the last two weeks. Her trailer sat on a hill looking over the delta; the haze of mid-morning spread over the marsh. As the thermometer inched up, the sound of cicadas increased. The sound had always calmed her before, but nothing would do the trick now. A dead husband, a terminal illness, and knowledge of something worse than Jerry's usual shenanigans going on in her little town kept her from peace. She looked down at her calf. While she sat there feeling sorry for herself, the veins in her legs continued to die. She couldn't lose her legs. She wasn't ready to quit walking.

The end of the cigarette brightened as she pulled off one last draw, threw it to the ground, and stomped it out. She knew what she had to do. She didn't like it, but she couldn't let anyone else end up like her.

Joelynn was sure no one would be willing to talk to her about the zubbing, but it turned out to be pretty simple. She went over to the local store, where you could still get Coke in a frosted glass bottle and Marjorie, the owner, would cut you a slice of baloney off as thick as your thumb. George Coontz gave her the information for free. He was one of the old men who spent their naval retirement sitting in a fold-up lawn chair under the large oak tree watching everyone come and go. Of course, after the talk he'd reminded her it was never too late to get right with the Lord. He apologized for Jerry's passing, but said he wouldn't miss the son of a bitch. She wasn't sure if her actions tonight would get her right with the Lord, but if they got her right with herself, she could die whole.

As the sienna sky of late summer evening shown through her windshield, Joelynn drove her 1984 Chevy Malibu to Earl's garage. She knew Jerry had been coming up here a lot before he died, but she hadn't realized what he was doing. The first person she spotted was Earl's bastard nephew, Justin. The boy was ugly, with mutated freckles, bucked teeth, and long shaggy greasy black hair. His were the eyes of someone who had dampened out the spark of life before it had time to ignite. Her insecurities about her aging body raged through her as she thought about her saggy tits and wrinkled face, but she shook it off, figuring the bag of meth in her hand would be sexy to him.

Joelynn strutted around to the hood of the car, tugging at her low-cut tank top. The boy ignored her. She laid down the bag of crystalized goodies on the carburetor. The ugly kid looked up with suspicious but hopeful eyes. "Mrs. Smythe, they ain't no such thing as a free gift. What you want?"

She leaned over, exposing her cleavage. "Little boy, I'm lookin' to get into a little zubbing. You know where I can do that? I need me a good time. I'm so lonely now that Jerry's gone." She didn't care if it turned him on or repulsed him; she just needed results.

From the boy's expression, it was a mix of both. Joelynn wasn't too happy with the idea of a nineteen-year-old meth-head who didn't brush his teeth loving up on her, but she had been sleeping with a sixty-year-old drunk who dealt drugs and fucked zombies. She could do what she needed to. What did she have to lose? The boy leaned in close to her, putting one hand on the baggy and the other on her breast. "I didn't think you the type to be into the ladies." He pinched her nipple through the padded bra.

She smacked the boy's hand away. "You don't know nothin' 'bout me. I'm as wild as Jerry ever was. Where's the club?" Joelynn grabbed the boy by his overalls collar, pulling him closer.

The young kid took the invitation to rub up harder on her. She could feel him pressing his small but determined manhood on her. He smiled. "Old lady, don't you think Jerry done caused y'all enough trouble with them zombie whores?" His breath stunk like rot. She could see inside of his mouth; his tongue was black and flopped around as he talked—it looked like it was detaching. So he, too, suffered from Z-38. The boy was going to lose his ability to talk first, if he wasn't already rotting in other places.

Her patience in letting this young sack of waste love on her was burning short. "All right, boy, take me to Earl then. He'll get me what I want for the right stuff." She pushed past Justin and grabbed the bag of crystal meth.

The boy stuttered and pulled back on the bag. "All right, I know Earl wouldn't want Jerry Smythe's widow upset with him. I'll show you."

The boy's shoulders sagged as though he had lost the championship game for the high school basketball team. He was probably pissed he couldn't intimidate an old lady with his wannabe-serial-rapist moves. He probably hadn't finished sixth grade; no doubt the only loving he ever got was from the undead vixens in the club.

He pushed his cap down further on his forehead as he headed toward the door. "You ain't going to like what ya see. The women never do."

Joelynn followed the boy. His coveralls drooped in the back where the boy's butt should have been. She traced his clumsy steps, anticipating the nightmare that she might see.

They headed down a path lit with outdoor solar lights shaped like fat frogs. They were most likely added by Earl's sister, who had an addiction for cheap lawn ornamentation. As they headed down the trail, thick with vegetation on each side, Joelynn could hear the sounds of the woods. On trails like this a copperhead was usually ready to bite under every unturned stone. The katydids chirped loudly; they sounded like they were bigger than her head. She would miss that sound. She wished she'd gotten off her ass in front of the television, sat out on the porch, and painted while listening to the sounds of nature.

Goddamn satellite television had been the death of her creativity. Maybe when she finished this, she'd go home, pull out all that old paint, and do what she'd sat there dreaming about while watching some soap opera.

The boy stopped abruptly, right where the frog lights ended, and yelled out, "It's me, Justin. Don't shoot. I brought the widow Smythe with me." There was either a trap or somebody sitting outside ready to shoot anybody who passed that invisible line without permission. She heard a loud voice yell back, "Clear." A light came on and Justin headed for it. She followed.

They arrived at a set of old trailers cobbled together under one haphazard roof. They were painted bright pink; next to the front door was a sign that read, "Entr at yur oan risq".

Joelynn looked at Justin. "You make that sign?"

The boy smiled. "I got more talents than just messing with cars."

Joelynn had a suspicion the boy didn't know how to work on cars either.

Inside, a familiar face welcomed them. Clyde Parker was one of Jerry's oldest buddies from high school. Joelynn clenched her teeth as Clyde grinned and shifted on his barstool. Joelynn turned away toward a young woman with long, dragon-like fingernails at an old table that looked as though it had been robbed from an elementary school.

The girl had big fake eyelashes to compliment the acrylic dragon nails. She looked up at Joelynn and smiled. "Hey there, Mrs. Smythe, you 'member me? I'm Macy. I used to come over to your alls place and play with LouEllen. How's she doin? Sorry to hear 'bout yer husband. He was a good man. Seems like all the good ones leave early, huh?" Joelynn observed Macy neatly sidestepped the fact her husband had been coming to this very club, fucking the zombies that subsequently caused his death.

Macy appeared healthy. She either wasn't screwing anyone associated with the club, or she was covering up her rot. Macy traced an invisible pattern on the table with her index finger, making a high-pitched scratching sound. She didn't look up as she said, "I'm supposed to charge one hundred and fifty dollars a person unless you're a member, but I guess since your husband just died and all, I'll let it go this time."

Joelynn cleared her throat, pushing back the bile. "Thank you, Macy, that's mighty fine of you." The girl beamed. Joelynn wished she could have told Macy how Lou was doing, but she didn't know.

Justin pulled Joelynn's arm. "You need to see Earl for the rules before you go looking and touching."

He led her through a long hallway that linked the trailers together. She could hear grunting and moaning through the thin metal walls. She had only heard the wails of hunger a couple of times during the rise of the infected. It wasn't hard for her to believe that Earl was using the undead to fill his pockets and satisfy perversions.

The original infected didn't die quickly like those infected with Z-38. The oldest zombie had lasted eight years before totally decomposing. Of course, he was being fed human flesh to help him along. With Z-38, the doctors said you could eat all the human flesh you wanted and you'd still fall apart.

They reached an open area in the old trailers. On a homemade wooden bench sat the massive Earl Thomas: entrepreneur and devil. He smiled. "Joelynn Smythe, I ain't laid eyes on you in 'bout twelve years."

She didn't think the rage would still be there, after all these years. "Well, Earl, that could be because the last time I saw you, you was trying to put your dick in my fourteen-year-old daughter." She choked, trying to hold back her tongue. She had so much to say to this piece of shit. Jerry had made an agreement with Earl to sell him their oldest daughter, JeriAnn. Joelynn had come home from picking up LouEllen from school and found Jerry sitting in the living room, counting a wad of twenties while her daughter cried in the back of the trailer. The girl never told Joelynn if Earl was successful in his endeavors, and she was too weak to ask. Jerry fed ruthlessly on Joelynn's fear of being without a man. With his help, that fear kept her there until his death.

JeriAnn ran away with LouEllen two years later, when she turned sixteen. Joelynn hadn't heard from them since. She was sure they loved her, but JeriAnn probably knew that her mother was not strong enough to protect them.

In the end, she was alone and unafraid. There was nothing left to lose; only everything to change.

"I'm here to see what you got, Earl. I'm ready to sow my wild oats." She looked Earl in the eye. *The zombie girls would have a good time destroying him*, she thought.

He didn't look infected. Earl had always been smart. Evil ain't stupid; Joelynn knew that. It was why she wasn't a success herself. Her heart was too soft and it made her dumb.

He gulped clear liquid out of a mason jar, belched, and said, "Well, I don't plan to keep anyone back from their desires, Joelynn. If you want to love up on some cold rotten flesh, I'll be the first to help you out. These are the rules, real simple. Number one: don't take the gag out their mouths for nothing.

Two: don't unhook 'em from the walls. Three: you can do whatever you want with 'em, but don't break anything, including the skin. These girls don't heal like they did when they was alive. You might even know some of these gals, but they ain't your neighbors' daughters no more. Just like with the rise of the infection. Still the same rules."

She nodded. Several girls that LouEllen and JeriAnn went to school with had become strippers afterward. From them, she'd learned to distance the person they'd become from the little girls she remembered. She just hoped Lou and Jeri hadn't ended up in the same kind of place.

Earl's sister Reba came into the room, dressed in a see-through teddy. They were the same age, but the world had been even less kind to Reba than Joelynn. Her breasts sagged and her legs wobbled with cellulite, but she proudly strutted across the room in kitten heels. The shoes were open-toed; Joelynn noticed several toes were missing.

"Earl, you didn't tell me we had an old friend visitin' us! How you doin', Joelynn?" Reba plopped down next to Earl. They looked like two hogs squeezed together in a holding pen. *Let the bitch smile*, thought Joelynn. She always knew Reba had her eye on Jerry.

Joelynn had forgotten that Justin was in the room when he said, "I'm going back to the garage to wait for more people. Mah, can you put some clothes on?"

Reba shooed the boy. "Son, you need to be more comfortable in your own skin. People who have a problem with their sexuality are the problem." Reba's saggy jowls moved up and down like a freakish puppet. Joelynn shuddered. She had hated this woman for a long time, even when Reba had been young and attractive.

She wanted this over with.

"I'm here to see whichever girl was Jerry's favorite," Joelynn said.

Reba laughed. "Jerry never did the girls, Joelynn! He liked to watch *me* do the girls, and then I'd do him." Her saggy nipples moved up and down with each laugh. Joelynn thought she would vomit. She was more repulsed that her husband would have sex with this living, breathing woman than by him fucking a corpse.

"Oh Jo, you always were a prude. Getting into that fancy college, letting your feelings get hurt so easy, running home the first time things got tough. Makes me sad for you, honey. If I was you, I'd at least gotten pregnant by some boy at that school whose family had a little something. You just came home and got knocked up by good-timin' Jerry Smythe. I guess you wasn't as smart as you thunk, huh?" Reba snorted.

Joelynn looked at Earl. "How'd you all start doing this, anyway?"

Earl grinned as wide as a Cheshire cat. "We just took the first couple strippers from the club that got sick and brought 'em out here. Been doin' it ever since. Reba couldn't stand to see her girls go to waste. This operation makes more money for us than the garage and strip club combined."

"I want to see the girls." Joelynn jutted out her chin. She felt compelled to witness what these two were doing with these kids' bodies. It would make what she was about to do feel more like justice than revenge.

Reba pushed herself up from the bench, the delight on her face made Joelynn's face sour. The mean girl that'd plagued her since childhood really was a monster. Reba moved away from the main room heading down a poorly lit, wood-panelled hallway. The smell of stale sex and death passed through Joelynn's nostrils with each step further into the dark. They stopped in front of a door with a small white board; written in red letters was, "Taylor, Paid for".

Joelynn entered the room. The walls were painted a light blue, muted by a glowing black light. She could see every speck of fluid that had ever hit the walls. She was already on her way to death. It didn't matter if she touched it.

An old iron bed was shoved against the wall. Feathers spilled from numerous tears in the mattress, glowing an ethereal white in the black light. Joelynn didn't realize that someone else was in the room until she heard the clink of the chain. Behind the head of the bed, a shadow moved, slowly slithering out of its dark crevice.

Joelynn shuddered as the dead being became animated, probably at the smell of a living person in the room. The girl was tiny, probably a hundred pounds soaking wet. Her skin shone waxy in the black light, her eyes were unnaturally wide and slanted to appear like a cartoon. Her mouth was contorted in a weird smile. She wasn't gagged.

Joelynn felt the cheap polyester of Reba's lingerie rub her elbow as the other woman leaned in close. "This is my pride and joy. Macy was going to school to be one of them folks that works on dead people at the funeral home. We're findin' her talents work better here. This is my Japanese cartoon girl. She don't need a gag 'cause we done sealed her mouth shut."

Joelynn looked at the girl. She did look like one of them Japanese cartoons from the satellite, but that didn't make it any better. "How you going to keep her going if she can't eat?" Joelynn asked.

Reba laughed. "We don't plan to keep her around much longer. They wear out." Reba looked at the girl's crotch. "This is going to be the new business: specialty orders right before we put 'em down. Some boy from New Jersey paid us fifteen hundred dollars to do this. He's gonna come fuck her, then shoot her."

Joelynn looked at the girl and saw the small muscles of her face contorting, probably in pain. She remembered this sweet little girl from vacation bible school, fifteen years earlier, walking up the aisles with a wicker basket as she took up donations for the church. Now she looked like a freak show, burning with the desire to eat flesh.

Joelynn felt dizzy. The room was very small and she couldn't tell the scent of the girl's rotten flesh from Reba's dirty, unwashed soul. Joelynn had always been a coward. She'd let Jerry run off her girls, beat the shit out of her, and lived in a trailer that was paid for with dirty deeds. She had let it all happen in front of her, which made her as guilty as the rest of them. All of the smells, the specks of flesh and blood on the walls, the feelings of hate, sadness, and fear welled up in her. She needed out. She went to push past Reba.

"That's enough."

Reba wedged herself in the doorway. "We let you see this; now you either participate or we'll tie you up and make you work for us."

Joelynn had been ready for a fight with Reba since high school. The old bitch bullied her back then, and she sure as hell wasn't going to take it thirty years later.

"It's a fucked-up world, old lady, and I'm about ready to make it right." Joelynn pulled a pistol the size of her palm out of her shorts. Jerry had given it to her, back when he sold drugs from the house. She'd never planned to use it, but now was as good a time as any.

"I'm dying already; you think a little pistol's going to scare me?" Reba cackled.

Joelynn aimed and pulled the trigger. The bullet seared through the flesh with ease. Reba staggered forward and fell on the bed. The girl stepped backward, repulsed. She must have known Reba was infected, and didn't want anything to do with her.

Joelynn knew she had only moments before Earl sent in one of his goons to take her out. She grabbed a set of keys from Reba's neck and unshackled the broken doll. The girl moved forward, struggling to open her mouth. Joelynn saw a jagged, bloodied piece of glass on the floor. She picked it up and sliced across the girl's face raggedly.

No air passed between the girl's lips as the hole was opened, but as Joelynn watched, she inhaled and began to moan loudly. *Oh shit*, thought Joelynn. She opened the door and pushed the big-eyed girl through. In the light, she could see that Macy had sewed the girl's eyes shut and painted the lids black, speckled with white dots. The girl couldn't see. She was running on some other instinct, one that all of the zombies seemed to have. If Joelynn's guess was right, the girl would hunt and destroy anyone without the infection.

In less than two minutes, she heard gunfire and screaming. She slowly walked out of the room to see the girl munching on a mound of Earl's belly flesh. One of his men was shooting at the girl, but she kept biting. Joelynn ran to the next room, pausing only to pop an unknown man in the head with her gun. She let the zombie go and moved on.

She only had four bullets left, and she needed to end this tonight. With each door she opened, Joelynn felt like an archangel, doing the Lord's work. For the first time in a long time, she felt she was doing something right. She was, in that moment, brave and strong.

She walked out through the last door onto a narrow set of steps leading down to the backyard. There she spied a tent made from tarps: a meth lab not even five feet from the trailers. She wasn't sure how to make it explode, but she knew it was all flammable. She could hear one of Earl's goons yelling, "Get that bitch!"

She shut the door behind her and ran for the propane tanks. Joelynn grabbed the first tank, pulling it away from the cooker. She turned the knob and pulled out her cigarette lighter, then realized she didn't have a wick. She looked around for anything to light up.

She heard the loud, angry stomping of feet; Earl's goons were coming for her. She used the butt of the tank to bust open one of the windows, then set the dime-store curtains on fire, praying the fire would meet with the gas. Quickly, she moved away from the trailer and headed for another tank.

The back door swung open as she passed back by. A short stout man wearing overalls screamed as a tiny zombie, dressed as a pixie, rode on his back. The undead fae ripped at his neck, his gun useless against her. Joelynn rushed toward him, pushing him back into the trailer with the zombie girl on his back. Looking around quickly, she found an old loose board on the ground and wedged it in place, securing the door. She headed for more tanks, broke open the last three windows in the back, and threw the spewing propane tanks.

The ignition of the curtains set the shack's meltdown into motion, and the propane tanks added a nice show to it all. Joelynn ran to the front to see if anyone had escaped. Macy screamed in horror. Justin stood motionless beside her.

One of the girls came out the front door, covered in flames, and headed straight for Macy. Macy kept screaming as the girl drew closer, but Justin pulled out a wrench from his coveralls and started beating the girl with it. He yelled at Macy, "Shut the fuck up, sis, you're drawing 'em out!" Macy kept screaming.

Macy wasn't infected, but she was as bad as any of them. Joelynn stepped out of hiding and shot her once. The bullet went through the girl's shoulder, dropping her to the ground.

Apparently overwhelmed with decisions, Justin stopped subduing the zombie and turned around to care for his sister. The infected got up from the ground and started toward Macy and Justin, while the boy was preoccupied with her wound. Joelynn shot Justin in the back of the head; he fell down next to his sister. She knew the boy had less time than her, but this way he'd be one less infected person spreading the disease. Behind the brother and sister, the maze of trailers continued to burn.

Joelynn decided to wait it out, to watch it all burn and make sure it was gone from the face of the earth.

The charred zombie girl stumbled over Justin's lifeless body and attacked the terrorized Macy. Through the burnt flesh, Joelynn could see it was the little cartoon character girl, getting her revenge on Macy for the mutilation of her body. Joelynn figured that maybe there had been a grudge in the past, like maybe the girl had beaten Macy out as a cheerleader, or stolen the girl's boyfriend. Maybe Macy was just a product of bad genetics and a horrible home environment. It didn't matter either way to Joelynn, not anymore. The mess had to stop somewhere.

Joelynn sat down at the edge of the trail next to one of the tacky solar frog lamps and watched years of debauchery burn. She lit up a cigarette, comparing the dull glowing end to the bright blaze of the burning trailers. The heat at twenty feet was scorching, but her legs were getting colder every hour. She had to admit, the warmth was nice.

When the fire was done, Joelynn figured she would go to Earl's garage, see if there was any money in the cash register. There were rumors that a guy in town could use the internet to find anyone. She hoped the rumor was true; she wanted to see her girls one last time before it was over. She hoped, with all her decaying heart, that she could finally make things right.

NEEDS OF A HALF-DEAD HEART
By Randy Henderson

I wake up next to Alice with my face pressed against the cool skin of her arm. She lies perfectly still, naked and nubile, staring at the ceiling. Zombies never sleep. I moan, sounding like a zombie myself, and crawl off of the mildewed mattress to stand. My jeans and jacket are stiff with the cold, and I scratch my beard as I look around. Concrete walls, a corrugated blue metal door, a single yellow bulb, the smell of stale beer… Bits of drug-hazed memory begin to flash in my mind. Some old guy let me have this storage space for a couple of days in exchange for—

I cough, gag, and push the memory back down, deep down. I continue coughing until my throat hurts.

"Nnnnnnnn," Alice moans. It is all she ever says.

I turn to reassure her, but then the need hits me. My hands shake as I quickly dig through my jeans pockets. This growing anxiety has become routine, this fear that I left no fuse for the next day, but I pull out the slick plastic sandwich bag and breathe a sigh of relief when I see several grey crystalline threads sparkle in the corner. The relief is short-lived when I realize that this is just enough fuse for the morning. I have no money to buy more with, and few real options to get cash.

I glance down at Alice. Some rich husband out in the 'burbs would pay me enough for an hour with her to buy a few hits. She wouldn't even feel—

"No." I kneel down to touch her cheek. "I know you feel something. I know you love me." The zom cocktail may have messed with her brain, but she still has a heart. My hand begins to shake on her cheek, and I feel the edges of nausea creeping up on me. I open the sandwich bag. "I'll find a way to get us by, I always do, right?" Then I dump the fuzzy threads onto my tongue, and close my eyes as they melt like cotton candy.

The mind bomb is a small firework flare of pleasure, nowhere near the orgasmic nuclear explosion of my first rush, but my entire body still sighs with relief.

I guide Alice to the drain in the corner so that she can relieve herself, and then get her dressed. I grab our brush and start brushing the knots out of her hair.

I don't know how she gets it so tangled.

Finally, I give her what is left of our peanut butter. That should keep her busy and quiet while I go score some cash and supplies. With Alice all squared away I kiss her on her pale forehead and then head out, locking the steel door behind me with a padlock.

I decide to go see my sister Natalie, ask her for another loan. She's one bridge I haven't burned completely—I hope. Regardless, she still owes me.

I hike to the city's free-ride zone and hop the buses. I see groups of zombies milling around the factories and warehouses of the industrial area, but there are no zombies allowed on the buses. The smell's still plenty bad though, a mixture of aged urine, vomit and body odor that makes my stomach curdle. The bus lurches to a stop in front of a temp worker building. The woman sitting next to me gets off and a large man plops down in her place, his bulk forcing me to scoot closer to the wall. He reeks of musk and alcohol sweat.

As the bus shudders and pulls out into traffic, he says, "Goddamn zoms are taking all our jobs, know what I mean?" I glance over at the guy. His brown hair and beard are ratty and peppered with grey, his eyes watery and red-rimmed. He nods out the window at a crowd of zombies lumbering around one of the warehouses. "We got more Africans than Africa," he says, and looks at me expectantly.

Great. I can't just ignore this racist asshole or he might start a fight. So I give him a maybe-or-maybe-not shrug, hoping he'll lose interest. I avoid his eyes and glance instead out the window at the zombie men and women, those with brown skin now an ashy color. Some of them probably are from one of the less stable African nations, it's true. Africa had been one big test lab for the early Haitian-inspired zombie cocktails. The cocktails proved the perfect ethnic cleansing tool for dictators, since the zoms could then be sold or used for labor. And AIDS victims would take the cocktail near their end so their families could sell them afterwards.

"Them zoms ain't American," the man says with his sour breath. "Weren't born here, sure as hell didn't swear no oath. What if some of them is terrorists, faking like they're zoms? Lot of Muslims in Africa, you know. Or they might be carrying some kinda disease, huh? Ebola or something. Am I right, or am I right?"

Several of the passengers exchange amused or disgusted glances, and a couple cast sympathetic looks my way.

"Yeah," I say. Then I stand and squeeze past the guy, and work my way to the back door to wait until my stop arrives. The zom hater doesn't take offense or follow me, thankfully.

ⓦ

It's past noon before I reach the old brick apartment building where Natalie lives. Hopefully she still works evenings and isn't out shopping, or still with a john somewhere. I climb into the entryway and jab the buzzer to her apartment.

There's a crackle from the intercom, and then Natalie's voice. "Who is it?"

"It's Mike."

"Ah. You don't have that zombie with you, do you?" I feel a surge of anger at how she says "that zombie", but there's no point in starting a fight about Alice. I'm here to get money, not argue.

"No, she's not with me," I say. "I was just over doing a job, and wanted to say hi." The door buzzes, and I snatch it open before she can change her mind. The hallway's walls are yellowed and cracked plaster, with flowery light fixtures from my grandparents' day. It might have felt all fancy, probably did when it was built, except now there's the ugly orange carpet, the stains, and the smell of mildew and bleach. I reach Nat's door and knock. The door swings open immediately. Natalie's eyes narrow, then she looks out into the hallway before nodding for me to come in. I slip past her, down her short hall and into her living room as she closes the door. "I like your hair," I say. Her long blonde curls are gone, replaced by short spikes.

She smiles and shrugs. "Easier to fit under wigs. So what's up, bro? Don't give me that working story, either. Working is the last thing you'd be doing."

In spite of my intentions to keep things friendly, I can feel my scowl as I say, "What's that supposed to mean?"

She sighs, not a real sigh but a sigh designed to tell me just how tragic a tale she could tell, if only she weren't so kind, so fucking better than me. Same old Nat.

She shakes her head. "Never mind, forget I said anything."

Yeah, right.

She moves towards her bathroom. "I've got errands to run, so really, why are you here?"

Okay, she wants blunt, I'll give her blunt. "I need some money. Bastards at the temp shack shorted me on my paycheck, and I just need a little cash to carry me through, pay the rent until I can get them to pay up."

"Forget it. I'm not giving you any money." Her expression is hard at first, but it softens, and she shakes her head as she puts one hand on my cheek. "Come here; look in the mirror, big brother. You look like shit—you need to get off the mind bombs." I jerk away from her touch, and look away from her blue eyes and the mirror as well. What does she know about it anyway?

"Come on, Nat! I am quitting, I just need a little more to help ease me off. It's not like you don't owe me."

"Don't!" Natalie shouts, and I'm shaken by the sudden anger in her voice. "I'm tired of you trying to blame your problems on me. I have enough fucking problems of my own without you trying to lay yours at my feet."

Heat flushes up my neck in response. I know I should be apologizing, saying whatever she wants to hear and keeping her happy so I can get the money, but reflexive anger fills me up like a rush, like a small hit of rage, and it feels good to shout at her, to just shout, period.

"If you hadn't run away, I wouldn't have quit school and gone looking for you in all those strip clubs and porn houses. I wouldn't have met Jake and started dealing, or—"

"Bullshit!" Nat says. "Okay, Mike, let's do this, let's get this out once and for all. I love you, but you're a fucking loser. Always have been, and my running away didn't have shit to do with it."

"Geez, thanks. I'm glad you love me or you might have said something mean! You know, it's not like I asked for this. Lots of people are homeless or jobless since the Crash, lots of people—"

"You were lazy and heading towards trouble even before I left, before the Crash or any of it," Natalie says. "You were skipping school, whined about any work you had to do, you ran away yourself, what, three times? If you can call spending the night at a friend's house and then coming home running away."

"You're one to talk," I say, but she waves a finger in my face before I can continue.

"Oh no, you're not making this about me, focusing on one thing I say and ignoring the rest. You used me as an excuse when you dropped everything to 'rescue' me and what did you end up doing? You ended up becoming a fuse dealer, and stealing yourself a zombie for a girlfriend instead and you know why you did that?"

Real anger at Nat is pumping through my head now, loud and painful. "I didn't steal her to be my girlfriend. That just happened, later. I rescued her because she reminded me of you, she was what I was afraid had happened to you and I didn't want to see her hurt or used."

"No. You didn't do it for her, Mike, you did it for you. Well, okay, maybe you did it partly because of me, I don't know, but like everything else, you took the easy way out and got yourself a girlfriend who doesn't require any actual effort on your part. You don't have to care what she thinks, what she feels, do anything to make her happy, she's just there, ready to go."

"You don't know shit, Nat! I do too care for her and I take good care of her. You think Alice is easy? You know how hard it is to keep safe with her, to avoid the zombie bashers and the rapists and the cops? Fuck, just to take care of her? How hard it is to be with someone who can't talk or show you how she's feeling or—"

"Feeling? She's a fucking zombie! She's dead. She doesn't feel anything."

"Yeah, you'd be the expert on that, wouldn't you Nat? I don't imagine you feel much of anything yourself. How else could you let all those guys fuck you?"

"You're an asshole," Natalie says in a quiet, dangerous tone. "And for your information, my clients don't just want a wet hole to stick their dick in. If they want that, they have a thousand zoms to choose from. They also want to talk or to play some kind of game—you know, human interaction? Or maybe you've forgotten about that, with your walking vagina."

"Goddamn it, her name's Alice! And whether you believe it or not, I really do love her."

"She's a zombie, bro. A zombie! How many times do I have to say it? She's not a person anymore. Just sell her already, and use the money to buy some rehab."

"I don't need rehab, I just need some money to get on top of things. Once the Crash is over, I'll get a good job, and register Alice, and quit the fuse, and even—"

"Bullshit," Nat says. "Nobody just quits fuse. And you'll have enough money to start over now if you sell Alice."

"Fuck you, Nat. Who are you to get all high and mighty with me, anyway? You're a whore, for Christ's sake."

"And you're a fuse-head and a zombie fucker, and a lousy fucking brother *and* you can leave now."

The shakes are starting, or maybe it's the anger. And why am I crying, damn it? My angry reply sticks in my throat. Instead, I walk to the door.

I stop with my hand on the doorknob. "Nat, I'm sorry," I say, and mean it. She seems as surprised by my response as I am, but I can tell she's determined to remain angry at me. She probably thinks I'm still just trying to get money from her. Fuck, maybe she's right. I don't even know what I'm feeling anymore, or why I'm feeling it. The fuse has my moods as scrambled as my thoughts. So I just turn the knob and leave. As I make a stumbling sprint down the stairs, letting gravity do my work for me, I try to figure out my next move. I need some fuse, and I need it bad *and* I need to get back to Alice. We both need food, especially me, and I'm starting to worry more and more that maybe I forgot to lock the storage unit, or that the manager did see me bring Alice in.

I need money. I reach the street, and find myself eyeing the cars that slowly drive by. Some of the drivers eye me back. *Just one last time—it would be over quickly and I would have the money I need.* Need. God, my brain feels like it's going to explode. I turn and run to the next block and into the dead white lights of the grocery store where the cars cannot tempt me. The security guard standing inside the entrance looks at me suspiciously, so I slow my pace and straighten up, and run a hand through my sweat-damp hair. *Just be cool. Maybe I can lift some stuff to trade for a hit.* I wander the thinly-stocked aisles until I get to the pharmacy section. I pick up a couple of things, put them back, and look around to make sure there's nobody in sight. Then I quickly slip some boxes into my pocket with my left hand while I pretend to be reading the ingredients of a bottle in my right hand. I put the bottle down, and wander as casually as I can to the door. As I step outside, I feel a wave of relief. Everything is going to be okay.

Then the security guard steps out behind me.

"Excuse me, but can you show me what's in your pockets, please?"

I try to run, but he tackles me easily, slamming me to the ground and putting his knee into my back. He drags me back to his office and then calls the cops.

♥

I'm taken to the local jail for the night. My shakes get so bad they dose me up with methadone to take the edge off, but it's like a handshake when you really want a fuck. The need is still there, throbbing; aching, but at least the pain and nausea are blunted. The worst part is that it clears my head enough to really think about my situation.

They give me my court date and let me go. I hop the first bus back towards Alice, and tap my head against the cold glass of the window as my thoughts race.

I'm screwed. I have no doubt I'll get prison for stealing meds. It is not my first time being caught. What is going to happen to Alice if I'm gone for five years, not able to take care of her, to protect her? And how will I ever find her again after I'm out, even if she survives? Hell, what's going to happen to me? If I make it in prison, I know it's going to be as someone's plaything. I am not intimidating or connected. I'm screwed, probably good as dead.

I need to run, to get Alice and flee.

Yeah. Right. Run away with an illegal zombie and no money, no plan, no destination. I'll get caught. I'm just not lucky enough to get away. Or rich enough.

I'm having a hard time breathing. My chest feels tight, constricted. Tears start to dribble from the corners of my eyes.

The thin wall of methadone collapses, and the need returns twice as fierce as before. Bile shoots up into my mouth when the bus lurches to a halt, and a guy plops into the seat next to me. He looks like a pasty-faced executive type forced into hard labor, his double-chin now covered in stubble, his suit traded in for the flannel jacket and jeans he probably bought once for a weekend retreat. He still has an air of superiority, though, as he looks at me with his bloodshot eyes. His eyes flare into bright fiery coals set in a leering demonic face, with tears of molten hate dripping down. I blink rapidly, and the image goes away.

Oh shit. I'm having fucking hallucinations now? I just stare, remembering the fuse-heads that used to come to me when I was a dealer, the ones who were really gone, the ones I found pathetic and sad. That wasn't me. Shit, I still took care of myself pretty well. I must have just got some bad fuse or something.

I stand up and make my way towards the exit. I need air. I need space. I fight an urge to vomit as the bus lurches and sways. The next stop comes not a moment too soon. I exit the bus outside an adult bookstore, stumble past a knot of hookers and hurry towards my next bus stop. I'm halfway home and no closer to knowing what I'll do once I reach Alice.

Nat's insistence that I sell Alice keeps nagging at me. If I did that, maybe Alice would be safe at least, and I could use the money to flee, or maybe buy a decent defense.

But the thought of being without Alice slashes at my gut, tears at my heart. I'd still probably end up dead, or in prison.

Then bus guy's rant from yesterday about Africans comes back to me for some reason. I remember the stories we heard in the early days, the ones about the mothers or fathers who were dying of AIDS or starvation, how they took the cocktail so their families could sell them for a little money. An idea whispers to me, but I try to ignore it. Shit.

"Jesus, or Buddha, or whoever's out there," I say. "If you're real then help me out of this, please, and I'll do good things, I'll help out all the people like me and tell everyone that you are real and good."

No god answers me, but a car slows down as it passes and a pale face leans down to watch me through the passenger-side window. His face melts, his eyes and mouth widening into huge black holes, cold dark pits that are trying to suck me in, to devour me. I slap myself, and the face snaps back to that of a sweaty man who frowns and accelerates away.

Maybe that is God answering me after all—isn't there some kind of saying that He only helps those who help themselves?

And the need—god, I need some fuse, I need it now. I brush back my hair with my hand, take off my flannel and jacket, and stand out on the corner, forcing a smile onto my lips as I meet the eyes of the men driving by.

♥

Alice is blue with cold when I finally get back to the storage unit and take her into my arms, murmuring apologies. I rub her arms, wrap her in a blanket, then clean her up. She does not shiver, does not return my embrace, but sits there quietly as I work. I am reassured to see she moved a little off of the mattress to relieve herself at least. Don't tell me she has no thoughts or feelings. More tears come to my eyes as I clean the peanut butter from her hair and tease her about it. I like to think she is pressing up against me for closeness, or as a thank you, not just from an instinctive need for warmth. I brush the long blonde curls, causing them to frizz even worse into a halo around her head.

Beautiful.

A laugh breaks free of my throat, and softly I kiss my Alice. Then I open the paper bag the dealer gave to me. The fuse is gone, used up already. I only bought enough to stop the need, to get me home to Alice. What I pull out instead are two old plastic soda bottles with the labels torn off. With Alice at my side, I hold the bottles up and look through them at the light. Inside the first bottle is a slightly yellow liquid, and in the second is a brown fluid that looks like dirty tea with bits of leaves and grit floating in it.

Alice sees the bottles and reaches for one. She must think it is food for her.

"No, Alice. This is not for you."

"Nnnnnnnnnn," Alice says, still trying to grab the bottle, and I kiss her cheek.

"Shhhh, everything's going to be okay, I promise."

By the time my sister checks her messages, the cocktail will have done its job on me—one bottle to kill, one to bring back. Natalie will know where to find me and Alice. With her connections, I'm sure she will be able to safely sell us, and get back at least some of the money I owe her. If she really loves me, she'll make sure that me and my Alice stay together. Because I know I'll be happier as a zombie with Alice than I'll be without her, in prison or out. I'll be happy, as long as Nat does what I asked.

I twist the lid off the first bottle and stare at its pale contents, my hand trembling. I don't know if I could go through with this if the process required only the zombie tea, not even for my Alice. As much as I love her, the idea of being a zombie myself is… freaky, upsetting. But suicide? Somehow, that thought is easier, more familiar.

After counting to three twice and taking several deep breaths, I finally just push thinking aside, put the bottle to my lips and guzzle down the contents. Cramps twist my stomach, and breathing becomes difficult, rapid, but the hard part is over. I have killed myself, so what does the second bottle matter?

I choke down the second bottle before the chance is lost, coughing and sputtering. Then Alice and the storage unit rush away from me down a dark tunnel. I reach out for her, dropping the bottles and grasping for her tiny hands.

I can't feel if I am touching her, but I hear Alice's voice echoing in the darkness.

"Nnnnnnn. Nnnnnnnno!"

WHEN THE LAST WAR ENDED
By Paul S. Huggins

Tom was still aware of his faculties, but radiation sickness had set in. His once magnificent mane of chestnut hair was now patchy. His gums were nonexistent. His eyes had changed from hazel to a vivid slate grey as the strontium and iodine circulated through his bloodstream. Every so often he would have a coughing fit that was bad enough to draw blood from his ravaged innards.

Unlike the rest of the dead that surrounded him, he had purpose.

Before the events in the Middle East escalated, Tom had been in London on business. He was meeting with various galleries and entrepreneurs in an effort to sell more of his art. Many scoffed at the desolate and dark imagery, but many more loved it for its futuristic landscapes. They hailed it as prize-winning work; he made a lot of money. Now he moved through the darkest of his own landscape creations.

He'd been an underground celebrity, though his true love was his girl, Cindy. They had been together as long as he could remember. They left the US and moved to Scotland, thousands of miles away from their small hometown.

It was unfortunate that Tom's artistic endeavours were not accepted in his native country. The British and Europeans, however lapped it up. All the time Cindy was by his side. As far as he was concerned, the rest of the world could rot, which of course they were doing. Luckily, he'd been passing through East Anglia on his way home when the bombs started to drop. Had he still been in London it would have been instant death, because the capital was a prime target during initial attacks.

Sometimes he thought it might have been better to die quick, rather than the lingering demise he now suffered.

Nothing shined in this new world. Everything was black and white and had the contrast turned down. Even the sun barely got a look in as the fallout clouds still hung heavy in the stratosphere. Dull, dusty and decaying.

Just like the mutants, Tom spent most of his time on the move, walking and cycling half the length of the country, towards the highlands. It was becoming an immense chore. Every day the sickness made him feel worse; love kept him marching on. He traveled only during daylight, hiding at night. The mutants seemed to be more active at night, and as far as they were concerned he was fresh meat. They hunted on instinct. They seldom ate their own type of human; too dry. The only time they did rip and attack each other was during heavy rain, when their bodies were soaked. For a brief time they looked almost normal. The mutants would then perform quite a spectacle. If many should meet up, a horde would be born. They would writhe and grab at their innermost members, looking for food in each other. Confusion and hunger would push them. From a distance it resembled a knot of slime-ridden worms in an orgy of bloodletting. Tom had witnessed it just once. Something he would prefer not to again.

Nutrition from any food was almost nonexistent for them. Mutated cells fed on healthy cells until domination of the entire being was made. They acted like Captain Smith on the bridge of the *Titanic*, and like the ill-fated steamship, the bodies were merely a vessel transporting these mutations like passengers until the body finally wore down to nothing and turned to dust.

Tom at least could still think freely. He could choose and he could question; the speed of mutation was slow in him.

Every water supply was now poison; Tom's radiation sickness was aided by every drop that passed his lips. Food was plentiful, though. Every supermarket was still well stocked. War had come too suddenly for most to get out and stockpile what they needed.

If vehicular transport had fared better, he would have driven up to Scotland. Unfortunately, electromagnetic pulses had disabled all but protected official electronics. It was a side effect of a nuclear explosion. Ironically, the people who had access to these working electrical items were either dead or wandering the wastelands. Most fuel had also burnt up in the firestorms that followed the first detonations.

Tom only ate canned food, even if the labels had burnt off. He didn't care. The contents could've been dog food for all he knew. His taste buds had long since burnt away. What kept Tom moving was his beloved. He knew she may be dead, but he would find her anyway. He knew death was hot on his heels, but he had to know before the end, he had to be with her… then he could rest.

His groin ached, saddle sore from being on the mountain bike for too long. Probably also unseen cancers in his testicles and bowels. Tom had been contemplating beside a deserted village green for too long, and the sky was darkening. Nowadays the nights drew in quickly and were very long. The ever present umbrella of dust in the atmosphere was always there to aid the night.

A row of houses bordered the circle of dead straw-like grass that used to be a vivid green, neatly trimmed. The old houses were small and whitewashed with roofs of tatty grey thatch. When the straw in the thatch was still yellow, they must have been quite picturesque.

He limped over to them, pushing his bicycle, and picked a central house with its door ajar. Dust and fallout was piled against it. The door scratched against the floor as he pushed it open; he slipped through into the musty shelter. The once-polished floorboards creaked underfoot. It looked as if the house had been the abode of someone elderly. Through the grime, Tom could make out the old-fashioned style of the living room furniture, and when he made his way under an archway he discovered a small kitchen diner and a staircase that led to a second landing.

After glancing over the kitchen he headed upstairs, where he could see through the open door directly ahead. Tom briefly looked inside the bathroom, finding nothing but more dust. He turned his attention to the last room.

Closed doors made him nervous.

Tom grasped the handle and twisted it slowly. With a click it released. He swung it inwards gradually, making its un-lubricated hinges grind together.

He faced a wrought iron double bed with a human-sized lump under the covers. The dust mote-infested air swirled as he walked in. The room stank of feces and urine with a hint of vomit, not recent but prevalent.

Respectfully, Tom pulled back the covers and uncovered an ancient-looking woman. Had her radiation-related death aged her further? Her skin was translucent, her skeleton almost visible, and there were no signs of obvious injury. Tom looked around, spotting an open pill bottle on the floor.

He brushed his fingers down the cold flesh of the woman's cheek. Despite the regularity of finding corpses in various states of decay, it still upset him to see them.

All of a sudden a skeletal claw-like hand slapped onto his wrist. He lurched backwards, forcing the body on the bed to sit up as he moved. The dry eyes looked into his as he pulled further back to distance himself from this thing. He tripped and fell backwards, unable to break his fall. The woman, still clamped to his wrist, was pulled from the bed and landed on top of him. She clawed at him fairly weakly, but to his horror she clamped her mouth over the bare of flesh of his other arm. Panic took him as he realized she was trying to bite into him. He pushed the woman up and back onto the bed, and her grip immediately released. She had no teeth.

Tom backed up into the dressing table, rattling the few items still standing on it, while the woman struggled with the bed covers in an effort to get to him.

Her eyes were dry and vacant. He knew the symptoms. She was in the last stages of radiation poisoning. Delirium and insanity had set in. Obviously the suicide attempt had failed, and by the time she awoke she probably didn't even know what suicide was, let alone the peace it could have given her. Tom was already tired, but managed a last burst of adrenaline and shoved the woman hard in the chest. This time she was taken by the momentum and slid with the aid of the covers over the opposite side of the bed. As she hit the floor, a sickening crack echoed in the room.

The only sound left was Tom's heavy breathing. He stepped around the bed to see the immobile body of the old lady. She was twisted, her head tilted at a severe angle against the wall. A small blemish on the wallpaper of fast-congealing blood indicated where her head had initially hit, finishing her for good.

He left the room after saying a brief prayer and closed the door behind him. On his return downstairs he cleared away the detritus obstructing the front door, pulled his bicycle inside, and closed it. He made the mistake of slapping the comfortable-looking high-back armchair; a cloud of dust enveloped it, and him, which in turn prompted one of his vicious coughing fits.

He didn't carry much out on the road as most things he wanted were readily available. He barely saw a soul; a few of the zombies, but never anyone still fairly human. Tom had heard the mutated humans on many occasions in the darkness of night. They were frightening creatures, made all the more terrifying by a variety of deformities. He almost always picked out a small house or barn to sleep in, if the fitful cat-napping he did could be called sleep. The ambient temperature of the earth had risen a few degrees; straw often made a good enough bed.

Today was a bonus. It looked like the old lady had been washing her spare blankets when Armageddon kicked off. The tumble dryer contained a clean and dry bed cover, having been locked away in the steel drum for a month.

When the dust had abated in the living room, Tom got as comfortable as his sores would allow in the surprisingly sumptuous armchair.

The morning would see him hunting around the woman's kitchen for a little breakfast, then traveling further up what used to be the main freeway up and across the Scottish border. In places, mainly near the large towns and cities, it had actually become more of a car park than a main arterial route. Tom always managed to get past the blockages one way or another. His top-notch mountain bike, liberated from a specialist shop, was now looking out of place, leaning against the heavy Victorian dark wood sideboard.

Tom pulled the blanket around him and drifted off into a slumber of sorts.

❦

He awoke to dull grey daylight. For once he had actually slept well, not that he was refreshed.

Tom groaned as he unsteadily got to his feet. Another coughing fit took him as he dragged his feet into the kitchen. He leaned over the sink, spattering dusty porcelain with flecks of blood, then spat a clot of blood down the dry drain hole. Afterwards, he slowly worked around the kitchen, placing items on the small wooden table. The cabinets weren't particularly full, but it was a veritable feast for Tom. A can of baked beans in tomato sauce: rich in protein and vitamins. Rice pudding: so creamy, it would slide down his dry throat with ease. Unfortunate that he could not taste it as when the world was alive, but it had been a favorite of his. Best of all were a couple of cans of pineapple segments. The juice alone would more than fill a large glass.

Half an hour later he was ready to go. The hearty meal, though eaten cold, had invigorated him. He was ready to ride.

Tom covered many miles in the following days. He avoided a few rancid inanimate corpses in various stages of decay, and within a week made it to the border.

He was a little shocked to see that the border now had a barrier. Prior to the bombs, the entrance to the Northern Territories consisted of two signs: *You are leaving England* and, a little further on, *Welcome to Scotland*. Now, though, the border was blocked by a hastily-built fortification of a couple of large semi-trailers with a few wrecked cars filling in the gaps. In front of it, empty cars stretching back for at least a couple of miles packed the border.

It was near dusk. Tom should have been looking for somewhere to hole up for the night. A couple of hours earlier, he'd managed to scavenge some cans of cola and some beans from a deserted roadside diner. He decided to scale the border first, then find a shelter and rest up for the big push through the dead-zone the next day. Picking his way through the abandoned traffic, he had to dismount as he got closer to the border. He saw large writing on the white sides of the trailers. *Go Back*, one read, and on another: *Death Awaits*. It saddened him, all these people pushing north to escape the horrors, but they were only jumping out of the frying pan and into the fire… a radioactive fire. They must have made an early bid for freedom to get their cars this far. Now, though, the cars sat, dead and inoperable. Tom wondered what had happened to all the people.

The idle thought suddenly resonated in the failing daylight. Where *had* they all gone? They had been turned back from the border, but what then?

He leaned his bike against the side of a station wagon and tried to peer through the grubby rear window. He pulled his sleeve down and rubbed at the glass, cleaning a small spot. Their luggage was still in place. He was perplexed.

Out of the corner of his eye he saw sudden movement from the front seat. He moved around to the side of the vehicle, then rubbed vigorously at the glass, moving in closer.

A spread-out hand slapped on the window from within, then a face came into view. It was the face of a child, a taut-skinned, malnourished child! The blown irises gave the impression that the eyes were almost totally black. Tom suddenly became aware of more noises around him. He'd been wrong: the refugees had never left their vehicles at all. As darkness fell, the wanderers of the night came out from their hiding places… and Tom was right in the middle of them.

He darted away from the car, desperate to get to shelter. He passed car after car, some with whole families staring out at him, trapped, having forgotten how door handles worked. He stepped over many bodies extricating themselves from their daytime shelter underneath the vehicles.

Just his being there was enough to get them riled up. They started to follow him.

Tom wasn't far from the border, but more and more people were converging on him. He let go of his bike, unable to drag it along while hands grabbed at his legs. Eventually he reached the last car, almost touching the barrier.

Tom jumped onto the hood of the car. The top edge of the semi-trailer named *Go Back* was just out of reach. Tom panted with exertion, but he could not stop. Fingers touched and grabbed at his legs. He jumped up, not quite making it, and landed with a hollow metallic thump back on the hood. He felt a hand under his foot. Jumping a second time, Tom finally caught the edge and tried to pull himself up, to no avail, only making it so far before his legs flopped down within the reach of the mutants. He kicked them away again.

As more and more of them scrabbled onto the car's hood, an idea came to him. Tom managed get one foot on the shoulder of a ragged-looking man; with the other, he trod on the head of a woman with matted dark hair. Using them as a boost, he sprang up, leaving them sprawling. Tom managed to hook one elbow on the roof of the trailer. From there, he pulled himself up, despite the lactic acid building up in his aching muscles.

Cindy's image spurred him on.

The mutants below grabbed at air as Tom lay on his back, panting. After he had regained his breath and survived another coughing fit, he peeked over the side. A large group of the mutants had gathered along the full length of the trailer, and more were approaching.

He had never seen so many in one place.

Light was fading fast, but the other side of the barrier was free of people. At the far end of the trailer he saw a ladder bound to it. Presumably the fortification had once been patrolled. It worked for him; in a crouch, he headed for it.

Tom eased his leg down until it met a rung, then descended cautiously. The sounds of the mutants on the other side of the trailer were muffled. He set out, walking along the empty road. There were no cars here; in fact, there was nothing at all. A layer of fallout obscured the road signs. The houses and buildings had already been few and far between on the other side of the border; now there was nothing, just rolling countryside, black but for the darkening horizon.

At last, a small hut came into view. It slanted on its foundation, probably from the nuclear explosion. As he approached, he saw that it was a road worker rest hut, basically a small cube with a door. Before entering, he took out his penlight and scanned the small but powerful beam around the windowless room. On the right was a long bench and table; opposite it was a single-ring gas stove and small wash basin. Above the bench and table was a fold-down cot. He went in, checked the closet underneath the cooker, shone the torch inside and pulled out a couple of cans.

His muscles ached as he sat on the bench. To save his battery, he took a half-burnt candle out, lit it, dripped a few drops of wax on the table and stuck it in place. Then he leaned back and sipped the cool thick liquid. He held the can towards the candlelight and rotated it so he could read the label again. *Cream of Chicken…* it would have been nice to taste it.

Memories of Cindy were comforting. The long walks they used to take together at the beach; during the winter they would cuddle in front of the open fire, cozy and warm, as bad weather raged outside.

Tiredness overwhelmed him. He had never walked as far as he had today. Instead of using the cot, he decided to wrap his coat around him and stay where he was. Sitting up, he was still comfortable; the coughing fits were worse when he lay flat.

The thought of the next day's trek through the dead zone intimidated him. From that point on, things would get harder. He would have to pass between Glasgow and Edinburgh. He remembered from the initial news reports that both cities had been pretty much obliterated. Radiation readings would be incredibly high, which could exacerbate his medical problems. It would be best to rush through as fast as possible. He would have to travel off the marked roads, but it would be faster. Then he'd only have about twenty miles over mountain passes and small roads to finally get to his home and his love. He might need some equipment for the last stage. His boots were still sturdy enough, although his lack of hair might benefit from a hat. An ice axe also would be essential.

In the early hours, a monstrous storm started to pelt down on Tom's shelter. The cabin rocked with gale force winds. Thrumming rain and winds buffeted the cabin while Tom held himself tight to the wall.

Then the unthinkable happened.

He felt himself tumble; the angle of the table had increased. A lull in the wind dropped the temporary building back onto its remaining foundation props, then a massive burst picked it up again and deposited it on its side. Tom was picked up and thrown across onto what used to be the wall. Once the motion stopped, he patted himself down as the storm thundered on. Thankfully, he had no broken bones, just plenty of tender spots.

He huddled in the corner and waited out the storm. The turned-over cabin swayed but didn't fall again. There was nothing he could do but wait.

It was long after the storm had passed before he finally plucked up the courage to go outside. It looked like the storm had cleansed the earth a little. Tom recovered his candle, the second can of soup and a can opener from the sideways cabin, then stood and stared around at the desolate landscape. A battered road sign indicated that he was only ten miles from a small town.

Maybe he'd find a new bike along with the gear he desired. Walking was far more wearing on his already tired muscles.

Three hours later, he walked into the ghost town. The buildings were in poor condition. Tom approached what looked like a general store; steps led up to shattered glass double doors. One side of the building was obliterated, rubble and non-perishable goods mingled all around. He stepped through the empty door frame as broken glass crunched underfoot. The shelves were a mess, contents spread around, all coated with a thick layer of ash. Finally, he discovered his grail at the back of the store.

Still bolted into its display stand, a near-pristine mountain bike greeted him. He left it for a moment, heading through to the grocery department. The damage was extensive, but he still hoped that there may be something he could eat. Unfortunately, the damage was too bad. The shop was wide open. Over what used to be the roof lay a large off-white cylinder with what looked like Russian characters written along its side.

The leviathan lay in the rubble as if it had been a toy rocket discarded by the child of some mythical giant. He remembered the names from old— ICBM, cruise, bloodhound, rapier—all now obsolete technologies. Tom wondered what name this modern one carried. In the eighties, the threat of a nuclear war was a real one. Paranoia and fear of Communist infiltrators was everywhere.

This time, the war had been televised. People weren't out in the streets protesting or building their bomb shelters and hastily stockpiling food. Years of fantasy through film and television had desensitized the population. Nobody knew they were involved until they drew back the curtains, looked out of their windows, then suffered blindness and incineration by nuclear weapons that had supposedly been decommissioned.

Tom gazed at the bomb. It was all that had been wrong with the world, and had eventually finished it. How he hated what the people in charge had done.

He coughed up another glob of deep red phlegm. He was exhausted. Love kept him going.

∇

The mountain passes were strenuous. The first day, he didn't clear as much distance as he had hoped. He quickly abandoned the bike; the paths were too treacherous. When he had reached the peak of one mountain, it offered him a 360-degree view of a landscape laid to waste. The journey had been bleak at the best of times, but now the greens and browns of the natural flora had disintegrated to an old black-and-white photograph. Off in the distance he could just make out the city, marked by a cloud of black smoke rising to join the fallout in the atmosphere. Glasgow was still burning unchecked.

Tom sat on a rock as another coughing fit racked his chest. It was hurting more and more.

He removed his thermal hat and brought it down to his lap, taken aback for a moment at the amount of hair on the hat. He felt his scalp; all he had left were a few tufts. After a couple of minutes contemplation, he stood up again. He would not die up there on the mountain. There was no way he was going to give up when he was so close to home and Cindy.

Darkness came. He continued to walk. The mutants held no fear for him now. What scared him more was not making it back. He feared sleeping; if he rested, he would never awaken.

As Tom reached the track that led to his home, he smiled. His limp had become severe, and his driveway was a good half mile up and around a sloping hillside, but he was happy to be so close.

As the road eased around the bend, his house came into view. It had always been an imposing building, overlooking all the land that came with it. Solid stone walls had combatted the harsh Highland weather for centuries.

When he stopped outside the front door, another coughing fit incapacitated him. The pain folded him in two and blood sprayed onto the gravel drive. Tom stood up and wiped his mouth on his sleeve, then dragged his feet to the solid oak front door. He leaned against the frame as he drew out the keys he had safely tucked in his pocket.

The door opened easily. He walked in and closed it behind him. Apart from the thin layer of dust on everything, it appeared just as he had left it a month earlier.

From the back of the house he heard a familiar clatter. He limped down the corridor and pushed through the door into the large kitchen. Flies buzzed about; strewn around the floor were dead wildlife—rabbits, game birds and even rats, some full carcasses and some partially eaten. The large flap built into the rear door still rocked. Tom walked over to it and unlocked the door, stepping outside.

He froze. The German Shepherd looked in a sorry state, bald patches breaking up its once-magnificent coat. It stood firm just five feet in front of him. Its teeth were bared, and a long drawn-out growl emanated from behind them.

Tom stepped back slowly. "Cindy?" The dog's growl stopped and it sniffed the air between them. Tom crouched as the dog slowly edged towards him, unsure. Tom's smile widened and he opened his arms. "Cindy," he repeated.

Cindy padded up to him and nuzzled her head in his shoulder as his arms closed around her. He looked along her back to see her hairless tail wagging to such an extent, he thought she might take off. "Oh Cindy, you would not believe the journey I've had to get back to you," Tom said as he stroked her vigorously. "Now, Daddy is very, very tired. So come on, let's go and have a nap."

Cindy dutifully followed as Tom looked through the kitchen drawers. Eventually he found the tub of prescription sleeping pills. He rattled the container and looked down into the doting eyes of his best friend. "Come on, girl." He headed towards the staircase.

The last war ended with the death of Tom. The victor was Planet Earth.

WHAT I WAS THERE FOR
By Matt Youngmark and Dawn Marie Pares

Maggie heard the crisp tap of heels on the concrete floor of the underground parking garage and smiled. It was a joke that very few people were in a position to understand: nobody heard Nancy North coming unless she wanted them to.

"Hey, Nance. I hear you've got a tip for me."

There was the flare of a match, the brief orange glow illuminating Nancy's clean profile, ash-blonde pageboy and grim expression. She took a meditative puff on her cigarette and exhaled, offering Maggie the pack.

"Virginia Slims is your brand, right?" That was another private joke. The cigarette company had used Maggie as inspiration for a superhero-themed advertisement a few years back (without her permission, of course), and Nancy knew it was a sore spot. So, of course, she brought it up whenever she had the chance.

Maggie shrugged, selected a coffin nail—*Lucky Strikes*, in point of fact—and lit the tip with her laser vision, inhaling the welcome burn of tar and nicotine. Nancy knew she was trying to quit. If she was offering smokes, then, all joking aside, what Nancy was about to tell her must be deadly serious.

"Tachyon dropped by my office last night," Nancy said. "In person." Tachyon was technically a member of Maggie's superhero team, the Liberty Patrol, but he wasn't big on field work. He was a time traveler, and a visit from him usually came in the form of a disembodied voice from God knows how far in the future or the past. Communicating with the guy was a pain in the ass, to be honest. If he had bothered to physically leave the grimy little apartment he kept on the East Side, it couldn't be a good sign. "It's Baron Von Zomb," Nancy said, taking another drag off her cigarette. "He's perfected a sort of viral contagion, apparently, and stuffed it into mail bombs in major metropolitan post offices across the nation. Could kill a lot of people, incredibly quickly."

Aces. "And somehow that's not the worst part," Maggie guessed.

"It's *Baron Von Zomb*," Nancy repeated. "Anybody killed by this thing will rise from the dead, highly contagious and under his control. If it gets to that stage, a global plague is almost unavoidable."

Maggie nodded. "Like you said, though, it's Von Zomb. He's not exactly the sanest rogue in my gallery, and he's tried to pull off this kind of thing before. You think it's the real deal this time?"

"Tachyon seems to think so," Nancy said. "Granted, I don't trust that guy as far as I can throw him, but I did a little legwork on my own, and so far it checks out. Maggie, if even one of these bombs goes off..."

"Got it. Sounds like a job for Magnifica. Any idea where I should start?"

"I'll contact the Liberty Patrol and start hunting for Von Zomb myself. Meanwhile, my intelligence suggests there are ten bombs, but I'm having trouble tracking down which cities they've gone to. It's most likely the biggest population centers, but honestly, they could be anywhere. I know you don't want to hear this, but with an operation this size you're better off clearing things beforehand with the powers that be. I'll call ahead."

Maggie checked her watch and shook back her long, dark hair. It was going on 5 AM. With her super speed, x-ray vision and laser eyebeams, she should be able to knock out most of the bombs before breakfast. A total cakewalk.

"Mags. One more thing. I've seen the blueprints. Von Zomb is using zyfronic gas as a propellant."

That gave Maggie a nasty turn, but she just nodded and drew her cigarette nearly to the filter. "Do you think he knows?"

"I don't see how he could," Nancy said. "Regardless, Maggie, I brought this to you because you're the only one who can stop it." She paused. "And because I trust you."

Maggie gave her a cocky smirk, but recognized the compliment for what it was. Nancy North didn't trust anyone, as a general rule.

Dropping her cigarette, Maggie ground it under her heel and gave Nancy's arm a reassuring squeeze. "Well, a woman's work is never done. I've got a world to save. Keep my gang out of trouble, will you?"

Nancy didn't smile, but she raised her Lucky Strike in a little salute as Maggie floated from the floor and roared out the front entrance, streaking straight toward Washington, D.C. with a sigh.

If there was one thing she hated, aside from injustice, it was paperwork.

President Carter had arranged for a light breakfast to be set out. "It's only bagels and juice, I'm afraid. No one could remember if you were vegetarian, Ms. Magnifica. But I thought you might need a little something in your stomach before you headed out on your mission."

Maggie hadn't paid a visit to the Oval Office since the Ford administration, and Carter's genteel charm caught her off guard. She might have expected as much, though, from a grown man who led the free world but still insisted that people call him "Jimmy." Maggie had little use for bureaucracy in any form, but she knew from experience that Nancy was right. This one quick stop could save her any amount of hassle for the rest of the day. It also helped that with Nancy clearing things ahead of time, she was in a position to go straight to the top. Not every journalist had a direct line to the President of the United States, but Nancy North was anything but your average intrepid reporter. As Maggie glanced down at the spread, a door opened on the rear wall of the Oval Office, and a woman was shuffled in by a small Secret Service detail. "Ah, here she is," the President said. "Magnifica, I'd like to introduce our newest Postmaster General, Ms. Abigail Francesca Hitchcock."

"Please, Mr. President, call me Fran. You too, Ms. Magnifica."

Fran was a short woman with broad shoulders and a vaguely military bearing. She was standing ramrod-straight, and looking crisp in a sort of dress version of what Magnifica recognized as a mail carrier's uniform. Her reddish hair was in a long, neat braid, and her face was round and very freckled. Only a slight puffiness around her eyes betrayed the fact that she had clearly been dragged out of bed moments ago.

"It's Maggie—only the papers call me Magnifica. Oh, and you two go ahead and suspend any regulations against tampering with the U.S. Mails for the foreseeable future. I'm going to be using my x-ray vision on a fuck-ton of packages, and I don't need a lot of whiny bureaucrats yelping at me while I do it." Both the President and the Postmaster stared at her. Maggie crammed half an onion bagel slathered in cream cheese in her mouth and gulped it down before continuing. "Believe me, it's come up before." When they continued to stare, Magnifica added, "Wah wah, it's a violation of federal law, blah blah blah."

The Postmaster General stepped forward, looking Maggie in the eye. If she was at all intimidated in the presence of the world's mightiest hero, it didn't show. "I understand what's at stake here, but a blanket exemption on federal privacy law is out of the question. What I can do is contact the Postmasters General of each individual state and have them appoint an official at each location to supervise, and to help you with your search."

"You don't understand," Maggie said with a frown. "These bombs could go off at any moment. I barely have time for this meeting, much less for red tape and pleasantries at every stop along the way." She tossed back a glass of orange juice. "Here's how this is going to play out: I zigzag across the country at several times the speed of sound using every tool at my disposal to locate these zombie bombs. As soon as I find one, I destroy it with my laser vision, or possibly my bare hands. Some of the mail around it, and in all likelihood a significant chunk of the building itself, may be lost as well. But as long as no one gets in my way, we shouldn't have to deal with casualties."

Fran narrowed her eyes. "Well, then take me with you and I'll supervise the operation myself. By all reports, you're plenty strong. One little passenger shouldn't be too much for you to manage."

She returned the woman's stare, considering it. The truth was, if anything unexpected came up along the way, having some top brass in tow might actually come in handy. And since she doubted she could convince Carter to make the trip, the Postmaster General would be the next best thing. Besides, bringing passengers along for the ride at top speed was always a good time. She had seen any number of hardened criminals reduced to tears (or worse, vomiting) by a short trip at Mach 5.

Maggie smiled. "Are you sure that's what you want?" The Postmaster swallowed hard and nodded. Maggie gave the second half of her bagel a cursory chew before bolting it, and slung an arm around Fran. "You might want to borrow a scarf," she said. "And button up tight. Otherwise everything flaps around." She gestured, indicating the annoying flutter of loose clothing. "That's the real reason I wear a bodysuit. The cape is just for effect. Nobody wants a gust of wind slapping their shirt into their face as they swoop down to stop a robbery."

"Thanks for the bagel, Prez," she added, hoisting the Postmaster General off the floor the way another woman might lug a squirming kindergartner to the car. "Next stop: New York City."

"Why there?" Fran asked.

"Because it's a nefarious supervillain plot. These things always start in New York."

When it came to overused villain clichés, Baron Von Zomb didn't disappoint. With her superhuman ears, Maggie could already hear an ominous ticking coming from the depths of New York's largest mail sorting facility as she made her approach.

"Set me down in front and I'll organize a search!" Fran yelled in her ear over the rushing wind. Maggie was impressed. They had made the trip from Washington at close to top speed. Normally at this stage anybody she was carrying would be a mess. Say what you want about Washington bureaucrats, that was some intestinal fortitude right there.

"Just tell your people to clear the building," Maggie yelled back, setting her passenger down on the post office steps. "I've got this."

She barreled through the front door and made a beeline for the back of the building—the nice thing about x-ray vision was that you always knew which door to take. It was still before 7:00, so there were only a few postal employees to dodge along the way. Within moments she had navigated the hallways to find the huge, cavernous room where the primary mail sorting was done.

And found a scene of utter chaos.

At first Maggie thought she was too late, but then it dawned on her: the New York post office always looked this way. Packages were stacked in slapdash, mountainous piles that looked like they might topple in a gentle breeze. It was a miracle, she mused, that anyone in the greater metropolitan area ever got their mail. She began scanning the mess of packages—between her advanced hearing and x-ray vision she'd be able to pinpoint the source of the ticking in no time.

Bingo.

There, beneath a stack of collector plates and a box that appeared to be filled with river rocks (seriously, the things some people send through the mail would boggle your mind), Maggie found a crate that her vision couldn't penetrate. Von Zomb must have lined it with aluminum siding, the one thing she couldn't see through. In general, this was fine by her, because although it meant she generally had trouble locating criminals in suburban tract housing, in most situations a glaring blank spot in her field of vision would lead directly to whatever any particular villain wanted to hide from her most.

Maggie noticed that the address label was smeared and nearly illegible—perhaps ensuring that the bomb would be undeliverable, and thus still be in the post office when it went off?—and the return address simply read 'YOUR MOM'. That sounded like Von Zomb, all right. She quickly tore the lid off the box... And stumbled, falling to her knees.

Zyfronic gas! It was a common industrial gas, and was also Magnifica's secret weakness. Trace amounts like they put in aerosol spray cans were all but harmless to her, but in a concentrated dose—like the cloud that just hit her in the face—it robbed her of all her superhuman powers! Unlike her difficulties with aluminum siding, however, the zyfronic thing was a carefully guarded secret. To the best of Maggie's knowledge, Nancy North was the only other person alive who knew, and she trusted Nancy unquestionably. She crawled away from the box, feeling her strength slowly return as she cleared the immediate vicinity. She was able to get a better look at the device from outside the zyfronic-infused area. It was a hodgepodge of explosives and biological components all cobbled together, and included an almost comically oversized clock that appeared to be set to go off at midnight. The most innocuous possible time for an explosion at a post office.

Supervillains loved scripted formula, though, and Von Zomb was a 24-karat nutcase, so who knew what that guy was thinking.

Also, as shoddy as the bomb's construction was, it was entirely possible that the zyfronic gas wasn't meant as an attack on her personally, but just a viral propellant that had slowly leaked into the box until she opened it and got a lung-full.

Maggie found some large, unassembled boxes and used them to fan the gas away from her. It would be simple to melt the timer into slag with a pinpoint laser blast, but the real threat was the contagion itself. She wasn't comfortable enough with her knowledge of bomb design to separate the weaponized viral elements from the rest of the device without accidentally becoming infected.

Conrad would know what to do. That guy was a mechanical genius, and had a kind of telekinetic control over machinery, to boot. He would be on the team that was hunting down Von Zomb, though, and she didn't want to pull him away from his other duties, much less have to carry him around all day in addition to the Postmaster General. Besides, she could always rely on Plan B. Maggie held her breath, hurled herself toward the bomb and grabbed it, rocketing out the post office's back door and turning straight up into the morning sky. She flew as fast as she could into the upper atmosphere, and hurled the package directly toward the sun.

Plan B was pretty much always throwing stuff into the sun. It was kind of her trademark, actually, and she'd developed quite an arm for it. The stuff took a few days to get there, but she had Dogstar monitor her various projectiles' progress (that guy spent all his spare time at his instruments peering out at the cosmos anyway), and so far she had never missed. Truthfully, she just had to get close enough for the sun's gravity to take over and finish the job.

Even without breathing it, she could feel the zyfronic gas weakening her constitution. Nine more trips like that was going to take a lot out of her. Still, she'd made good time. If all the other bombs were set to midnight, she should have no problem finishing. She turned and headed back for New York, swooping through the front door to find Fran giving orders to a crop of post office officials.

"Ready to go? I figure Los Angeles is a safe bet, and we can hit Chicago on the way over." To her surprise, the Postmaster grinned wide. Maggie figured the woman would probably have had enough non-vehicular supersonic travel and might just let her handle the rest without supervision. Instead, she seemed all but giddy at the prospect, drawing in close and throwing an arm around Maggie's shoulder.

"Ready when you are," she said.

Chicago proved as fruitful as New York had—on their third post office fly-by, Maggie spotted the tell-tale box lined in aluminum from high altitude, right through the building's roof. She dropped off her passenger and rocketed the whole kit and caboodle into the stratosphere unopened, but the box's structural integrity buckled during her ascent and she somehow managed to get covered in an even bigger cloud of the gas in the process. She was going to have to be more careful getting rid of these things. With the next one, she decided to carefully burn open the box from a safe distance with laser beams, then fan away any built-up zyfronic fumes before tossing it into the sun.

Curiously, Los Angeles turned out to be a waste of time. They spent a couple of hours searching before finally giving up and making a quick jaunt up the coast to San Francisco, where an explosive care package awaited them inside a lovely, scenic post office just off the bay. Still, they were making excellent time. All three bombs had been set to explode at midnight, and it was barely ten in the morning. Or seven, rather, on the West Coast. The clocks in the packages so far had all been ticking away on East Coast time. She decided to make a quick stop at a pay phone to check on her team's progress. Conrad had worked up some big, bulky communicator devices that could transmit over long distances via radio waves, but she found it much more convenient to simply carry dimes.

"Talk to me, Olivia," she said into the receiver. Olivia was technically just the sidekick of Professor Medium Maximus, but it was just as well that she was manning the switchboard today, because Maggie refused to deal with that guy on principle. It was a long story.

"We think we've found Von Zomb," Olivia said. "He's hiding out in that old, hollowed-out volcano lair he used to have. The robotic defenses have been beefed up, though, and it looks like Mofongo's back, too. We're sending Tina, Conrad and Chuck to investigate."

Mofongo? How did that minion not stay dead? He was Von Zomb's right-hand muscle, an enormous, undead, semi-intelligent gorilla who had given the team plenty of trouble in the past. He was strong enough to go head to head with Tina the Tank, and utterly devoted to his master.

"Understood," Maggie said. "Any intel on where the rest of these bombs might be hidden?"

"Nightwatchman is consulting on that front. But he hasn't come up with anything yet."

It looked like Maggie was going to have to keep doing this the hard way. "Keep me posted," she said, hanging up the phone. As she did, she heard Fran in the booth next to her, finishing her own conversation.

"How could I possibly know what they're doing there, Freddie? I don't know, call public works or something. You understand that the Postmaster General is not an appropriate point of contact for this type of problem, right?"

"Trouble back at the ranch?" Maggie asked after Fran ended the call.

"Oh, it's just the guys back at the post office in Casper. It's my hometown. I was Postmaster there until last year, but since my promotion they seem to think they can call me up to fix every little problem."

"You're a lifer, huh?" Maggie said. "I assumed the people at the top of the heap were just political appointees."

"Second Postmaster General in history to have risen up through the ranks," Fran said proudly. "My great-grandfather was actually PG years ago, under Taft. He packed the department to the gills with relatives, and it's been the family business ever since."

Casper, Wyoming. Maggie was slowly realizing the sheer number of post offices in the sheer number of cities they would have to search today. "Now that we know what we're looking for, maybe make some calls and get some more bodies in on this search?"

"You know, I've been thinking about that," Fran said, "but I think you had it right this morning. A nationwide alert is just going to create panic, and that never makes anything easier. Besides, if someone does find a bomb, isn't there a chance some local cop will want to play hero, try dismantling it himself and get zombified in the process?"

"It's less of a chance and more of a tradition," Maggie said with a sigh. "If you want something done right and all that… Okay, let's get a move on. God willing, we'll find the rest these things before we make it all the way down the list to Wyoming."

"Oh, but it's beautiful this time of year," Fran teased, hopping up into Maggie's arms.

My, this is starting to get cozy.

Maggie figured they'd check San Diego and Seattle, then head back East for Philadelphia and Boston and some of the larger population centers on the other coast. The bombs they wound up finding, though, were spread throughout the country seemingly at random. They flew through a dozen cities with nothing to show for it, before finally stumbling across explosives in Indianapolis, Atlanta, and Fort Worth. Maggie didn't think it was worth mentioning that the USPS was apparently trafficking enough Mary Jane to fill a football field. Fran seemed pretty buttoned up and it would probably make her mad. Bombs in Tucson and Kansas City eventually followed, and by the time they found the ninth device in Raleigh, North Carolina, the sun had already set. Maggie was starting to feel awfully tired, too. The truth was, the one time she had been exposed to this much zyfronic gas before, it had almost killed her.

She couldn't afford to slow down, but she was starting to worry that if she didn't find the final package soon, she might not have the strength left to hurl it out of the Earth's atmosphere.

Maybe she could just throw it into the sea? Zombie mackerel would probably be trouble. Plus, Olivia would be pissed if she thought Magnifica was *poisoning our beautiful oceans*, and Chuck would probably mope for weeks.

City after city, however, yielded no results. By the time they were flying over Madison, Wisconsin, the nation's 82nd largest metropolitan market, it was past 10:30 and panic was starting to set in.

"Checking them by population size isn't working!" Fran yelled in Maggie's ear. "There must be something we're missing!"

Maggie had been in touch with Nancy over the course of the day to keep her informed of each bomb they found. If Nancy North hadn't uncovered a pattern, Maggie was confident there was no pattern to be found. "He probably just picked city names out of a hat or something," she said.

Fran was still chattering, mumbling the target cities they'd found to herself under her breath. "Fort Worth. Raleigh. Atlanta. New York." She paused. "Oh my God. Is it possible he's trying to send a message to me, personally?"

"I suppose so," Maggie said. "Why?"

"Because if I had a city starting with U, I could use the first letters in each one and spell out the words '*Suck It, Fran*.'"

"You know, that actually kind of sounds like Von Zomb," Maggie said. "And it's the best lead we've had all day. What cities start with the U?"

"Not too many," Fran replied. Maggie slowed to a gentle glide so they could talk without screaming at each other. "There are a handful of Unions and Union Cities. Urbana, Illinois isn't too far from here."

"Point the way," Maggie said.

The nice thing about smaller towns was that each one didn't have a million post office buildings to check over. They rapidly crisscrossed the country working their way down the list, and finally found the aluminum-lined box they were looking for in a place called Utica in upstate New York.

"About goddamned time," Maggie said. She barely had enough strength left to break orbit, but in moments the final package was out of her hands and on its way to the center of the solar system. This had definitely been one of Maggie's more grueling days at the office, but at least it was over, and with forty-five minutes left on the clock, too. She had to admit that it had been unexpectedly nice to have company while she'd raced across the countryside. Even as a member of the Liberty Patrol, her raw speed and power generally set her apart, so thwarting villainy tended to be a fairly solitary affair.

Maggie didn't generally give much thought to the way she presented herself to civilians, and therefore was completely oblivious to the way the moonlight framed her as she landed, adding silvery highlights to her long, dark hair as her cape flared behind her majestically. "Want to grab some dinner?" she asked, floating gently to the ground in front of the Postmaster General. "Saving the world always puts me in the mood for pasta."

"Thanks for stopping by my apartment first," Fran said. "I need a shower like you wouldn't believe."

"I wasn't going to say anything," Maggie teased, plucking a mangled insect from the wisps of hair that had escaped Fran's braid in-flight. Magnifica's hair seemed to generate a localized field that repelled small particulates when she flew, but her passengers weren't so lucky. They landed directly on the twentieth-floor balcony of Fran's Washington high-rise and entered through a sliding door which Maggie was slightly mortified to learn was left unlocked. Honestly, anybody could fly up there.

Fran disappeared into a back room. "You know," she called out, "I could always whip up a pot of spaghetti if you don't feel like going out. You did all the heavy lifting today—if I'm this tired, you must be exhausted."

She didn't know the half of it. Repeated exposure to the gas had left Maggie utterly drained and she felt like she could collapse right there in Fran's apartment and sleep for a week. "Sounds like a plan," she said.

"Help yourself to whatever's in the fridge, then. I'll be out in a few."

Maggie found a battered coffee mug, filled it from the tap and wandered around the apartment listening to the roar of water from the shower. The decor was mostly 1970s ultra-modern, but there were more than a few touches that had clearly made the transition from small-town Wyoming. One tiny room was filled with a battered old desk and comfy-looking chair. The walls were covered in shadow boxes showcasing a selection of Girl Scout sashes and merit badges and a framed photograph of a smiling woman in what appeared to be a space helmet.

"Hey," said Fran. "I see you found my little office." Her long hair was dark and wet, combed out over the shoulder of her white terrycloth robe. She looked smaller somehow and tired around the eyes, but her skin was pink and rosy and she smelled like lemon and lavender.

"Nice badge collection," Maggie said. "Who's the movie star?"

"Movie star? That's Valentina Tereshkova! First woman in space? Flew the Vostok 6 in 1963? You don't remember her?"

"I guess I wasn't big into international news when I was in my teens."

"I was just out of graduate school," Fran said. "And pretty sure I was going to be the second one. I wanted to be an astronaut so bad, and I had such a crush on her."

Oh. *Ohhhhhhh.*

"Well, why not?" Maggie said. "She was an astronaut! A tough, smart, daredevil pilot. Kind of cute, too... you know, if you like that sort of thing." Maggie was babbling. She couldn't recall having babbled since she was fourteen and her mom had tried to introduce her to Muhammed Ali in an airport. Fran's freckles had almost been blotted out by her blush, and the color didn't stop at her cheeks. Where her neck sloped under the bathrobe, her skin was just as charmingly pink. Maggie found herself wondering just how far that rosy glow extended—and then stopped herself from using her x-ray vision. She took a hasty sip of her water, half-choking herself in the process.

Fran gave her a few pats on the back. "Are you okay?"

Maggie nodded and tried to regain her distant, super-heroic dignity by standing tall and tugging surreptitiously at her cape. Thanks to her magenta boots, she was significantly taller than Fran and found herself again eyeing the strangely beguiling curve where Fran's robe closed.

Meeting her eyes, Maggie did her best to seem as unlike the ogling creep she suddenly apparently was. Fran's blush seemed to redouble as she ducked her head.

"Um," Magnifica said.

"Yeah," Fran replied. Fran's eyes had little golden flecks, and her upper lip had a single cinnamon chip of a freckle that Maggie found indescribably appealing. Fran lifted her little round chin, and Maggie felt herself considering pressing her lips to the clean, pink, pretty mouth of the nation's first female Postmaster General… "You know, if it hadn't been for that ridiculous villain's evil plan, I might never have met you," Fran said softly.

"Tell me about it. Remind me to send Wilhelm Krauthammer a thank-you note," Maggie murmured, leaning forward to meet—

"Wait," Fran said, pulling away slightly. "Baron Von Zomb's real name is Wilhelm Krauthammer?"

"I know," Maggie grinned. "With a name like that, it'd be a miracle if he *hadn't* turned to supervillainy." She leaned in again, only to be shoved back by Fran's square little hands.

"You don't understand," she said, agitated. "Krauthammer was up for Postmaster General before I exposed his massive corruption. It's how I got the job—he swore revenge on me and everyone I ever loved! Maggie, what if all those packages we found today were just decoys? On the phone, Freddie said there were a bunch of workmen messing around the post office today. There could be an eleventh bomb hidden in Casper!"

Maggie glanced at her watch. "Crap—it's almost midnight! Sorry, Fran, we'll have to continue this conversation later."

"Don't think that you're going without me."

"You're not even dressed! We don't have time to—"

"I'll be fine," Fran said, jumping into Maggie's arms. "Now move it, sister!"

Magnifica wasn't about to argue. She took a running start toward the balcony and leapt into the night sky, barreling westward at maximum speed and cradling Fran as close as possible to keep her warm. In her diminished state, the trip took an excruciatingly long time. When they finally arrived, Maggie scanned the building for a tell-tale aluminum blind spot. What she found instead was several tons of explosives piled up in a back room. Von

Zomb hadn't even bothered to shield it.

"My God, Fran," Maggie said, making a hasty landing in front of the building. "It's enough to blow up half the city!" She burst through the heavy double doors and raced down the hallway, only to find herself flying into clouds of zyfronic gas, losing control and skidding across the floor into the back wall, twisting her body around just in time to protect Fran from the impact.

"Maggie! What's wrong? Jesus, it smells like a factory in here."

Maggie's head was swimming from the collision. "The gas—" she said. "Robbing me... of my... powers." This couldn't just be residual gas from the bomb, either. The stuff was pouring out through the vents. "The bomb's in that room," she said, stumbling to her feet. "I don't have the strength to destroy it—I'm going to have to try to disarm it."

"How can you do that without becoming infected yourself?!"

"What choice do we have?" She took a step toward the explosive-filled room, but felt a hand on her shoulder.

"Maggie, I have to be the one to do this."

"I won't let you take the risk," Maggie said. Powers or no powers, she was used to taking her own life into her hands. "If you're exposed—"

"Then you'll be here to stop me from spreading it. Think about it, Maggie. If you get zombified, then what? You die, stop breathing whatever this gas flooding the place is, and suddenly you're back from the dead with all your powers, but under Von Zomb's control. You'd be unstoppable! That's the risk we can't afford to take!"

"Fran, you can't!"

"It's not your decision," she said, pushing Maggie backward with a hard shove. It was an amount of force that Maggie wouldn't even notice under normal circumstances, so she was shocked to find herself losing balance and falling to the floor. Fran gave her a tiny apologetic wave as she slipped into the other room, shutting the door with a loud click.

"Fran!" Maggie leapt to her feet and lunged at the door, but found it locked. She reflexively tried pulling the door off its hinges, but of course now she was no stronger than an ordinary human being. There was a muffled scream from the other side.

No!

The door had a glass window set into it. Maggie hit the window with her fist, but it only resulted in a loud thud. Jesus! She couldn't even break plate glass with a single blow? How did people live like this? Through the small rectangular glass, she could see a mountain of explosive putty that nearly filled the room. The clock affixed to it was showing 12:01, with a little red light flashing away. Fran was lying on the grubby tile floor in the corner, a mess of red wires tangled up in her clenched fist.

Maggie didn't need superhuman hearing to know that Fran's heart was still. Nevertheless, a small noise was coming from her mouth. "Nnnnnnng," she moaned.

No, no, no.

"Maaaaaaster… I hear and obey." She opened her lifeless eyes and started crawling toward Magnifica. "Infect. Infe-e-e-ect."

Maggie felt utterly devastated, but didn't have time to stop and mourn. How did the contagion spread? By touch? Was it airborne? She couldn't afford to stick around and find out. She bolted down the hallway, feeling just a hint of her strength return as she passed through the front door and was hit in the face with the chilly night air. She found a yellow Volkswagen Beetle parked on the street and shoved it up the steps with her shoulder to barricade Fran inside. Then she took off down the street, running as fast as she could until recovering enough to fly.

At first she could barely make it a few feet off the ground, but what she lacked in power she made up in rage. Before long she was rocketing over the Pacific Ocean, on a southwestern trajectory, toward a certain volcanic lair tucked away in the Hawaiian islands. She hoped her teammates hadn't finished with Von Zomb yet.

Five thousand miles seemed to pass in a heartbeat. When she arrived, she found Conrad and Chuck—or Mechaman and the Human Torpedo, as the world knew them—lounging in big, plush, comfortable-looking chairs, watching over Baron Von Zomb, who was locked up tight in about forty pounds of mechanical shackles. Tina the Tank was perched upon the chest of a fallen, fourteen-foot gorilla, staring at him through a huge grin as if daring him to get up and have another go at her.

"Good to see you, Mags!" Chuck said, taking a big bite from a turkey leg he had apparently confiscated from the secret base's kitchen. "You're a little late for the action, though. This guy's been defeated for more than an hour and he's still in full-on cackling monologue mode. It's amazing. I've never seen anything like it."

Baron Von Zomb's maniacal laughter sputtered to a halt when he saw her enter the room. "You think this is over, fool? Ah, Magnifica! I assume you liked my little zyfronic gas trick?" She just glared and waited for him to continue. "You thought your friend the Major took that secret to his grave, did you? Well, it's amazing the tales dead men will tell when properly motivated."

"Hey, you want some more of this, buddy?" Chuck said, waving his fist at the villain, turkey leg and all. "I told you to shut up, already."

"Do what you want with me!" Von Zomb taunted. "Beat me up! Lock me away in prison! I already got what I wanted. I could feel that bitch Hitchcock die the moment the infection took her. The psychic bond between zombie and master is unbreakable—she'll obey my commands from halfway around the globe as long as she has strength in her lifeless, perfectly-preserved limbs. In fact, I'm proud to say that she's almost found her way out of that old post office already. She'll be rousing the townsfolk any time now, her only desire to infect, infect, infect."

"Wait, what's he talking about?" Conrad asked. "Hitchcock? Is that the Postmaster lady you were flying around with all day?"

"Oh, don't worry about her," Von Zomb said through a sneer. "She won't mind the work. Hell, she'll even enjoy it if I tell her to. Watch this—Mofongo! Enjoy punching yourself in the face!"

The big gorilla worked his right arm free from under his torso and started clobbering himself in the jaw and giggling. "That's fun, boss," he said in a deep growl. "You want I should keep going?"

"Lord, what I wouldn't do for a hundred more like him," Von Zomb said. "But then, I had to create him the hard way. This new method is so much more efficient! Even in the godforsaken barren wasteland of Wyoming, the zombie plague will spread like a wildfire as soon as it hits the general population." He gave Magnifica a wild-eyed stare. "Whatever will you do? Put your little friend out of her misery with your bare hands and risk infection yourself? Burn her up with lasers from high orbit, just to be safe? You'd better hurry! In fact, you may already be too late! Fly away, little birdie, and try to save the world again! Fly! Fly!"

Maggie stretched one arm, took hold of Von Zomb's neck gently but firmly, and snapped it like a twig.

There was a gasp from somewhere in the room. "You all heard him," Maggie said, her voice flat. "He was commanding his zombie to infect the population. Would you rather have had me try it his way, racing back, hoping to stop her before she could spread the plague? Is that what you would call an acceptable risk?"

Chuck and Conrad simply stared at her. It was Tina the Tank who finally broke the silence. "Tank find rabid dog once, had to be put down," she said. "Tank sadder then."

Beneath her, Mofongo let out a low moan. "Oh, God," he sobbed. "The things he made me do. I didn't want to, but I can remember every single thing. Take me away. Lock me up. Please, I need to pay for my crimes."

"Maggie," Chuck said at last, looking stricken. "What are we going to do about the Postmaster General?"

"The only thing we can do," Maggie replied. "Conrad, how quickly can you whip me up a plague-retardant, gas-resistant suit?"

▼

"It's been a while," Fran said with a smile.

"A superhero's work is never done," she said. "You know the drill. I brought presents, though." Maggie set down one crate full of scientific equipment and another full of books (for Fran) and magazines (for Mofongo). The third-generation space suit Conrad had built for her was form-fitting and amazingly resistant to tearing, contagion, and radiation, but she was still very careful when she hugged Fran, who, after all, remained a danger to every living thing on Earth. Conrad's decontamination routine included a forty-eight hour quarantine and an excessive amount of Listerine, but it was worth it to visit with Fran.

"Maggie!" Mofongo, as always, was delighted to see her. "Lookin' good, lady. Hey, how's Tina liking that Ferrigno guy in *The Incredible Hulk* show?"

"She'd like him better if she was getting a percentage, but they've been going to schools together and teaching kids about strangers and bad touching, that kind of thing. They sign a lot of autographs."

"I wouldn't mind an eight-by-ten glossy of that Loni Anderson, if you should bump into her at some point," said Fran.

"What, Tereshkova's photo is getting lonely?" Maggie teased, rolling her eyes and smiling. Mofongo and Fran watched a lot of television. Conrad had rigged them a solar generator for their modest electricity needs and an enormous, dish-shaped receiver to catch television signals. Neither of them needed to breathe or eat, and because they also didn't need to sleep, when Fran wasn't conducting experiments for NASA and Mofongo wasn't tending his zero-gee garden in the atmospheric dome, they caught up on soaps and reruns of *Gilligan's Island*. "I'd watch less TV if you brought me books more often," Fran said. It wasn't exactly a reproach, but Maggie felt a twinge even so.

While NASA appreciated the research Fran was doing for them, they didn't have the resources for regular supply runs, and it fell to Magnifica to be their link to the moon base. With a busy crime-fighting schedule back on Earth, she couldn't visit as often as she'd like, and in many ways the visits were hard on both of them. Fran and Mofongo were still a danger to the living and it was likely that their exile on the moon would be permanent. With Von Zomb dead and his research gone with him (his laboratory had self-destructed moments after his death), there wasn't much hope for reversing the infection, and Fran had decided that giving tissue samples to the U.S. government to experiment with couldn't possibly end well.

There were fail-safes, of course. If Fran decided she'd had enough of the isolation or if for some reason she and Mofongo became a threat to the planet, three people had kill switches that would trigger their instantaneous destruction via tiny implanted explosives that had been designed by that creep Reginald Thorpe over at Crexidyne, Inc. There were hidden charges on the face of the moon as well, should either of them attempt to disable their own devices. It had been Fran's iron-clad caveat. Magnifica saw the wisdom, even if she hated the idea.

"Come on in, I'll put some music on," Fran said, stepping into the haphazardly constructed but cozy shelter she and Mofongo had built. Maggie heard the sounds of Billie Holiday's 'Blue Moon' coming through her helmet's speakers. "Cheesy, I know," Fran said, "but thought it was appropriate. We can play it as loud as we want, too. It's not like the neighbors will complain."

They spent the rest of the afternoon together, but before long Maggie had to bid farewell and make her way planet-side. In addition to time spent on the moon, each visit meant two days of the Liberty Patrol protecting the planet without her while she waited in quarantine. She shuddered to think what the world's supervillains might get up to in that time.

To be honest, though, she looked forward to these tiny vacations after a visit to the moon. She had the cleanroom set up with a big, soft bed and an office workstation—every time she stayed there she told herself she was going to get started on her memoirs, but she never did. She had taken some decorating tips from Fran's apartment back in Washington, too—shadowboxes hung on the walls with Maggie's old socket wrench from her steel-working days, and the cowboy and Indian toys she used to play with as a kid. And above the desk sat a framed photo of her own hero, although she hadn't worked up the courage to ask for an autograph yet… It was a copy of the official portrait of the first female Postmaster General of the United States of America.

And first woman ever to set foot on the moon.

THE SECOND BATTLE OF GETTYSBURG

By Kriscinda Lee Everitt

Caleb Hollings ran his hand across the rough, splintered bark as he circled the trunk of the oak, inspecting the ground around it for disturbed earth. His eyes fell on an area that looked as if it had been dug up by a squirrel. He squatted down, pushed his fingers into what he figured was the hole, and pulled out a soft-lead minié ball. Grinning, he stood, brushing the dirt from his find, and was about to triumphantly call out to his friends. Mary Ziegler picked her way across the plain of corpses, not looking for anything in particular. Jacob Kyle was on the other side the field, having managed to hook a medium sized branch into the buttonhole of a Confederate's jacket, and was currently pulling with all his might to turn the body over. Caleb's brow creased and his mouth sank.

There was good money to be made in town for authentic battle souvenirs, but Caleb couldn't bring himself to rob the dead. Not directly, like that. And the men on burial duty didn't much care for it either. Dipping into the pockets of the spent soldiers was tantamount to dipping into their own, since digging didn't pay much, and most were assigned the duty as a penalty for some rule broken, so weren't paid at all.

Jacob yanked until the body, bloated by the harsh July sun so that its clothes looked two times too small for it, rolled over to reveal the buttons and buckles Jacob coveted.

"You're gonna get in trouble, Jacob. You're gonna get caught," Mary said as she approached. She wore a faded-blue gingham dress and the mud from the heavy rains earlier in the week clung to the toes of her boots. Her hair was mousy, but her eyes were a captivating shade of green. Jacob waved her off as he dropped to his knees and began working his jackknife against threads that held the tiny trophies to their owner. After a moment, he crawled off to the side, gagged, took a deep breath, and continued his grisly work.

Caleb stood at the edge of the field watching his two friends. Just last year, he was able to catch frogs with Mary without looking at her twice, but this year was different and, try as he might, he couldn't quite pinpoint why.

He watched Mary turn from Jacob and look around the field. Jacob acted as though she wasn't there. Or, that's what it looked like from Caleb's vantage point. Caleb didn't understand—she was exactly the kind of girl that a boy should want to grow up and marry. She caught critters, stomped in the mud, and could outrun even him. Jacob, he thought, must be crazy.

Caleb sighed, then continued scouring the woods for small arms shot, sabers, caps, knapsacks, and blankets. Some trinkets were good for the sightseers, others could be given to the families whose houses and farms had been looted during the fighting. Some of the blankets he would drop off at the college. Old Dorm was transformed from classrooms and sleeping quarters to a hospital, and though there were darn near seven hundred men inside, there were many more about the grounds, and it got chilly after the sun went down.

It was July 7, 1863, and Gettysburg was trying to pull itself together. Three days of fighting had ended and now all that was left to do was clean up the mess. Men worked as quickly as they could to take care of the Federal dead, but the Rebels were left to bake. Talk in town, though, said that Rebel or not, they had to get buried, if for no other reason than to suppress the stink that filled the streets. Most of the corpses in town had been attended to, but the surrounding fields and farms sizzled with rotting, cooking flesh. They had to do something. In the meantime, girls like Mary sold flowers and townsfolk got used to recognizing each other despite the handkerchiefs tied around their faces.

Before the first day of fighting was through, six days earlier, the out-of-towners began to move in. Some were distraught and desperate—looking for loved ones they'd hoped had survived the onslaught—but many others were just there to see, because the opportunity was there. Some locals expressed disgust and openly scolded men and women in the streets, calling them vultures and daring them to go look—to go see the horror and see what war really was. So people did, and many came back into town flushed or pale. Still others returned wide-eyed and gossiping, unable to really process what they'd seen.

All Caleb knew was that there was a wealth of goods strewn about those fields amongst the bodies, and over the few days since he'd emerged from his cellar with his family on York Street, he'd heard enough stories of the battle to be able to entertain the guests.

Currently, the three friends were in a field north of Chambersburg Road and south of the railroad cut. It was late afternoon and Caleb's cotton sack was heavy with solid shot that never made its intended target. He also had one small saber thrust into the back of his belt, one beaten cartridge box, and a blanket. Thus weighed down, he decided he had enough to carry and began to make his way toward Jacob, who was just finishing up with the Confederate, standing and brushing off knees caked with dirt and gore. Caleb picked his footing carefully; while one could easily avoid the bodies, big and bloated as they were, one couldn't always miss the parts. He'd learned that the hard way the day before, his heel slipping and causing him to pitch on account of a segment of hand and just three fingers.

His eyes scoured the ground in front of him until he stopped short in front of a hole punched perfectly into the earth. He knew immediately what it was and dropped his load, fell to the ground, and began to dig with his hands. A few moments later he was smiling up at a grimacing Jacob, now standing over him. Caleb cradled a fully intact, unexploded artillery shell.

"All the luck," Jacob snorted and shook his head. "Not fair."

Caleb grabbed the blanket next to him and began wrapping up his precious find. "It's because I don't go around worrying the dead," he chuckled, and Jacob grunted a reply. Caleb grinned, knowing he could make as much with one shell as he could with a hundred pieces of shot. Mary joined them now, having filled an apron full of whatever flowers she could find at the edge of the field that hadn't been decimated by artillery. Caleb gathered his own battlefield harvest and stood, shielding his eyes from the sun. He looked off to the northwest, toward John Forney's farm. "I think we should head out that way tomorrow."

"I think we should go to the other side of town. I heard there was more fightin' there," Jacob said.

Caleb had heard the same thing, but disagreed. Other kids were going south of town because they had heard the same thing—the fighting was more vicious, more brutal, and there were more horrific sights to see there. That's why he preferred to cover the ground bloodied on the first day—fewer people, more treasure.

The two boys looked at Mary, who shrugged. "I don't care," she said. "I'm going where the flowers are."

"You go where you want. I'm going out toward Forney's," Caleb said to Jacob.

"Suit yourself," said Jacob, and they all began their trek back into Gettysburg proper.

The little town of Gettysburg, with a population of about 2,400, was crawling with people: Federal soldiers and officers who stayed behind to survey the damage and round up prisoners and deserters; medical practitioners who came from all over the country, jumping at the chance to practice their art (particularly the art of amputation); relatives either in a state of desperation to find their missing loved one, or devastated at having found him; and the sightseers.

Caleb had never seen it like this in all his thirteen years.

The range of emotion was wide; people wept and laughed, men walked gallantly and some limped. Some men couldn't walk at all and needed to be stretchered to the station. Then they were shipped off to whatever sacrificing state they'd come from—or off to Fort Delaware as a prisoner of war. The thread to all of this emotion was talk. Caleb couldn't walk from one end of Baltimore Street to the other without gathering half a dozen battle stories, even if he covered his ears.

After a stop off at his bedroom to squirrel the shell away under his bed until he could gather enough information on the street to devise a good price, he struck out to hear what there was to hear. Just steps away from his own doorway, he stopped short upon hearing the words 'Devil's Den'. The massive collection of boulders just south of town had always had a kind of mystical quality about them, but the yarns that were spinning as of late—the intense fighting, the depositing of Confederates, both dead and alive, into the cracks and crevices as a kind of quick and dirty burial—were the stuff that made your scalp crawl.

A woman behind a floral printed kerchief spoke to the man who owned the print shop. She described how some women acting as nurses had gone down through the fields to help the men who had very nearly drowned when the run had come up too high with the rains. Some actually did. But the women had not returned before nightfall, and they hadn't been seen since. Caleb lingered, pretending to investigate some bug on the ground and thinking of the downpour on the evening of the last day of the fight.

"There might still be Rebels in the woods," the man said.

"Oh, pray not!" cried the woman, hands going to her heart as if it might stop at the very thought. "Let's pray to God not. We were assured those woods were cleared!" The woman looked about to leave, so Caleb left as well, continuing down the street, and wondering what had happened to those poor, well-meaning nurses.

"Hey!"

Caleb swung around at Mary's voice and smiled without being able to help himself.

"Hey," he replied.

The flowers she'd collected that morning were now neatly arranged in a small barrel that she carried. A rainbow of color from their myriad petals reflected the sun in a kaleidoscope below her chin.

"Gettin' anything good?" she asked.

"Yeah."

He had become aware that from the day he'd perceived the tint of her eyes—the first time he'd observed the shape of her nose and the delicateness of her fingers—he'd more often than not found himself at a loss for words.

"Well," she said, and paused. He was pretty sure she'd noticed as well. "Let's walk around," she continued. "You can get more stories, and I can sell more flowers."

Caleb nodded and let her go first, following red-faced.

As they headed down York to Hanover and to the Square, past businesses and houses, his discerning ear picked through the gossip for the most valuable information, and soon he was upon it. The moment they turned the corner and entered the Square, he narrowly missed bumping into a man who was in mid-story.

"I got it from Forney," the man said, scratching his nose. "Said there's damn near five hundred boys up in his field… doesn't know what to do with 'em. Says he gone out there yesterday mornin' n' saw the damnedest thing you'd ever see. Seventy-nine of 'em—he counted 'em—seventy-nine of 'em lyin' all in a perfect row, toes up, 'cept for three. They fell face first. Damnedest thing."

"Out on Oak Ridge? In John Forney's field?" Caleb interrupted, but the man flicked a hand and shooed him. Another man ignored Caleb and took up the conversation.

"Serves 'em right, God-damned Rebs," he said. "I say best use 'em for mulch." Caleb turned and they continued down the street.

The following day Caleb rose bright and early, pulled the stash of Confederate blankets from under his bed, stuffed some of yesterday's cornbread into a sack and headed off toward Forney's farm. After meeting Mary in the Square, they passed Old Dorm on the college grounds. Upon seeing a limping soldier appear from around the building, pushing a wheelbarrow full of feet and arms between reclining, injured men, to be buried a little way off, they both quickened their pace. They walked briskly up Mummasburg Road, toward the farm. The smell was pungent and, though Caleb found himself getting used to it, it was getting worse as they neared the railroad tracks and the steep incline up toward Oak Ridge.

They breached the summit and kept going.

To their left was what he assumed to be the very scene the man in the Square had been talking about, and it was every bit as gruesome as he imagined.

The field was indeed littered with the dead, some on their backs, some on their faces. He preferred them face-down, as the sun had swollen their tongues almost out of their heads and their eyes bulged. Mary stopped him and pointed to a solitary woman, skirts raised, picking her way carefully across the carpet of bodies. She was looking for someone.

"What brigade?" Caleb called out to her. She seemed startled for a moment, then called back that she was searching for someone in the 6th Alabama. Caleb turned northeast and pointed away from the field she was in, to another. She looked for an instant like she would crumple, but then, heaving a sigh, she pulled her skirts up and began trudging toward the field indicated.

"Sad," said Mary as they watched her plod along awkwardly.

Mary's mother had died last summer, just over a year ago. When it happened, Caleb had no trouble hugging and crying with her, but it felt different now. As if any gesture was magnified a thousand times, and therefore more vulnerable to scrutiny.

"Yeah," was all he could manage. It was easier when Jacob was around.

They watched her for a moment and then turned back toward their destination: Forney's farm.

The barn doors were flung open to allow as much air in as possible. The two paused, looking in.

Wounded Confederates lay on the hard dirt floor, packed like rolled tobacco in a tin, with barely a handful of hay for cushion. Many moaned as they felt infection creep its way through their veins, and the pain of shattered bone beneath flesh kept some mercifully unconscious. They called out for water, their mothers, or merely an end to it.

This seemed so much worse than the corpses on the field.

"Should we go in?" Caleb asked.

Mary stood silent for almost a minute, which felt like an eternity to him.

"It's why we came, isn't it?" Her answer implied yes, but her body language spoke differently.

Caleb took a deep breath and took the lead. He felt Mary close behind and again thought of how he was pretty sure this was what his father meant when he talked about his mother having been 'the marrying kind'.

After his eyes adjusted to the murky atmosphere, he scanned the men, searching for one who might seem in the least pain and therefore have the most clarity of thought. He knelt down beside a man whose side was brown with old blood, but seemed to be still bleeding, as the center of the stain was dark and wet. Mary stood in the center of the barn, stiff and fidgeting with the hem of her pinafore.

"I'm looking for anyone who fought out on Oak Ridge," Caleb said. The man looked at him vaguely and then pointed weakly to another man across the barn. Caleb rolled one of the blankets he carried and placed it under the soldier's head, who immediately closed his eyes and either slept or died. Through sparse and scattered hay, filthy with dirt and blood, the boy crawled his way over to a Confederate who wore a dirty bandage over one eye and stared with his good eye through a crack in the barn wall, out into the sunshine. He was dressed in grubby butternut that was stained with blood here and there.

"'Scuse me, sir," Caleb began, and then paused to see if the man had heard. He didn't seem to, so Caleb touched his arm gently, which made the soldier jump and grab the boy. He almost cried out as the dirty fingers squeezed his wrist and one glassy eye held his. "I got cornbread," Caleb wheezed.

The soldier loosened his grip, shaking his head. "Can't eat no more," he said, the South in him drawling out sweetly. Caleb wondered how someone whose voice was that softly soothing could fight on the wrong side.

"I got a blanket," he returned, as he pulled it out.

"Now, that I can use," the soldier smiled with difficulty. Caleb moved to put the roll beneath his head like the previous soldier, but this one stopped him. "Don't move my head. I can use it tonight, when it gets cold." With that, he took it under one arm and pulled it close to his side.

For an instant, Caleb thought he smelled lilac, then he felt Mary's presence kneeling beside him.

"You're from Iverson's Brigade?" Caleb asked as he pulled his knees out from under himself and sat directly on the ground. The soldier's eye flared wide, and he grabbed Caleb's collar, pulling him close. He felt Mary's hand on his shoulder.

"You don't say that name to me, boy," the soldier spat, then just as quickly released Caleb and sank down again, as if every bit of energy he had left was spent in that one gesture.

"What happened out there?" Mary asked. The Reb stared into a dark corner of the barn, and for a moment, Caleb wondered if he was still of this earth.

"We was ordered to go. We had to push forward, had to take that ridge, to push those Yanks back down. I'm in the 23rd North Carolina. We went out with the 12th, 20th, and the 5th. Something went wrong. O'Neal attacked first and everything just fell apart from there. We marched right up to the stone wall—didn't see hide nor hair of 'em, 'til they stood up, plain as day, and let 'em fly, close as you are to me right now." The soldier's one good eye watered and a salty tear cleaned a streak through the dirt down his face. He turned the eye to Caleb. "The boys went down—so many of them went right down, right in a line. I dove behind the wall, pushed up against it. I tried to wave my hat, but it was gone. I looked up and saw musket barrels pointed out, killing me and my boys. And that bastard..." His face twisted into a grimace. "That bastard, he said 'give them hell,' he said. Give them hell. And then he hid... behind a tree." He sputtered those last words between clenched teeth, his eye rolling to and fro, grasping for something to hold onto in his absolute rage, then softened again, his eye slowly turning over toward the bright crack in the boards of the wall. "We've lost before," he said so softly that Caleb wondered if he was still speaking to him. "How often has Billy Yank spilt our blood on our very own soil? This Yankee town done us wrong." Then he was silent for several minutes.

Mary dug into Caleb's knapsack and placed a piece of cornbread next to the soldier, just in case. They made to stand, but the soldier spoke once more.

"They're up and about at night," he whispered.

"What?" Caleb asked, and bent down once more.

"My boys. I can hear 'em out in that field." Caleb couldn't quite understand what he'd meant. "... out on the field..."

And then it hit the boy, accompanied by a jolt of horror and pity.

"Sir, those boys are dead," Caleb said in as measured a tone as he could muster, to make sure this poor, delirious man understood. "I'm sorry, sir, but they're gone."

The soldier turned to him once more. "The shelling stopped days ago. Did we win?" He looked desperate, but also as if he knew the truth.

Caleb shook his head slowly, and although he was glad of a Union victory, at this moment, he felt sad. He heard Mary sniff, but when he turned to her, her eyes were dry, but her mouth turned down like a horseshoe.

The soldier's eye again turned toward the crack. "They're not done fighting," he said. "My advice to you, boy, would be to turn tail an' get outta town." He looked at Caleb once more evenly. "We will take this town."

The look he gave was one with such conviction that Caleb believed for a moment it would all start up again—that the bullets and shells would again whiz through the air, and through bodies, as they did just days ago. The soldier eyed the crack again and Caleb felt as though they'd been dismissed. He looked over the lot in the barn, discerned the dead ones from the live ones, then he and Mary distributed the remaining blankets and cornbread as best they could.

Wagon wheels ground to a halt outside, so they squeezed through a space of a missing board and sneaked away, turning back to see that a nurse had arrived and was hauling buckets of water into the barn. Caleb thanked her silently and they headed back into town.

As soon as he walked through the front door his father called from the kitchen.

"You sit down," his father said, brow furrowed and a kind of anxiety etched into his features that were completely unfamiliar to Caleb. He did as he was told, feeling anxious. "Jacob Kyle is dead. Both he and his father are dead." Caleb blinked at him, and was opening his mouth to speak, not actually knowing what he would say, but his father continued. "They were walking out on Emmitsburg Road. Henry said..."

"Henry's all right?' Caleb interrupted. Henry was Jacob's little brother.

"The boy lost a hand," his father continued. "He said they could get money for shells, and they were just all over the road up there. They were trying to empty them... to get the shot out."

"And they blew up," Caleb finished, his mouth feeling formless as he spoke, but the words were clear. His father grabbed his arm roughly and shook him.

"Now, I know you're making some money, and I don't care about that. You sell what you find; it doesn't matter. The whole thing's ugly—may as well get something good from this mess." He pushed his face close to Caleb's, tightening his grip. "But you don't touch those shells. You hear me?" Caleb nodded, somewhat frightened of his father's intensity. "I mean it, Caleb. You see one of those things, you don't go near it."

Caleb thought about the bundle under his bed, bouncing back and forth between the money he could get for it and the image of Jacob Kyle, blown to bits. His father released his arm and pulled Caleb into a hug not wholly foreign to the boy, but rare enough that he threw his arms up and around, soaking it in. "Now, you get," his father said, straightening up. "Why don't you go play?" He said the word 'play' as if it was something he hadn't seen Caleb do for years, although it had only been just over a week since Gettysburg was serene enough for the playing of a child.

"There's nowhere to play right now, Pop," Caleb said. Quickly, he added, "But I'll find somewhere."

He stepped out onto York Street and stopped, gazing out into the bustle of the townsfolk, thinking. After some wandering, Caleb found Mary sitting with her knees pulled up and her back against the brick wall of the general store on the Baltimore Street corner of the Square. Her barrel was empty. He squatted beside her.

"You sold all your flowers," he said.

She looked at the barrel and nodded. "I guess I did," she said, as if she hadn't been there when any of the exchanges took place.

They sat for a few quiet minutes. It was a kind of quiet. The space between them hung empty while the town moved around them, squealing and squawking. They didn't hear it.

"You heard about Jacob," Caleb said. Mary nodded.

Caleb thought of her stoicism in the barn and watched her eyes. The lids held her tears in check. He could see them brewing, but they never spilled over and onto her pink cheeks.

She suddenly heaved a deep sigh that came from her toes. Her accumulated grief hung about her head, dulling everything about her—her hair laid limp, her dress worn. The toes of her boots were scuffed, maybe from their trips out to the fields. But the moss green of her eyes, as they gazed out onto the busy street, seemed to exist in another reality, shining glossy like a new leaf.

"What are you gonna do with all your money?" Caleb asked, hoping to distract her. He expected the life to return to her face, but it didn't. Instead, she reached out and pressed a line into the wooden rim of her flower barrel with her thumbnail.

"Mama still doesn't have a stone," she said. Caleb's heart sank. "But I don't think I'll have enough."

Another stretch of their private silence. Caleb thought.

"I know," he said. "You can come with me, when I take people out to the fields. You can sell your flowers twice, maybe three times as fast that way."

She scratched the side of her nose. "Really?" she asked, less looking for an answer, but expressing that she felt she was somehow unworthy of this gesture.

"Well, yeah," he said and smiled.

When she returned it, he knew at once that any money he made himself from his own business of trinket-selling and battlefield tours, he would gladly give to her. She would argue with him, but he would make it impossible to refuse. He wasn't sure how, but he would.

Caleb spent the following morning gathering tourists and selling small shot. He meandered around the square until he saw people who were clearly not local, and if they didn't look like surgeons, and they didn't look like troops, he'd approach them quietly and ask them if they needed a guide.

"There's a sight to see up on Oak Ridge," he'd say. When the people inquired as to what, he would just grin, shake his head, and tell them they just had to see it to believe it. Once he got five or six people to agree to go, he would pull out a red handkerchief from his back pocket and pretend to blow his nose. In a moment, Mary would appear.

"Flowers!" she'd call to no one in particular, ignoring Caleb. "Flowers!"

Then he would garner the attention of his tour group and serve them his pitch.

"Ladies and gentlemen, if I might suggest, perhaps purchasing a few flowers to take with you might be a good idea." He gestured to those passing by, who employed their own flower-filled rags to their noses. He pointed to Mary, whose back was to them. When most everyone agreed the idea had merit, he would tap Mary on the shoulder and she'd feign surprise. "Excuse me, Miss," he'd say. In this manner, Mary sold five times as many flowers as she did on any other day.

The group would then rally on the corner of Carlisle and the Square and start trekking out to Oak Ridge, leaving Mary behind in town to sell more flowers. He made three trips just that morning, and at a nickel per person he was making more than his older brother Ben did at his smithing apprenticeship.

On the last trip, as they made their way up Mummasburg Road, the women complained of the dirt on their shoes, and Caleb's mind went to work, trying to figure out how much of a cut a trap driver would want. The barricades hastily thrown up by troops with nearby farmers' fences were pushed out of the way enough for at least a pony and trap. His thoughts were interrupted by complaints of the smell. As they came over the ridge, the field opened up to the left of them and his group gasped. Caleb reminded them of their purchases in town and as they wrapped their flowers in their handkerchiefs, he pointed over to his right and slightly behind them, and began to tell his tale.

"O'Neal's Alabama came over from this way," he announced, and pointed back over to the left, more into the distance, toward Forney's farm. "The North Carolinians, under Iverson, came from that way." Caleb wondered briefly how the one-eyed Tar Heel was doing, if he was doing at all. He then pointed toward a stone wall in the middle of the field, "And that's where Baxter repelled 'em." Pointing back up to the farm, he yelled, "Iverson said to give 'em hell, and then..." Caleb paused here for effect. "... he hid behind a tree."

The women clicked their teeth with disapproval, and the men shook their heads.

Caleb continued the bloody account as he led them to the fence. The ladies passed through the gap easily, though clearly disturbed. Before them lay hundreds of bodies, a field of grey, light-blue and butternut, dirty and rotting. The ladies begged the men to cover up the faces of those nearest them, which the men did reluctantly, lamenting that they all didn't carry more kerchiefs.

Caleb led them to the line of soldiers.

"See, they came right up to the wall before Baxter's men stood up and fired. These boys fell where they stood," he said dramatically, punctuating it with a swoop of his hand down the line. The group looked on, fascinated, murmuring at how horrific and uncanny the whole scenario was. One man lined himself up with the boots of the dead men, shut one eye to get perspective.

"You sure you didn't come up here, boy, and line these men up like this?" he said, still squinting at the boots of the line.

Caleb became indignant. "No sir," he replied. "No sir, as they lived is as they died, right there, God's honest truth."

The man smiled, conceding.

Caleb noticed some men pacing the field. He let the group wander around inspecting corpses and what was left of the scattered personal effects of the dead, saying they'd regroup at the wall in fifteen minutes, then headed over to the men. One was scribbling on a pad of paper, while the other pointed and surveyed the land. As Caleb approached, they stopped.

"I'm afraid, little man, your business days on this field are going to be over," the surveying man said, smiling. "Morbid as it is." Caleb stopped in front of them and the puffed-up Confederate at their feet.

"What d'you mean?" He put his hands on his hips.

"I mean, we're burying these boys tomorrow," the man said and then seemed set to continue with their work. "Right there," he pointed out to the scribbling man the line of dead soldiers. "Work's practically done for us. Just dig a long trench and roll 'em in." Scribbling man scribbled some more.

"When? What time?" Caleb asked, again gaining the man's attention.

"Startin' early, goin' all day," the man replied. "So, if you want to bring up any more of those vultures, you'd better get 'em in today."

Caleb cursed his luck, but resolved to get back into town and rotate as many people through as possible before sundown. As he walked back to the wall, he had a sudden entrepreneurial thought and grinned at his own genius. He would get a few more groups in today, and tomorrow's selling point wouldn't be the line, but the event of the burial. Watch these bastard Rebs put in the dirt! See bodies swing to and fro until they drop into the hole! Macabre, yes, but at the same time, he found he couldn't accept that Mary's poor mother lay as unknown to anyone but her kin as these Confederate would soon lay. And he couldn't accept that each time Mary visited her up at Evergreen Cemetery, she had to count the stones until she found the shallow dip of her grave, the only signal to her location.

As he approached the stone wall, the group was waiting for him, but dismissed him as soon as he arrived. One of the men paid him his fee and said they could find their way back to town, so his services were no longer needed. Thanks went around, and one woman even passed him a sweet, which he stuffed into his back pocket. He offered to run into town and fetch them a carriage, but they declined, saying they needed to walk this off. Some of the ladies looked as though they might have regretted their Gettysburg adventures, which, Caleb was sure, seemed like such an exciting idea when concocting it. He wished them a good day as they walked off, and then turned his attention toward the Forney farm. He thought again of the one-eyed, dying soldier as he fingered the candy in his pocket. A moment later he was on foot to the barn.

He could hardly believe that the stench from the day before could possibly be worse, but it was. The barn doors were closed, which struck Caleb as odd, since the heat of the day had already gotten unbearable a couple of hours ago. He looked around, found no one outside the barn and no one coming up the road, so he swung one of the doors open and was met with a mixture of cries. Some of the men, with their weak, raspy voices, thanked him, begging him for water, and others pleaded that the doors be closed again. The cacophony of intonations—some angry, some afraid—rose to a buzz around him as he strained to see the back of the barn, where the one-eyed soldier should have been lying. He stepped amongst the soldiers, narrowly escaping the grasp of a few who'd gone a little funny, and made his way to the rear.

A man sat with his back against the wall, staring at Caleb, and sitting next to a form beneath a blanket, which Caleb assumed to be the one-eyed soldier.

"He's dead," the man said. "When's the woman coming with the water?" This man had already been serviced by surgeons, his left arm gone from the shoulder.

"Don't know," Caleb replied, still looking at the blanket. He involuntarily reached for it, but the man struck out with his one remaining arm and stopped him.

"No," he said. "I cover 'im up durin' the day 'cause I don't wanna look at 'im. But it's cold in here at night…" He trailed off and his eyes moved toward the same big crack in the boards that the one-eyed soldier had stared through.

"Why were the doors closed?" Caleb asked. "You'll all roast alive in here." The man shot his gaze back to Caleb and the fear that took root there struck the boy immediately as contagious. He found himself creeping back a half step.

"Last night," the man's voice quivered, "they came." Caleb could only squint at him, not understanding. "Angels or devils, I don't know which," the man continued, and the soldier to his other side rolled away and groaned.

"What are you talking about?" the boy asked, becoming somewhat impatient, not so much at this poor soldier, but because he suddenly, very desperately, wanted to be out and away from that barn.

"I don't know anymore if we was fightin' for right. If so, they was angels. If not, they was devils. Whoever they are, they's comin' to take us, heaven 'er hell." The man paused. "They come last night. We could hear 'em comin' from over the ridge out yonder." His eyes floated again to the crack. "They come, an' they got all up around the barn. I managed to get up an' get the doors closed and the bolt down, but they damn near shook the place 'til I thought it'd come down on our heads. An' they moaned n' groaned, like they's belonged in here, with us, all tore up an' hurtin'." He stopped and was lost in the memory, then didn't seem like he'd continue.

Caleb reached out and placed the piece of candy on the man's chest, who didn't seem to notice, so he stood to leave. "You shut that door behind you," the man said suddenly, startling Caleb. "An' you tell that woman who comes to shut it behind her too." The boy nodded, knowing he probably wouldn't even see the woman, but he did what he was told and pulled the doors shut tight, to the sounds of distress and relief inside.

⚜

The first thing Caleb did the following morning was to count his take. He'd managed to wrangle three more groups up, two of six and one of three. He'd made so much—and planned on making at least as much today—that he no longer cared about losing the shell sale. He thought about it tucked away under his bed and made a mental note to get it out of the house and back out into the field as soon as convenient; he'd have to do it when everyone was out of the house—father and brother at work, mother out shopping. Until then he saw no harm in it sitting there a few more days.

By dusk, he was showing his seventh group around the field on Oak Ridge. Where bodies once lay was freshly turned soil. The Oak Ridge Line was now deposited into four trenches, though just barely. Caleb noted a marked difference between the way the Federal dead were interred, and the way the Confederates were dealt with. The Federals were given as decent a burial as possible, and marked when identified so they could be found later. Rebels were tossed into shallow trenches and had just enough dirt thrown over them to keep the stench and carrion at bay.

All day, with each group, Caleb watched the men work. Some were Confederate prisoners, not yet shipped off, while others were Yankee deserters, now considered no better than the Rebs. There were a handful of Negroes as well—the only men getting paid for this repulsive and back-breaking work. Some groups would dig while others hauled bodies to the area of burial. Caleb watched one man double over and vomit after an entire sleeve of skin from a dead arm came off in his hand. By afternoon they were primarily using hooks to snag and carry them. Now, as the sky changed gradually by turns from blue to pink and eventually to orange, the men moved slowly, faces haggard and arms, when not digging or hauling bodies, hanging limp at their sides.

Suddenly one of the women from his tour group screamed and the man with her cried out, "This man's alive!"

Other men ran over to where they stood—over to what, to Caleb, looked like just another Rebel corpse. And then he heard, coming from over the field, from John Forney's barn, such a racket of screaming and calling out for someone to save them, for God's sake, save them. The boy strained to see as far as the source and noted a man running as best he could away from the barn, with another following. The soldier in front had only one arm, and Caleb wondered if it was the man he'd talked to the day before. His remaining arm on the right flailed wildly, trying desperately to find the balance that two arms gave, but he fell to the ground hard, and that's when Caleb realized the man behind him was not merely following—he was in pursuit. Another woman screamed, but the boy paid no notice, figuring it was nothing more than the field of dead they stood in, as he watched the pursuing second man fall upon the one-armed man. His head went down and then came back up violently, blood spraying into the air. It was some distance and Caleb couldn't tell for sure, but it looked like a fox he'd once seen out on Lightner's farm, tearing up the coop. The one-armed man screamed and screamed before falling abruptly into a deathly silence.

Now there was chaos around him, men and women shrieking and dashing toward him haphazardly. He scurried out of the way. The corpse they had been investigating for signs of life was on its knees, crawling unsteadily. Caleb saw a line of black ooze falling from its mouth and nose, trailing along the ground collecting dirt. Then eyes that had already formed a skin angled toward the boy, just as another cry took his attention toward a couple of grave diggers. He looked in time to see one disappear into a trench just before a mass of bodies rose up to claim the second, pulling him down into the dirt as well. And then all around Caleb was undulating; all that was once stone dead and still was now shifting and stirring. He ran, tripping once, then snatched a fist-sized rock from the ground . He scrambled to his feet and was off again.

He didn't slow until he reached the college grounds, and only then was he able to think. As he walked quickly toward Old Dorm he wondered how on earth he was going to explain what he'd just seen, but as he grew closer, the panicked yells became louder. Caleb stopped behind a tree, gripping the stone in his hand. Peeking around the trunk, he could see men streaming from the massive white columned building, once majestic and now blood-spattered. There were at least twenty black iron steps that led up to the main doors on either side—hardly a thing a wounded man could navigate—and they tumbled painfully down, stumped appendages flying wildly about their heads and knees, crying out in pain and fear. Behind them other men staggered spastically, swiping at the retreating soldiers and occasionally catching one. The ones who were caught were taken down unceremoniously, their throats torn out with teeth that hadn't chewed meat since they were alive, just days ago, possibly just minutes ago.

The men on the grounds were no better. They spread out in all directions, some heading toward him, others toward town. Some could do nothing but grab fistfuls of grass and drag their lame bodies forward, until they were fallen upon by their comrades. Then, something moved beneath Caleb's feet as he stood transfixed. He shifted his gaze down to see fingers, and then toes, squirming up through the dirt at the base of the tree. The boy stepped back, confused, watching the movement of the earth spread and the dirt fall away to reveal a pit of squirming limbs, twisting this way and that. He was standing on one of the trenches they'd dug to dispose of the immense number of amputated limbs they'd been accumulating.

A screech that in any other circumstance would have been embarrassing flew from his throat and he was off again, darting past trees and soldiers, past the murdering dead and the dying, past the great stone edifice that was Old Dorm.

He needed to find Mary.

Once he reached Washington he cut across Water Street toward Carlisle and headed into the Square, where he'd hoped to find stability, but there was none. As he made it to the center, he looked all around with views down all four roads that converged there. All was bedlam. Men, women, and children ran into and out of doorways, depending on which way they were chased. Horses reared wide-eyed as their riders pulled the reins in all directions, not knowing which way to go. A driverless carriage careened past the boy. From where he came up Carlisle Street, there were only more like him—people running, baffled.

He found Mary with her back against the general store again, standing this time, her eyes large and bewildered. He ran up to her, dodging all moving people and things, grabbed her hand, and pulled her with him.

Down Chambersburg and York was more of the same. It seemed that for every person Caleb could recognize as living, there was a blackened, grey-clad fiend limping and shambling behind, tongue lolling in and out from its distended lips. On Baltimore they watched Mrs. Creary bash a Confederate in the face with a large block of wood the old woman had managed to get up and over her head. It lurched awkwardly toward her and then, with that blow, went down and convulsed on the sidewalk. Caleb towed Mary toward home.

They got inside and Caleb pulled the door shut behind them, latching it, then rushed to the back door and did the same. There was no sign of his family anywhere. Although he wanted to stay downstairs, he saw figures gathering outside the windows. Soon the light inside dimmed under all the bodies at the panes and the occasional meaty palm slapping against the glass.

"What is this?" Mary asked, her face calm but her voice tight. "What's happening?"

"Don't know," he answered. "You have to get into the cellar."

"Why?" Now her eyes flashed with fear. Something shattered; it sounded as if it might have been the small window in the back of the house in the kitchen.

"That's why," he said, and began pushing her towards the cellar door.

"No." She struggled against him.

Although she was as afraid as he was, he knew it wasn't because she didn't want to be by herself. It was because she needed to know why. She needed a plan. She was smart like that, which is why he loved her.

And he did love her.

He pulled her into his arms for a moment and squeezed. She returned the embrace.

"They're going to get in. Go down into the cellar, board the door, and don't make a sound," he said into her hair. Lilac. "Once they've followed me upstairs and the downstairs is clear enough, run. I'll meet you at Old Dorm."

When he pulled away, she was crying, but her mouth was still determined and she nodded to him.

He yanked the cellar door open. Before he could guide her in she kissed his cheek and went in herself, pulling the door behind her. The warmth where the kiss was planted lingered as the sounds in the kitchen grew louder.

Caleb brought himself back around and took the stairs two at a time, pausing at the top landing just long enough to hear more windows give and the sound of heavy feet hitting the living room carpet.

Caleb's room was very small and not well furnished. There was the bed, and a dresser, and aside from a few of his own personal belongings—some neglected wooden toys, books, and his grandfather's cane—that was it. He clicked the lock over once he slammed the door and then pushed the dresser up to it. Next, with his back against the foot post of the bed and his feet against the dresser, he pushed his knees straight. Footsteps stomped clumsily up the stairs—first one set, then another, until it seemed twenty men were taking the stairs at once. He could hear them in other rooms, fumbling around, knocking things over, along with the screams from outside. It all came together in a symphony of absolute terror. Finally, a thud came to his bedroom door, then another, and another. With each, Caleb jumped and cried out, although he tried to remain quiet. On the fifth thud his hands involuntarily flew up to protect himself, though the fiends had yet to break through the door. He found he was still holding the stone he'd picked up on Oak Ridge.

The door above the dresser began to splinter. Before long, fists were punching their way in, pulled back bloody and then punched in once again, making the hole just a little bigger every time. Caleb looked desperately around the room. There was nowhere he could possibly go except to jump straight out the window. He doubted his situation would be much better doing that; in fact, with two broken ankles, it would be much worse. Wood flew down onto his lap as he closed his eyes as tightly as he could. It was only then that he remembered the shell.

The shell, in the blanket, under the bed.

He fell to one side, stretching his arm as far to his left as possible to reach the cane that had been knocked over in the rush to get the dresser in front of the door. It had been passed down from his grandfather to his father, and finally to him. It had been earned painfully in the California campaign of the Mexican-American War.

His fingers scratched at the polished wood before finally attaining some grip, and slid the cane over. He then propped the cane in his place, between the bedpost and the dresser, and scurried frantically under the bed, retrieving the shell.

By this time there were whole arms thrust through the hole in the door above the dresser, writhing in all directions like snakes. It sounded as if the house was being taken apart, board by board. With the shell under his arm, Caleb crawled over to the window and peered out. The street was full of them now, having choked out the living. Still screams were heard, and with every one Caleb wondered if Mary was safe.

Stories he'd heard on the streets flooded his brain—those Rebels'll skin you alive; they'll rape and pillage; they'll roast yer babies an' eat 'em fer sup; they'll kill you as soon as they look at you.

He prayed she'd gotten away.

The dresser scooted forward slightly as the cane began to give, and the hole in the door got larger. One brute began to push his face through, gouging away skin against the fractured wood, and revealing a soft wet brown beneath the dry, dark sun-baked black. Of all the stories he'd heard of the Rebs, none of them had prepared him for this.

Caleb got on his knees and wedged the shell between them. It was one with an older model paper fuse, which was missing. He aimed the brass cap ring upwards and with both hands brought the rock down hard.

Clank!

Best case scenario would be releasing the entire cap and getting straight to all of the powder inside. He'd be lucky, however, to get a little spilt from the fuse hole to ignite the whole thing. Caleb brought the rock down again.

Clank!

Nothing. Caleb stopped and lifted his head, straining to hear. Beneath the grunts and howls of the dead, beneath the cries of the living, he could have sworn he heard the sound of a bugle, faint but repeating, and for a brief moment he thought he'd be saved. The monstrous Confederates attacked the door with renewed force, the cane began to splinter, and the bugle sounded again, closer. Just then, Caleb recalled the words of the one-eyed soldier in Forney's barn: we will take this town. The boy suddenly knew whose morale that bugle was lifting, and whose call to charge it was. It was the second battle for Gettysburg. The boy heaved a loud sob as he began wailing on the shell with all of his might, over and over.

Clank! Clank! Clank!

The cane gave, and the dresser flew as the door opened wide.

▼

Mary Zeigler found herself high above the commotion.

She stood in the cupola of Old Dorm, unable to barricade the trap door, so she stood on top of it and hoped none of those things had followed her up. The Union flag above her head flapped madly with the wind as she strained her eyes to see the town, fast disappearing under the cover of twilight.

She used to walk through the college campus and admire the stately old building, eyeing the cupola and wondering how she, Caleb, and Jacob might sneak up there and play pirates. They would transform the structure into a rocking, creaking ship, sailing green seas. They would spy their enemies from the crow's nest and launch cannon fire out into the ocean. That seemed like years ago, and she felt decades older.

She scanned the rooftops in the near distance, and just as she thought she'd located York Street, where Caleb lived with his family, there was a loud explosion. Flames leapt from where her gaze rested, sending a shock wave of fear through her chest. She jerked her head in all directions, searching the horizon of Oak Ridge to the west and then Seminary Ridge a little to the south. There were no white plumes, no artillery. She waited for another, thinking the battle was about to start up again, but there was nothing.

She continued to look for Caleb, expecting to see him running across the lawn of the college, dodging the moving and the unmoving, leaping over corpses and grinning up to her triumphantly. She looked and looked until night fell.

And then, it was dark.

THOUGH SHE BE LITTLE, SHE IS FIERCE

By Michele Roger

"Are they Princess roses?"

"Yes, Joan. I double checked with the florist that you recommended in New York. Twice." Melissa said.

"Have the fresh scallops arrived for the Coquilles Saint-Jacques?" Joan stared at her slender silhouette in the long mirror.

"The sous chef texted me to say all of the fresh ingredients arrived at 5 AM," said Melissa, checking off a long list in her phone. "That ends the preliminary list to go through before we get you to the church on time." She smiled.

"The press is covering the entire day. There can be no mistakes, Melissa."

"You're the most beautiful bride in the world and, as your sister and maid of honor, I will see to it personally that you are the happiest bride to ever walk down the aisle."

Joan smiled her perfect, soon-to-be-senator's-wife photo-op smile and turned to Melissa. "Well? Am I going to take his breath away?"

"In that dress, you're going to take every man in the room's breath away." Church bells rang on Melissa's phone. "That's the wedding planner. Your groom has arrived at the church."

A fanfare of press and onlookers filled the sidewalks and the little side street leading to the cathedral. Police kept the public at bay behind tape lines, while security checked invitations in the alley behind the church before re-routing each guest to the carpet where they could be filmed walking in. Inside, the guests were electric with anticipation at the sight of their local 'royal' couple.

Joan checked her makeup one last time in the limousine mirror. She bit her lips together to plump them, then applied one more layer of long-lasting lipstick. Taking a deep breath, she gave one last smile at Melissa. The chauffeur opened the door.

"Show time!" Melissa beamed and gracefully exited the car.

Joan followed, taking her father's arm just outside the cathedral door. Through the sound of cameras and well-wishers, Joan picked out the prelude music. Her heart began to race when the large wooden doors opened and she watched Melissa gather her bouquet and take her timed steps to *Minuet in G*.

Joan felt her father's hand grip hers a little tighter. As instructed by the wedding planner, who was tapped into the radio for the camera crew, Joan and her father counted in whispers to twenty, then stepped to the archway opening to the church. *Canon in D* trickled over the balcony and rolled over the sea of guests in a wave. The groomsmen, who had been facing the altar, now turned, with the exception of the groom. Joan wondered if it was the film crew's idea for Jack to turn at the last minute. All eyes were on her anyway. The wedding was being broadcast live on all of the Detroit stations. Joan smiled and tried to make eye contact with each important guest as she stepped in time to music. She felt her father tremble a bit and Joan prayed to God he wasn't getting emotional. Not in front of all these people. She shot him a quick glance of disapproval when she detected a trace of tears in his eyes.

"Hold it together, Daddy. Stick to the script. You can always cry when Melissa gets married." She smiled at the crowd as she squeezed the old man's hand.

As they approached the center steps of the altar, Joan's father gave her a quick kiss. Melissa stepped up to collect Joan's bouquet, but as Joan and her father turned to meet Jack, a million things happened in one split second.

Joan and Melissa gasped when Jack turned to meet them. The Senator's press secretary saw Jack's face and cued the camera crew. A huge bang echoed in the cathedral; the guests panicked and hit the floor. Jack, Joan, Melissa and her father were whisked away by a team of bodyguards. To the audience, one minute the bride and groom were there, the next they were gone. The Detroit Police flooded the side aisles and instructed everyone to remain calm. The SWAT team looked for the gunman.

Joan paced in her wedding dress, only stopping to tap her perfectly manicured fingers on the lead glass window and stare out at what should have been her adoring fans and spectators. Jack's personal physician had been snuck into the side entrance of the sacristy, and was currently running tests. Melissa came in to report what she had learned. Jack had come in from Zimbabwe sometime in the middle of the night. Apparently he had met up with his best man at the hotel and complained that he was exhausted. Jack had gone to his room and presumably went to sleep. When they met this morning, he looked disconsolate, growling more than talking. The best man said he was so angry, he tried to bite the makeup crew prepping him for the wedding. Then the hotel lobby said that the Senator walked to the church. By the time the best man found Jack, it was too late to do anything save straighten his tie and get him to the altar.

"I don't believe a word of it. This is some underhanded scheme. You just wait, in an hour we will find out that some Republican put drugs in Jack's coffee or something."

"Ron would like to talk to you." Melissa interrupted Joan mid-tirade.

Ron, Jack's press secretary, entered the small room just off the sacristy. "Joan, I know you're upset, but…"

"Upset? Upset! That word doesn't even begin to express what I'm feeling right now. This is some kind of conspiracy, I'm telling you!"

"Presently, we have our own conspiracy to take care of. Security set in place an emergency deflection plan. That was the loud bang you heard. It was meant to make the guests and press think that one of you had been shot. Until we know Jack's prognosis, you and Jack must remain out of sight."

"Shouldn't we be at the hospital? Just look at him!" Joan barked.

"The doctor doesn't think we should move him yet, not until we can determine what the problem is. A car has been sent to the hospital and the press has followed it, thinking Jack or you must be inside of it."

"Brilliant," Melissa said.

Ron smiled. "Yes, I kind of thought so."

"Really?" Joan moaned. "Do you think a car is going to throw those blood-suckers off for long? Quit patting yourself on the back and get to work. Both of you! I want to know what could do that to Jack! Have you seen him? Do you have any idea what that kind of damage this will do to his career?"

Hushed voices came from around the corner, and both the cathedral priest and the doctor entered the room. "His condition worsens. I've asked Father O'Carolan to administer the Rite of Dying, just in case. Can he have your permission?"

"I suppose we need all the help we can get. Go for it, Father." She turned to the doctor impatiently. "Now, divine intervention and miracles aside, what the hell is going on? Why does he look that way?"

"The metamorphosis is spreading. The decay of the epidermis is deepening into the soft tissue and working its way into the bones of his face and neck."

"Who is the best plastic surgeon in the area? Better yet, Melissa, find me the best doctor period. Fly in whoever is the most qualified. Get them here this afternoon. He can be in bandages for the press. He will look all the more a hero if he does. Be sure to brief the surgeon as soon as they arrive that I need 'well placed' bandages. Nothing that will mess up his hair."

"That's the problem," the doctor said grimly. "No plastic surgeon in the world can fix dead tissue. It needs to be kept alive and have a blood and oxygen source." He paused and ran his hands through his salt-and-pepper hair. "By all medical definition, Jack is dead. He is decaying like a corpse. I just can't figure out why he is still conscious. He has a pulse and basic brain function."

"My father is still very upset," Melissa said quietly. "Were you able to reattach the, um, piece?"

"No. Your father's firm handshake, combined with the compromising bone deterioration, took Jack's finger clear off. Both the finger and the hand are dead. There is nothing to reattach it to. I'm sorry."

Ron took Melissa's hand. "We can't really tell your father anything, but he seems to be a very honorable man. Please tell him that he acted completely appropriately and anything that the Senator is suffering is not his fault. Can you tell him in those exact words?"

"Yes, thank you," Melissa said.

"Now," Ron said, his demeanor changing as soon as Melissa left the room. "Between the three of us, what is really going on?"

The doctor went pale. "The CDC has released warnings regarding any travelers returning from Zimbabwe. There is an outbreak of a disease that local missionaries call *'Mors Comedenti'*. It means *Eaters of the Dead*."

"Careful, Doctor, you're not just breaking bad news to a bride. You are about to drop a bomb on an entire political party," Ron warned.

"I am afraid that the Senator is becoming what in modern America, we would call a zombie."

❦

"Man down! Man down! Code red in the sacristy!" Ron heard the call through his earpiece. "Team Something Blue, keep redirecting the guests to the reception in the back. Team Runaway Bride, meet me at the scene."

When Ron arrived in the sacristy he found two bodyguards kneeling over a third man.

Ron recognized the priest and sighed. "Anybody know what happened? Where is the Senator?"

"We checked on the two of them fifteen minutes earlier. The Senator was sleeping and the priest was reading from the bible. A few minutes later we heard screaming. When we got here, the Senator was gone and we found Father O'Carolan on the floor. Sir, I would have administered CPR if there was anything left of him." The bodyguard choked on the last sentence. Blood was smeared all over the floor; the priest's jaw had been broken, and most of his cheek and left side of his neck was completely gone. His chest cavity had been bitten into. The softer parts not protected by his rib cage had been devoured.

"Confirm the time of death and then leave the body. We might need to feed it to the press later." Ron pushed a button on his intercom headset, "All staff. Put everyone in high alert. The Senator is armed and dangerous. All staff has permission to use tazers to subdue and hold the Senator. Whatever you do, don't let him bite you. Subdue and hold. I repeat, subdue and hold until I get there."

"We've got a lead on him, sir!" A young woman's voice chimed in over the radio. "He's headed into the kitchen. One of the snipers has him in his sights."

"Don't shoot! Just get a team over there. Evacuate the kitchen staff and contain him, before he makes it to the guests."

Ron ran down the stairs and through the church. He stopped when he felt his cell vibrate in his pocket. The text was from Melissa. *I've Googled this zombie theory. If the doctor is right, the last thing Jack had on his mind will be his one consuming thought, aside from eating. What was Jack working on in Zimbabwe?*

He was working on passing a bill that would distinguish his career. Set him up for bigger things, Ron replied. He wasn't used to sharing information about Jack with anyone.

His cellphone vibrated again. *Joan said he was angry with some people. She thinks he might have some scores to settle?*

Ron stopped in his tracks and hit the call-back button. Melissa answered and for a moment, his heart beat a little differently. "First off, are you and Joan safe?"

"Safest place I can think of," Melissa laughed darkly.

"Where are you?"

"The limo. I'm in the driver's seat using my laptop. I figure we can drive out of here if we need to. Meanwhile, Joan can raid the mini-bar. How's Jack?"

"Joan's theory may be closer to the mark than I care to admit. He's killed Father O'Carolan and the team last spotted him in the kitchen." Ron could hear Melissa giving Joan the run-down.

"Terrance!" Ron heard Joan shout. "Terrance is always hiding out in the kitchen away from the press!"

"Jack was pissed at Terrance. She's right, that bad speech he wrote nearly cost Jack the election."

Ron disconnected and ran to the kitchen, but it was too late. "Sir, no sign of the Senator, but this one is still alive."

The young sous chef lay on the ground clutching a blood-soaked white uniform. A huge bite had been taken out of his abdominal area. The man's eyes were white and his face was already beginning to darken, particularly around the eyes. Ron stood up, clicked the safety off his semi-automatic and shot the man in the head twice.

"I want all the rest of the corpses or those bitten by the Senator shot accordingly. Do I make myself clear?" The team members nodded their heads. "Good. It would appear that these attacks may not be random. I want a guest list sent to my phone in the next three minutes. Anyone else found?"

"Just this one, and he was dead when we got here." There, lying face down on the floor, was the overweight speech writer. A piece of *fois gras* was still in his pudgy hand. He had been attacked from behind; with the back of his skull completely missing, exposed brain glistened in the artificial lighting. A look of shock was forever chiseled on his face as a result of the attack.

Ron reached into his pocket and typed a message to Melissa: *Joan was right. We need to talk. Drive over to the rectory. Meet you there in five.*

Ron hopped into the passenger side of the limousine, turned to ask Joan more questions, but found her passed out in a pile of tiny liquor bottles.

"Sorry," Melissa said. "Things go downhill quickly when there aren't any chasers and your dream man turns into a zombie on your wedding day."

"You need to sober her up and fast. We can't spend the day continuing to chase Jack while his political rampage runs through the guest list of top Capitol Hill players. Most Americans might think Washington is run by a bunch of zombies, but we certainly don't want to confirm that."

"Why do you need my sister?" Ron could see that he had frightened

Melissa. Usually he liked that kind of thing, because the more someone feared him, the more control he had. As a press secretary and the head of security for a Senator, that was as good as gold, but this innocent woman, brave enough to stay by her sister's side, organized, smart—he couldn't bear to upset her. "What are you going to do to her?"

"I'm going to put a sniper on the roof and give him permission to shoot Jack. The only way to save his legacy and his career is to kill him while he's still on top, but I need bait, Melissa. Your sister is my only hope for drawing him out. With the press watching, and a bullet in his head, I can give them a body and a story that the world can believe. Not the truth."

Chaos broke over Ron's intercom. "We have total meltdown! Help! Call in back-up! He's bitten three guests at the reception."

Ron looked wildly at Melissa, but she looked towards Joan, down for the count. "I have a better idea. Jack loves revenge far more than he does my sister." She paused. "What you don't know is that behind the press, the glamour, the French caterer and the Italian designer dress, we are looking at the world's biggest shotgun wedding."

"Joan's pregnant?" Ron gasped.

Melissa nodded. "Jack tried to talk her into having an abortion in Europe. He would quietly get her away from the prying eyes of the press. She was heartbroken that he didn't want their baby, but he insisted he couldn't have a child out of wedlock and still move up the political ladder. That's why he hates me."

"You? Why?" Ron asked, spellbound at the secret tumbling from Melissa's perfect lips.

"Because I'm the one who talked her out of it. If Jack wouldn't love her, the baby would, at least. Then I told my father. Together, we made Jack see that his only option was to marry Joan. If he didn't, we would go to the press." Melissa took a deep breath. "I helped Terrance write that terrible speech, because I knew that Jack couldn't take another negative hit, especially as big as my sister's broken heart and growing belly. If Jack wants revenge on anyone today, it's me." She touched Ron's arm. He couldn't help but want to kiss the petite crusader before him. Melissa sighed. "I better clean up my mess. Where is this sniper?"

Ron could feel his heart pounding as he stood on the roof of the office building just beside the cathedral. From his vantage point, he and the marksman could see directly into the courtyard where the remaining guests were hiding, or running and screaming.

"I'm testing the mic. Can you hear me, Melissa?"

"Loud and clear, Ron. Although I still say this Kevlar vest is wickedly uncomfortable and I look hideous."

"You look fantastic. It stops bullets and zombie teeth. Just mind your hands and feet."

"I'm going in." Melissa held her breath as she pulled out Ron's semi-automatic. She walked through the garden gate. There was little time to think. Well-dressed wedding guests with opaque eyes reached for her. One waiter tried to grab her hair. She pointed the gun in his direction and squeezed the trigger. He went down, but he was still moving.

"Aim for the head. That's the only way you know they're dead. Don't panic," Ron shouted in her ear. The tennis player from Arizona, fairly famous and once good-looking, now walked stiff-legged towards her, swinging his arms out to grab her, growling. His face was already beginning to decompose; chunks of his cheek were missing, revealing a bright set of white teeth. Melissa took a deep breath, aimed for those impressive teeth and squeezed the trigger. He went down and never moved again. "Call for Jack. We need to get him in the open courtyard. While you look, the shooter is going to try to clear off the infected guests," Ron told her. "Hurry! At the rate you're going, we're going to run out of bullets before we run out of zombies."

Melissa ran back through the kitchen, but there was no sign of Jack. She spotted a security guard and ran up to him. The man turned to reveal half of his face had been chewed off to the bone. Melissa screamed and aimed her gun. He knocked the gun from her hand and tried to grab her with the other. Melissa fell backwards, landing on the hard floor. The security guard grabbed at her left foot. In a desperate attempt, she kicked off her shoe as his teeth sunk into the thin leather. Struggling to her feet, Melissa grabbed at drawers, opening them in a panic. She found a paring knife and threw it at her attacker, missing him. She threw another knife and it pinned itself in the zombie guard's forearm. Confused and distracted, he tugged at the foreign object stuck into the bone, giving Melissa the opportunity to throw cooking brandy at him. She doused his pants and feet, breaking the bottles of alcohol as they hit the floor all around him. Then she ran to the stove and found a box of blue-tip matches. The security guard lumbered for her, coming closer and closer. Melissa's trembling fingers finally found enough strength to ignite the spark, then blindly threw it in his direction. She felt the rush of the flame, and heard his screams behind her as she ran for her life.

"Melissa!" Ron shouted. "He's at the church front steps! Can you get there and keep him busy long enough that we can film the shot?"

"I'm running as fast as I can!"

"When you get there, hold him at gunpoint so we can get a clean shot."

Melissa rounded the corner and ran towards the steps via the garden gate. "No!" She grabbed an old real estate sign post from out of the ground to use as a weapon. "I lost the gun." At the church steps, she ran up to Jack and hit him over the back of the head as hard as she could. A large chunk of his skull went flying.

"Try to hold him in one place!" Ron yelled.

"What the hell kind of sniper is it? Tell him to hurry the hell up!" Melissa screamed back. Jack turned around. As soon as he saw Melissa, he became enraged. She took another swing, but he caught the post and tore it from her hands. Melissa landed on the concrete steps with a thud.

In her earpiece she heard Ron yell, "Take the shot! Take the shot!" Her head spun. Her ears rang with the sound of gunfire, but just as she breathed a sigh of relief, a crackle came back over her headset. "Melissa, get up! Run!"

Wasn't Jack dead? Survival instinct kicked in. Ron was shouting, her head hurt, her ears rang, she couldn't make sense of what he was saying. The church was before her; she ran to the sanctuary of her childhood. Inside the cathedral, Melissa stumbled to the altar. Something warm was running down her face. The logical part of her brain told her it was bad. It was… That was bad too.

Something heavy landed with a loud thud next to her. He had missed. Another sound, this one was light, a swish in the wind. Pain registered in her brain, clearing the fog. Melissa screamed for help. The post had come crashing into her shin bone. She was sure it was broken. With her other leg, she kicked at Jack who was grunting and roaring. He grabbed her shoeless foot. He opened his mouth. With her good leg, she kicked at him even as his mouth grew closer. She screamed again and it echoed through the cathedral. Melissa reached for anything she might throw at Jack, but there was nothing. She was sure his next tug would mean his jagged teeth in her flesh. She would become one of them. Ron would have to shoot her. She would never see Joan again. She would never meet the baby that grew inside Joan's belly. With her last breath, she prayed for help.

A blast from the side window was followed by protective arms around her. It was too clumsy for an angel. It was too warm for a ghost. It was Ron.

"Did you get the shot?" Melissa asked wearily.

"Yes."

"Did the cameraman get it?"

"I have no idea. I hope so. Right now, none of that matters." Ron leaned in to kiss her and she welcomed it. "It's all over. We're all safe," he said against her lips. "Jack's legacy is safe. Joan and the baby are safe… and it's all thanks to you."

CHURCH OF THE RISEN DEAD
By Tom D. Wright

Reverend Marcus Stillwell sat on his Valkyrie outside the alley leading to zombie skid row, debating which to discard: his wedding ring or the clerical collar. The image of Jesus stared up at him, hanging from the flaming cross painted on the gas tank between his legs. Taped to the tank below Jesus was the photo of his recently deceased wife, Annie, which had been used in the wake he left to come here. A bitter cold wind stung his cheeks as he cinched his black leather jacket, but he couldn't zip it up due to the bulky rows of C4 explosive strapped around his midriff. His hand twitched when he touched the electronic detonator in his coat pocket, reaffirming why he was parked outside the zombie reservation that now took up most of The Bronx.

His friend was more than twenty minutes late, and the longer he sat waiting, the more stupid this whole idea seemed. He should have known better than to implicate someone from his bike riding club, but he didn't know who else to turn to. Retired ministers typically didn't have the kind of underground connections needed to get the material that his plan required.

Wiring the vest with explosive and ball bearings had been remarkably easy; in fact, finding plans on the internet was the hardest part. Marcus tried not to look down at Jesus as he checked his cellphone for the time, any messages or missed calls. Nothing.

Not only had he been unable to protect Annie, but he couldn't even avenge her.

He was about to switch on his bike when he heard the unmistakable deep-throated growl of another Valk approaching. Lizard rode around the corner at the end of the block and glided up to him. With leathery skin, a long drawn-out face and drooping hooded eyes, it was hard to think of calling the man anything other than Lizard, though someone once did tell Marcus what the man's real name was. He simply couldn't recall it.

After dropping the centerstand and rocking the bike onto it, the biker switched off the engine and dismounted. Marcus swung off his own bike to join him.

"Hey, Rev! Sorry I'm late, bro. It took longer than I thought, because my buddy had to make it up especially for you, but here it is." The gaunt man pulled a brown paper sack from the carrier and handed it over.

"Thanks," Marcus mumbled and reached into his pocket. "How much do I owe you?"

"Man, I know what you're gonna to do. I don't blame you for wantin' to take out those sumabitches. Someone's gotta do it. Annie wasn't an official house mouse, but we still felt like she was one of us. So anyway, don't worry 'bout it. We took a collection and paid for it ourselves."

"I don't know how to thank you," Marcus said. He opened the bag and pulled out a dark, unmarked squeeze bottle of lotion. "So how does this work?"

"It's easy, man. The guy who made it said just put it on, like it's suntan lotion. Only this is untan lotion… get it? Undead? Untan?"

Marcus shook his head as he opened the top and squeezed out a palmfull of cucumber-green lotion. The substance felt somewhat oily. He began to spread it on his neck and face. Immediately his eyes stung and a stabbing pain shot through his nostrils.

"What the hell is this?" Marcus paused to examine the ointment.

"Some kinda horseradish stuff mixed with wasabi. Zombies fucking hate that shit!"

Though he constantly heard profanity when he rode with his riding club on Saturday mornings, it still grated on the minister in him. He gave the lotion a skeptical look. "Are you serious?"

"It's real, man. Look, if one of those bastards left the res and showed up on the street, what would we do? Shoot the fucker in the head! This green shit makes you feel like you just got shot in the head, right? So imagine what it does to them."

What the hell. Marcus let out a deep sigh and resumed applying the repellent. It just needed to get him deep enough into the zombie ghetto that he could exact his revenge.

"Dayum! You should see yourself, Rev," Lizard laughed. "You look like the fucking Hulk. Might be, they'll just run when they see you coming."

"Thanks for everything. Listen, you better go, but I do have one last favor to ask."

"Anything, bro. Seriously. What do you need?"

"My bike. She's a sweet ride, and about the only thing I have left that I care about. Can you find someone to take good care of her?" Marcus held out his keys.

"I feel ya, man, it would be an honor. I'll head over to the club and bring someone back to fetch it."

Lizard looked like he wanted to say something else as he took the keys, but thought otherwise of it. Instead he gave Marcus a bro-hug before sitting on his bike and riding off. The reverend watched his riding companion drive away, then wiped his hands on the bag and tossed the lotion in an abandoned dumpster next to the alley. He wasn't going to need that stuff again.

He slipped the clerical collar off his neck and dropped it in the trash as well.

Where had God been when Annie needed Him? Where was God now?

Marcus entered the alley leading into zombie territory. The far end of the alley opened onto a deserted street, and Marcus faced an open lot lined with rows of unfilled graves. He walked across the street and stared down into the nearest pit, where the body of an old woman was simply dumped. One token shovel of dirt had been tossed over the woman's face.

When the zombie phenomenon came out of the closet, it didn't take long for large cities to take advantage of the zoms. Creating zombie reservations not only wiped out huge swaths of urban blight overnight, disposing of the deceased poor and indigent no longer required the expense of cremation or pauper's graves. The politicians called it interment reclamation, but the bottom line was that feeding the zombies actually served a useful purpose, especially for families living on welfare or minimum wage.

The late afternoon sun slanted across the field, highlighting a single zom that crouched down in one of the graves on the far side of the lot, but Marcus wanted to find a large group of them, so he could take out as many as possible. His finger caressed the trigger as he walked around the lot and down a street, past crumbling brick façades. As he walked deeper into ZomTown he saw numerous figures, some sitting and others shambling about. A few of them appeared to be in advanced stages of decay, but most simply looked pale and sickly, as if stricken with an awful flu.

Several times he passed near one of the walking dead, but when they were within fifteen feet they shook their heads and turned away. It was almost as if he was invisible to them.

A few more blocks, and the street opened onto what must once have been a city park. Now it was just a salvage yard of un-human debris. Most of the benches were lined with zombies looking remarkably like the strung-out addicts he once ministered to. Beyond them, a large dirt field dotted by small tufts of grass was littered with prone bodies.

This was precisely what Marcus wanted. He carefully made his way toward the center, occupied by the crumbling edifice of what had once been a small fountain. Weaving through the crowd, he stayed a few arm lengths from most of them, but the bench-bound zoms didn't even stir. He got to the fountain, closed his eyes, turned around and gripped the trigger.

The reverend silently mouthed a prayer, asking the Lord to forgive him for taking his own life. At least he would bear no guilt for the murder of others, since there was no Biblical commandment against taking a non-life. Even local law considered acts against zombies as animal cruelty, although the Supreme Court was deciding a case about whether zoms had the right to own property.

He opened his eyes to take one last look at the world before he pressed the button, and then he saw her.

His wife.

Annie sat on one of the benches, staring at the buildings on the other side of the park. Her silvery hair, which she always kept cut in a cute style that reminded him of elves, was somewhat disheveled, and her face didn't wear the Mona Lisa smile and sparkling eyes which he fell in love with the day he first saw her. But it was definitely her.

When she turned to look in his direction Marcus turned away. Part of him wanted to run over and gather her in his arms, but the other part was repulsed by the monstrous thing she had now become.

His hand grew sweaty as he handled the switch inside his pocket. He tried to make himself press it, but he glanced sideways again at Annie and slowly removed his hand. It wasn't really her. The woman he had known was gone. But even if it was just her body, he couldn't press the trigger.

Marcus stepped down off the fountain and noticed a zom staring at him. Unlike the others who were in a stupor, this one looked intently at him. It was a medium-sized male, a bit shorter than Marcus, with a slight build. A red wool cap partially covered a cascade of dreadlocks, but in the fading light he couldn't determine what race the zom had once been.

"What do you want?" Marcus shouted at the zom, unnerved by its attention.

"What do I want? One of those MRI machines," it called back, in a voice that was surprisingly deep and with an accent Marcus couldn't quite place.

"Why, you think that might help them?"

"Are you kidding? I want to use it as a microwave oven. You've seen those corpsicles, lying out there in the field all night. Cold cuts are fine for these guys, but I prefer my food warmed up. Better yet, if you can get one with a tanning bed too, then I can put them on a spit and brown 'em while they're warming up."

"I'll, uh, see what I can do," Marcus muttered, then slowly walked away. The zom turned back to sitting up one of the figures that had fallen over.

Dusk grew while he walked back toward the alley. Marcus sent Lizard a text to say there was no need to pick up the bike. He couldn't get the image of Annie's face out of his mind, her slack expression and the lack of life in her eyes. At the same time, memories of their last trip to the beach came up as well, as she stretched out on her towel and he spread suntan lotion on her back and shoulders.

The acknowledgement from Lizard came back by the time he reached the field of graves, where a couple of figures knelt down in the hole in which the old woman lay, devouring her. Shuddering, Marcus hurried past them and emerged from the alley to find his bike still waiting for him, which was no surprise in this neighborhood. Once the zombies took up residence, the surrounding streets became remarkably deserted. A few hard-core drug dealers and gang members had defied the evacuation orders when the reservation had been declared and the area turned over. By the time the border guards returned a week later to check on things, no trace of the dealers could be found. Not that they tried very hard.

After retrieving the hidden spare key, Marcus carefully removed the bomb vest and placed it in the luggage carrier. As he navigated the empty streets leading to the Triborough bridge, he kept thinking about that beach outing. Annie had been so relaxed and happy, looking forward to their first vacation since his retirement. They were supposed to leave for Europe and the Holy Land in a few weeks. He ached thinking about making that trip alone. It wasn't just the trip. He couldn't think about going through life without her.

A couple blocks before the bridge, a Humvee moved to block his way. A soldier swung out and walked up to examine him. Border Enforcement was printed in large white letters across her chest and back. Please, God, Marcus prayed, don't search the bike.

"Just checking." She held up an infrared scanner toward him, then wrinkled her nose. "Okay, you're warm enough to be alive. Say, is that wasabi you've got on?"

"Yeah, I guess I went a little heavy with it," Marcus admitted.

"Ya think? You know that's just an urban myth, don't you? Doesn't do jack shit." Then she walked back to her vehicle and nodded to her buddies as she climbed aboard.

When he was halfway across the span, he put his flashers on and pulled over. The traffic was light and vehicles had no problem moving around him, but several drivers still honked and gave him the bird as they drove past. It only took a minute to pull the vest out and toss it over the side. Marcus expected it to detonate when it hit the water, but the garment simply splashed into the river and vanished.

While Marcus continued his journey home, he kept thinking about the zom that watched him in the courtyard. Unlike the others, it seemed alert and intelligent *and* it spoke. Did that mean that something of Annie might remain in the body he saw in the courtyard? And if there was, how much was there?

Nothing in Bible College had prepared him for this.

Marcus woke up just before noon the next day, the whiskey bottle next to him empty of all comfort. He vaguely recalled picking it up on the way home; the hardest thing he and Annie normally kept in the house was cough syrup. He did recall that the clerk stared at him when he entered, and reached under the counter for something, but it was only when he got back to his bike that Marcus remembered he was avocado green.

As he lay in bed, head pounding, the image of Annie sitting on the bench haunted him. But was it really her? When the news and the media talked about a zom, it was never referred to as him or her, just as it—with the exception of the few celebrities who turned and kept their living identities. In fact, the latest trend in Hollywood was to put all your assets, including intellectual property, into trust funds, with a Zombie Clause. Then, if someone turned like Charlie Sheen did one weekend just for the hell of it, their zom would still be escorted everywhere by the same bodyguards, ostensibly to protect the public. But in reality life, or rather unlife, went on for the celeb the same as before. Sheen had been almost as disappointed as his dealers when he found out that zoms didn't react to cocaine like the living. So really, Marcus shouldn't have been shocked to see Annie's zom sitting there, but, as in all other things, celebrities somehow seemed different.

Even before he wrestled himself out of bed, Marcus knew he had to go see her.

When he came up to the alley, he noticed the door of a service entrance slightly ajar. He had to give it several shoves, but then the door screeched open. He found a small freight entrance to the long-abandoned tenement. A few minutes later Marcus had cleared out enough debris to carefully ease his bike inside. The door didn't lock, but having his ride behind closed doors was far better than leaving it out in the open.

He found the zombie repellent where he dumped it the previous day. From the smell of the dumpster it had been a considerable time since it had last been emptied. This time he just smeared a small amount of the lotion on his cheeks, as though it were aftershave.

So far the zoms hadn't seemed particularly threatening. According to the newspapers, the city morgue kept ZomTown well fed.

When he got to the square, Annie was still in the same spot. It wasn't clear whether she had moved from the day before. As he looked around at them, these creatures resembled homeless residents more than fearsome monsters.

Marcus reminded himself that it was a zom like these that had left the enclave and attacked Annie.

He started to turn around several times, more fearful of what he wouldn't find than what he would, but finally he walked up to her and crouched down to look his wife in the face.

She was wearing the same jeans and chiffon blouse she had worn to the church book club meeting on the night she was attacked. The orange blouse, stained with blood on the right shoulder, partially covered the deep gash where she had been bitten. After the zom attacked her, she broke free and fled into the night, which was why they didn't recover her body before she turned. The lack of a body was why her wake had been closed casket. However, she appeared to have no other injuries aside from the bite wound and some bruises to her delicate face, even though she was quite pale. Slowly, her gaze shifted toward him, and then her glassy eyes focused. She stared for a few moments and then quietly moaned something.

"What, are you trying to say something?" Marcus asked, his pulse quickening with hope, despite his deepest fears.

"Ennngg thhheeen eechooo eeeeey oooo."

"What are you saying, Annie? Try again; I know you can do it." She moaned a couple more times, then slowly shook her head and turned away.

"Dude, she's a newt. She hasn't learned to talk again."

Startled, Marcus looked up. It was the Rastafarian zom that had stared at him the evening before. "Whaaa?" Marcus hadn't heard it approaching.

"Yeah, she's a newt. Newly Turned." The zom walked up to Marcus and held out its hand. "I'm Chris. Go ahead, you can shake my hand, I promise not to bite." The zom made a playful gnashing motion.

Marcus instinctively jumped back, then stared at the zom's palm and slowly reached to clasp hands. The zom's grip was cold, but surprisingly firm and steady.

"Marcus," he said. "I'm her husband."

"I figured it was something like that. The only living that come around here are relatives, looking for their lost loved ones. Few come, and never more than once. So I'm surprised to see you again."

"So you *can* talk?" Marcus asked. Chris nodded. "What did you mean about her learning to talk?" The zom looked at him askew, crossed its arms and circled around Marcus, examining him up and down. A chill ran down his spine as he wondered whether the zom intended to eat him. Reflexively his hand gripped the lotion bottle in his jacket pocket. If it came to it, maybe he could squeeze hard enough to squirt the thick liquid in its eyes.

Finally, somehow satisfied with what he saw, Chris replied. "When a zom is turned and wakes up, it's similar to a baby among the living. She won't starve to death, but your wife needs to be taught how to function again. When they can care for themselves, we call them walkers."

"Is that what you're doing here?" Marcus glanced around. It didn't seem like much of a school. "Teaching them how to..." He almost said live. "Function again?"

"No, not me. There's far too many here. I'm a Guardian, just looking after them until someone can take them on and care for them. Every night I round 'em up like a little flock and guide them into that building over there. Then in the morning I bring 'em back out, and make sure they get fed now and then."

"Kind of like a homeless shelter?"

"Yeah, I suppose. So, what's her name?" Chris turned to face the woman.

"Her name was Annie. How much of her is still there?"

Chris sat on the bench. "It'll take time for memories to start coming back, just like learning to talk. They won't all return, but some will. Inside, she's still the person you knew." He took her hands. "Your name is Annie. Can you say at least part of that?"

Annie slowly turned her gaze to Chris, then after a few moments made some sounds, with what was obviously enormous effort. "Ahhh. Ahhh… eeeeee. Ahhnnneeeee."

"Yes, that's very good!" Chris stood up and gestured for Marcus to sit. "Go ahead and work with her. I've never seen such a quick response, which means there must be a very strong drive inside of her. Just talk, encourage her to respond and be patient. When I was among the living I was a rehab therapist, and this isn't very different."

Marcus spent the afternoon working with Annie, coaching her to first make sounds and then to begin piecing them together into words. At first it was creepy, but by the time the sun was getting low, it was Annie that he was leaving behind, not a monster. Still, when he stood and gave her a hug, it felt strangely awkward, and the thought of kissing her almost made him puke.

The bike was safe in his impromptu garage.

While Marcus drove back to Queens, he wondered whether it was really Annie that was coming back, or maybe just some sort of reflection. And real or not, did this Annie have a soul?

When he first learned that Annie had been attacked, he questioned why God would allow such a thing to happen. For the first time, he wasn't sure what it might be, but perhaps there was a purpose to all this after all.

⚜

The next morning Marcus arrived just as Chris was guiding the first zoms out into the yard.

"Can I help?" he offered, setting a backpack on the bench where Annie normally sat.

"Some of these new arrivals are a little unpredictable, so I better take care of them," Chris said. "Just in case they bite. You never know, and rabies ain't nothing compared to what these nips pack."

Marcus didn't argue the point, and instead went to look for Annie.

From that day, he worked with her every morning.

Every so often a functional zom, the ones called walkers, would come by and lead away one of the newts. Initially the walkers regarded him with suspicion, but over the weeks that turned to curiosity and then finally acceptance. As quickly as newts were adopted, new ones seemed to drift in.

Marcus slipped into a routine of getting up and making breakfast, watching some of the local news so he could be prepared for the day's weather, and then putting together whatever he needed to take to ZomTown with him. Usually, he brought some small token from their home for Annie to handle, such as the small statue they brought back from their trip to New Zealand. Also, every day he picked out an outfit for Annie, trying to match up items that he could recall her wearing together. Although zom-Annie didn't seem to care, he knew the old Annie would've. So the first thing he did when he arrived at the zom park was lead her into a nearby building where he brushed her hair and changed her clothes. Initially she simply complied, but by the end of the week she was actually helping with the dressing process, even if she fumbled helplessly with the buttons.

One morning, after he zipped up her skirt and started brushing her hair, he began to sing one of her favorite hymns, one that she had often sung to herself while brushing.

The trumpet sounds, the dead shall rise,
Christ lives, Christ lives, risen from the dead

It was only when he reached those final lines that he realized she had begun humming along with him. He repeated the last stanza a couple of times, and she followed along, her humming growing stronger and more confident. Marcus then sang another hymn, "Abide With Me," and she accompanied him through the whole tune, smiling at the end. The hymn seemed to have awakened something inside of her. Annie stood up on her own, took the hairbrush, and headed out to the courtyard without having to be led. By then Chris had just finished leading all of his charges out into the fresh air. He stopped in amazement as he watched Annie sit on the bench and begin brushing her own hair.

"That's amazing, she's really coming along," Chris said when he came over. "Usually it takes them a few months to become this responsive."

"It was when I started singing to her that she really perked up."

"I wish I could have that success with some of these others," Chris said. "They could certainly use some perking."

"Yes, I've noticed," Marcus said. "So far all of these new zoms have been pretty mellow. I haven't seen any crazed killers, like they show on the news all the time. Nothing like the one that attacked…" He couldn't finish.

"The one that turned Annie," Chris said. "Those are the ones that we don't get to in time. Just imagine, if you were born and everyone in the hospital ran away, your parents screamed at the sight of you but you had no idea why? We all have bad in us, living and zom alike, so it shouldn't be surprising that the way we're treated brings out the bad in us."

"I guess we didn't know any better. It was like that with the living as well, when I ran a mission for the homeless. The ones no one loved."

"Like these," Chris said, sweeping his hand around the park. "I don't think you're going to be able to stop with Annie, you know. They need your help as much as those homeless did. Why don't you try your singing thing with them?"

The next morning, when Chris brought his charges out he gathered them all together, facing the fountain. Marcus started off singing "Amazing Grace," and to his surprise all of the zoms responded, even the newest ones. It seemed that even if they couldn't sing the words, they could hum. By the third verse the whole courtyard echoed with the humming of a hundred voices. Heartened by their response, Marcus then led them through several more gospel songs. By the time he wrapped up his last song, "The Day of Resurrection," at least two dozen walkers had wandered into the area, drawn by the singing.

For Christ the Lord hath risen, our joy that hath no end.

He paused at the end of the last stanza, and felt the silence of expectation weigh upon him. For the first time in years, he faced an attentive group that waited for him to say something, but what should he say? How was he to save souls that he wasn't even sure were really there?

"Talk to us," one of the walkers who wandered in during the singing called out. "Give us some good words."

This was something he hadn't seen coming. The only other time Marcus ever froze in front of a crowd had been the first time he gave a sermon, when he forgot his own name during the introduction. Facing an audience that he had no clue how to connect with, he had no words to give them at all, let alone good words. Silently he stepped off the fountain edge and walked through the crowd of zoms. He didn't even say farewell to Annie. He just hurried back to the place where he stored his bike and headed upstate, taking the interstate to no place.

By the time he reached the first exit for White Plains, Marcus was ready to stop and collect himself. The more he thought about it, there wasn't any real difference between ministering to the living or the undead. The Lord instructed that the Word was to be spread to all the ends of the world. If zombies happened to be part of that world, who was Marcus to say they shouldn't hear the Gospel? They were all the same as Annie, and if there was any part of Annie's soul remaining, how could he not minister to her?

Maybe the Lord was calling Marcus out of retirement.

Taking the highway onramp back to the city, he began to consider the best way to reach this new congregation. Nothing in seminary could have prepared someone to preach to the undead; this was unknown territory. Like being the first missionary into the Americas, except hopefully this would turn out better.

When Marcus got home, the first thing he did was choose a clerical collar from his dresser drawer and put it on.

When Marcus entered the zom park the next morning, Chris looked somewhat surprised, which was rather remarkable for a zom.

At first, Marcus followed the same routine of preparing Annie for the day, although this time she did most of the work herself. Mostly he just handed her the new clothing and took the old, then handed her the brush. She even used some of the makeup that had sat unused for weeks.

They sang several hymns, and by the end of the last song she was actually forming the words, but when he started for the door, Annie reached out and caught his arm.

"I know you," she said, her diction slightly slurred but otherwise clear. "I'm not sure where from, but we knew each other before. Didn't we?"

"Yes, Annie." His voice trembled. "I was your husband."

She stared at him, then whispered, "Oh, Marcus. Your name is Marcus." She stepped toward him, and without thinking he folded her in his arms. Awkwardly at first, then she wrapped her arms over his neck and laid her head on his chest. Her body felt cold as he held her against him, but her shape was familiar and he began to caress her. Annie's voice, never as strong as it had been before she turned, was muffled in his shirt. "I don't remember everything, but it's starting to return. Thank you. You brought me back."

Marcus began to cry and the tears fell on her shoulder.

She leaned back, still within his embrace, and put her hand on his cheek. "The hardest thing about being a zom is not being able to cry." She buried her face in his chest again, and he didn't want to ever let her out of the protection of his arms. After all this time, he hadn't been sure that he could reach the Annie he once knew, but here she was. Then, Marcus remembered that he had a new flock to tend to.

When he went out to the square, it was packed with more zoms, both newts and walkers, than he had ever seen gathered in one place. Scattered throughout the crowd he even saw some living humans, probably individuals who had come to look for a loved one. There had to be several hundred living and undead altogether.

Marcus started out leading them through half a dozen songs, wishing he had brought his guitar. What this crowd lacked in sophistication, it more than made up for in enthusiasm. The park echoed with the sound of humming.

After the songs, Marcus raised his hands for silence and took a deep breath. "I know many of you have felt forgotten, alone, abandoned by the world that now shuts you in and wants nothing to do with you. But I am here to tell you that you are not alone. You do not have to wander in darkness. For God so loved the world that he sent his only son. Christ died for the sins of the world, and he was raised from the dead, so we may live."

At that, the entire square erupted in a chorus of cheers and moaning attempts to cheer. Heartened by the response, Marcus gave his standard introductory sermon. The content mostly concerned searching for goodness and eternal life, free of the corruption of the flesh, and seeking for more than what the earthly world had to offer.

Afterward, a small group of living came up him, a couple of boys and several girls, none of whom could have been over eighteen. "We came looking for our friend," said a thin, wispy blond girl. "And then your whole church thing just blew me away. This is the bomb!"

Marcus felt a wave of relief wash over him. Saving the souls of the living was something he knew well enough. "We all come to the Lord, seeking in many ways," he replied. "What's important is that we come to the truth and are saved, it doesn't matter how we found it. I'm Reverend Marcus. What's your name?"

"I'm Rachel." The girl held out her hand. "So, how does it work, this being saved thing?"

"It's really very simple. Just ask the Lord Jesus to come into your life. He'll send the Holy Spirit down on you, and you'll be born again."

"Really? That sounds so cool," one of the other girls gushed. "What is that like? I'm Alia, by the way."

"It's like nothing you've ever experienced before. I've heard people describe it as being washed in the spirit, and the Apostle Paul says it is dying to the world. Then you are reborn, and once you are part of the body of believers, you can join together with us in communion, where we eat of his body and drink of his blood." Beyond them, Marcus saw Annie wandering away, following the walking zoms that had come in attendance. Up to this point he hadn't done any exploration of ZomTown, and he didn't want to have to start by trying to find his wife. "I'm sorry," Marcus said. "I have to take care of something, but I'm happy to answer all of your questions."

"Are you going to be here tomorrow?" asked Rachel. "We'll come back."

"Absolutely." Then he hurried after Annie.

The next morning, when Marcus came out to lead the singing, the crowd had grown in size, extending onto the side streets leading into the square. Although he had a loud voice, developed from preaching over the years, he knew that if this congregation continued to grow, he was going to need some type of sound system. That fell into the category of a good problem.

This time, he kept it simple and gave a sermon based on the Beatitudes. It was hard to go wrong with those. As Marcus proclaimed each *'Blessed are the'* statement, a cheer rose from the crowd, especially when he said blessed are those who hunger and thirst for righteousness, for they will be filled.

It wasn't until he neared the end of his talk that he realized there were a lot more living among the crowd than the day before. Instead of about a dozen, now there had to be more than fifty; they accounted for much of the increase. Up near the front, on a blanket together with Chris and Annie, sat Rachel and Alia along with about two dozen other young people. They appeared to be rather listless and lethargic, as if sick.

After he gave the benediction, Marcus stepped down and walked over to the youngsters. The group scrambled to their feet.

"We are so excited!" Rachel said, somewhat breathlessly, and slightly swaying from side to side. "We're going be reborn, just like you said!"

"What are you… ?" Then Marcus saw the small gash on the side of the girl's neck. In fact, every one of the youth had a similar bite wound. "What have you done?" he asked, aghast.

"We are becoming part of the body, part of The Church of the Risen Dead. We're going to die to the world just like you said, and by tomorrow we will be born again. Raised from the dead, like Jesus."

"That's not what I meant!" cried Marcus. "Who did this to you?"

Rachel pointed to Chris, who shrugged and said, "Ask and ye shall receive, right? Well, they asked—and very politely I should point out—so they received."

"This is what we want," Alia said, grasping both of Marcus's hands. "And you'll be so proud to know, we told all of our friends, and a lot of them are coming to join now too. Like you said this morning, we have to spread the word to everyone."

"Sweet Jesus, not *this* word!"

"Why not?" Rachel frowned. "Jesus rose from the dead after three days. Obviously, he's a zom, and now we are joining him too."

Stunned, Marcus shook his head, took his wife's hand and stumbled toward the building where he worked with Annie every morning. Nothing he could say would derail the train crash taking place in front of him. Marcus sat heavily on a chair in the small room and hung his head. "What have I done?"

"What do you mean? Is something wrong?" Annie rested her hand on his shoulder.

"I've created a blasphemy, a perversion of everything I've ever learned and taught. They took everything I said and twisted it inside out."

"How do you know they're wrong?" Annie asked. Marcus started to answer, then stopped. What just happened out there in the courtyard went against everything he had been taught about religion. Then again, so did the very existence of zoms.

"If they're not wrong, then I don't know what to believe anymore, Annie."

His wife sat in the chair next to him and took his hand. "Then you accept that you don't have all the answers, and… maybe some of the ones you had were wrong. Welcome to the human condition. That's all any of us can do."

Marcus let out a long sigh and felt his tension flow out. In its place came clarity. He stood up, and squeezed Annie's hand. "Wait here." He went out into the courtyard where Chris was sorting through the remaining newts, guiding them across the yard and settling them into their spots for the day. As Marcus walked up to him, Chris paused and gave Marcus an apprehensive look. Marcus pulled off his clerical collar. "If someone wants to be turned, where is the best spot to get bitten?"

"On the shoulder, near the neck." Chris gave Marcus a quizzical look. "It won't hurt as much as some other places, and spreads quickly."

"Do it, then." Marcus unbuttoned his shirt far enough to slide the shirt and bare his shoulder. "Don't ask, just do it."

Chris shrugged, then stepped forward and sank his teeth into the exposed shoulder. A fiery pain stabbed through his upper body, and then he felt a heat slowly spread through his muscles, working toward his heart. It was as if the wound had been infected with muscle ointment.

Marcus hurried back to the building where Annie waited for him. He sat down on the floor, leaning against her legs, almost collapsing as he settled into position.

"Are you all right?" she asked.

"Not yet, but I will be soon."

The heat was spreading quickly; already Marcus was getting woozy. He didn't know what the truth was, or where heaven and hell were any more. The one thing he did know for certain was that, wherever Annie was, wherever she ended up, that was where he wanted to be as well.

He reached up and pulled her arm over his shoulder. "Hold me close, Annie. It's going to be a long night."

POST BOMB ZOMBIE ROMLAND
By Dana Wright

"Get down!" Naya reached up and yanked Paladin back underneath the rubble. It wasn't dark enough to move yet. The Roms were out again, combing the wastelands, searching. Luckily the rag-tag group of survivors huddled inside the alleyway, safe for now. There were only five of their group left, and if she had any say, it would stay that way. The Roms moved like automatons as they searched the streets with their undead eyes, looking for more survivors to add to their masses. "Do you want to get taken, you idiot?" Naya whirled on Paladin, hissing in rage. "Is that what you want?"

His expression tightened, gathering righteous indignation at being called out, and by a girl no less, until she remembered what had happened the previous night. They had lost Jesse…

"I'm sorry, Naya." His dark eyes followed her, aching to fight, but knowing she was right. Scuffing his sneakers in the dirt, he pulled the old navy blue hoodie over his head and lowered his eyes.

The Rom crews had unleashed the zoms, hunting them like dogs. Life after the bombing was only for those in the protected walls of the city, which means that if you were on the outside, you were expendable.

They needed bodies to rebuild. Bodies they didn't have to feed. Basically there were only three choices: You could run, get eaten, or volunteer to become a Rom—a zombie run by computers.

The elite had their lives back, and they were built on the backs of the undead. Zombie slaves were put in place to do their bidding, all run by a computer. There was no muss, no fuss, because the undead never needed to be fed. Not really, unless their programming failed, or they didn't get to a victim soon enough, like the wild zoms that still roamed the darkened streets.

They only unleashed the zoms to drive the human chattel out, though. More bodies to recruit for the cause…

"We have to be careful, Pal." Naya lightened her tone and stared at the group through the violet twilight.

Chester swallowed. His expression turned sallow. "There might be food over in the old Meta-Mart." His stomach rumbled; none of them had eaten in days. The old plaid shirt and holey jeans he wore hung in tatters on his gaunt frame. "Do you want to try and go there?"

She nodded. "Yeah. What do the rest of you think?" A series of nods and hopeful looks met Naya's whispered question. "Okay, Hannah. I need you to check the map. Have you updated it since last night?"

They had an old gas station map of the city with the areas of Rom occupation noted.

"Done." Hannah pulled out the map and quietly unfolded it. "Zoe, hold this." She handed the map to her sister Zoe, her long blond hair tied back in a ratty ponytail. Hannah's jeans were smeared with all manner of dirt and the old white T-shirt she wore was almost completely grey with grime. "We can't go this way." She pointed at a pocket of streets where they had been just yesterday. "I think the safest way is to take the back alley on Southern Street and turn right on Bammel." Hannah blinked in the fading light. It was hard to read the map, but everyone crowded in for a close-up look.

Naya nodded. "Okay. Let's get ready to go. Does anyone know what Jesse might have done with the water?"

Four heads shook in unison. The water bottle they had shared was gone. Naya fought against the crushing despair that threatened to push in on her. They would find more tonight, she was sure of it. Getting out of the city was imperative, but they had to have food and water to do it.

The alleyway was quiet when they reached it, and the darkness spread its inky tendrils with little light from the moon overhead. The Meta-Mart was across the street, but overturned cars littered the highway, bodies of the fallen left to rot in the open, making it difficult to maneuver across without trouble. The smell alone made Naya stop in her tracks as she tried not to vomit. Some of the bodies were still fresh; there might be some wild zoms in the area.

"Be careful, guys," Naya whispered.

They began the dreadful task of navigating the field of the dead, hoping they were all truly gone. Gore slicked the soles of Naya's sneakers and she almost slipped, then found her footing.

The small group ran as fast they could, lured by the promise of canned peaches and packages of beef jerky.

At the edge of the darkened parking lot, the faint shuffling of a probable zom halted Naya in her tracks. Pulling the baseball bat out of her backpack, she listened closely. Once she located the sound, Naya turned to face the zom, holding the baseball bat at the ready. The zom was a fresh kill and didn't look much older than twenty.

"Heads up," Naya whispered.

"Got it." Paladin unsheathed his latest sporting goods store find, a long sword. He approached the rogue zom and, with a potent swing, decapitated it without making a sound.

"Thanks. Now let's get moving before we have more visitors." Naya peered into the darkened windows of the store, but couldn't tell if there was movement within or not.

"Something's coming," whispered Hannah.

Several rogue zoms lurched into view. They were of different shapes and sizes, and in various degrees of decomposition.

"Come on!" Paladin called from the darkened doorway. It was hard to tell what was more dangerous, the open air or the pitch black of the store. "Quick!"

"Everyone in." Naya pushed the kids into the darkness and prayed the zoms would pass by without noticing that there was some fresh meat nearby.

Once they were inside, Naya was overwhelmed by the sour smell of rotting food, which was almost more rancid than the zombies outside. In the uncirculated store, the rampant odor of decomposing lunch meat and the butcher counter was nauseating.

"Oh God, that reeks," Chester moaned in disgust, covering his nose with the back of his hand.

"Sorry, kiddo. Let's find some canned food and get out quickly." Naya clicked on the flashlight and moved carefully down the canned aisle. As she moved, the haunting moans of the damned were heard from outside.

"I think we might be able to rest here behind the deli counter for a couple hours. We need to get some sleep." Paladin motioned for the others to follow.

"Why can't we just go back to the warehouse?" Hannah argued. "This place stinks."

"We can't." Naya motioned for everyone to move forward. "They found us there last night. Don't you think the zoms would still be there?" Her gaze met Hannah's and she reluctantly nodded her head, albeit slowly.

"Okay, Naya. But just for a little while." Zoe made a face, holding her nose. "I'm not sure what's worse. The rotten meat or the zoms."

Naya rolled her eyes. "I hear you. Now come on. Hurry. We might not get another chance to visit this part of the city again for awhile."

Paladin cocked his head, listening. "We need to hurry. The Roms keep coming around. It's like they know we'll have to come at some point. I don't like it."

"Yes. I know. It's making me really nervous." Naya pursed her lips. "We can't go on much longer without more supplies. Let's just get what we need and get back onto the streets. I think there is an abandoned building we might be able to stay at for a couple of days. When I scouted out the street a few days ago it looked clear."

Zoe and Hannah grappled with arms full of food, both canned and prepackaged, stuffing bunches into the knapsacks at their feet. They had to take some things with them, but hunger took over and they all paused to quickly inhale some food.

They each had grabbed some packaged foods. Zoe passed a container of pudding and a package of crackers to Naya, which she accepted with a grateful smile. Chester brandished a beef jerky stick and bit into it with enthusiasm, making Naya giggle before she peered into the darkness ahead.

"Thanks." Naya crept behind the counter and into the back kitchen to make sure it was clear of danger while the echoes of the undead coming from outside continued to sound deceptively close. "Okay. Let's sit."

Everyone piled into the small space behind the counter with a collective sigh. Hannah had found a small case of water and was distributing the bottles around to the rest of the party. Soon the sound of slurping filled the air. Naya unscrewed the cap and brought the bottle to her lips with relish. When she was finished, Naya leaned against the counter and closed her eyes, soothed. Hunger clawed at her gut, but her nerves were on overdrive. Half nauseous, she was almost afraid to eat something until they were safe in the abandoned building. Weariness wared with the hyper-awareness that had become her survival mode. It bore her down and as she shut her eyes just for a moment, she began to drift off.

Just for a minute, she thought as she held on to her uneaten food. *Just recharge for a few minutes.* Slumber found her, even though she tried to fight it off.

Naya awoke with a start when someone shook her arm. Chester held his finger over her mouth and pointed into the store, gesturing that they weren't alone.

Paladin was already awake. He had roused the girls quietly.

"Hurry," Paladin barely whispered as he took his sword out and scanned the darkness. Something fell onto the linoleum floor. "Get back to the front door, fast." Gesturing to them to pick up whatever they could carry, Paladin stalked off into the shadows with his sword at the ready.

Chester nodded and took off with Hannah, while Zoe looked at Naya nervously and took off in the other direction.

In seconds, she was alone.

Something fell over and the sound of shuffling feet grew closer, along with soft moans of the undead. Panic twisted Naya's guts.

"Paladin!" Naya hissed, running her flashlight down the aisle. Nobody answered. They were still scavenging for food but the threat was imminent. "Paladin," she tried again as she rushed into an aisle and grabbed a few things on her way. Batteries, peanut butter, whatever might help them get through the journey was pushed into her backpack as she searched for her friends, flashlight held firmly in her hand. "Anyone?"

They wouldn't leave me. Would they? Naya looked around the dimly lit aisle and her heart sunk. *Would they?* She backtracked towards the front entrance slowly, keeping an eye open for both friend and foe, before she knew she needed to leave.

"Activity in sector three."

Wren looked up from the city map and had to resist rolling his eyes at the Rom seated at the switchboard that was stating the obvious, as usual. The headquarters of City First was a buzzing center of activity, with beeping signals, flashing lights and Roms running sector reports. Three other Roms were busy tracking rebel activity on the flashing screens and it was starting to get on his nerves. The internal artificial intelligence system only allowed for minimal interaction and communication on a human level. Frankly, it was a waste.

"Yes, Number Three. Thank you." Wren stood up stiffly and went to investigate. It could either be rogue zoms or the band of resistance that the Organization had been tracking inside the city for the last few days. Jeffers's group had gotten one rebel last night, but the rest had eluded them.

Secretly, he was glad.

He agreed that the city needed to be rebuilt, but at what cost? How many humans were they going to turn into zombified robots for the sake of rebuilding the city? His father had started something good with the Rom chip, but it had quickly became something else... something that sickened him.

"Ah, Wren." His father approached, wearing the uniform of an Organization official. He had been put in charge of keeping order and making sure they had new recruits for the restoration efforts recently, but power suited the old man in some twisted way.

"Yes, Father." Wren closed his expression and stared at the reports in his hand. Any reaction from him would be considered weakness, and he had had just about enough of drinking the company Kool-aid. He believed in the Organization, but not at the cost of humanity as a whole. It was a major point of contention between Wren and his father. The older man couldn't resist prodding him into acting rashly. Sometimes he thought that his father would rather have him as a Rom. Like his mother.

Everyone he had known before all of this happened was gone.

He shuddered and stoically met his father's gaze.

"You are going on patrol this evening?" Captain Wallace glanced over the blinking maps, completely disregarding the Roms at the controls.

"Yes. I am heading over to sector three. There are some rogue zoms that need to be put down." Wren looked away from his father's frosty blue eyes. It had been his father's idea to bring the reanimated to heel as computerized lackeys. His work as an artificial intelligence engineer had served him well, and after the bomb hit, he took full advantage of the situation. His talents were used well and no other city he knew of had this technology unless they paid dearly for it. It was the one resource they had an ample supply of… the undead.

"Hello, Captain Wallace." Jeffers strode in, clad in a dark blue uniform and black boots.

The captain shook his hand. "Good capture last night, Jeffers. The subject is already being fitted with the necessary programming to complete her transfer into the western part of the city's restoration unit."

"Thank you, sir." Jeffers smiled, sending a smirk towards Wren.

"Rom Two, what is status on sector three?" The captain walked up to the screen and watched the movement of the red dots.

"Rogue zoms at the Meta-Mart, Sir." The empty-eyed Rom had no expression, only data.

"Have a good run tonight, Wren." His father smiled distractedly and turned back to the screen.

If Wren didn't get out of there soon, he was going to vomit. Back when the bomb had hit, he had been home working on a project for the artificial intelligence course his father had forced him to take. He'd wanted to be hanging out with his girlfriend Naya, but he still had an hour's worth of work ahead of him. He'd been working on an analysis for networking solutions when suddenly the lights went out and all hell broke loose. Soon thereafter, the streets had begun to teem with the undead. Reports of the widespread damage were staggering; it became common knowledge that no one was spared. Wren was moved into the compound early on, though, even if he didn't want it.

Scientists like his father had searched frantically for a solution.

After mass slaughters of the animated corpses and burnings of the bodies on every street corner, his father took his work in artificial intelligence and was able to bend dead flesh to his will. It was nothing short of miraculous, even Wren could admit that. What he couldn't stomach was the killing of human beings. The death of his own mother to meet those ends was something he could never forgive his father for. She had been the experiment that had launched the program. The Rom Solution, as it was dubbed.

Need a body to do a job? Why not program a system already in place? Just charge up the brain with electricity and a rom chip and you are in business. Animated corpses to work for the greater good, for a brighter tomorrow!

And it was sound, in theory… until the killings began. Only the healthiest and richest were allowed to remain human. There was simply not enough to go around, and the dead were oh so expendable.

"Have you looked at the report I left on your desk regarding the farming conditions in the east part of the city?" Wren asked.

"Yes, I have. Something I might bring up at the city meeting next month. No hurry." His father smiled, without warmth. It didn't make sense that they weren't trying to create new ways of feeding the people that were left.

"Fine, we'll discuss it later. Thank you." Wren gritted his teeth and left the control room before he said something he shouldn't. He needed to get to the other side of the compound and check on his patient before his run. In a lot of ways he should have been happy that his father had forced him into medical and artificial intelligence training when he did.

His co-worker, Carol, had been bitten on a run the previous week. He needed to make sure the implant he had given her was still performing. As far as anyone else knew, she had the flu. Her son Toby was none the wiser. It wouldn't be easy to tell him. Roms had only been used as mindless slaves. Having a rational and aware undead would scare the pants off of the Organization. Wren himself was just getting used to the idea.

"Hey! Wren!" Toby ran up beside him, clad in his white lab coat, old T-shirt and ratty jeans. "Did you tell the captain about my breakthrough?" His hopeful eyes scanned Wren's.

"Yes. He saw it." Wren's mouth turned up in a grimace. He needed to get away from Toby before he followed him back to the lab.

"He didn't read it, though. Did he?" Toby frowned, hurt shining from his eyes.

"I did, Toby. It was really good. I love your idea for using the organic waste from the fish market to stimulate crops in the city."

"We need to do something. At the rate of food usage, the compound is going to be in danger of starvation in a matter of months."

"There are still supplies at some of the outlying stores that haven't been collected in the sweeps. I can have the Rom crew do that tonight. We can drive out the rogue zoms while we're at it."

"Great! I'll let the food bank know. We appreciate what you're trying to do, Wren. Just don't let it get you in trouble with the Organization." Toby's gaze was furtive. "You don't want to hear the rumors going on about your dad. That's all I'm saying. Son or not, you don't want to cross him."

"I know, Toby. Believe me." Wren thought about the last image he had of his mother and shuddered. "I have to go on patrol. I'll see you later."

Naya froze in the doorway. She was surrounded by zoms. They streamed in from the city streets like they were being driven by some unseen force.

She hoped the others were safe.

Resting her hand against the side of the building, she accidentally sliced it on a piece of protruding metal and withdrew it in a hiss. The sudden movement and smell of blood was a beacon to the zombies. They shambled toward her, moving as a horde toward the entrance of the store.

Damn it! Naya cussed under her breath as she looked at the small pool of blood in the center of her palm. She grabbed hold of the hem of her shirt, tore a piece from the bottom and quickly wrapped her hand. *How long have the others been in the store? Are they even still there?* Her thoughts were interrupted as light shone over her from somewhere, making her even more of a target.

"Oh God! No!" Wishing for Paladin's sword, she unslung her baseball bat and whaled at the first head that got close enough, wincing at the pain in her palm. The crack of the wooden bat on a human skull used to make her sick; now it just made her determined. She was not going down without a fight. Not yet. Shambling towards her, the zombies closed in. With each swing, her arms grew tired, but Naya wasn't giving up. She couldn't. The others were depending on her. "Come on!" Naya shouted as the bat collided against a wild zom's skull with a sickening crack, before it fell to the ground. Hesitating would have gotten her killed. Naya raised her bat for a second time and brought it down on the already cracked skull again. Taking advantage of the gap she had made, she grabbed for a metal spike from the broken plant stand outside the store and alternated beating the zoms with her baseball bat with stabbing them in the eyes. The stabbing didn't use up as much energy, but they had to get a whole lot closer and that was just plain unnerving. Naya plunged the spike into another zombie's eyeball and shuddered. "Ugh!" Gore splattered down her arm and onto the front of her filthy, torn shirt.

Movement in the alleyway made her look up, almost costing her dearly. She swung and smashed the face in on a zombie trying to take a bite out of her arm.

Roms. The blue uniformed zombie force corralled the rogue biters and began to effortlessly put them down. A broad-shouldered man in a blue uniform and armor approached her as she swung again at a zombie. Before she could hit it, the man had tazered the undead monstrosity to the ground, scrambling its reflexes.

Oh God. The Rom crews had finally caught up with them. *Oh God...* Fear, so much fear coursed through her veins.

Naya looked at him in terror, and then her eyes widened in recognition. "You."

Wren stared at the brown-haired beauty in front of him and almost swallowed his tongue. He had been so sure everyone he knew had died in the bombing. His father had drilled it into him every chance he got, so how was he to know?

No one left to mourn. Build the future.

Now the past and the future were colliding in violent waves around him. Naya... Naya had survived, and with dawn approaching she looked like a cross between a dream and a hallucination.

"Naya," Wren whispered, staggering forward and embracing her. "Oh my God. Naya." He sucked in his breath. "I thought you were dead. God, forgive me. He said you were dead."

She stared up at him with wide eyes and touched his face. "Where have you been?" Wren was speechless. "Where the fuck have you been?" She beat at his chest with her fists, tears running down her face. "I lost them all. Mom. Dad. Charlie." Naya shook her head, closing her eyes. "But you. Losing you almost killed me!"

The shuffling behind him made his hair stand on end. Wren turned around and saw that a Rom was approaching him in the same way one of the rogue zoms would have. He pushed Naya behind him and frowned.

"Stand down and report to your station," Wren ordered. The Rom kept coming.

In the faint light he could see that the Rom's throat was missing, exactly where the implant would have been. It had gone full zombie again. A chill ran down Wren's spine.

His father's plan was fallible. Take out the chip and the dead were just like any rogue zombie: a violent killing machine. Wren's implant was different. With the combination of specialized drugs and the implant that he had created, they would save lives, not make slaves of the undead.

It made Wren angry to see the lifeless force lumbering toward him and Naya, knowing that his father could have done things differently, but had instead chosen to be a dictator in this new and seriously fucked up world.

The zom at his feet twitched.

"We have to get out of here." He scanned the open area and pulled the sword from his scabbard.

"No. I can't. The group…" she started to say, then backed away from him. "Oh no. You're here for us, aren't you? The zoms… you drove them in." Naya shook her head. "I'm so stupid." She turned to move, but the tazered zom latched onto her leg and sank its teeth into the soft flesh of her thigh. Naya screamed as she hacked at it with the spike, before impaling it through the eye socket. Clutching her leg, she fell to the ground.

"Naya!" Decapitating the approaching Rom, Wren threw the head into the sea of corpses behind them before he slid through the gore to her side. He pulled her into his lap and studied the damage, wide-eyed.

"Well, you have me," she said as blood pooled around her wound. "Go ahead. Do your worst." Naya gritted her teeth, the pain in her gaze obvious. "Just tell me one thing, Wren. Where are the kids? Did you take them too?" Tears ran from her eyes as she stared at him.

"No! I mean, yes. I came here to drive out the zoms, but I didn't know you were here. I am not Jeffers. He gets off on collections. I don't." He stared down at her, at war with himself.

"What did you do to her?" A dark-haired teenage boy wearing a blue hoodie stood over them, a sword in his hand. Three other kids clustered behind him, eyes wide with fear. They looked like they had seen too much terror in such a short lifetime.

"Naya!" A sandy-haired young boy knelt down and hugged her.

"You were bitten." Two girls that looked like sisters stood close together, tears running down their faces.

"Paladin. Stop." Naya touched his jean-clad leg with her hand and he frowned at her.

"He let you get bit. He just wants to take us back to the city to be Rom drones. I'd rather freaking die." Hatred shone from younger teen's eyes.

"No." Wren felt a fissure in his heart tear as he shook his head.

"Do you know this creep, Naya?" Paladin lowered his sword, but kept his eye on Wren.

"Yes. Now help me up." Naya groaned. "We have some talking to do, and there isn't much time." Wren stared at the group and hoped to God they would listen to what he had to say.

Naya looked awful; Wren knew the infection must be blazing through her body. Her skin was already taking on a pale cast and shadows pooled under her eyes. Despair filled him. He had just found her only to lose her again. Only maybe he didn't have to.

"Paladin, help me." She leaned into him and reached for Wren's hand. "You have to get these kids to safety." Tears ran down her cheeks. "I need to know that, before it's over."

Wren shook his head. "It doesn't have to be over, Naya."

Paladin scowled. "What? Making her a Rom slave? No way!" Chester hugged her and she could feel his warm tears soak through her shirt. He had been the little brother she had missed so terribly when she lost Charlie. It broke her heart to think of leaving him out here in this wasteland alone. She felt the same about Hannah and Zoe.

"What are you talking about, Wren?" A cough shook her body and Chester looked up at her, awareness freezing his features into shock.

"You should all come back with me to the compound. You would be safe there, I promise. I could put you to work with Toby in the food bank. Naya, you will undergo implantation as soon as possible, before the infection takes over." Wren met Naya's eyes. "It isn't without risk, but you can have a normal life with the Rom2 chip, if we do it soon enough. It has been tested." He looked away. "Please let me try to save you."

"What do mean tested?" Paladin wrapped his arms protectively around Naya.

"Do you really want a big debate now? We have to go." Wren moved to pick up Naya, but Paladin stopped him.

"No, I'll carry her."

Naya leaned against Paladin and tried to walk toward the armored vehicle.

Stepping over the bodies of the fallen was difficult before she was injured, now it felt impossible. Naya felt herself losing her footing, but before she could fall Wren's arms were around her and she was gathered against his chest.

"Come on. Bring the kids. We haven't got time to lose."

Naya slipped in and out of consciousness, but felt the start of the vehicle moving and a small hand in her own. Opening her eyes was too difficult, so she lay as still as possible and let the movement of the vehicle lull her to sleep. She awoke to the sound of crying and strange voices. Someone named Toby was speaking with Chester and Paladin, and then there was silence. She strained to hear the conversation, but the darkness dragged her deeper until she couldn't fight it any more.

Wren looked at Naya stretched out on his table and felt a tremor in his hand. Cutting into her beautiful flesh was the only way to save her, he knew that. The fever was taking over and if he didn't move soon, she would be beyond his reach.

Looking at the chip in the tray to the right, he placed the small electrical conduit on the table next to Naya's head. He had mere seconds to implant it before the potential for nerve damage was too great, so Wren turned her neck toward him and carefully sliced into her skin. Lodging the web of electrical impulse reactors, he popped the chip into place and sealed the wound. Ripping off his gloves, he used the electrical therapy machine, which would stimulate her nerve endings. The electrical pulses would hopefully be enough to boost the wisp of activity in her brain to that of a normal living human, which would ensure her life. Not just the shambling existence of a moronic revenant punching buttons in a lab all day, or driving zoms in for the kill, but quality life. The life she was meant to lead.

Wren watched Naya as the pulses moved through her body. The warm curves brought back memories of the time they had spent together before the bomb, before life had changed from a normal teenage romance to something almost unrecognizable.

He had to have faith that she had come back into his life for a reason, even if it was only to save her. He was selfish. Just when he found her again, he didn't want to lose her. Wren hit the notch on the electric shock and brought it up to a stronger setting.

It simply had to work.

Darkness blurred into spiral formations behind Naya's eyes and slivers of light blossomed into colors. Suddenly the stillness that had ensnared her body was lifted. Zings of feeling burned through her limbs and she blinked open her eyes in amazement. Wren was staring down at her with a peculiar tilt to his lips.

"Well, you decided to join the land of the living, then?" He smoothed his cool hand over her cheek, sending warm feelings rushing to the innermost parts of her body. Her mouth was dry and when she tried to speak, only a whispered acknowledgement tumbled out of her errant lips. "Here."

Wren pressed a button, elevating the table she was resting on to a more upright position. "Have a sip of water." He held the glass to her lips and watched as she swallowed greedily.

"Thanks." Naya smiled, her voice cracking only a little.

"You gave me quite a scare." Wren pushed the surgical tray out of the way and tilted her neck up. Naya frowned. Wren was here, but why was he looking at her neck? Memories came flooding back and she jerked her head out of his hands.

"Am I dead?" Panic fluttered through her body and her heart pounded. Could a heart beat if she was dead? What was he looking at? Her hands wandered to her neck and felt a small bump. Unsure, she stared at him for a long moment, before looking down to find that she was nude, with only a thin sheet covering her. A deep blush crept onto her cheeks. "You had to strip me?" she demanded.

"I couldn't let any of the zom blood contaminate you, I'm sorry. It was the only way." Wren moved closer to her and lifted up the sheet to show her the wound, which should have killed her, on her thigh. Imagining his hands on her bare flesh made butterflies take flight in her stomach. The weight of all that she had lost faded away as she looked into his steady gaze. God, she loved him. What if this was their second chance? "Do you want to try and get up?" Wren held out a robe and draped it over her knees.

"Yes." She leaned into his body and the sheet draped low around her chest. Wren looked down and a blush ran across his face.

So, he's still interested. Hmmm. She had just come back from the dead and she was still obsessing over the boy who broke her heart.

He put an arm around her waist to help move her forward, but Naya couldn't help herself. Her lips melted against his and she kissed him deeply. He kissed her back for a long moment, then moaned into her mouth and pulled away, breathing hard.

"You saved me," she whispered as she looked at him. "I don't know how, but you saved me. Thank you."

"Well, it's going to be different." Wren looked at her and smiled tentatively, trying to compose himself. "There are a few things we'll have to work out."

"I don't care." Naya smiled and pulled him toward her hungry lips once again.

Wren broke the kiss and smoothed the hair on her brow. "Let's get you up."

Naya grinned. "Are we plotting to take over the world?"

Wren hugged her as she slipped the robe over her shoulders. "You could say that, even if it sounds slightly sinister. But before we do, how about a nice trip to the food bank? Your friends should be settled in by now and there are some people I want you to meet."

"Only if you promise that we'll pick this up later." Naya wiggled her eyebrows at Wren, making him chuckle.

"Naya, I wouldn't miss it for the world."

Neither would she.

MAMA
By Jay Wilburn

Kelly pressed her back to the wall and listened to its cold breathing around the corner. She reached down and adjusted the harness. Only one pipe remained. Kelly gripped the handle of the bat and twisted her hands nervously on the peeling duct tape. Her hands felt sticky and raw.

Something inside her backpack clinked; the breathing stopped. Kelly gritted her teeth and waited. She heard a foot slide forward a few inches on the gritty ground and stop again. Her own breath hissed out between her teeth.

Breathe again, you dead beast. I need to know where your head is.

Air rasped over its dry gullet and a whistle sounded between teeth—gapped, or broken. She heard a puff of air escape from somewhere lower. No, it hadn't lowered its head. The puff of air had escaped from a hole in its chest and a tear in its lung.

The feet scraped forward. She raised the bat. The tape creaked as she twisted the handle one last time.

The breathing became a growl as it rounded the corner. Kelly whirled the bat hard and high, twisting her hips. She pushed up on her back foot the way David had taught her before he died. The fat metal imploded the creature's forehead and blew dust out of both sides of the crumpling skull. The corpse grunted, fell, and stopped breathing. She saw the man's mangled suit, his blackened tie, his torn throat, and the rotten shreds of flesh under his lifeless face.

Kelly drove through the swing as if she were hitting a home run. David had told her to swing into the target, but swing like she was trying to hit the building across the street, the wall across the room, or someone she hated across town.

She watched the body drop motionless off the end of the bat. It struck the ground flat without bouncing, revealing the mob of the dead meandering behind it. They turned their milky eyes and crooked heads toward her and the sound of her bat, then breathed out in one harsh chorus of cold, dry air. They turned their shoulders and raised hands to reach for her.

Kelly cursed and ran along the wall of the warehouse ahead of the wave of dead. Creatures crossed through the lanes of the street in front of her. Some of them began to turn toward her and the sound of their brethren behind her.

This is going to be tricky. I don't have much lead time.

Kelly lifted the last pipe out of her harness. Holding the bat in one hand and the head of the pipe in the other, she twisted the cap, flung the pipe out in the street ahead of her, and dropped down into the space between concrete steps and a drainage pipe. Shadows of the monsters caught up, but she stayed put, listening for the click of the timer. The blast shook the earth, making her jump, but the dead in the alley clawed at her, unaffected by the explosion. She scrambled out ahead of their grasps as smoke swirled up from the street, beyond the warehouse. Bits of flesh landed on the broken pavement.

A woman, smoldering from head to toe, stood at the corner of the warehouse blocking Kelly's way. The walls were too close to swing her bat, so Kelly lifted it above her head. The undead woman flexed her fingers; the charred flesh of her arms split, revealing lifeless, grey muscle underneath.

Swing down like you are hitting the center of the world. Kelly breathed and swung downward, splitting the woman's skull. She crashed to the floor and ash wafted into the air.

Cold hands reached her shoulders, nails scraping against her backpack. She leapt over the body and charged through the smoky street. Covering her nose, she dodged the craters in the road. The monsters closed in on her. She knew the bombs only opened a small space, but she felt she deserved more for her effort.

Kelly made it to the entrance of the opposite alley, only to find it filled with the waiting arms of the hungry dead. She ran for the next block, finding a fire escape. She worked the ladder down using a rope strung behind bundles of soggy phonebooks. Kelly started to climb, but a grey splotchy hand clutched her ankle and tugged lazily. Kelly screamed, trying to pull free. A scarred face with broken teeth emerged from the stacks of books, toppling one bundle into the alleyway.

She had done exactly what she had been told not to do.

Kelly kicked the dead face as hard as she could, feeling the cartilage in its nose crush as pain shot through her toes. She finally pulled free and limped up the ladder while he fumbled at the steps. Once on the landing, she pulled the fire escape back up and wound the rope out of the monster's reach.

Don't give them something to eat. They don't feel pain from hitting or kicking, but you'll feel the bite, Kelly reminded herself as she stared down at the reaching, growling body.

She pulled in a deep lungful of air and shuddered. "You are dead now. What do you know?" she said to the zombie. More creatures shambled into the tight passage under the fire escape, roaring and hissing, reaching towards her. Shaking her head, she climbed to the roof and decided to cross the boards between the structures. Looking down at her feet and ignoring the drop, she carefully walked across the boards. They shifted slightly from side to side. When she made it to the other side, she let out an exasperated breath and bit down on her lower lip. "I'll have to remember to go back and drop that rope later. I might need it again."

Crossing another bridge of loose two-by-eight boards, she heard one crackle under her feet, making her grit her teeth.

"Life would have been easier if you had hit your head when you fell, instead of just breaking your legs, David," she mumbled to herself.

Eventually, Kelly descended the metal stairs on the opposite side of the building and climbed through the open living room window. Buck sat with his back to her. She lifted the bat off her shoulder and set it against the wall.

Buck turned, scratched at his two-day beard with a screwdriver, and asked, "Are you okay?"

"I had some close calls, but I'm not hurt."

He bent back over the open radio and continued working. Kelly took off her backpack, opened it on the counter between the living room and the kitchen, and studied her finds.

Buck opened his mouth and breathed with his tongue out. "I could hear you coming the whole way. Did you use up all your bombs?"

Kelly unbuckled her harness and dropped it. "You can see I did. You didn't take a break from diddling your radio to come see if I needed help, Buck?"

He smiled with his tongue between his teeth. "I stuck my head out. The last blast was right out in the street. I figured you'd be back by the time I got to you, and here you are."

Kelly sighed. "Yes, here I am." She unpacked her bag, placing a bottle of wine and a sleeve of fancy crackers on the counter. Pulling out a plastic container of dried fruit, she sighed. *I miss fresh fruit.*

Buck set down the screwdriver and retrieved a knife from the table. "You made it tricky for us to get out this afternoon. You knew we had plans."

Kelly set the fruit down. "If we have to postpone, I got wine and a couple treats. We can use one of the batteries and watch a movie. I'll even let you pick."

Buck pulled his tongue in. "My mother is expecting us. We can't cancel again."

Kelly walked away from the counter. "I'm low on bombs. It might be safer to wait until I make more."

He set the radio down and held his back as he stood up straight. "I can't radio her to tell her that we're canceling until I fix this. She'll worry, Kelly. Did you draw the dead in on purpose to put off this visit again?"

"That's stupid, Buck. I can't believe you would even say that."

He licked his lips and set down the knife. "We'll need to get ready to go soon. My mom has a recipe for bombs that she says are easier than the pipes you use. She wants to show you."

Kelly walked back toward the bedroom. "I can't wait," she said sarcastically as she closed the door and sat on their bed. Kelly swept Buck's clothes off her side and onto the floor and shuddered. The room smelled like old socks and mildew, and the sheets felt tacky underneath her hands. Kelly closed her eyes.

I want to love him. I want to feel about Buck the same things that I felt for David. The same intensity I had those days right after the dead rose… the way that I never wanted to be away from him and how I never wanted to be out of his arms.

She whispered to the empty room, "You are being foolish. We thought we were going to die. We weren't thinking about the future. Everything was more intense. Living with someone feels different than dying with them. Grow up."

Buck shouted through the door. "Are you okay? We really need to go soon. Traffic is getting thick outside, if you get my meaning."

Her heart raced. "I'm fine, just give me a minute. I need to change clothes and gather the pipes." She waited for him to say something else, but he walked away over the creaking floorboards. Kelly bounced herself a little on the corner of the mattress, making the springs protest, as she got herself back in the game.

We need to flip the mattress.

Shaking her head, Kelly stood up and opened the closet, looking at clothes she would have never worn before the dead began ripping open the living. She looked down at the sweat stains under her arms, the dark blood splattered on the front of her shirt. A bit of rotten brain stuck to one sleeve, a bit of gore on the back of her leg.

"I should have undressed on the fire escape. I can't believe I brought this into the bedroom."

I wasn't planning on storming in here when I got back. I'm just going right back outside. Why am I bothering to change clothes anyway?

She sighed, answering herself. "Because Buck's mother will say something about it." Kelly stripped off her clothes, trying not to let the filth spread across the carpet. She stood naked in front of her closet and wondered what to wear. She took out two sets of clothes and walked toward the door.

Kelly carried the clothes in front of her as she crossed the living room to the rain barrel at the front window, dropped them on the chair and ladled out a pan full of water. She rubbed the sponge slowly around the water as she bent over in nothing but her boots. Glancing through her hair, she noticed how Buck looked away, returning his attention to the guts of the radio that was strewn about the living room. Kelly sighed as she sponged her sweaty skin.

David would have never let me stand here like this without putting his hands on me, she thought. *You see right through me in more ways than one.*

<hr />

The Rover bounced off the wall of bodies on the driver's side, but Buck overcompensated and Kelly felt the vehicle begin to tip. Grabbing the handle above her door, Kelly braced herself for the crash. Buck adjusted again and brought the cab back onto all four wheels. Dead fingers scraped down both sides of the truck and fell away behind them.

"I should have brought an extra pair of underwear," she mumbled.

Buck snorted. "I appreciate the vote of confidence. They're thinning out as we get closer to the bridge, so I think we'll be okay."

"Don't say that. It's bad luck."

He nodded. "Sorry."

She reached over and brushed his hair back behind his ear. He smiled, sticking his tongue through his teeth. She squeezed his shoulder and dropped her hand back to her side.

As they reached the bridge, he slowed a bit, weaving around the wrecks and abandoned vehicles before he came close enough for Kelly to see through the thick guide wires to the river. "I think the water is cleaner now."

Buck kept his eyes forward. "Yeah, probably. We might want to stay a night or two to let the bodies thin out around the apartment."

"I think we'll be okay."

Buck laughed. "Don't say that. Bad luck."

Kelly stared out at the water. "Yeah, right."

"We should think about moving out of the city, closer to my family. They're building better defenses, and their town isn't as exposed as it used to be."

"I don't know, Buck. I know how to maneuver in the city. Crime isn't as bad here as it is out in the country."

Buck clicked his tongue. "That's true. Raiders don't come across the bridge often, but if we're going to have kids, we'll want a doctor and some help, right?"

"You're asking me about kids as we swerve on a bridge in the middle of an apocalyptic city?"

"Come on, Kelly, we've crossed this bridge a dozen times. We have these wrecks memorized. I could do it with my eyes closed."

"Don't."

"I'm not. I'm just saying, we've talked about kids before. They have an optometrist, and my mom can help."

Kelly shook her head. "That's an eye doctor. And I don't want to think about your mother anywhere near my birth canal."

Buck made a face. "Yeah, me neither. Thanks for that, by the way. I meant she can help after the baby is born. And eye doctors go to medical school, right?"

The Rover pitched hard into the air. They both screamed as the truck landed hard, clanging metal against metal. The wheels spun on the body as it continued to claw at the underside of the vehicle.

"We're fine," Buck yelled, as they worked free.

"You can't run over them like that! The bones break and puncture the tires."

"Yeah, right, sorry about that."

"Just focus on the road, for god's sake. We'll talk about this later."

They cleared the bridge without further incident. Despite the effects of Kelly's explosions, the clusters of wandering dead remained spread apart in the rest of the city. The creatures turned slowly to follow the Rover as it whizzed by, but they would lose focus before they followed for very long.

Outside the city, Kelly could see the bodies out in unplowed fields and between smaller buildings. Their clothes had lost their color from exposure to the elements. Wounds lost their definition. Decay took its toll on the lifeless flesh that still moved and pursued the living.

Kelly stared at the ugly undead through her window. They should have rotted away by now. She still couldn't figure out what held them together. When she bashed their skulls open, they rotted to nothing within a few days or weeks, depending on the time of year.

"That's not living."

Buck glanced over at her. "What are you talking about?"

"Just thinking out loud."

Buck turned the Rover onto a road with barbed wire fences on both sides. "It's still awful to see them all up and walking around like this. The closer I get to home, the more of them I recognize, too."

Kelly closed her eyes. Pain built behind her eyes as she clenched her fists. Caffeine sometimes helped, but there wasn't much left. Back in the day, when she felt like this, she would take half a dozen capsules of pain medication. Her mother warned her that she would shut down her kidneys, but who listened to their parents? Now she missed them.

David had tried to take her back to check on her parents. The streets had been bloody and thick. Finally he told her that he was sorry, but they couldn't make it.

Kelly heard the tone change under the tires. The grit continued to crunch under the wheels as the Rover moved slower. The wheels bounced through ruts in the dirt path, making Kelly's headache grow.

I only met David's mother twice, and the second time she was being torn apart. He pulled me away from her and used his bat to get me back to his truck alive. He picked me over his mother.

The Rover stopped. Kelly opened her eyes, staring at the cottage at an angle. Her vision pulsed in time with the pounding in her head.

She looked back along the trail, checking that nothing followed them, and then saw the gate sitting open. Kelly opened the door and looked on top and underneath the Rover before stepping out of her seat.

Buck closed his door. "Stay by the truck until I deal with the chain."

"Why is it open like that?"

Links clinked as the chain extended across the ground. Kelly pressed her fingers into her forehead and faced the front of the Rover, not wanting to see the dead body wearing the collar at the end of the heavy chain. Her body had bloated more since the last time. The spongy flesh folded over the collar and padlock, and her bathrobe hung open. Her nightgown sagged down, exposing the body in unsavory ways.

Kelly dropped her eyes to look at the grimy slippers that the creature wore and thought: *Why do they keep her in pajamas like this?*

Buck stepped in front of the Rover's grill. The woman shifted her cataract eyes from Kelly to him. The woman's skull plates could be seen through the thinning hair and split scalp. When she reached the end of the chain, the metal clanged. She gagged sickly, her blue lips rolling back from black teeth, but the voice came out as a choked hiss.

Pitiful. Kelly shook her head.

Buck walked around the Rover, making the woman lean into her collar, reaching and hissing for him. Her chain rubbed against the scarred bark of a tree and then started to wrap around it. Before Buck completed his turn, the chain jerked backward, dragging against the tree, and the monster stumbled back, clawing at her own throat. Buck stopped and stared for a moment as the gate slammed behind them.

Kelly turned around. She didn't recognize the man in body armor who was busy connecting the latch with his back to her, so her hand dropped to the timer cap on one of the pipes in her harness. Something was wrong. "What's going on?" she whispered as the chain rattled and the zombie fell to its back in the thicket where its chain was spiked to the ground.

A woman shouted, "Get on up to the porch, while I hold her."

Buck started running and took Kelly's hand, dragging her along with him as he led her up the porch. She watched the man stand guard by the gate while the corpse wandered back out on her chain, just before Buck's mother strolled up to the cottage to greet them.

She wore her broad-brimmed gardening hat and a black vest with a high Kevlar collar over a flowered dress. She clomped up in heavy boots and wore a rifle strapped to the back of the vest. Kelly stared at a duffel bag slung over the woman's shoulder and heard glassware clinking inside.

"Does that chain and biter system actually work, Mom?"

The woman removed her hat and stared at Kelly for a long moment, then shifted her eyes over to her son. "The smell covers our scent from the ones in the wild. Also, we got them all around the property now. If we find one brained, we know someone is sneaking in."

Buck stepped off the porch to hug his mother. "I guess that makes sense."

She hugged him with her forearms, but held her hands with the heavy gloves out to the side. "Careful, Son, I've been working in the field and had to down a couple rotters that chased a deer onto the property. I need to wash up."

He kissed her on one large cheek and stepped back.

Kelly smiled. "Pleased to see you again, Mrs. Dollard. What do you do if one of the creatures pulls up its stake?"

Buck's mother paused on the steps and looked up at the girl slowly. "It's good to see you too, Kelly… far too long between our visits. And I listen for the chains and do the same thing I do to anybody that wanders in uninvited—aim for the head and ask questions never."

Kelly looked away and nodded.

Mrs. Dollard looked back over her shoulder. "Besides, I played bridge with Catherine-Kay for years even though she was a Yankee. I'll brain her in a second if she gets loose or feisty, but I like to keep her around until then."

Mrs. Dollard reached the top step of the porch, then looked back. "Girl, have you been crying?"

Kelly shook her head. "I have a headache I can't seem to shake."

"Are you getting dehydrated, or not eating enough?"

"No, ma'am, I had to set off a few explosives coming back from shopping today. I think it just caught up to me."

"Good girl," Mrs. Dollard said. "I got a recipe that might have a little less kickback on you. Buck, I need you to put on a kettle so I can make your young lady some tea. You remember where the kettle hangs?"

"Yes, ma'am." Buck kissed Kelly's cheek and went into the house.

Buck's mother took Kelly's arm and led her inside. "What do you pack those pipes with?"

Even in the darkness of the cottage, Kelly could see the walls lined with folk art—license plates, bicycle parts, even animal bones. It looked like a meth addict lived here, but then again, in a post-apocalyptic world, décor didn't really make it onto the list of necessities.

"I use a modified gunpowder mix. It's fairly powerful."

"It would have to be to blow open a pipe, dear."

Kelly gritted her teeth. "The metal becomes part of the explosion. It tears through muscle and brain better than glass and faster than fire."

"Of course." Buck's mother led her into the kitchen where Buck stoked more wood into the burner under the stove. "You can also add shards of metal to mix in a bottle and get the same shrapnel without losing force from blowing apart the solid pipe."

"Anything else, Mama?" Buck asked.

Mrs. Dollard added tea bags to empty cups next to the stove. "Yes, will you please fix the settings on my VCR remote again? I messed it up switching the batteries the other day."

"What happened to the DVD player I got you, Mama?"

"I have it on the downstairs TV." She added oil to a frying pan on the burner next to the kettle. "I still want to watch my tapes upstairs. All the family stuff is on tapes."

"Mama, I can get those copied and burnt onto DVDs that will last you forever."

"Are you arguing with me, Buck?" She peeled potatoes into a basket.

"No, ma'am."

"Run up and fix it for me then. Some of the tapes are personal from your father to me and I don't need them to last forever. Even if I do, I won't be watching video tapes from a chain in the yard, will I?"

"No, ma'am."

Mrs. Dollard held out an extra peeler and Kelly joined her at the basket. Kelly liked to leave a little skin on her potatoes, but Buck's mom liked them stripped naked, so they prepped them Mama's way.

"Well, fix my remote while the roast finishes and we start these potatoes. I should have your dinner ready and your girl's head fixed by the time you're done with that and the shower curtain."

I hope she means just fixing my headache, Kelly thought glumly.

"Shower curtain, Mama?"

"You'll figure it out, once you're up there."

"Yes, ma'am," Buck sighed.

"Let the peeler do the work, dear. Just skin them; don't gouge."

Kelly adjusted her touch without answering. The kettle whistled and she squeezed her eyes shut. The headache pounded as the high-pitched sound continued. Mrs. Dollard lifted the kettle away and poured it over the two cups. Soon the oil in the pan began to spit and sizzle. Buck's mother took the peeler and handed Kelly the warm cup. "See to your head while I do the slicing, dear."

"Thank you, Mrs. Dollard." Kelly heard the knife snick through the potatoes as she brought the cup to her lips. She tasted the bitter mix.

Herbal. No caffeine. Might as well drink hot water. She shuddered.

"Thank you, Mrs. Dollard, this hits the spot." Forcing a smile, Kelly took small sips of the tea.

"Call me Mama, dear." She dropped the first handful of potato slices into the sizzling oil. "I miss the kick of caffeine and bourbon myself, but I'm glad it seems to be helping."

"You could probably figure out how to make bourbon again, ma'am. Mama."

Buck's mother dropped the next handful of slices into the pan without answering. Kelly took another sip as Mrs. Dollard checked the roast over the coals in the belly of the oven.

"I could, but we need the corn to feed the livestock and the human-stock. Maybe in a few years, if we're all around that long, I imagine we'll be making cornbread for a new generation of Dollards before we start brewing whisky again."

The popping oil punctuated the silence that followed.

Kelly lifted her cup and took a large swallow as Mrs. Dollard began slicing potatoes again.

"Buck gives me so much grief about trying to give him my old ring. He talks about luck and tempting fate even though he obviously wants to spend his life with you. Is that coming from him or you, dear?"

Kelly set her cup down. "I don't tell a man when to propose, Mama."

Buck's mother snorted, making her jowls shake. "Dear, women always tell them exactly what to do whether we do, it in words or not."

"Tell me about this bomb recipe that Buck won't leave me alone about."

Mrs. Dollard began re-peeling the potatoes Kelly had already done. "It's a Molotov cocktail using oils instead of gasoline, but it has the same rag fuse, but scorched and twisted tight."

"I prefer the twist timers, because that way I can gauge the amount of lead time I need."

Buck's mother returned to slicing. "Nonsense, the fuse gives you a visual. You don't need lead time, if you aren't blasting your way out of solid metal. It isn't about power. Bombs are for breathing room. You will only ever get the skulls within a few feet. Anything more is just a bunch of show that will ruin your hearing and bring the whole city down on top of you without dropping a single extra corpse for your trouble. The metal from one of those heavy pipes can give a dozen Dollard Bottle Blasters. I'll show you I'm right, dear." She dropped the last of the potato slices into the pan. Kelly became aware of ringing in her ears again as well as the pain behind her eyes. Mrs. Dollard lifted the roasting pan out and kicked the oven closed with her heavy boot, then set the meat out to rest. "You want me to show you how to mix a Dollard bottle?"

"Maybe after we eat." Kelly looked out the window. "Who is the fellow guarding your gate?'

Mrs. Dollard cleared her throat. "He's a friend. We have a lot more people in our community now. He's actually from Tennessee, but he's okay... He came here looking for family that didn't make it past the first week, I'm afraid. I use him to plow my fields."

"Sounds like a helpful man."

"Yes, when he's done plowing me, he helps with the crops too."

Kelly laughed and choked.

Mrs. Dollard nodded as she forked the potatoes out on a platter. "Just seeing if you were paying attention. Help me carry all this to the table."

She called the boys to supper and introduced her broad armored man as Bubba. He nodded at Kelly and shook Buck's hand as Buck thanked Bubba for all he was doing for his mother. Kelly coughed and Mrs. Dollard started serving roast. During the meal, Kelly's headache finally began to pass, until Buck started arguing college football with Bubba.

Kelly took the last bite of her second helping. "You realize those teams no longer exist."

Buck's mother said, "Don't bother, girl. They don't even hear you. I'll make you a to-go package while they punch themselves out."

Bubba argued offensive lines and Buck interrupted him with opinions on coaching staffs.

At least David stopped talking baseball after we saw his mother chewed apart.

Kelly narrowed her eyes. "All the players are probably flesh-eating monsters tearing their families into bite-sized chunks." She watched and saw Buck's mouth twitch, but he did not look at her. He plowed back into his pointless debate with the man who was plowing his mother.

He probably doesn't even realize it.

Buck's mother rolled her eyes. "Come on, Kelly. Help me clear the table. I need to show you that recipe anyway." Kelly carried a stack of plates into the kitchen.

Mrs. Dollard set the oils out and began explaining each one.

Kelly sighed. "Mrs. Dollard, Mama, I have my way of doing things and I'm a bit attached to it. No offense."

"We all do, dear. Just pay attention. It is good to have options." Buck's mother kept mixing. "Buck and Bubba still want to argue college football like the world is still there. I keep my husband's tapes and Catherine-Kay staked in the yard. One day the tapes may snap or my neck may get snapped in the hands of a rotter. Catherine-Kay may need braining. You have your old boy still staked inside your brain, even though he's been dead a spell too." She shrugged her shoulders. "Be sure about the portions on these and it will explode right every time." Kelly stared at Buck's mother as she spoke, but did not really hear her any longer. Mrs. Dollard pointed at the fuse after she finished. "You can put the fire out by stamping out the flame or dousing it, but you never really know. It could still be cooking inside the twist and blow up anyway. Once it's lit, you're probably safer just to let it burn and throw it."

Kelly stared at the pink gel inside the Molotov they had created. "I want to love your son… I do love him. I mean, I want to love him the way I felt about David. Sometimes I believe I can and that I can choose to." Kelly dropped her eyes and stared at the floor.

Buck's mother didn't look up from the sink as she used powder to remove the extra oil. "Listen, I'm obviously a big fan of my son, and maybe less obviously I'm a big fan of yours. Being able to make your own bombs makes you worlds better than the starving waifs eating trash that he could end up with. If you could convince yourself to love him or convince yourself enough to settle and to start a family in what's left of this world, well, I'd consider it quite an upgrade to the Dollards' genetic stock. I'm sure Buck loves you enough to be too thick to know the difference between the two options, really. If you can't do that, you might need to cut loose and look for a different man, or convince yourself you don't need a man at all. Not many are wandering out of Tennessee these days, you understand? Buck's father threw himself on a mob of the rotters to let me get away. Him dying like that makes it hard for any other man to live up to my standards. Do you understand, dear?"

"Yes, Mrs. Dollard."

Buck's mother washed away the powder. "You can call me Mama."

"Yes, ma'am."

On the way home, Buck and Kelly reached the bridge in the last rays of sunset. The dead filled the spaces between the cars and poured across toward the headlights of the Rover.

Buck shook his head. "We should probably go back to Mama's. They've clogged the bridge and it's almost dark."

"I'm not spending the night out there in the open, Buck."

"You are so stubborn at the worst times, Kelly. The absolute worst times."

She hit her fist against the dashboard. "There are other bridges, Buck. I want to sleep in my bed tonight. You want to drive back to your mommy's house and listen to Bubba bang her against the headboard, go for it. I'll get out and walk across the bridge myself."

Buck turned the Rover sharply and followed the road along the river ahead of the creatures' reaching hands. "They are all gathered together because of how you handled yourself earlier."

"I told you I'd walk!"

They parked outside after dark and got up into the apartment in a full run.

Kelly forgot to bring in the to-go package of roast and vegetables. They faced away from each other in bed. Waking up before Buck did, Kelly slipped outside. She crossed the rooftops and climbed down the fire escape to drop the rope she had pulled up the previous day.

I should pull the Rover into the garage, so he doesn't have to do it. It will make up for our spat.

She pulled the rope free and began to lower it behind the stacks of phonebooks. Then she saw the same speckled hand from the day before grab hold of the top of the stack and pull itself up. The creeper crawled back out and stood below the raised ladder as the monster licked its lips and growled at her. Kelly held the rope and sighed as she sat there, considering whether to climb down and deal with the issue or not.

I'll deal with this later.

She moved back to the apartment across the rooftops. Back to Buck. Mama was right. Sometimes you just have to make do with what you have. Right now, all Kelly had was Buck. He may not have been David, but he didn't need to be…

SOUL TIES
By Katie Jones

Her heart was a ticking time bomb; at least this was how Casey felt about the muscle inside her thoracic cavity when she was alive. Once she was informed she was born with a congenital heart defect, the continuous thud dud seemed to drown out the entire world around her. It felt like a clock, with small hands that monotonously struggled to tick deep inside of her and at any moment, it could cause a shock wave to burst through her body. The muscle itself over time became enlarged, so much so that the engorged walls made it impossible to fill the ventricles with the blood her body so desperately needed to survive. As a result, she had literally drowned in her own vital fluids, and the sponge-like lungs soaked up the blood that couldn't be forced into the cavities of such a vital organ.

Unable to breathe, Casey had clutched helplessly at her chest, her fingers clawing away madly at the blouse covering her breasts. It felt like an explosion from within; pain intensified as though the muscle had torn into bits of shrapnel, flung against the inside of her rib cage. The agony was something she had never felt before. It seared and burned like fire licking at her insides with a white-hot tongue. Brilliant light behind her eyes blinded her vision as though she was staring directly into the searing hot orb of an oncoming sun. And then nothing. It was over, and darkness descended upon her life.

And now she was dead, with a useless heart wedged inside her body.

But somehow she still felt overwhelmed by the love that had resided inside her, connected by some sort of invisible thread to the one she loved in a world she had lived in. She didn't understand this. How can you feel love when you're dead? Was she even dead, or was this all a bad dream? Casey had always believed that you felt love somewhere deep inside the cavities of your heart, locked away inside an unknown corner where the darkness and blood could nurture it into something tremendous. But she knew that the heart that had failed her in life was now necrotic in some places. The enzymes and bacteria inside her body were rapidly breaking down her membranes, and this caused those once-functioning organs to become nothing but a giant, decomposing soup that dribbled and sloshed out of a puncture wound created by a rib that had torn through the now thin, decayed skin which covered her skeleton.

Yet, somehow she was still capable of love. It was the only thing on her rotten mind. And with that alone to drive her, she found herself suddenly flung from the darkness that once encased her mind. The shock was intense, being dumped back inside the wooden coffin in which her body had been laid; she felt like a baby suddenly pushed from the comfort of her mother's womb. In this case, the mother would be Death itself.

She started inside the cramped, wooden box, and realized at once that this was the final place family and friends had placed her. An image of a man with hazel eyes that smiled and dark hair swamped her vision, and she knew instantaneously she had to make her way to him, to her Aaron.

With that her journey began. There were no questions as to why she was here on Earth, under the soil when she should be dead; the one thing that swamped her was how she could find him. Her fingernails worked furiously at the wooden slab above her head. She dug her digits into the roof above, tearing off splinters and bits of wood. The wood wedged inside her flesh, but she felt nothing of the pain that she would have if she was alive. Meat ripped against the surface, and her ivory-colored bones extended through the skin that was damaged. Triumphantly, she hit soil, and it began to pour through the funnel-like opening above her. Wet and damp it tumbled through the roof. Slime-covered worms and shimmering beetles greeted her with the gentle scuttle of many legs. Unfazed, she moved on, her hands now scooped like spades into the dirt. It covered her on all angles now, and if she was claustrophobic in life it didn't show now as she worked with a furious determination. Casey dragged herself up, inch by painfully slow inch. She worked with closed eyes, and soil filled her nostrils, clogging her sinuses. After what seemed like an eternity, one quivering, skeletal thin hand stretched up and into the air above.

The decomposed flesh tensed tight as tendons pulled, fingers coiled frantically to grip hold of the ground above, and finally her head popped through the tunnel she had made. Thick blonde hair now matted with mud and grit fell over her face, and as she shimmied her thin waist out of the ground below, she flung her head back and revealed herself to the world.

In life, Casey hadn't been tremendously good looking, and death didn't make her any more attractive. Her eyes were sunken into the hollows of her skull, and her nostrils were occluded with wet, dark dirt. The skin on her face was thin, pulled taut over the cheekbones that rested prominently on her skull. The dragging of her body through the dirt below had torn shreds of skin from places. Clear, black and white fluids leaked from these wounds now, dribbling over the side of her chin.

Casey stood under the morning sun, her dull eyes soaked in everything around her. The light summer dress she was buried in had been a favorite, but now it was a dull brown and yellow, splattered with mud. Those magnificent legs she once showed off were nothing but skin and knobby knees that leaked and squelched with each movement.

But the thought that somehow Aaron might not think she was still the Casey she had been, the girl he had loved, did not even cross her mind. Perhaps this was because she was dead, maybe it was because her liquefied frontal lobe was now slowly seeping into her clogged nostrils and had caused her face to bulge in places. Either way, no one could be sure, not even Casey herself.

She set off, unable to care about anything other than the hunger pains she had. Starved of love, she moved off and began to follow an unseen path, as though a coil of thread was pulling at her body, some sort of umbilical cord that tensed and led her to the soul which she desired so much. She didn't even flinch when she heard the sound of a lawn mower starting, and she didn't seem to hear the terrified yelp of the groundskeeper as he moved past the grave where she was once buried and laid eyes on the obvious signs of interference.

She simply stumbled through the tombstones that peppered the cemetery around her; at times she tripped over low memorial stones and had to crawl across the higher tombs that towered up into the sky. But each time her feet hit the squishy green grass beneath her she moved on in the same beeline, unable to defer from her path. Her little toes stubbed into rocks and caught on limp flowers that covered the ground in some parts, but she didn't even notice. Even when the clump of her big toe hit the side of a gravestone, she didn't falter. The bone snapped clean off and she lost her balance, but her journey continued and she wobbled with each laborious step, intent on only one thing.

Casey didn't even know how long she had been dead. Now she cursed herself silently for not stopping to check her own stone before she moved on. Had it been days or weeks? She couldn't know. The sun had risen swiftly into the cloudless blue sky and the heat of the day was fast upon the land. This sort of weather would take its toll on her body, and as the sun seared in the sky above, it seemed to make her flesh sizzle beneath the tight skin.

When Casey looked down at her chest, a rasp-like gasp escaped her throat and the bones of her fingers prodded at the Y-shaped incision that ran from her collar bones down beneath the flimsy fabric of her dress. She soon came to the conclusion that they had cut her open, and her fingertips ran down over the lumps and bumps created by the sutures. Whoever had sewn her up had done a shitty job, and she was not impressed.

Casey found herself crossing a paddock. She ducked under the white slabs of wood that fenced in the horses. The oversized beasts flung up their heads, ears flattened as they watched with big, rolling eyes. The horses flared their nostrils. The stench of death caused them to become edgy; they watched as she twisted and weaved through the slats of wood that were in her way.

"What's your problem?" she cried out to one of the animals, slightly offended by the way they didn't welcome her.

The buzz of a motor caught Casey's attention and she quickened her wobbly gait. She moved faster towards a road nearby and waved frantically at a car as it came into view. It glimmered like a mirror under the hot sun. The sedan pulled up, the window rolled down, but the eyes that met Casey's were filled with terror and the burning of rubber on tar filled the air as the automobile took off in the opposite direction.

"Asshole!" she shouted, flashing them the bird. The flesh of her middle finger peeled down the bone like the skin of a banana. Casey's eyes fell onto the disfigured member. Somehow she understood that maybe she wasn't delightful to look at, and doubt began to niggle at her mind. Would Aaron really want her around? Would he be terrified of his girlfriend coming back from the grave?

Defeated, Casey slumped down under the shade of a tree; droning flies settled at the corners of her eyes and sucked liquid from her tear ducts. She didn't even try to shoo them away; they seemed to be the only thing that wanted to be close to her. Maybe it was the smell that was bad, not just the sight of her, she thought. She couldn't sniff, the holes in her nose were clogged, but that didn't bother her. She doubted she would even be able to recognize what she smelled like even if she could. When your body is made out of rotten meat, can you really tell how disgusting your aroma is?

This was a truly horrible fate. At the time of her death, all she could think about was Aaron and how she would give anything to see him again, just one more time. Now she was given the chance. And though she wanted to sit under the tree and rot away to nothing under the shade, she could not help but feel that tug at her body, something that she knew was going to guide her back to Aaron. She fought it for as long as she could, and she dreaded getting up, but she had to. Her feet moved without her wanting them to, and before Casey knew what she was doing she trudged along the road again, head held high. Her limp became more severe with every footstep. She couldn't control the urges within. They overflowed to the point that she was robotic now, moving toward something that was calling her from far, far away.

In the state that Casey was in, this journey should have killed her, but because she was already dead, all it did was cause her body to fall apart in places. The constant movement of her legs enlarged the rips and tears in her skin, and the stitches that trailed beneath her dress bulged. Three hours later, a suture gave way and the lump that protruded from her belly caused Casey to explore under the dress. What she found was a slippery, wet bag of intestines that had been packed inside her body after the autopsy. The clear plastic that encased her organs poked out from the tear. She stopped to hold it for a moment in her ragged palms, contemplating what would happen if her entire insides fell out. Would she still move toward this undying force? Would she drag her body along the road, wriggle and squirm like a legless maggot until she found the thing that she wanted most? Casey had seen those movies of the undead, but somehow she thought she wasn't *that* sort of monster. For starters, if she was, wouldn't she want to eat people? She had no desire to consume another human being; the thought made her feel a little strange. With this in mind, she pulled down her dress and held her palms over her stomach before she walked on, confident that whatever she was wasn't evil.

Aaron lived a fair way from the cemetery, and the walk to his house was tough. Not only on Casey, but other people too. Once she started to pass oncoming walkers, she knew she must look terrible. They stared at her, then quickly averted their eyes, before glancing back, unable to believe what they had seen. The human mind is usually quite logical, and the thought of a dead girl walking the earth is not something that would occur on your daily walk to work. Cars slowed down and heads turned, but they soon sped up. The wrinkled noses and looks of total disgust were evident on most faces.

A lady walking a dog passed by, and the canine moved towards Casey, sniffing and snuffling at her meaty legs. The owner tugged on its leash and had to struggle to move the pooch. The stench of her body was just too tempting to the animal.

Finally she came to the flat on the corner of a very familiar street. Casey moved toward the rock which held the spare key. She turned it over and used it to open the door. Once she was inside the small unit, she moved into the darkness of the room around her. It felt nice in here, away from those eyes that burned like lasers, judgmental people staring at her as though she had two heads.

The first thing Casey did was walk over to a table that contained photographs. Her eyes fell onto images of her and Aaron. Smiles and laughter shimmered on the photos, and she felt sadness dawn upon her. Casey knew that somehow things wouldn't go back to normal. Even though she was here in Aaron's home she still couldn't stop that urge inside, that thing which constantly pulled at her and wanted her to follow. She knew Aaron would be here soon, but would she be able to withstand the urge? Could she stay here long enough until he walked through the door?

The night shift must have been over by now. She didn't want to walk to his workplace. The people out there made her feel like a beast; this place felt safe for now.

Casey settled onto the couch and waited in silence. It felt like her heart all over again, that ticking time bomb just waiting to happen. Only this time, the explosion would take place inside Aaron's home.

When Aaron pulled up, the familiar hum of his engine filled Casey's ears and she trembled in anticipation. He slid out of the car, then slammed the door shut with a thud. It took what seemed like forever for him to take those few steps to the front door, fumble with the keys and unlock it.

᛫ ♥ ᛫

He walked inside his house and the first thing he noticed was the smell. His hands moved to his face in revulsion, and he shielded his nostrils with closed palms, shoving the door closed with the back of his heel. It was dark, but he could feel someone was in here. When Aaron thought he could remove his hands without vomiting, he flicked on the light switch. It took a moment for his eyes to adjust.

His gaze fell on the grotesque image of a girl. It took a moment before he recognized the rotten features of her face. This was when his body hit the floor.

Aaron's eyelids fluttered for a moment before they slid open. His wide, brown eyes locked onto Casey in disbelief as he watched her struggle from the couch, the leather seats stuck to her skin as she pried it from her body. Unable to move, he watched her hobble unsteadily towards him before she knelt by his side. His mind was groggy, but the deafening pop that came from her knees startled him a bit. He could not force himself to speak, a mixture of fear and disbelief overwhelmed him. Finally, he lifted a single hand that trembled and touched her ever so gently. He slid his fingers over her ruined face, wiping away the slime that slid from her eyes. Then he propped himself up on his elbows as he fought back the sudden urge to gag.

"How can this be?" he whispered. Her skeletal hand reached out and wrapped around his wrist, the bones of her fingers stroked at his skin.

"I don't know," she muttered. Her words were slurred. She had lost some control of her tongue as it decomposed inside of her mouth.

Aaron instantly recoiled from her touch; he wanted to pull away from the slick ooze that seeped from her open wounds. Yet, he forced himself to gather enough courage to glance up at her face and saw the relief in her eyes as he did so. He recognized the girl inside this monster. He took a deep breath as it suddenly dawned on him that this was the girl he loved. With that thought in mind, he reached forward and gently pressed his lips to hers. Aaron's lips were firm but plump. They moved over hers slowly. The sensation of kissing dead lips was strange to him, but he didn't care as she kissed him back. A sludge-like mixture of flesh and gunk streamed over their open mouths. Distaste rippled over his face as he pulled back. The smell of rotten flesh lingered in his flaring nostrils, but he sat up and really looked at her.

Neither one of the lovers could quite believe that they had been given a second chance to be together for one last time. The reunion was overwhelming, but Aaron could feel the presence of the girl he loved and for now, no matter how bizarre, that was enough. He found himself reminiscing about old times and with that in mind he switched on the television and the late night movies flickered upon the screen, somehow it made this odd meeting seem a little less strange.

But this couldn't stay that way for long. The brain that had liquefied inside Casey's skull caused her to become slightly disorientated at times, and she couldn't shake that desire within. It was welling up inside her now, and the sensation pulled at her self-control. She tilted her head as it lay on Aaron's shoulder and tried to inhale his scent, but there was no use. The clogged nostrils made this impossible.

The taste of that kiss lingered on her tongue, sending fire flaring up from within. This was something new, an urge that was so much more powerful than the initial need to find the one she loved. Her dress was completely soaked by this time; those intestines sealed inside the clear bag, along with other organs, were empty. Casey didn't quite understand what she was feeling, but it felt similar to the hunger she had experienced when she was alive.

Aaron seemed to notice her uneasy nature. He tore his eyes off the glow of the television screen. His fingers trailed through her mucky hair and caught on a clump of dirt. "What's up, babe?" he asked, concern evident in his voice.

Casey propped herself into a sitting position. Her eyes had sunken back into her skull, and the look on her face had become more severe, her deadly gaze settled upon Aaron and she saw a mixture of uncertainty enter his gaze.

She didn't speak as she moved in closer. Her skeletal arms wrapped around his muscular neck. He tried to push the fear out of his mind as he kissed her oncoming lips. The taste of decay was fierce on his tongue, and after a moment he needed to breathe, but she wouldn't pull away. Before Aaron knew it her lips mashed furiously with his and her rotten hands trailed over his chest. This evoked a mixture of disgust and lust in him. Naturally, the decoposition of her body was vile and strange to him, however he could not simply think of her as dead. He could still recognize that somehow she was still the girl he'd kissed a thousand times before.

The thought that this might be necrophilia plagued him. He soon found himself struggling in her death-like grasp. He pulled away, and the plump flesh of her ruined lips hung from her upper jaw, the teeth beneath visible now in a grotesque sneer. This was too much and it rudely awakened terror in him, his body was rejecting her and he could see the confusion in her eyes. Fear continued to rise as anger rose up in what was left of her monstrous features and she spat words at him as though they were shards of glass.

"What the fuck is wrong?" she growled with a lisp. "Why don't you want me anymore?"

Aaron's eyes softened and he spoke gently, he couldn't stand to see that he'd hurt her. "I know it's you, Casey. I love you."

His words had barely finished before she was on him again. She pressed her sunken breasts against his hard chest. Aaron loved her, he really did, but his gut was churning. Something wasn't right about this and the only thing he could concentrate on was how he could escape.

As though she read his mind, Casey snarled close to his face. Her eyes now showed no emotion but the rejection was clearly hurting her. It wasn't just the way Aaron had reacted, though, the situation had changed. Something inside Aaron screamed at him that Casey wasn't just seeking his affections anymore. The teeth in her face smiled at him demonically, that sinister smile seemed to prove that she was no longer human.

Before Aaron could fight back the ravenous Casey, her teeth moved frantically forward and she lunged onto him. Those teeth snapped and sunk into his face, her dead weight pinned him down and her jaws locked tight as pain engulfed his senses.

Aaron's scream penetrated the room; it rung off the ceiling and deafened his own ears. He frantically tried to push her away, but those hands came up and clung to his neck. The bones of her fingers were like talons that dug deep into his flesh. Agony seared through his face, and as he pulled away, Casey was there before him, a wet hunk of meat with white fat and skin glistening between her jaws as she chewed. The shock wave hit him like a tsunami. Instantly his hand moved to his face. Hot, wet blood splattered onto his palm, and Aaron dived towards the door.

"How the hell can you do this to me?" he screamed, voice shrill and intense with pain. He bounded across the room.

But Casey was hot on his heels. Her skeletal arms stretched out for Aaron. They clung like a vise to his side. He reached for the first thing he could find, a vase, and flung it in her direction. The ceramic pot shattered over Casey's head, and wedges of it stuck into her skull like horns. By now she'd finished swallowing the lump of meat; black blood was thick like lipstick on her mouth. And as the chase began the harsh reality of the situation dawned upon Aaron, the truth was in the ferocious squelching of her feet hitting the carpet and the murderous gaze that met his eyes each time he glanced over his shoulder. The state of her dead mind and body was no longer remotely the person she once was. And after she had tasted human flesh, the need consumed her features and blazed in her eyes.

She came again and again. Aaron scrambled in the direction of the exit. Nails ripped into his side and tore his shirt to shreds. His heart pumped; he couldn't believe what was happening. He hoped like hell this was a dream, that he would wake up, but the blood on his face had leaked down his neck by now and the pain was all too real. Aaron knew he had to escape or kill the woman he loved.

Conflicted, Aaron stopped in the hallway. The monstrosity that was his dead girlfriend moved towards him with a limp. He refused to give up.

"Casey," he called through the darkness of the hallway. The light that flickered in the room illuminated her silhouette and caused her dead eyes to glow as though they were covered in a sheen of moisture. "Please, Casey, you know who I am." By now his voice was breaking and salty wet tears rolled down his torn face. They irritated and burned the throbbing wound like acid.

She didn't stop, she just continued along the path. Each movement closed the gap between the two lovers. "I love you," Aaron said before he suddenly turned to flee. Casey's outstretched fingers reached toward him as his feet thudded toward the door. He moved swiftly to his car and got in. He pulled out, then reversed back; the headlights shone onto the woman, illuminating her in all her grotesque glory. The car left in a cloud of burning rubber, smoke rose high into the night sky above them.

As Aaron drove into the early morning, he held a hankie up to the wound on his face. Blood seeped through and saturated the cloth in no time as his slippery hands held the steering wheel. He hoped to god this wasn't like the movies, that he wouldn't be transformed into the demon Casey had become.

The wound was severe on Aaron's face, and he was afraid to look in the rear-view mirror. He didn't want to see what had happened, but eventually he found the courage to peek. What he saw caused him to cry out in terror. She had taken the flesh off in one bite. Teeth marks ringed the edge with jagged marks and red, raw flesh seeped with blood. The bone of his upper jaw glistened in the image before his eyes. He was severely disfigured, and the blood just would not stop. It filled his mouth; all he could taste was the metallic liquid. He continued to drive, until his movements became sluggish and his eyelids started to droop. Before he knew it, Aaron's head slumped forward against the steering wheel, and the car veered off the road, then slammed into the thick trunk of a nearby tree. The hood crumpled back as though it was a tin can, and his body was flung through the windshield. In his hurry he had forgotten to buckle up.

Shock overwhelmed him at first, unable to move he lay beneath the shattered glass that covered his limp body. After all the pain and terror Aaron had recently endured, he found himself welcoming the darkness beyond as peace finally crept in.

Casey had well and truly lost her mind by now, what was left of it, anyway. Time had taken its toll and the hunger was all she could think about. But it didn't seem quite as strong as the feeling she had when she was with Aaron. His flesh was the one thing she wanted and that pull was still there. She knew it would lead her to him.

And so the walking dead girl followed the pull. She walked on with ragged legs, and the surface of the road continued to wear out the putrefied flesh on her feet right to the bones.

Hours later, Casey shuffled along the winding roads of her home town; the sun rose up into the sky, staining it with vibrant colors. Very few cars were on the road; the ones that drove past didn't wait around to find out if she was what they thought she was. She followed that invisible path. It led her to a crumpled car. The front was wedged up against a giant tree. Instantly she felt Aaron was here. The hunger inside her was enormous. She got down on her hands and knees, crawling like a dog in search of a bone buried beneath the sand.

She came upon the lifeless body of Aaron. His face was infested with a million tiny bodies that moved in a mass; ants had begun to work away at the meat left beside the road. Casey didn't have what it took to process what was happening. She just found herself sitting beside his body like a swan beside its lifeless mate, unable to move away from the one she loved. The pull had stopped for now, and that was all that mattered.

Twenty minutes later, Aaron's fingers twitched slightly. Casey turned her head like an owl, her vertebrae popping with the motion. She knew he was moving, but something was different. She didn't have that incredible urge to consume him this time.

Aaron was dead, and as he moved into a sitting position, his lifeless eyes locked onto Casey.

Her body was in an advanced state of decomposition, his was relatively fresh. Nothing pulled at their empty souls, because they were together.

The two lovers gathered themselves. Aaron shook his head and the shards of glass fell from his black hair, glistening in the morning sun. He reached his blood-drenched hand out to Casey's palm that consisted of not much more than skin and bone, their fingers intertwined.

The two of them began another journey, this time together. They already had the one they loved and so they hungered for something else entirely. It wouldn't take long for Aaron's body to reach an advanced stage of decomposition, because unlike Casey, he had not been embalmed.

Their bodies would cease to be able to move at the same time, side by side, together.

Until then, they would hunger for flesh.

UNTIL THE END
By Patrick D'Orazio

The sound of the explosion was muted by distance, but Jason's back went rigid in anticipation of the shockwave all the same. When it came, it was little more than a tingling sensation shooting up through the soles of his black Gucci loafers, past his feet and on into his legs. The effect dissipated before it hit his chest, where his heart was already beating like a jackhammer.

The screams of the people running pell-mell across DeSoto and the screech of fighter jets high above was far more jarring to his nerves. The rapid fire of automatic weaponry echoing through the canyons of skyscrapers only served to compound the disruptive effect on his frayed nerves.

Taking a deep breath, Jason looked both ways before crossing the street. He needn't have bothered. The four lanes of traffic were at a standstill as far as the eye could see. Though most people remained in their cars, huddled in confusion, a few had thrown open their doors and joined the mad onslaught of pedestrians doing a frenetic panic dance on the roadway. They looked like an ant colony with its internal radar on the fritz. Everyone was rushing in different directions, bouncing off one another and causing madness to spread like competing ripples on the surface of a once-tranquil pond.

Jason's first step off the sidewalk was wobbly. His legs had gone rubbery and each breath he took sounded like it was coming from a straining locomotive. He bounced off the grill of a Mercedes SUV and pinballed into the middle of the intersection, but managed to avoid getting creamed by a group of screaming teenage girls rushing past. A jarring bleat of a car horn at Jason's back caused him to jump like he'd been bitten by a snake.

It might have ended for him right there.

At that moment, the youngest corporate executive in the history of Randis Corporation was on the verge of losing it. He would have been almost relieved if his heart had seized up and struck him dead in the middle of the street. If something snapped inside his head causing him to yank off his Kiton tie and tear off his Valentino suit while running down the street hooting like a madman, that'd be just fine by him. But that was the exact moment *she* caught up with him.

She'd been chasing him for at least twenty blocks, but he wasn't really sure how long he'd been running. It had been after the first explosion, the one that had caused half the windows in a three-block radius to shatter. A strangling fear had gripped him, because he knew what it meant. That's when he'd let go of her hand and taken off running. *And that had been what? Maybe thirty minutes ago?*

Of course Theresa had followed him. She knew where he was headed and it wasn't like he could grab a taxi to get there quicker. Not with the city under siege. So it wasn't surprising she managed to catch up with him just as he made it to his destination.

She grabbed his wrist and spun him around. He almost lost his balance but managed to stay upright. He stood slumped-shouldered, his chest heaving.

"Jason! What the hell are you doing? Are you insane?"

She was hard to hear over the blood pounding in his ears, but he caught the gist, and when he heard Theresa's words, spoken with that Irish accent, all Jason could do was swallow hard and stand there, mouth agape. That was the effect Theresa Finn had on Jason Watts from the first moment he ever laid eyes on her.

He had a speech prepared. It was a good one. It explained how he wanted to keep her safe, and why he had run. He would grab her by the shoulders, stand tall, look her in the eyes and tell her why he needed to do this on his own, but that was before she managed to cast the spell which always left him tongue-tied and befuddled: she looked at him. It wasn't just her eyes that mesmerized him. Theresa's long flowing red hair was a blast of vibrant color in a world whose palate was all dim greys and blacks. The splash of freckles running across her otherwise pale porcelain skin was a feature Jason didn't find appealing on most women, but on Theresa they drove him to distraction. Of course, that was the point. That was why they had chosen her. For Jason, she was impossible to ignore.

It took the bite of Theresa's fingernails digging into the palms of his hands to jar Jason out of his stupor.

"—did you run? We need to stick together!"

Jason clamped down on Theresa's delicate fingers to prevent her from drawing blood. The pain, along with the tumult of battle surrounding them, allowed him to focus. He did his best to steady his breathing before replying.

"We're too late. They've already completed the experiments. There's nothing we can do to stop them."

"No! All of this—" Theresa screamed, gesturing with a flip of her hair to encompass everything surrounding them "—is just the beginning, and you know it! The government will keep working with Randis and the next time will be even worse, unless we do something to stop them NOW!"

"Okay... But I can go there to get what we need and get it over to the HLF. You don't need to go with me—I can handle it on my own. You need to get somewhere safe." The words were like gravel in his mouth, hard to spit out. They sounded far less noble and brave than he'd hoped for, but he felt relieved he'd gotten them out.

Theresa shook her head, slipped her hands free of Jason's and grabbed hold of the lapels of his suit, pulling him down next to her. He had to lean in, since she was a good six inches shorter than him.

"There's nowhere safe anymore, and besides, we're in this together, until the end." The heat from her breath made Jason's heart race with excitement despite the crippling madness of what was going around them. She tugged harder on his suit, pulling him close enough for her lips to graze his earlobe. "We stick together, no matter what. Remember? Me and you forever." Before she let him go, she kissed his cheek. It was just a peck, but when Theresa's lips touched his skin, Jason could feel goose bumps rising up all across his body. Still, he wondered if she was telling him the truth.

They met at a charity benefit. She'd been alone, which should have been his first clue. She ignored the come-on lines of some of the most eligible bachelors there, which should have been another clue. But even when Theresa walked across the room to say hello to him, Jason still didn't suspect a thing. And when he heard that lilting Irish accent, any skepticism he might have had about her intentions had vanished.

They spent every available second together over the next month.

Jason met many of Theresa's friends and didn't think it strange that their polite dinner conversation always turned toward his role at Randis and the genetic research they did for the government.

After only a few weeks, Jason confessed his love to Theresa. She did as well, and admitted that she was part of the Human Liberation Front, a radical organization dedicated to stopping corporations like Randis from carrying out illegal genetic testing. Theresa admitted she'd been assigned to befriend him and to work to get him to join their cause, but instead had fallen for him.

Hurt, but unable to deny his feelings, Jason worked to make the most out of his newfound situation.

To prove that HLF were dead wrong about Randis, he decided to do some research at work, but his sniffing around got him more than he'd bargained for. A project he came across, code-named BCR-23, raised his suspicions. Paper trails related to funding led to a dead end, and certain prominent government officials were attached to the project. That was a strange finding, but not abnormal, even when the government officials in question were heads of more than one covert entity.

It was some of the data Jason unearthed which caused his blood to run cold, though. Words like *reanimation, corpse, chromosomal transmutation,* and *weaponize* were prevalent throughout, and descriptions of what Randis was doing to their animal test subjects were ghastly.

Jason kept digging, and discovered there were plans to move forward with testing on human corpses. That was when he made the monumental decision to work with Theresa and the HLF to stop Randis.

They devised a simple plan: Jason would go to his corporate headquarters, retrieve as many files as he could on BCR-23, and then share them with the HLF so they could expose the illegal experiments to the world. Theresa insisted she would accompany him when he did so, despite Jason's miserable efforts to try and stop her.

They discovered the dates on the experiments, and all hell broke loose, despite their efforts to put an end to it all.

The HLF were probably the only people outside of Randis—and parts of the government—who knew the truth when the morning news broke a story about a series of violent assaults occurring at one of Randis Corporation's largest labs in the city. Within an hour, half of downtown was a war zone.

It came as no surprise to Jason or Theresa when the National Guard was called in, or the fact that they were immediately available.

Jason stared at the Randis Building. The skyscraper's sleek lines and dark, tinted windows made it look like an exotic rocket ship. It had been a cool place to work. Now it looked sinister, like the lair of wicked monsters that wanted to devour his soul.

Theresa let Jason take the lead when they reached the sidewalk outside the building. Smoothing his ruffled suit, he did his best to regain his composure. Trudging up the steps that fronted the building, the couple spied the twin lion statues which guarded the entrance. Theresa had always given Jason grief about the lions. To her, they weren't intimidating, they looked more like two oversize kitty cats with a few extra tufts of fur on their necks.

The twin sets of revolving doors were stationary; Jason could see a man beyond the tinted glass, working at something above them. Moving in the direction of the handicap-accessible door to the right, he pressed the handle. It was locked. Shadows shifted behind the door and Jason looked up to see a security guard behind the glass staring at him.

Squinting, he realized he knew the man. Bob, he remembered. The middle-aged, slouchy guard looked different than usual, though, but that was probably because Jason had only ever seen Bob sitting in the lobby booth where employees had their ID's scanned before using the elevators. Jason assumed the man would be taller, but despite Bob's pot belly and stooped shoulders, he looked menacing enough from where he stood, with a scowl on his face and a hand poised over the Taser on his belt.

An acidic lump formed in the pit of Jason's stomach and bullets of sweat poured down his face as the staring match with the security guard continued. Theresa's hand slid across his back, which gave him a small surge of confidence. Puffing out his chest, the young executive returned Bob's scowl and mouthed the words "*Let me in,*" and then added "*god dammit*" for effect.

It was like a cartoon light bulb turned on above Bob's head. His eyes widened and he leaned forward to shove a key in the lock. Pulling the door open, Bob ushered Jason inside. Theresa, who was glued to his back, slipped in before Bob pushed the door shut and locked it again.

"I'm sorry I didn't recognize you immediately, Mr. Watts. But things have been a bit crazy around here, if you know what I mean. The building's on lockdown." The words flew from Bob's mouth while he backed up to give Jason and Theresa some space. The other guard, who had been tinkering with the revolving doors, stopped what he was doing and stood next to his partner. Bob's heavily lined face had a sincere, apologetic look on it, while the younger man looked a bit more skeptical. Bob gave Jason a nervous chuckle. "But we very well couldn't keep *you* out, now could we, Mr. Watts?"

Jason nodded and felt his rattled nerves settling. The fear that had threatened to overwhelm him outside was subsiding.

"We need to see your employee ID's."

Jason felt a jolt of surprise when Bob's partner took a step forward and glared at him. Built like a brick wall, his thick meaty fists were clenched at his sides.

"Now Jake," Bob scolded his partner. He made the effort to maneuver between him and Jason, but there wasn't enough of a gap. "Don't you know who this is? He doesn't need to show ID. He's one of our top vice presidents, after all."

Jake's face was impervious stone, and his eyes remained locked on Jason's.

After a few moments, with what could best be described as begrudging reluctance, the blocky security guard shifted his shoulders and redirected his attention to Theresa, who had moved out of Jason's shadow to stand at his side.

"And what about her?" Jake thrust his square jaw out at the redhead, looking at her like she was a slab of meat. One of his hands shifted until it rested on the canister of mace attached to his belt.

The lump of acid in Jason's stomach transformed into something more akin to lava and he felt his blood starting to boil.

"She's with me."

Jason hadn't intended for his words to come out sounding like a growl, but he didn't like the way Jake was eyeing his girlfriend. Not one bit.

Something that might resemble a smile on appeared on Jake's face. He lifted a finger to point at Theresa. "She an employee too? Only employees are allowed in the building when we're on lockdown."

Bob took a step toward Jake and dropped a hand on his partner's shoulder. Jake shrugged him off and when he did, the older guard's nervous chuckling returned before subsiding suddenly. For a few seconds, silence reigned in the lobby while outside, the world cried out in agony. Blurred shadows passed by the windows and they could hear the screams of people crying out for help from a few feet beyond the glass.

"Sorry, Mr. Watts," Bob crowed. "Jake here is new and he's a bit overzealous. You'll have to forgive him."

"Shut up, Bob." Jake didn't look at the man he'd ordered to silence. His eyes remained glued on Jason, even while his words continued to be flung at Bob. "We were given explicit orders that no one except employees with proper ID get into the building. So I'm not going to take the fall because you're too busy kissing ass to do your job. Not with all the crazy shit going on outside."

Jason could feel a vein in his temple starting to throb. Gritting his teeth, he shoved a hand into his jacket pocket to fish out his wallet. He wasn't sure how showing his company ID would help Theresa, but he hoped showing this goon he was indeed an executive VP might get Jake to back down.

Before Jason could get his wallet out, Theresa stepped forward holding something in front of her. She'd retrieved it from her purse. As far as Jason could tell, it was some kind of ID holder. She shoved it in Jake's face and sneered.

"Don't get your panties in a bunch, princess. I'm not an employee, but you better think twice before you try and toss me out." Theresa's terse words didn't just stun the menacing oaf in front of her, but her boyfriend too. All Jason could do was gawk at her. It wasn't just her words, but the fact that they had been spoken in a flat, Midwestern accent. Jake's eyes narrowed. He did his best to keep glaring at Theresa, but when she glared right back, he blinked first, then studied her ID. Jason couldn't see it from his angle, but the way Jake's eyebrow arched and he ground his teeth, it must be impressive. "Now, are you going to stand aside and let me and Mr. Watts go up to his office so I can conduct my investigation, or am I going to have to call down to the station and run a background check on you, Jake?"

It was as if a switch had been flipped. Jake's chest deflated and the hand that had been itching to grab his mace flopped to his side.

Bob cleared his throat. "Well, now that that's settled, I'd suggest you two head over to the elevators. We're going to be pulling down the storm shutters since it doesn't look like things are getting any better outside." Bob's watered-down smile was back, and he was gesturing at his partner to get moving.

Jason stumbled after Theresa, his mind racing. He was still thinking about the stunt Theresa had pulled when they neared the bank of elevators, which was probably why he didn't hear the loud thud. It took the sound of Bob yelling to make him turn to see what was happening.

The older guard was gesturing and shouting at Jake, who was running along the front wall of windows with some sort of pole in his hands. Jason could see him poking the device at something metal above the windows. Inserting the pole into some kind of loop of fabric, Jake yanked with all his might, sending the metal shutter sliding down to the ground. Not wasting any time, he slid sideways and worked the metal rod into the next loop above the windows. Bob had moved to the opposite side of the front of the building with a pole similar to Jake's in hand. He reached up with the hooked end of the pole and snagged the loop attached to another metal shutter. When it came sliding down, it sounded something like a garage door slamming shut.

Jason wouldn't have bothered continuing watching the two men if it weren't for the fact that his eyes were drawn to what was going on past the windows. His blood ran cold.

Four people had moved up to the door he and Theresa had passed through and were slamming fists against it. Three more had slipped into the gaps between one of the revolving doors and were ramming their shoulders into the glass, attempting to force the turnstile to spin. If that wasn't strange enough, all of them were covered in some sort of muck, though it was hard to tell what it was through the tinted glass. One thing was obvious, though: they were in a panic. But there was also something else.

They weren't just begging to be let in; they were pounding, kicking, and scratching at the glass. Their cries were raw, barbaric. It was like they were speaking in tongues, splattering the window with spittle as they raged against it and pleaded with the security guards working as fast as possible to slam the last few storm shutters into place.

Jason almost jumped out of his skin when Theresa's hand slid inside of his.

"Come on," she whispered. The Irish accent had returned. "There's nothing we can do for them." Before she could tug on Jason's hand, the sound of shattering glass caused them to turn and look back across the lobby again.

At first, Jason couldn't figure out what was happening. It looked as though one of the people pounding at the doors had suffered a psychotic break. The man, dressed in a natty silk suit, had grabbed the woman next to him by a hank of her long dark hair and was slamming her head against the glass door. A spiderweb of cracks had already formed where her forehead had met the glass and something black was oozing into the cracks. It looked to be similar to the substance everyone else was covered in. Jason's stomach churned when he realized it was blood.

The other people who had been pounding on the door had scattered, or at least most of them. One, a teenager dressed in baggy jeans and a tank top, had been tackled by two other people before he could make a break for it. They dragged the kid to the ground and were attacking him, tearing at his clothes while clawing and biting him. He fought back, kicking and scratching, but they ignored his feeble efforts to defend himself and tore into him like wild animals. One of his deranged attackers leaned down and with his teeth ripped a gaping hole out of the boy's neck. A spurt of blood shot out of the wound and sprayed the window, blocking Jason and Theresa's view.

It was the last thing they saw before the final storm shutter slammed down, closing the lobby off from the outside world. Jake, who had pulled the last shutter down, leaned against it, his shoulders rising and falling as he tried to catch his breath. Bob, standing next to him, appeared to be less winded, perhaps because his partner had done most of the work. The older guard turned and spotted Jason and Theresa across the lobby.

Bob's face contorted with rage.

"Didn't I tell you two to get upstairs? Move your asses! It's not safe down here!"

The man's sudden change in demeanor made Jason jump with surprise.

"Come on," Theresa urged him again, this time with her hand squeezing Jason's fingers as hard as she could. He didn't resist, and let her tug him toward the elevators.

After Theresa pressed the 'Up' button, it took only moments for them to hear a ding from above. One of the elevator doors slid open and they moved toward it. Before the door closed behind them, Jason heard the sound of more glass shattering and screaming out past the storm shutters.

Reaching into his pants pocket with a quivering hand, Jason's numb fingers retrieved his elevator keycard. After he almost dropped it, Theresa covered his hand with hers and held it for a few moments. She looked up at him with solemn eyes and Jason's agitation faded. Sliding the card into the slot beneath the bank of buttons labeled L through 84, he waited for the red light next to the slot to turn green. When it did, he pressed '82' and slid the card back into his pocket.

Jason leaned back against the wall of the elevator. For several seconds the couple was quiet. The only sounds they could hear were the steady hum of the mechanisms pulling them upward and Jason's breathing, which was heavier than usual. The near silence was eerie after the endless parade of loud, jarring assaults to their senses that had taken place over the past few hours. Looking over at Theresa, Jason wasn't surprised to see her looking back at him, though her expression did catch him off guard. The look on her face surprised him. She was smiling.

"Go ahead."

Jason blinked at the odd command. "I'm sorry—what?"

The smile blossomed into a full grin and Theresa almost laughed.

"Go ahead, ask me anything. I'm sure you have some questions."

Jason could do nothing but stare at Theresa for several long seconds; long enough for her smile to falter.

"Did you ever really love me, or was I just a means to an end?"

If Jason had slapped her, Theresa couldn't have looked more stunned.

That was when he saw her tough veneer crack for the first time. Theresa had always been strong. She never cried, at least as far as Jason knew. When she had first admitted that she had fallen in love with him despite all her efforts to remain aloof, he had seen something new in her eyes—vulnerability. For the first time since she had told him that, the look returned.

Jason's lip quivered and the urge to blurt out an apology for his callous question was strong, but he held his tongue, refusing to retract it. He had to know the truth, especially now, with the world going off the deep end.

He waited, watching Theresa working hard to regain her composure. She blinked away what might have been tears, but none fell.

She tried to smile again, but it faltered. "And here I was, thinking you would ask me about the badge or my fake accent." She laughed, but her throat hitched when she did. "But no, you go straight for the jugular, don't you, J?"

Jason winced, but his mouth remained shut.

Theresa took a shuddering breath and closed her eyes. When she opened them again he could see the pain in them, but also something more, something more profound. She continued, "I was assigned to convince you to see our side of things, like I already told you. You'd been a target of ours ever since you were promoted to upper management. We did our research, studied your profile. You're a corporate climber, but you were also an activist in college. Perhaps even an idealist. When they asked me to reach out to you, I was skeptical, but I studied everything about you. I got to know you before

I ever met you. I... was afraid. I think they saw that." Theresa sighed. "I was afraid because I could see it in you too. You were someone we could convince to champion our cause. Someone who would believe in it as wholeheartedly as we do, but I... I didn't want to be the one to convince you, because I knew they wanted me to manipulate you. We knew about your past—the girlfriend with the red hair and green eyes who broke your heart, who you never really got over. But I—"

"But you what?"

Theresa could only look into Jason's eyes for a moment before her chin dropped and her pale face flamed red.

"I didn't want to hurt you. I didn't want to seduce you or anything like that. So I tried to just become your friend and make you understand our cause. I thought if I could do that, my conscience would be clear. I thought that despite all we knew about you, you had probably become some greedy corporate stooge since you'd joined Randis, but I *still* didn't want to hurt you." She looked up again, and this time her eyes remained fixed on Jason's. "But that was before I got to know you. The *real* you. Not just another corporate executive, but Jason Watts, a man with a good heart. Someone with a rare quality: he does the right things for the right reasons. I realized you didn't join Randis because you wanted to get rich. You joined this company because you believed in what they claimed their mission to be: to help people.

"And that was one of the reasons I fell in love with you."

"I, uh. I don't know what to say—"

DING

Jason and Theresa turned toward the opening elevator doors and took a step back when they saw who was waiting for them on the other side.

"Mr. Watts." A man carrying a submachine gun peered into the elevator. His eyes gravitated to Theresa and one of his eyebrows rose. "And you must be... a guest?"

Jason recognized Mr. Wirtz, head of corporate security for Randis, though he had never seen the man armed with anything more than a handgun.

Unlike the guards in the lobby, Wirtz was no wage slave. He was responsible for maintaining the safety and security of Randis's executive staff, from

CEO on down. He was a distinguished man in his mid-fifties, greying, but with sharp, alert features and eyes that drilled right through you.

There were rumors about Wirtz that gave him the mystique that he was not a man to mess with. He had allegedly made a few 'troublesome' issues disappear for several of the C-level execs, though Jason hoped they were nothing more than exaggerations—stray rumors that didn't mean anything. But as he stared at the H&K MP5 in the man's hands, he wondered if those stories might be more than just rumors. The barrel of the compact weapon had been pointed toward the ground when the elevator opened, but rose when Wirtz acknowledged Theresa.

"If you'll allow me to get my ID out without shooting me, I'd be happy to show you who I am," Theresa said, this time with an impeccable southern drawl. Wirtz chuckled and lowered the weapon. "Certainly, and my apologies, ma'am. We weren't expecting any guests today; especially not on the executive levels of the building."

Wirtz continued staring at Theresa, but Jason knew the accusatory words had been directed at him. Jason waited for her to pull the same ID holder out, but this time Theresa retrieved something that looked more like a driver's license. Wirtz took the proffered ID and studied it for several seconds. His eyes darted to Theresa's face, then back to the card. His expression never changed, though his lips tightened and it appeared as if he were grinding his teeth.

Returning her ID, he gave Theresa a stiff nod.

"My apologies, Dr. Hale, but as you can probably guess, we're on high alert around here. Things are a bit tense today."

Theresa waved off the apology. "Well, I hope you treat *other* high-level government scientists with more respect when they come around."

Before Wirtz could offer a retort, Theresa turned to Jason. "Now, if you please, Mr. Watts. I'd like to discuss your findings on the Rensellari project so I can share your information with my team back in Atlanta."

Jason cleared his throat and nodded, gesturing down one of the hallways in front of them. "Right this way." Theresa marched down the hall before Jason could say another word. He glanced at Wirtz, who scowled back at him. Jason shrugged and took off after his girlfriend. He managed to catch up with her just as she was turning a corner. Making sure they were out of Wirtz's line of sight, he grabbed her by the elbow. "Where did you get that ID?" he hissed. "Better yet, where the hell did you get either of those IDs? You could have given me some kind of heads up at least."

Theresa smiled. "*Now* you ask." She gave him a flirtatious smile. "Sorry, I can't kiss and tell." Jason opened his mouth, but before he could say anything else, Theresa raised a finger to her lips and looked up at the ceiling. "Shhh."

Jason looked up and spotted one of the countless security cameras Randis had in the building. Frowning, he shook his head in frustration and stepped in front of Theresa, leading the way down another hall and past several large meeting rooms to his office. When he slid his index finger over the biometric reader on his door, there was an audible click and he tugged on the knob. It opened and he gestured for Theresa to enter first.

She smiled and touched his hand as she passed. "Always the gentleman."

Goose bumps rose on his skin and Jason felt a tingling sensation in his chest. He couldn't help it. It didn't matter what doubts he may have about Theresa's true intentions, he was hopelessly, helplessly in love with her.

Shutting the door behind him, Jason moved to his desk. Overhead lights flickered on the instant they had stepped into the room, though they were hardly necessary. Theresa studied the room while Jason took a seat behind his desk and began tapping on the keyboard located behind three large monitors. His desk was an oak piece, but it wasn't extravagant. Neither was anything else in the office. There was a leather couch situated between two matching bookshelves, but little else—besides a print hanging on the wall—that could be considered a decorative touch. The print looked old and dusty, as if it had been on the wall for years.

Overall, the office was rather drab.

The only thing that drew Theresa's eye was the floor-to-ceiling picture window behind Jason's desk.

"This'll take just a few minutes. Once I'm done, the HLF will have enough to hang these bastards out to dry." Theresa nodded, but her eyes remained fixed on the view of the skyline outside the big window. Gravitating toward it, she slipped past Jason's desk.

"Won't your IT staff be able figure out what you did?"

Jason shrugged. "Yes, but they won't for at least a couple of days. Besides, it's a little late to be worrying about stuff like that, isn't it?"

Theresa stopped her progress toward the window and looked at Jason. He gave her a shrug before turning back to his monitors. Theresa felt a pang of guilt for what she had put him through. She had stepped into Jason's life and turned it upside down. After this, it wouldn't just be Randis coming after him; it would be the government. They never liked it when someone exposed their secrets. His life had changed drastically and permanently, all because of her. At the same time, she felt an undeniable sense of pride. She had been right about Jason all along. He was willing to give up everything to do the right thing, regardless of the consequences, and that was another reason she had fallen in love with him.

Turning back toward the window, she walked up to it and looked out across the skyline, then down on the streets below. When she did, a frown creased her face.

Five minutes later, Jason hit a few last keystrokes and smiled. He beamed at the information flashing on his middle monitor. "All done. Hopefully, this will put a stop to this madness. Randis won't be able to get away with anything like this ever again."

"I think we might be too late for that."

Jason spun around in his office chair to look at Theresa. She was leaning against his window, her head resting on the glass.

Forcing a smile onto his face, he stood up and walked up behind her. Touching her shoulders, he rubbed them gently. "I recall you trying to convince me we weren't too late all that long ago."

Leaning forward, Jason rubbed his cheek on Theresa's soft hair and buried his nose in her curls. He could never resist the smell of the shampoo she used... or perhaps it was just her natural scent. It was intoxicating. Looking out the window, his body stiffened.

Smoke was billowing from countless fires burning out of control. Military helicopters streaked across the sky in every direction. Jason could see that the Militran tower, one of the more majestic buildings in the city, had a gaping hole on one side that ran from its fortieth floor up to its roof. It looked like some kind of giant had taken a swipe at it with a massive clawed fist.

When he looked down, it was hard to understand what was happening below. From eighty-two stories up everything is supposed to look peaceful, but that was far from the truth. The streets were awash in blood and splattered with corpses. It looked like they had been tossed around like dismembered rag dolls. Jason did his best to ignore the dead and focus on the living, but they were just as bad.

When he'd been down there the people running around had reminded him of ants, only with no method to their madness. From what he could see now, there was definitely a method. Those who still lived were doing one of two things: running toward someone or running away from them. The former group far outnumbered the latter and when Jason saw one catch another, he felt his gut clench in revulsion and had to turn away.

The nausea he was feeling was replaced by a growing feeling of outrage as he stepped away from the window.

"We have to stop this. Somehow."

Theresa turned away from the window and looked up at Jason's face. He could see his own sadness and regret mirrored in her eyes. She shook her head. "We can't stop what's already begun. The city is gone. The military has probably already blown the bridges and set up blockades all around downtown."

Stepping backward, Jason slumped into his office chair and put his head in his hands. "I had no idea how big this would get. I thought it would be bad... but not *this* bad."

Theresa knelt down in front of him. Leaning forward, she laid her head down in Jason's lap. "The information you've shared with the HLF might bring everything crashing down on Randis, and the government too. If the public hears about this, they'll be hung out to dry." She snorted. "But that's a big if." Looking up, she gripped Jason's hands. "I'm so sorry I got you into all of this, but I promise you, I'll make sure what you did will have meaning. I'll do everything in my power to stop these people so this can never happen again. I promise you."

The look in Theresa's eyes unnerved Jason. There was no doubt in his mind that she was telling the truth and that scared him.

Before Jason could formulate any kind of response, the overhead lights went off. The room dimmed, though the daylight coming from the window kept the darkness at bay.

Jason squinted at the ceiling. "The motion sensors must be glitching," he mumbled, though he wasn't very confident of that assessment. A blaring alarm invaded Jason's office. It was coming from out in the hall and despite being muffled by the closed door, it threatened to shatter their eardrums. *"ALL EXECUTIVE PERSONNEL REPORT TO THE NORTH CORRIDOR STAIRWELL IMMEDIATELY."*

The couple jumped up and wrapped their arms around one another. Jason looked down at Theresa and could see that she was as shocked as he was.

"This can't be good."

Jason turned to face the door. Relinquishing his hold on Theresa, he walked across the room.

"Are you sure it's a good idea to leave your office?"

Jason bit his lip. "I don't think we have much of a choice," he said with a shrug.

Theresa took a deep breath and nodded in reluctant agreement. Together, they went out into the hall. The lights were out there as well, but emergency overhead lighting cast a dim glow. They spied the outline of several people further down the hall, all moving in the same direction. Jason gestured for Theresa to follow him and they fell into line with everyone else. Moving through several halls, they came across more people, all of whom were heading toward a door across a common area with a red "Exit" sign. A few frantic people with smartphones were trying to make calls or were texting, but no one seemed to be having any luck. Jason recognized some of his peers among the crowd. He also saw someone up ahead who gave him pause.

"What's happening?" Theresa asked.

"It's Wirtz," Jason said. Theresa frowned at the response, but said nothing. Jason sighed as he continued to watch what was going on up ahead. "He's taking people out of line and not letting them go up the stairs."

"Why? Who?"

Jason felt queasy.

"Only executives are being allowed to go into the stairwell. Everyone else is being taken out of line by his goons."

Jason spied one of Wirtz's security team moving down the line, heading their direction. He yelled at him. "Hey! What's going on?"

Other people in line were also yelling. At first, the guard ignored the shouted inquiries, but after several people stepped out of line to crowd around him, he raised his weapon—a submachine gun similar to Wirtz's—and shouted above the noise of the crowd.

"The building has been breached. We're working on re-securing it, but for now, all executives are being evacuated to the roof."

A hundred questions raced through Jason's mind, including asking what the man meant by *breached*. Before he could shout another question, several other people beat him to it.

What about the rest of us? was the one question Jason heard the most.

The security officer shook his head in frustration and pushed his way through the crowd, ignoring the shouts of anger. Pointing the barrel at anyone who got too close, he walked past where Jason and Theresa stood.

Panic was rippling through the crowd, but Jason and Theresa managed to migrate up to where Wirtz was standing before things got out of hand. More of the security team had arrived, and their presence kept anyone from getting too rambunctious.

The last people were pushed back and out of the way and Jason and Theresa found themselves standing in front of Wirtz. The scowl on his face changed into a smirk when he saw them.

"Ah, Mr. Watts and Dr. Hale. Long time no see."

"Are you going to let us go up, or what?"

Jason's angry words were met with indifference by the security head. He looked at the younger man, his dark eyes narrowing. Theresa watched the staring match between them and resisted the urge to clasp Jason's hand in hers, knowing it would sabotage their efforts to get to the roof. The one thing she knew for sure was that they *needed* to get up there.

It surprised Theresa when Wirtz blinked first. He glanced over at her but didn't spend more than a moment studying her. There was loathing in his expression. Without a word, he gestured at the door behind him.

Not waiting for the head of security to change his mind, Jason grabbed hold of Theresa's hand and pulled her through the open door. The stairwell was dark, but the emergency lighting was adequate for them to see their route to the roof. When they came to the top landing, more security personnel were standing at the door. Seeing the couple, one opened the door and motioned them outside.

Jason and Theresa had to shield their eyes from the bright sun. The sounds of blaring alarms and the message urging executives to the stairwell had faded, only to be replaced by the chop of helicopter blades and the echoes of distant gunfire. An occasional police siren or scream would bounce off the surrounding buildings, but they sounded even further away.

A crowd of people moved across the expanse of the roof, away from the vestibule housing the stairs and toward another set of steps leading up to the helipad. It was a veritable rogue's gallery of C-Level execs, VP's, and division presidents.

The atmosphere on the roof was convivial, people laughing and chatting. At first, Jason wondered if perhaps it was nervous energy; relief that they had been saved from whatever had *breached* the building. He didn't want to think too hard about it, especially after what he'd witnessed in the lobby. He latched onto Theresa's arm; she looked at him and smiled. There was a distant look on her face. He wanted to ask her what was wrong—besides the obvious—but one of the security guards stepped onto the roof with a bullhorn.

"Attention everyone. Can I have your attention please! A cargo helicopter will be here soon. We will be evacuating to McGreevy Military Base. Please be patient. It will be arriving in the next fifteen minutes."

The news was met with a rousing round of applause from everyone except Jason and Theresa. The implications of what was being said were clear.

Randis's executive team was fleeing the scene of the crime, and leaving behind everyone else to face the consequences.

"Until it arrives, we have some liquid refreshment and hors d'oeuvres for you."

Behind the man on the bullhorn came two more guards, their submachine guns strapped to their backs while they carried trays full of food and drink. The pair moved toward Jason and Theresa. Seeing the looks of disgust on their faces, they kept moving. They were better received by the people standing near the helipad.

"This is sickening," Theresa hissed.

Jason, embarrassed by what he was witnessing, could only nod in agreement.

"Jason! Glad to see you made it!"

The words, coming from the stairs, caused Jason to whirl around. When he did, he saw Samuel Trent lumbering up the steps. Following him was a young woman, hidden by the shadow cast by the bulky executive's shadow. Sam was all smiles, while the girl, who was perhaps in her mid-twenties, looked rather skittish, her eyes darting about the roof while she clutched at an iPad like a security blanket.

Jason lifted a hand and waved at Sam. Samuel Trent was the chief technology officer for Randis and for all intents and purposes was the most powerful man in the company. The CEO, Mark Trayper, was on his way out, having lost the confidence of the board of directors when his pet research project drained the company's coffers of several billion dollars in less than eight months. Sam, on the other hand, had the Midas touch. Every project he championed was a winner. In a few short months, after Trayper resigned, he would become the top dog.

Reaching out with a meaty paw, Samuel shook Jason's hand and slapped him on the shoulder with his other. "I didn't think you were in the building today," the balding, saggy-faced man said to Jason, though his eyes were on Theresa. Turning to face her, he gave her a toothy grin. "And who is this lovely young lady?"

"Dr.—"

Theresa put her hand on Jason's arm to stop his introduction. She was smiling, but there was something off-putting about it. Her teeth were clenched and her body was rigid, though she looked calm, almost serene.

"My name is Theresa Finn, Mr. Trent."

Jason was once again stunned by what had come out of Theresa's mouth. This time, she had used her real name and her words were spoken with the Irish accent he knew he knew so very well. "Ah, so you know who I am!" Sam responded with a delighted chirp of laughter. Reaching out with stubby fingers, he pawed Theresa's hand, tugging it toward him. Leaning down, he squashed his moist lips against the back of it before letting go. "It's a pleasure to meet you." He winked at Jason, and gestured for him to step away from her.

Theresa was fuming and Jason was worried about what she might do, but he turned and followed the man who had been, in many ways, his mentor during his time at Randis. Jason breathed a sigh of relief when Theresa didn't follow him and Sam as they walked across the roof of the building toward the corner furthest from the helipad and the rest of the executives.

"So, you managed to get your assistant past the guard dogs, huh?" Sam asked.

Jason was about to shake his head and correct Sam on who Theresa was, but thought better of it. He nodded. Sam looked back over at Theresa and licked his lips. Putting an arm around Jason's shoulder, he guided him a few steps further away from her. "Irish lass, huh kid? I bet she's a real firecracker in bed."

Jason could smell the stench of Sam's body odor and the gallons of expensive cologne he bathed in to cover it up. The combination was almost as repulsive as the man's comments about Theresa.

Sam gestured at the woman who'd come up the stairs with him. "She's my newest assistant." Jason glanced at the girl. She was fidgeting, her fingers tugging at a blond lock of hair that hung down past her shoulders. When she saw Sam looking at her, she attempted a smile, but it faded quickly. "It'd be a waste to let her get caught up in all this mess, if you know what I mean." Sam elbowed Jason, who grunted from the shot to the ribs. The old man looked out over the city and shook his head. "Can you believe this shit? It's a crying shame."

Jason nodded, but didn't offer any commentary. When Sam continued to stare out at the city, Jason's could feel a prickle of sweat dripping down his neck. He was anxious to get back to Theresa, but knew his boss had grabbed him and pulled him away from her for a reason. It was time to cut to the chase.

"So, uh—what's going on, Sam?"

Sam let his arm slip off Jason's shoulder and reached into his jacket pocket. Pulling out a case, he retrieved a cigar. A lighter appeared and he lit the cigar, puffing on it several times. Jason waited, knowing Sam would answer the question when he was good and ready and not a second before.

"You knew about BCR-23, didn't you?"

Sam kept his eyes on the skyline, looking out over the city. Jason felt the urge to lie, but he knew Sam would know.

"Yes."

Sam took another puff on his cigar and smiled at Jason. "I knew you had dug around. I get reports on anyone who accesses information on any of my pet research projects—at least anyone who isn't authorized." Sam raised a hand to stave off Jason's protest before it even started. "I'm not upset with you, Jason. On the contrary, I consider it a show of initiative that you took it upon yourself to learn more about these projects we've been working on for the government. After all, they're game changers."

Jason could feel his heart pounding against his ribcage. "It was what caused what's happened in the city, isn't it? Human test subjects were used this time, weren't they?"

Sam smiled and raised an eyebrow. "Smart boy," he said with a snort. "Of course, of course! You read the files. You knew we were ready to move up to the big leagues. No more chimpanzees or dogs." He paused and shrugged. "Well, at least we *thought* we were ready to test it on humans." He barked out a loud laugh. "I guess we were a bit ahead of schedule, if you know what I mean."

"The experiment was a catastrophic failure."

Samuel squinted at Jason's proclamation. He looked confused. "How can you call it a failure?"

Jason hesitated for a moment. "Because… the city is under siege after the test subjects came back to life and turned violent. They escaped from the lab and have gone on a rampage. Isn't that what happened, Sam? And whatever genetic degeneration the testing caused to the test subjects is now being transmitted to the victims they attack."

Sam shook his head. "Jason, have you ever heard the expression *you have to crack a few eggs to make an omelet*? This experiment was a success, boy! We reanimated dead tissue, for Chrissakes! How could that be considered anything *but* a success?"

"But Sam, we lost control of the experiment—lost control of *everything*!" Jason paused, realizing his voice was getting louder with every word he spat out. He looked around and saw that the only people looking at them were Theresa and Sam's assistant. The rest of the executives were having a good time on the other side of the roof, oblivious to anything else. Jason did his best to compose himself, but the urge to throttle the fat bastard in front of him was getting stronger by the second. "The entire city is decimated because of this experiment," he growled. "So many people have died… saying that somehow this is a success—that's insane!"

Sam shrugged, unperturbed. "Jason, you better get with the program. Mistakes are made all the time in the course of scientific progress. Lives are lost. While it's tragic, and I am sorry about that—truly I am—if we don't take risks, we don't get rewards." Sam puffed on his cigar one last time before he dropped it to the surface of the roof and stubbed it under his loafer. "We deal with minor bumps in the road and keep moving forward, because *that* is when great things happen."

"But if anyone ever finds out, won't that ruin everything?"

Sam rolled his eyes. "The government won't let that happen. They've invested far too much and their hands are far too dirty to allow the country, let alone the world, to know what really happened today. No, they'll keep funding this project and all the others we're doing with them, because they know how close we are."

Jason swallowed hard. "How close we are to what?"

Sam smiled, exposing his yellow teeth. "To controlling our own mortality, of course. We'll have soldiers we can patch up and send back into battle regardless of how many times they get killed, and we'll be able to offer anyone who can afford to pay for it the ability to live forever—or for a very long time at the very least. We just have to work out a few bugs… oh, and find a new city in which to build our new lab." Sam turned and began walking back to his assistant. Jason remained stationary, unable and unwilling to follow the man whom he had admired for so long. "Just keep one thing in mind, kid. Make sure you remember where your bread is buttered, and you'll do just fine at Randis." Sam tossed the words back over his shoulder and kept walking.

Jason tried to control his breathing. He turned to look out over the city. Peals of laughter from the people standing somewhere behind him clashed with a far-off scream for help from below. He listened to those sounds and all the others with tears rolling down his face.

Moments later, he sensed Theresa behind him.

"You were right all along," he said. "They don't care about anything or anyone, except what they can control, and what gives them power." His shoulders slumped. "And they're going to fly away now, out of this city, to spread their madness elsewhere, and when they find out what we did, they're going to have us killed."

"That's why it has to end here and now."

Jason looked over at Theresa. She had wrapped her arms around her midsection and was rocking back and forth while looking out at the city. There was a miserable look on her face. "You know how much I love you, don't you?" she asked. Jason nodded immediately. "That's why it hurts me so much to have to leave you."

"What do you mean?"

Reaching down, Theresa undid the buttons on her suit jacket. Jason watched as a couple of very thin plastic containers strapped to her chest were revealed, each filled with a different colored liquid. One was orange, the other blue. A single wire ran between the containers and down one of her jacket sleeves. Jason's eye widened in realization at what she was showing him.

Theresa turned to him, an agonized look on her face. "I was hoping I'd make it out of here alive today, but these people need to be stopped. I can't let them get away with this."

Jason shook his head. "You can't be serious. That's a bomb?"

There was pain in her eyes. "I didn't want to do this. I prayed that I wouldn't have to, but what choice do I have? I can't just let those bastards leave this mess behind."

Grabbing Theresa by the arms, Jason resisted the urge to shake her. "You *do* have a choice! You don't have to do this. We can get on that helicopter when it comes and fly out of here. And we stop them after we make it out of here alive, together."

There were tears in Theresa's eyes as she shook her head. "No, you said so yourself. They'll just keep doing this. They'll cover up what happened and do it all over again somewhere else, and maybe the next time, there won't be anyone around willing to do what it takes to stop them." She reached up to caress Jason's chin with her fingertips, but he flinched away. "You need to go back downstairs. If you get to your office, you'll be out of the blast radius. I'll make sure I give you enough time before I do anything."

Jason was shaking his head once again, but Theresa ignored it. "You can hide from them; barricade yourself in your office, until the military comes to rescue you."

"And what makes you think that'll happen?" The words were angry and filled with desperation. "What makes you think I'd want to try and survive without you anyway? No—I think if I'm going to die anyway, I'd rather die up here with you." For the first time, he could see her breaking down. Tears were pouring down her cheeks, matching his own. Because of that, he felt a quiver of hope. They fell together, their arms wrapped around each other. Jason nuzzled Theresa's ear and whispered into it. "Remember what you said to me. We're in this together, until the end. Me and you forever, right?"

Theresa fought the urge to collapse to the ground. She felt so warm and safe in Jason's arms and couldn't imagine living without him, and couldn't imagine leaving him behind either. She had sworn an oath to the HLF, but it wasn't worth it. It wasn't worth losing her life and it wasn't worth losing Jason.

She nodded. "I know. I know," she whispered over and over before moving her face up to kiss him. "I won't leave you. I promise I won't."

He moved his head back so he could look her in the eyes. "Do you mean it?" There was fear in his eyes that hurt Theresa's heart.

She nodded again. "I won't leave you. I promise."

They kissed again, and held one another near the edge of the roof. Moments later, a cheer went up among the group of executives waiting next to the helipad. They were all jumping up and down and waving at an approaching helicopter. It was still a several thousand yards out, but making steady progress. It was a big, bulky bird with twin rotors, large enough to carry everyone who was on the roof.

"So, do we stay here, or go with the others?" Jason was still far too happy to give it much thought. The idea of losing her had terrified him. At the moment, he didn't care if they stayed in the building or left, just as long as Theresa was by his side.

An ear-piercing scream shattered Jason's serene thoughts. For a moment, he thought it had come from down below, but it was far too loud and close. He turned to look and saw that it was Sam Trent's executive assistant who had screamed. She had moved with Sam over to the crowd of other executives. The assistant was looking across the roof and pointing at the steps. Jason looked in that direction and was confused by what he saw. The doors were hanging open and one of the guards was helping someone who had perhaps tripped and fallen on the landing. But that didn't seem right, because a second guard was waving his machine gun at the two men rolling around on the floor, screaming at them. Jason watched with a growing sense of dread.

"Oh God, no."

It was all he heard Theresa say before there were several loud cracks and they saw the muzzle of the second guard's weapon light up. Blood blossomed across the bodies of the two men in the landing. They convulsed for a few seconds and then stopped, but the guard continued to unload on them until he had burned through an entire magazine. When the gunfire stopped, the screams began in earnest. Several of the women and men near the helipad were wailing. Their party was over.

The guard didn't bother checking either of the bodies he'd riddled with bullets. Instead, he slammed the doors to the stairs and backed away while he reloaded his weapon. Once his submachine gun was ready to fire again, he reached for the walkie-talkie strapped to his hip, but before he could get a call out, there was a loud thud on the door he'd just shut and it vibrated in its frame.

Turning, he looked out over the crowd of people watching him in terror from across the roof.

"Get to the helipad, now! Move it, move it, move it!"

He whipped around, scanning the expanse of the roof. He almost missed Jason and Theresa, but paused for a moment, then screamed at them to get to the helipad before turning back to face the doors. The sound of more fists pounding against it was matched by increased vibrations. It was pretty clear the doors weren't going to hold.

"I think we should do what he says," Theresa said.

Jason nodded and they took off running. They were halfway across the roof when the doors gave. They didn't look, but could hear screams of rage for a split second before the chatter of submachine gun fire started up again.

Jason had a tight grip on Theresa's hand as he looked up and spotted the helicopter getting closer. Several people had made it onto the helipad, but most were on the steps, pushing and shoving against one another.

When they made it to the steps, Jason risked looking back at the vestibule and wished he hadn't. Several people lay dead or twitching on the ground, but even more were streaming out of the doors, howling and crying out with subhuman rage as they charged toward the security guard, who was in the process of fumbling with another magazine. He was backing up as he did so, but was running out of space. It appeared as if he finally managed to get the weapon reloaded, but by then it was too late. He didn't get a chance to raise the weapon before three men and two women slammed into him and drove him to the into the asphalt surface of the roof. The submachine gun went flying, and any screams the guard had the chance to let out before he was ripped to pieces were drowned out by the screams of the people pushing against one another on the helipad steps.

With the guard out of their way, the horde turned as one and began sprinting toward the crowd, which only encouraged those filing up the steps to scream even louder. Turning his back on the monsters coming for them,

Jason forced his way up the steps, pushing his way through the crowd with his fist and shoulders, moving older executives out of his way while he maintained an iron grip on Theresa's hand.

One distinct advantage to being a young executive was the fact that he was stronger and faster than just about everyone in his way. Forcing his way through the crowd, he ignored the grunts and curses of anger as he bulled his way through. When he was halfway to the top, the sounds of bodies slamming against one another from below mingled with the screams coming from the people near the bottom steps who were begging for their lives.

The next minute or so was a blur. Jason kept hold of only two things: he needed to get the top of the steps, and he needed to retain his grip on Theresa's hand. He scratched, bit, and clawed his way past everyone, kicking and gouging anyone who got in his way. When he reached the top and Theresa was still with him, he felt no remorse even though the people he had pushed out of his way were fodder for the monsters.

Looking back, he could see more of them filing onto the roof. A glut of the raging creatures fought with one another, throwing themselves at the last of the living people on the roof. They pressed against one another, trying to force their way up top. As they did, they tore through the poor unfortunates who remained in their way.

Jason could see that Sam Trent was one of the last survivors. The look on his face was one of pure terror.

Jason thought he would enjoy watching the old man get dragged down into a sea of waiting hands and teeth, but he couldn't bear to watch.

Turning to look for the helicopter, Jason couldn't spot it at first. Looking across the sky, he saw it off in the distance, but there was something wrong. It was too far away. It had been closer—he was certain of that—before he fought his way to the top of the steps.

"It turned back," Theresa whispered. "We're not going to be rescued."

Jason refused to believe it, even when several other people on the helipad started crying out, begging the copter to come back for them.

"Come back! Come back, you bastards!"

Jason held Theresa tightly as he shouted at the machine moving further and further away every second. She had already accepted it was gone, but it took Jason a moment longer. He turned to look at the steps and could see the horde had torn through almost everyone. The first few of them had already burst through the blockade on the steps and were charging across the helipad toward the few cowering individuals left alive.

Theresa touched Jason's cheek and he looked down at her. She ran her fingers up along his jawline and he felt it once again—that shiver of goose bumps when she touched him.

"I love you," she said.

"I love you too."

She moved her hand down to the sleeve of her jacket and pulled out a device that looked like a pen. It was connected to the wire that ran to the explosives. She pulled a cap off the top and held the device so Jason could see it. He reached down and wrapped his hand around hers so that both of their thumbs were right above one another.

The howls of rage were getting closer, louder. The two lovers held one another and shared one last kiss.

"Until the end," Theresa said.

Then she pressed the plunger.

FROM SAFETY TO WHERE
By Kris Freestone

Ava took her first few steps across the stage with a song pulsing from the wall-mounted speakers. Loose hair cascaded down her bare shoulders and tickled her back on her way over to the silver pole. She closed her eyes for a moment, swaying to the familiar song. When she opened them, she gazed fiercely out at the clients. She slid her hands down her light brown hair, then ran them down her slender neck. It wasn't difficult to work the room on a Friday night. She knew all of the tricks of the trade from two years at The Skullery Club, but her classic beauty didn't hurt. The waitresses were dressed in black leotards with a shine to their toned legs, aided by pantyhose, and miniature white aprons tied around their waists.

The girls restricted to the floor made far less from the big spenders.

Tourists, frat boys, military, and married men frequented the club along with the occasional girlfriend hoping to spice up a dying relationship. Ava lost track of the growing numbers of women accompanying their flames to the champagne room, but didn't mind the extra show for the extra dough. Security was tight at The Skullery, with the watchful eyes of the local underground Russian mafia alert. Las Vegas remained the City of Sin even a century after the first claims were staked. The club was hidden behind the guise of a mattress warehouse; only clients with a set of Iberian runes inked on their inner wrist were able to make it in.

Luka watched from his usual perch a few feet away with a cigarette balanced between his long fingers. The table on the far right sat close to the stage for the elite and men assigned to document every move. She felt Luka's eyes burning a hole into her with a mixture of interest and possessiveness. Ava chose to ignore his intensity, leaning forward in front of a man at the bar that rounded the stage. His fingers felt meaty, thick and cold against her skin as he placed a ten-dollar bill in her short skirt.

Ava twisted expertly on the silver pole and sneaked a secret glance at her admirer, then continued to work the room. He watched with jealous eyes as the music continued, easing into another song. She willed time to pass by as she lost herself in the act of stripping down to her panties and a set of pasties. Hungry eyes watched her shamelessly collect the large bills that were tossed on the stage or tucked into the flimsy string of her underwear.

She left the stage with a coy wink and wandered backstage.

The backroom was surprisingly empty. Ava was pleased to avoid conversation with the other exotic dancers. She removed the pasties, dressed quickly into another skimpy black skirt and revealing lace-trimmed black bra. She sat down in front of her assigned dresser and stared at her reflection without blinking. Then she reapplied her makeup and opened the bottom drawer of the dresser. She removed a partially filled bottle of vodka and drank straight from it. Every drop reminded Ava of the power she carried within her. It oozed out of her on the stage, the saccharine illusion seeping out of her pores, fooling every man below her. It made up for the high levels of control exercised by the stoic Russian men running the club.

Another drawn-out taste of vodka and numbness set into her rosy cheeks.

Ava winked at her reflection and stalked out of the dressing room with confidence. She felt the eyes of the men on her as she made her way to the bar to find out which clients were in need of a drink. The floor girls had taken care of everyone besides the elite group of men in charge, out of fear. She eyed the table, and counted, and taking took notice of particular men.

"Can you get me a round of the usual for the guys? I'd appreciate it, Mac," she said with a shy smile to the bartender.

"As you wish."

Mac was the newest bartender, but by far the most respectful she'd met at the club. He was a baby at twenty-one, seven years Ava's junior. His youthful, pale face and hazel eyes held an eerie sense of innocence. The girls on the floor mooned over him, but all remained unsuccessful in their missions to obtain a date.

"Thanks, Mac." Ava picked up the round tray and walked over to the table the other girls feared. Two years ago, she had dived in without giving herself a chance to overthink the situation and had succeeded at her first attempt. "Hello, boys." She greeted them with a bright smile, balancing the tray on a flat palm with expertise.

"How are you doing this evening?" Anton inquired in his thick Russian accent, giving her a wide smile in return.

"Peachy keen, Anton." She set his drink down and walked around the table. The men watched her appreciatively as she put their poisons of choice down. Anton, Nikolai, Oleg, Lev, Grigory and Boris thanked her immediately. They were all dressed in their usual dark suits and a variety of ties. Each of the men were well groomed, a requirement of Kristoff's. She paused at Luka, setting his drink by his hand. He nodded in acknowledgment, but said nothing. "Is everyone behaving tonight?" she asked with her hands on her hips mockingly.

"They better be or there will be hell to pay," Oleg said with a chuckle.

Grigory tucked a hundred-dollar bill into the waistband of Ava's skirt. She smiled graciously. "Why thank you, boys. Can I get you anything else?"

"Keep the drinks coming and tell Ana she needs to watch her girls. Some of them are gossiping together for far too long and not paying attention to the clients."

Ava picked up the empty tray and saluted with her other hand. "I'm on it." She let out a small squeak when Oleg smacked her butt lightly on her way back to the bar. Ava turned around and waved her finger at him. She dropped the tray off at the bar.

"You're brave," Mac commented.

Ava laughed. "It's not so much bravery, as it is stupidity."

Another one of the strippers pushed her into the bar and it dug into her stomach. Ava heard a giggle and didn't need to turn around to identify the stripper. "Maybe you shouldn't stand in the way, Ava."

Ava gritted her teeth but held her tongue. She stood up straight, took a deep breath and met Mac's inquiring expression. "Don't worry about it, this is normal."

"What? It's normal for you to knock into things?" Bri laughed wickedly.

Ava turned around with a smirk. "Good thing I don't have to belittle others to feel better about myself. I find myself thankful for that."

Bri's cold blue eyes narrowed in on Ava, but Lexis looped her arm around the heavily inked stripper's waist and steered her away. Ava watched as they walked off, giggling at one another and talking in hushed tones. Mac whistled lowly. "What did you do to piss her off?"

"She's just jealous."

"Uh-huh. Are you sure that's all it is?"

"It's a long story. Care to make me a Long Island iced tea?"

"But of course. So she gets her jollies from torturing you?" Mac set to the task.

"Sort of. It's very childish. We were once friends; she tried to lecture me and implied that I wasn't smart. I stood up for myself and it blew up from there. It's the whole reason I change the code on my locker once a week."

Luka sat down beside Ava, much to her dismay. "You want me to do something about Bri?"

Mac set the drink down in front of Ava. She shook her head and focused on sipping on her drink. "I can stand up for myself. If I react, it will only make things worse."

"You're sure?"

"Positive," she said, then looked up with a faint smile. "Thanks for the offer, though."

Luka nodded, ordered a whiskey on the rocks and fell silent. The music played louder. Ava peered up to see Lexis strut across the stage with extreme inexperience. She smiled and shook her head.

"What's so funny?" Luka asked.

"Lexis. She's like a newborn colt even after three months here. I think the clients only like her because of her tits." Luka chuckled. "What? It's true! She made fun of me for being fat, yet I'm smaller than her. I keep myself toned. I've never received a complaint."

"No complaints here. The other men would agree with me." Luka finished his drink. Ava studied Luka's profile from the side, taking note of his long, thin nose. His squinted blue eyes seemed to always be watching his surroundings. His skin was worn, yet youthful. His lips were small, his chin almost perfectly curved.

She felt her annoyance simmer down. "I'm sorry," she whispered quietly.

"For what?"

"Being mean. It's just if I started up with anyone here everyone would resent me."

"You're afraid of what everyone else would think?" Luka laughed. "Since when have you been afraid of anyone?"

"Since always."

He watched Ava take a long sip of her drink before responding. "The Ava I know doesn't let anyone get in her way. I'm surprised you let Bri and Lexis get to you so badly."

"I mean, come on, who names themselves after a car that no longer exists? It's ridiculous." She tried to stop the smile from peeling over her lips, but failed. "I don't even know what a Lexus looks like anymore. My dad used to like them."

"Still keep in touch with him?"

"Too personal." Ava drained her drink.

"Sorry."

Ava stood up abruptly and slid her empty glass closer to Mac, who kept a watchful eye on the pair. She walked away without a word.

🝆

Luka stared after Ava, watching as she walked around the room to each client for a few minutes. He returned to his original table.

"Busy mooning over the beautiful Ava?" Oleg joked playfully.

"Like you don't," Luka scoffed and sat down between Oleg and Boris. He averted his eyes from the stage as Bri stripped down to sheer black underwear and exposed all of her tattoos while half the men at the table stared. Anger brimmed within him. When Anton moved with a twenty-dollar bill towards the stage, Luka pinned his shoulder down and tugged him back.

"What the hell?" Anton glared at Luka.

"Don't feed her any money tonight. She disgraced our dear Ava."

"How did she disgrace our Ava?"

"She pushed her into the bar intentionally and tried to start a fight, as did Lexis. Ava chose to be the adult and ignored attempts."

Anton sat down in his chair, although Bri moved across the stage in his direction. "A shame. I had such high hopes for them. Do you know why?"

"It's been going on for a while, but Ava did not want to bring attention to the situation," Luka explained. The men around the table nodded in agreement.

"What should we do about this? Do we demote them to be floor girls?" Anton asked.

"Yes, it seems to be the best plan of action," Oleg agreed. "I will schedule a meeting with each of them tomorrow."

Ava strutted over to the table with a bright smile and an expertly balanced tray. "Gentlemen, I thought it was time for another drink." Each of them thanked her and tucked another hundred-dollar bill into her skirt, which was surprisingly bare.

"You are not getting very many tips?"

"I'm afraid Lexis has been raiding the floor, along with Lilah and Devon. Business will pick up later."

"Would you like a more secure place for your personal belongings?" Oleg asked.

"Why would I need that?"

"With Lexis and Bri harassing you, it can't be easy," he pointed out.

"Did Luka say something to you?"

"We have taken notice of their actions," Oleg said.

"It's a sweet offer, but my combination lock seems to do the trick."

"We have a special state of the art lock that only unlocks with a precise fingerprint. How does that sound?" Boris offered.

"Very sweet, but again, unnecessary."

Suddenly the ground shook, harder than the usual earthquakes, and Ava fell against Luka's shoulder. She tried to move away from him, but the ground shook again. Particles of the ceiling dusted the table. The emergency siren sounded above the music and echoed within the city.

Luka cursed under his breath in his native tongue. "It's begun," he whispered. Ava almost didn't hear him.

"What's begun?"

"Not now." He pulled Ava closer to him. "Come on, let's get backstage." Her legs shook with every step, despite Luka's arm wrapped around her shoulders. The other girls were huddled in the back in confusion. Waitresses were in the dressing room strictly reserved for the stage girls.

Bri rushed into the dressing room shortly after. Ava moved closer to Luka as more of the girls crowded into the room.

"I'll tell you later," Luka said, and left the room.

The shaking stopped; everyone tried to catch their breath. Ava squirmed against the bare skin of the other strippers, easing her way closer to her dresser. Bri pressed up against her.

"Have you checked your stash of nail polish recently?" Bri asked with a smirk.

"No. Do I need to keep an eye on you?" Ava replied with a smile.

Bri didn't respond. Ava opened the bottom drawer of her dresser where a bag full of nail polish sat above a pile of clean clothes. Color oozed out of the bottom of the netted bag. She opened it and the colors spilled across. Bottles of nail polish were opened completely, freshly pouring over the bag and onto the clothing. The colors spilled over her fingers and ran over her nails. Ava took a deep breath before looking up. It was a flashback to the high school days she dreaded more than words could express. She practiced the breathing lessons she'd been taught from endless yoga and Pilates classes. Ava felt Bri's and Lexis's eyes on her, but kept her expression neutral. She maintained a blank look as she wiped the wet nail polish off on the ruined skirt. The colors smeared across her fingers. She pushed past the girls crowded in the room and went in search of Luka.

Particles of the ceiling had shaken down during the heavy earthquake. The room still reeked of cigarettes and cigars. Ava wove between the tables until she reached the doorway where Luka was talking to the owner, Kristoff. She sat down at the nearest bar stool and waved Mac over. "Can I get a glass of white wine?"

Mac obliged and poured her a glass. "What the hell just happened?"

"Hell if I know," Ava muttered.

"Time is money," Kristoff tossed a one-liter bottle at Luka. He caught the glass bottle, but not without a near miss.

"This is insane," Luka hissed. "You don't know what you're bringing in here. If the bomb unleashed anything like the rumors entailed—"

"Give the antidote to the best girls, take some yourself and spread it out amongst our men." Luka watched his father begin to greet the gentlemen waiting by the doors for shelter and spirits. The men piled in one by one. He rolled his eyes and followed the orders.

Luka found Ava nursing another drink at the bar and sat down on a stool next to her. She stared up at a television screen mounted to the wall with captions scrolling across the bottom during the news broadcast. Luka motioned to Mac, requested three empty glasses and poured an inch of the antidote into each glass.

"You need to drink this," he insisted and slid the drink over to her.

"And what makes you think I trust you?" Ava's eyes didn't leave the television screen.

He swallowed the bitter drink and slammed the glass against the wet bar. "It might taste like ass, but I drank it. If you don't drink it, the sickness from the bombs will affect you soon. Kristoff opened the doors and he's letting in clients. I don't know what the gas released, but I'm not ready to chance the consequences." Ava dragged her eyes away from the screen, lifted the glass and drank. She looked back up at the news as she set the glass down. Luka slid the remaining glass over to Mac. He consumed the drink with no questions asked.

"Come on, ladies, back to work!" Kristoff's voice echoed off the walls. "Time is money!"

"You told me you'd explain later." Ava got up and headed to the end of the bar. "This is some weird through-the-looking-glass shit right now."

Luka followed her. "What should I tell you? The truth?"

"That would be nice."

✦

Luka followed her into the dressing room where an excess of girls were hiding. He clapped his hands together loudly. "Come on, ladies! I have direct orders from Kristoff to continue on, business as usual! Please evacuate the dressing room and make your way to the floor. Clients are beginning to flood in for shelter."

"Good to know you weren't following me for a reason," Ava huffed.

"What good would it do? It's not like you care about me."

She met Luka's squinted eyes with defiance. "I never said such a thing. You're putting words into my mouth."

"Really now? So what do you think of me?"

Ava shifted uncomfortably under the gaze of the dawdling strippers and floor girls.

"Get a move on!" Luka shouted gruffly in his thick accent. The girls evacuated the room quickly. Ava sat down in front of her vanity and closed the nail polish stained drawer. Luka pulled over a chair. A silence fell.

"Are you going to tell me what the earthquake was? You obviously knew it was going to happen." Ava smoothed her hands over her bare legs, wishing for something far less vulnerable.

"Does it matter anymore? The world is ending…" Luka trailed off. "There were bombs spread across the United Regions of America. The president went against the agreement he made with Russia and there were consequences. I've only heard whispers of what the bombs contained."

"Bombs?"

"Yes. They went off simultaneously across the URA. I thought it was just a rumor traveling through the underground, there wasn't a set date. I hoped the president would come to some sort of an agreement with Russia, but that clearly didn't happen."

Ava watched Luka lower his head in shame. "You knew about this?"

His eyes met hers fiercely. "You expected me to be able to do something? It was going to strike the country either way and there wasn't a damn thing I could do about it." She shifted uncomfortably. "I gave you the antidote. Whatever the bombs released, you're immune to."

"What about the other girls?"

"I can selectively pass it out."

"Be a friend and skip over a certain duo?"

Luka smiled. "Would that put you me in my your good graces?"

"Maybe. It would be a far better world without Bri and Lexis. Am I a horrible person for admitting that?"

"No. I won't give them the antidote. You're not horrible for wanting them out of your life."

"What did the bomb release?"

"A toxic gas." Luka leaned forward and paused for a long time. "I only know that it will transform everyone. Kristoff once said it will expose the true greed of America. He spoke of transformation and a new age."

"Greed," Ava echoed.

"Yes, the true greed. Whatever that means."

"Why did you want to save me?"

Luka let the silence ring for a moment, then paced around in thought before speaking again. "There's a spark. I see it every time I glance at you and try to ignore it. It's no secret I've been promised to someone else, but there's no spark. I don't feel anything when I'm in the room with her. I feel alive and electric whenever I'm around you. It's unlike anything I've experienced before."

She tangled her fingers together on her lap, bit her lip and searched for the right words. Only a faint nervous laugh erupted. Ava shook her head, then closed her eyes tightly.

"Say something. Anything. You asked why I saved you and I told you the truth. Isn't that worth something?"

"You're better than that and far better than me. I'm not even an option with your betrothal and all." Ava stood up. "I better get back to work. You heard Kristoff. Time is money."

Disappointment flooded over Ava when Luka allowed her to escape without a fight. She couldn't shake the shiver she felt as Luka spoke of a new age. His confessions echoed even deeper, but she pushed them aside and forced herself to focus on work. She wandered around the room, but found the other girls keeping a good eye on the incoming clients. Mac pointed out a new arrival without a drink in his hand. She started to make her way over when Bri scurried ahead and swooped in on the client.

Bri returned to the bar, rolling her eyes. "Ugh, I should have had you take him on. He's practically drooling on the table and sweating. He wants a whiskey on the rocks."

"Sure thing," Mac responded.

"So, no hard feelings, right?" Bri asked, turning to face Ava with a sly smile.

"Of course not, I feel better now that you have the disgruntled customer. Mister Aimes doesn't like anyone; he isn't a big spender either."

"Huh. So that's why you let me take him?"

"He's all yours."

Bri glared at Ava, picked up Aimes's drink and stalked off.

"Wow, you're definitely on her bad side. What's Bri short for anyways?" Mac asked.

"Briana."

"Not an Ana, is she?"

"Nope, because I'm an Ava."

"Really?"

"Yes, but she'd never tell you that. I overheard the other guys chuckling about it one evening."

"Excuse me?" Bri's voice shrilled loudly over the music. Mac and Ava stared while Aimes tugged at Bri's arm. The surly client stood up and pulled the girl closer. She screamed when her eyes met his. Even from the bar, Ava could see that his dark eyes were covered with a strange cloud of white. Bri screeched loudly as Aimes drew her closer. Her arms flailed wildly as his mouth nearly closed on her awkwardly bent shoulder. She hit him in the head with her free arm then kicked his nearest knee hard. Aimes lost his grip and sent Bri barreling into a table. One of the biggest and burliest of the security guards managed to take Aimes down, but another fight broke out at the other end of the room during the chaos. Aimes regained his balance and knocked Lou clean off his feet.

Mac pulled Ava, breaking her stare, and motioned for her to get behind the bar. She used the stool to pull herself over the bar and ducked down.

Lou screamed loudly. Ava, looking up again, saw Aimes bite into his shoulder hard. He pulled a chunk of flesh away from the security guard. Aimes then focused on Bri, charged at her and met her head on. "GET OFF OF ME!" Bri squealed at the top of her lungs with the crazed man biting into her cheek.

She kicked at his knees again, but he held onto her securely. Blood flowed out of the wound as Aimes went in for another bite. Bri's arms went slack, but her pale face twisted in horror. The pain was obvious in the nineteen-year-old's face, although none of the other security guards came to her rescue.

Then the earthquakes began again, shaking the glasses off of the back of the bar. They shattered on the stone tiles. Mac pulled Ava down again, holding her against the bottom of the wet bar.

He reached under the register and drew out a pistol. "The job required some lessons." He moved to his knees and scoped the room out, then ducked down. "It's a mad house out there. Are those earthquakes?"

"No, they're bombs," Ava corrected.

"Bombs?"

"Let's just say you're lucky to have had that nasty drink earlier. Luka didn't say much, but Russia is attacking."

"So much for the United Regions of America," Mac muttered, shaking his head. Rapid gunfire went off in spurts in the bar, but neither dared to poke their head up. They listened to the cries of the floor girls and strippers. A tune meant for Ava's next act played over the speakers and gunfire ceased. Mac dug through his pockets and withdrew a white handkerchief. He waved it over the bar.

"You can come out!" a gruff voice with a Russian accent boomed.

Mac placed the pistol in Ava's hands, stood with his arms over his head and waved the handkerchief. "Ava is behind here with me. She hasn't been bitten or attacked."

"Ava?" Luka asked. Ava rose, holding the pistol, but was completely thrown off by the bloodbath in the middle of the club. Several of the girls stood on the stage away from the war scene. Four strippers and five floor girls were tangled together with other bodies in the middle of the room in a growing pool of blood. She stared, unable to drag her eyes away from Bri's tattered body. It rested near the bar on a pile of overturned stools. Her throat was ripped out down to the center and straight to the collarbone. A piece of her stomach had been torn out and a portion of her esophagus peeked out.

"Come on, Ava," Luka urged her gently.

Mac had left the back of the bar and spoke in hushed tones to a surviving security guard. Ava walked around the bar slowly, held the pistol tightly and stopped in front of Luka. "Why didn't you tell me the bombs were releasing something so vile and violent?"

"I didn't know."

"You had to. There's no way you're Kristoff's blood and he didn't tell you." She shook her head and walked closer to the bar. "I can't trust you."

"Ava, he didn't tell me."

"So you buy his lies? What did you expect these bombs to bring? You didn't think of maybe warning someone? Anyone? Did it ever cross your mind?" Ava drew the pistol close to her side and looked around the room cautiously.

"We can't do this right now."

"He didn't know," Oleg put in. Ava glanced at Oleg skeptically.

"Come on, Ava. We can deal with this later. First we need to get out of here alive." She obliged wordlessly and stepped closer to Mac. Lev, Oleg and Boris were the only men from Kristoff's crew that remained unharmed. A few of the security guards sat perched on the side of the stage beside the surviving girls.

Lexis leapt off the stage to a barely moving Bri. She held Bri's head up and started to laugh. "See? She's fine!"

"Did any of you give her the antidote?" Luka glanced at the men. No one had a chance to respond before Lexis cried out in pain. Bri attached to her left arm, ripping off a piece of flesh. Oleg fired at the infected stripper, but a bullet to the chest failed to work. Lexis's screams heightened. A bullet tore straight for Lexis's head; she fell limply in Bri's damaged arms. Bri's eyes were clouded and hazy as she took another bite, reaching bone.

"Oh for heaven's sake." Ava stepped forward, aimed the pistol and fired at the stripper's head. Bri lurched forward over the other dead body, finally ceasing to move as the bullet penetrated her skull. The men stared at her with a mixture of shock and awe.

Kristoff emerged from the backroom, shouting. "Come on! Let's get a move on!" The girls standing on the stage rushed over to Kristoff but were stopped as he aimed a large gun in their direction. "No, no, no. You are not going with us."

"We will need women," Lev pointed out.

"They are unnecessary evils. We have Russian women waiting for us."

"What about Ava?" Luka stepped forward.

"Ava is expensive trash. Dressed up, sugar and spice, everything nice, but not as good as Nina. You will marry Nina as planned, merge with the family."

Luka measured up the other men. He stood beside Ava, wrapping his left arm around her shoulders. "I'm not leaving without her." Lev and Oleg joined his side. Boris didn't move a muscle, eyeing the divided parties.

"So what will it be, Boris?"

"What harm does she do?"

A bullet tore through Boris's chest. He fell forward on his knees and stared at Kristoff in disbelief. "You shoot a comrade?"

"Comrades do not go against one another."

Luka pulled Ava behind him. Oleg and Lev stood their ground beside Luka with their firearms pointed at Kristoff. The last of life fell away from Boris. Panic spread over the mobster's face.

"Lower your weapon," Lev warned him. Kristoff bent down carefully, set the shotgun down and stood up straight. His salt-and-pepper hair fell out of the ponytail at the nape of his neck, but he didn't make a move to fix it.

"Mac, get Ava behind the bar and don't come out until I give you the word," Luka said. Ava ducked down and followed Mac. They knelt behind the bar, careful of the broken glass. Mac reached for Ava's cold hand and comfortingly squeezed it. She offered a weak smile.

"You would betray your father? What do you think they will do when you show up without me?" Kristoff's voice increased in volume with every question, until he was shouting. "What about when you tell the Yagudins that you refuse to marry their only daughter? You think they will protect you?"

"I will tell them the truth. That you shot one of your comrades and forced my hand." Luka stepped closer. "How you always tried to control my life, forcing around your thirty-seven-year-old son. You didn't tell me what would happen when the bombs dropped or how many there would be." He drew close enough to kick the shotgun away from his father.

"Have forgiveness, Luka—"

"Have consideration for someone who never considered my life or how I might feel? You're supposed to care about me more than some damn merger or destroying the United Regions of America. Can you tell the truth for once?"

"If it helps."

"If it helps what? If it helps you? Did you know people were going to attack each other after being infected?"

"Gogil said it looked like the horror movies from a century ago. The kind you watched as a boy with zombies in them. I received top secret videos of the successful experiments," Kristoff confessed.

"You knew this was going to happen?"

"Yes."

Luka paced back and forth in front of his father. "You're just like those—" he broke off. "Zombies can't trust their feelings."

"So leave me here. I can fend for myself."

Luka ceased pacing. "Lev, get the plastic zip-ties from the back and attach him to the bar." Kristoff tried to dive for the discarded gun, but his wrist met with the heel of Luka's dress shoes. He cried out in agony and was dragged up shortly after by Lev with Oleg pointing a gun at Kristoff's head. Lev bound his uninjured wrist to the metallic piping on the edge of the bar. His former boss glared up at him relentlessly.

"Mac, take Ava to the back loading bay and prepare two of the aircrafts," Luka barked. "Make sure they're fully fueled and find any provisions in sight. We need to get a move on."

The look on Luka's face was stone cold as Ava passed by him. She followed Mac into the back where they stopped in the dressing room for her few belongings. She found her emergency firearm in her locker, a backpack and clothing. Mac waited silently for her to change into clothes, then accompanied her to the loading dock. Ava was far more comfortable in a pair of black denim pinstripe pants with a gun belt hanging off of her right hip, and a dark shirt advertising a rock band.

Mac finally broke the long silence. "He's sacrificing everything for you."

She searched for the correct response, but came up empty. "I'll check one of the aircrafts and you can get the other," she said, stepping into the large loading dock.

The Halycon aircrafts in the dock were reputable for being substantially large enough to carry six passengers with meager living quarters. Mattresses wrapped with plastic lined the sides of the walls, merchandise for the warehouse that fronted for the strip club. Ava entered the aircraft through the loading dock, walked up to the cockpit and turned the control panel on. The aircraft was fully fueled, emergency reserves filled to the brim and the solar panels were primed. She smiled for the first time in hours, turned off the control panel, left her backpack behind and went in search for Mac.

"I think Kristoff was prepared for an escape," Mac informed her as he stepped off the loading dock to the other aircraft. A low moan echoed in the loading bay. Mac motioned for Ava to join him; they stood back to back and moved slowly together to avoid surprises. The world shook violently as another bomb landed nearby, far closer than the others. Two infected girls from the floor peered around the dock in confusion, searching for the source of the human flesh that invaded their senses.

Ava stared at the new girls, unable to fire. "Ava, come on!" Mac hissed.

"I can't. I just trained those girls." A portion of their stomachs had been feasted upon along with sections of their legs, but they managed to walk at a slow but steady pace. Mac fired at each of their heads and they fell into a pile. Oleg and Lev rounded the corner cautiously, relieved to see Mac and Ava were safe. Five girls trailed behind them, barely dressed and scared out of their wits.

"Oleg and Lev, take the girls on one aircraft and follow my lead. Mac and Ava, come with me." Luka ran around the corner quickly, narrowly missing the pile of bodies. The doorway to the docks groaned, then creaked open painfully. It was nearly pitch dark outside and buildings nearby were on fire. Ava ran to the aircraft she'd secured, picked her backpack up from the co-pilot's seat and waited for the men to join her. She sat down in a passenger seat and buckled up as the back of the aircraft closed up. Luka situated himself in the pilot's seat and Mac sat down in the co-pilot's position.

"Ever fly one of these?" Luka asked Mac, starting up the engine with a loud roar.

"Raised on them."

"Good, then let's get started." The aircraft glided out of the docking bay of the mattress warehouse seamlessly and into the dark of night. Buildings all across the Las Vegas strip were on fire. Mac guided the aircraft into the safety of the clouds and stared straight ahead.

"Where are we going?" Ava dared to ask Luca.

"Russia. The United Regions of America isn't safe anymore. I don't know where else to go," he admitted uneasily.

Ava nodded and looked out the side window at the burning buildings. Holes were left in the ground where larger bombs had been dropped; people ran around like ants illuminated in the firelight. She bit her lip, glanced back at Luka and knew to place her hope in him.

THE TOWER
By Joshua Brown

Hooves came to a halt upon the stony ground, which in the dim light seemed to have a peculiar bluish glow. The animal snorted and tossed its head under the bridle as the wind stirred through the rancid air. The sky was black, and filled with clouds that sailed from east to west. There was no moon. The place was ringed in by natural walls of jagged rock; cliffs of dark rock that formed a basin where it stood. She regarded the structure. It was enormous, made of stones with a set of stairs winding up from the base to a strong iron door. There were no windows until the very top of the towering spire. The horse reared slightly, and snorted again in displeasure. She rubbed the horse's neck to calm it, then looked around.

Numerous people walked toward her with slow and unsteady steps. Her horse became more frightened, difficult to control. The 'people' closing in upon her were merely shells of what had been humanity. They staggered, shuffled, and dragged toward her—they who had once been peasant or noble, warrior or wife. She gripped the reins tighter.

She was Lethella, a warrior of a special sect, and she had been sent here by a calling which few understood. She watched the beasts emerge from every shadow, from the crumbling wrecks of wagons or carts, and seemingly everywhere else. If they actually reached her, their clawing hands would burrow into her and their gnashing teeth would bite into her flesh. These were the living dead, and they now sought to feed upon the living. They were relentless; the only thing that would stop them was to destroy their rotten brains. She drew her sword from the scabbard and swept her gaze around once more. The dead continued to come—now more than a hundred.

She spurred the horse forward; it ran toward the tower. However ominous, it was the only structure in the basin, and it was why she had come. Surrounded by the wailing and growling hordes of walking corpses, Lethella directed the horse onward. It would be close, and narrow, but she was an excellent rider. She put the sword away as the horse reached the base of the stairs. Without hesitating, the animal started up the stone steps.

Thelos lay quietly with his hands behind his head on a dilapidated old bed. Suddenly he sat up. A rider! He ran across the room toward the heavy iron door. It was bolted and barred against the terrible, ghoulish things below.

He began to work the bolt open as he heard the horse approach. The rider should find the door open, especially if the zombies were following. There would be no escape from them at the landing. Thelos then began to remove the two heavy planks. The horse was coming fast. Thelos dropped both planks, worked the latch, and dragged the door open.

The horse had reached the top of the stairs. Thelos looked past it at the dead things staggering up behind. The horse rushed past him, knocking him back as it entered. He scrambled to his feet to shut the door. The rider was beside him, helping him. The ghastly figures outside closed in on the landing; the noises they made drowned out everything else. He shoved harder as the first of them brought its glaring, snarling face into the gap between door and frame. Together, Thelos and the newcomer slammed the door. Thelos knelt, grabbing one of the bars. There was pounding from outside.

The woman grabbed the other bar, and soon, they were worked into position. Thelos fixed the bolt on the door before turning to her. She was some sort of warrior; he gave a deep bow as he stepped back, his breath still rapid. She accepted his bow with a nod, then removed her helmet to reveal a lean, beautiful face, framed with a long mane of silver hair.

Thelos smiled. "A rather dangerous way to spend an evening, eh?"

She nodded toward the door. "Will it hold?"

"It will," he answered. "It would take a thousand of them to push it in, but there is no room on the landing for even a score."

"We are trapped here," she said, and walked into the center of the entry chamber, taking up the horse's reins and patting it on its neck.

"Welcome to my plight," Thelos said, flashing a smile. "Near three weeks I have been here. The food is barely tolerable, but the local taverns are closed…"

Now she smiled, looking around at the decaying old furnishings, the rotten tapestries, and the man who had opened the door for her. He bowed to her, extending his arms outward. "I am Thelos."

"You may call me Lethella." She pulled back the folds of her fur-lined cape to reveal her armor—a suit of leather that seemed to have been crafted specifically for her. Thelos gazed at her with wonder as she looked over her horse, and ran her hand across its shoulder.

"Lethella," he said. "Then you must be…"

"I am," she affirmed. "The East."

She and her fellow warrior maidens were known as "The Four," one from each direction. They had been myth to Thelos until he found himself taking cautious steps toward the shapely, if somewhat silent, Lethella.

"The East…" he breathed. "Never did I expect I would see one of you."

"And yet, here I am," she said. "Is that so amazing?"

"Well, yes. What would bring you to such a place?"

"Three days ago, I was awakened by a dark terror in my mind. The vision told me that this place was the start of a great, spreading evil. I was to find it, and stop it."

"Stop it?" he asked. "But how?"

Ignoring his question, she reached out to place her hands upon his face, gently. He did not dare to move. "The source is here," she said, at last.

"How do you know that?"

"I can feel it," she said, removing her hands from his face.

"Evil?"

"Power," she corrected him. "Have you searched the tower?"

"No," he admitted with a sheepish grin. "After my arrival, and the loss of those with whom I came, I decided it was best not to… disturb anything further."

"Come, then," she said, drawing her sword. "We must explore the rest of the tower."

"We… must?"

"Yes."

She walked over to utter quiet words into the ear of her mount. The horse tossed its head, then settled. Lethella returned to Thelos, and nodded toward one of the walls, just as there came a renewed thumping on the iron door.

"Bring a torch," she said. "We'll go up."

He retrieved the torch, and they headed toward the stone stairs. As they began to make their way up, the pounding grew more frenetic. After they'd climbed several flights, they found a closed wooden door.

"Locked?" he wondered aloud.

"Perhaps." She approached it with her sword.

He stopped her with a smile. "Hold a moment." He set the torch on the stone floor. "I have my secrets."

"Oh?"

He extended his hands and uttered a single loud word. The door burst inward. He glanced at her; she looked somewhat impressed.

"Oh yes," he said. "Forgot to mention. I came as apprentice to Vanayx the Cold Eye. I was nearly beyond his tutelage when he… met his end."

"A most welcome surprise, Master Thelos," she said. "If we may continue."

He nodded, then lurched back as a ghastly face, half of it gone to reveal the skull, sprang from the doorway. The thing growled viciously as it came from the dark, followed by a pair of others. Grasping, bony hands reached for him, but before he could react, the sword jammed through the throat of the lead zombie. With a flash of her arms, Lethella wrenched the sword sideways, decapitating the monster.

Thelos lifted his hands again and shouted a magical phrase. There was a blinding flash, casting back the other two ghoulish things. Lethella bounded forward, her sword swiftly dispatching them.

Thelos picked up the torch. "Well, that was certainly not ideal." He joined her in the chamber. "Let us hope there aren't any more of those."

She gave him a stern look, but said nothing.

This room was much smaller than the main level below them. The furnishings were destroyed, and part had been scorched. Thelos saw more than a dozen skeletons in the blackened part of the chamber, lying in various poses. Lethella moved on, looking for more stairs. "I wonder what happened here," Thelos said, his foot brushing against a burnt skull. It dislodged, rolling away.

The dreadful creature had risen to its feet, its dead, milky eyes directed toward the back of Lethella as she had taken the first of the stairs. What was left of the tattered tunic covered the emaciated form of what had once been a traveling merchant. A worm-filled hole was exposed where the tunic did not cover him, telling the story of his descent into the ranks of the living dead. A hole had been chewed into him by another of the zombies, while the man had been alive. Now, a caked, cracked layer of blood surrounded his mouth, which fell open. The thing moaned softly as it closed in on Lethella, and its hands reached her cape. She spun back, but got caught up as the ghoul pulled at her from behind, and she stumbled back, losing her grip on her sword. It clanged upon the floor below, and Thelos looked up to see the confrontation, breaking into a run to reach them. As he arrived, the zombie had just been kicked in the jaw by Lethella.

Thelos grabbed it by the shoulders. Lethella looked for her sword as the thing turned with a wail toward Thelos. Grasping its wrists, he could cast no spell, so he tried to pull it away from Lethella while she dove for her sword. The monster bit at the air as she reached the weapon; Thelos shoved it back. There was a swish as the blade cleaved its head from its body.

"Are you all right?" she asked.

"Thoroughly horrified, but not injured," he said. "You?" She shook her head. "All right, let's go." Thelos snatched up the torch he had dropped in the struggle. Then he paused, noticing something. She seemed... uncertain. "What's the matter?"

"I... had not anticipated this depth of darkness."

"Surely you have seen, and vanquished, evil before," he said. "Is this so different?"

"Our calls to arms are rare indeed," she said with a noticeable quake in her voice. "In the years I have been the East, never have I had to face such evil."

"Well," he said, and put a hand on her shoulder. "Good thing you will not be facing it. *We* will." She studied him, then nodded.

"Then we must go forward," she said, and started up the stairs. He followed, carrying the torch. Peculiar smells began to fill the air; the room below them was no longer in sight. The torch flared brighter. Suddenly Lethella took it from him and tossed it back down below.

"What the devil?"

"Careful with your words," she cautioned, sweeping her gaze around. "For he may very well be here."

"We may find out," Thelos said. "We must be near the top."

Soon they found another wooden door. It looked as though it had been clawed at. They stared at it a moment before she tried the latch, then glanced at him.

"Can you open it?" she asked.

"For you, my lady? I would open a thousand doors."

She raised an eyebrow. "For now, this one will do."

He gave a quiet laugh and extended his hands toward the door. There was a crackling sound, and he recoiled, nearly tumbling back down the stairs. Lethella grasped him by his robes, but the loose garments were not enough to keep him steady. In the tangle, they were suddenly face to face. Thelos blinked, smiled, and stepped back.

"Nice to know you care," he said.

"You... That is..."

The door clunked as a bolt was undone, and then, with a hiss, smoke erupted around the edges. She lifted her sword. With a creaking of hinges, the door swung inward, revealing an older man, tarnished metal skull cap atop his head. His dark beard was longer than usual, and his eyes hard.

"Are you them?" he demanded.

"Them?" she asked.

"You speak," he said. "You cannot be them. Are you injured of their teeth? Have they bitten you?"

"No, we are unharmed," Thelos answered. "Who are you?"

"I will ask the questions," the man said. "Why are you here? Who are you?"

"We have come to put an end to this," Lethella said. "What has caused this?"

The man looked them over again before stepping back from the door. "You'd better come in." They followed him. As the door swung shut they could hear the magical force sealing it into its frame. The man slid the bolt, then walked toward the center of the chamber, where there was a large, round object suspended by ropes. The man put something into a hole in the side of it, then turned to them. "There is much going on that you do not know about," he said.

"You would do well to explain it," Lethella said, putting her sword away.

"I am Nysyx of the Dread Solace." His tattered ebony robes flowed with the wind from the open windows. Thelos could hear wails and moans from below.

"The Dread Solace…" Thelos growled. "I've heard of your sect. You are meddlers between this world and others. Of darker places."

"Well, a studied young man," Nysyx said, his fingers winding into his beard. "From your robes of violet, I would guess you to be an apprentice of the Brotherhood of the Arcane… Such weakness of magic."

"What madness have you unleashed here?" Thelos asked.

"It was not I," Nysyx said. "A brother wizard, Luqara, thought he had found a new gate. A portal to bring forth a demon he could control. The power would have been almost limitless."

"What happened?" Lethella asked.

"He opened the gate," Nysyx said. "But no demon waited on the other side. All he found was a river of venom which consumed him and drove him to madness before he was finally allowed to die."

"This does not explain our situation," Lethella said.

"He did die, but he awakened a terrible zombie. He soon had infected two people, then seven, then dozens, then hundreds. The more there were, the more there became. Now all that remain within miles are the two of you, and myself."

"So what are we to do?" Thelos asked.

"There must be a way to close the gate," Lethella said. "The only thing that stays my blade from your black heart is that you obviously know that way."

"The gate is closed," Nysyx said. "I closed it, some two hundred feet below the base of this tower, in catacombs carved out centuries ago."

"Then why are these creatures still here?" Thelos asked, walking to the windows. He gazed out into the basin, which had filled to its edges with the things. Hordes of creatures crammed up against the tower. Lethella joined him as Nysyx remained by the large, round object. "Why do they gather?" Thelos asked. "Do they seek to reopen it?"

"They gather because I called them," Nysyx said, grinning.

"You… called them," Lethella growled, her hand descending toward the handle of her sword.

"I called them," Nysyx said. "Lethella the East. Yes. I know who you are. I can feel your power."

"A power you will soon feel with the sting of my blade," she said, and drew the sword. As she stepped forward, there was a dark flash. She froze, unable to move. Thelos stepped around her and lifted his hands, unleashing a ripple of energy that crashed into Nysyx. The sorcerer growled as he tumbled backward, landing close to the black orb. Nysyx looked up with wide eyes at it as it swayed. He shifted his gaze back at Thelos and uttered a quiet word, unleashing a beam of light. Thelos cried out and fell to his knees.

"Thelos!" she called out, but got no response.

"He will be fine," Nysyx said, grunting as he got back to his feet. "Until the end."

"What do you mean?" she demanded. "Release me!"

"Oh, I couldn't do that," Nysyx said. "It couldn't have worked out better that one of the Four has arrived, as well as a man who possesses the gift of magic—however inferior."

"What do you mean?" she asked. Lethella, unable to move, tried in vain to see Thelos, who groaned as he turned over.

"I called them here for a purpose some may see as noble. You may call it what you will. I have only a little time left, and I need all the power I can conjure."

"For what?" Lethella asked.

"Why… to destroy them, of course." Nysyx pulled back one of his sleeves to reveal a number of horrible wounds on his left arm. "If for no other reason, I will have my revenge against them for taking my life. Once bitten, there is no way to avoid becoming one of them."

"It is a fitting end to you," she said.

He gave a quiet, sinister laugh. "The end? The end will not come for me as one of them."

"Then how?" she asked.

He turned and placed his hands on the round object. "With this. You see, our sect has long sought to improve and expand our powers beyond magic, into the world of chemicals and anything else that garners power for us. This… creation is a concoction of many different chemicals, as well as a powerful spell. When it falls and strikes the ground below…"

"You are mad," she said.

"The fire should destroy them all," Nysyx said. "Alas, it will take the tower and us as well, but the power you each radiate will not only make the explosion larger, but hotter."

"And if we refuse to be a part of your plan?" Lethella asked.

"You have no choice." Nysyx approached her. His gnarled, blackened hand reached out to stroke her face. "Such a lovely girl. Much like Dransa the East, so many years ago."

"Dransa? What would you know of her?"

"I was quite familiar with her. I was the one who killed her." Lethella roared, making Nysyx laugh. "Oh, the situation is only too sweet," he said. "It will be the second time I have necessitated a new warrior maiden in the East."

She struggled against the spell which held her fast.

"When the moon is at its highest point, I will destroy them and us along with them," Nysyx went on. "A fitting end, I think." He turned back to the device, checking the chemicals and powders within, then went to a large book on a pedestal.

Lethella closed her eyes. A moment later, she felt a hand cover her mouth. Her eyes darted left: it was Thelos. He put a finger to his lips.

"Quiet," he whispered. "I have an idea, but you must let me act first." She couldn't nod, but her eyes told him that he could trust that her. He let go of her, and went back to where he had been lying before.

Nysyx approached the device again, then turned to Lethella, before sneering at Thelos on the floor. "You see? So weak with magic that he cannot even withstand the lightest of spells. Apprentice? You would have been wiser to have been your master's valet and spare him the hell of realizing you know nothing." Nysyx looked out the windows, down at the mass of walking corpses and then up at the shadow of the dark moon. With a twisted smile, he turned back to the chamber. "It is time." He walked to his device and ran his hands over it. "A life to learn and to practice. So many years spent in the pursuit and the development of magic. Now, to bring it all to one final, fiery end. When they speak of Nysyx of the Dread Solace, they will regard it as legend."

"No," Thelos said. "Just a sad tale of a man who fell to an apprentice."

Nysyx wheeled around, his eyes wide as a blast of purple energy crashed into him and sent him to the floor. He roared with pain. With a flash, Lethella was freed from the magic holding her. She started for Nysyx, but Thelos stopped her. "The ropes!" he cried. Nysyx looked up in terror as Lethella swung her sword, cutting two of the ropes holding the large orb. It swung dangerously; Nysyx scrambled to steady it. Thelos cast another spell—a bright light flared, and the chamber door burst from its frame. Thelos grabbed Lethella by the hand and they ran for the stairs. Nysyx began to chant his spell loudly, shoving the damaged sling with the device toward the windows.

Lethella took the lead, running down the stairs with Thelos behind her. The frightening voice of the dark wizard echoed through the place. They reached the second level of the tower, not pausing as they dashed for the stairs to the main level. Lethella ran to her mount while Thelos went to the door. He removed the bars and undid the bolt, and then pulled on the door even as he was helped by shoving from the other side.

"Thelos! Come!" Lethella cried out, starting the horse toward him. He backed away from the door as the ghastly, leering creatures poured in. She rode up to him and with a powerful arm pulled him onto the saddle.

"Can we make it through them?" he asked.

She drew the sword again, and her eyes narrowed. "We are about to find out." She spurred the horse. It reared, then thundered forward, crashing through the creatures on its way to the landing. She started the horse down the stairs, trampling and scattering zombies as they went. Once they reached the bottom, they would be thicker.

"Hold onto me, tight!" she screamed. He squeezed as the animal ran toward the floor of the basin.

Above them, Nsyyx laughed hysterically and uttered the last word of his spell. With a dreadful cry, he shoved his device over the edge of the window and it began to fall. The horse plowed through the monsters in the basin, Lethella's sword flashing back and forth.

The orb continued to drop.

Thelos cast a spell, scattering a number of the zombies. Lethella gazed ahead, spying the path that had initially brought her here. She swung the sword, removing the head of a zombie as she rode past it, then glanced behind them. The dot of a black object tumbled from the tower.

The orb struck. There was a tremendous, ground-shaking crash, then flames poured from the tower, which was quickly consumed by the magical bomb. Lethella urged the horse faster. Flames roared through the basin, incinerating the living dead, spreading toward the high walls. The horse reached the path as the flames closed in on them. Lethella felt the growing heat on her back. The horse grunted, carrying the riders up the incline as flames reduced the many zombies to ashes. Just as the heat began to sting and the roar was growing deafening, the horse reached the top of the incline. It raced away from the lip and further into the night.

Some time later, Lethella brought the horse to a halt by a flowing stream. It took to drinking, while both riders slid from the saddle. She put away the sword and looked at the man. He looked right back at her.

"I... thank you for your assistance," she said, which earned her a smile.

"That was a close one," he said. "We could both be dead."

"Thankfully, you had a plan that worked."

"Yes," he said. "But your riding definitely saved us, and this fine fellow..." He stroked the horse's neck.

"Where will you go now?" she asked.

He shrugged. "I suppose I will travel for a time, find my place in a new realm. I'm on my own now. No more master to serve, but I think I'm ready."

"You are," she said. "But… You could return with me to the east."

He looked into her eyes, then took her hand. "If you would like, I would be more than glad to come along, so you could keep saving me from certain death."

"I would like that," she said.

"We're going to have a lot more adventures, just you wait and see."

She smiled, continuing to enjoy the feel of his warm hand in hers.

Later, the sound of the horse's hooves filled the night, and they were headed east. Behind them, the basin lay dark and burnt, the rubble of the tower in the center of it. Amidst that rubble, a charred body lay. As it crumbled, a ring tumbled to the floor of the basin, before the echo of laughter swirled through the air.

TILL DEATH WE DO NOT PART

By Killion Slade

BOOM!

Heather scuttled across the container towards the peek hole, searching desperately for what blew up the outer rim barricades. It was her job to protect the south and watch the east. Her eyes ached. Heather punished herself for not remembering to pack the Visine.

Since the deader outbreak, each howl from the coyotes and every tumbleweed blowing up against the edge of their metal container, kept her awake. Sleep had become a rare commodity since the CDC had declared the rising dead a real threat in Montana and across most of the continent. Rubbing at her eyes, she focused on the eyepiece in the telescope.

"There! One o'clock—southeast. They're coming down the ditch road from old man Flannery's ranch."

Logan looked out the west side of their prepper's fort with his binoculars. He knew this was going to happen; it was simply a matter of time before the walking corpses arrived. Logan cricked his neck from side to side and took in a slow breath of air. He remained calm to help ease Heather's anxiety.

"Yep, it's happening. Our first line of defense has been breached." He wanted more time with Heather to ask her to marry him the proper way. Now he wasn't sure they would last through the night, let alone long enough to find a preacher man. "Why did it have to be zombies?"

BOOM!

Heather and Logan fell forward from the aftershock of the C4 blast. Their container took most of the aftershock, but it still pummeled the hell out of them.

"Holy crap!" Disoriented, Heather raced to the north wall. "It's only a matter of time until they breach the fence. They must know we're in here. There's a massive hole in the ground about a hundred yards out."

Logan checked the west gate of the ranch. With his binoculars glued to his eyes, he watched in horror as he listened to bovine screams bellowing over the land. Echoing down through the coulees, the non-stop eating deaders consumed the cattle as though it was a buffet at the local Moose Lodge.

He dropped the lenses to his chest and spat on the floor. "Dammit, I knew we should have butchered more cows."

Heather grabbed a pair of neon orange disposable earplugs from her ammunition bag. "Gah! Listen to them. That sound is crawling up my skin."

Logan reached around to his back pocket and pulled out a tin of beef jerky where tins of tobacco once wore the threadbare patch on his ass. How he wished he had tobacco now.

"Check the south. See if we can make a run for the bug-out location. We might still have time."

Heather checked the forest line to the south; maybe they could get out. The deaders were busy with the cows, which might buy them the time they needed to get to the boat. "Oh no. No, *NO!* Baby… they're coming from the lake too. We're surrounded!" Heather backed up against the wall and slid down. Her knees scrunched up into her chest as she bit at her nails. Her stomach roiled. "How the hell are we gonna get outta here? What are we gonna do now? Sit here and wait it out?"

"Breathe, baby. Just take a deep breath and focus. We've done this drill before. We just have to do it before they get in the fence."

Light faded faster than a prairie dog trying to outrun a bullet. It was only a matter of time before they wouldn't be able to see past the compound barricades. Heather reached for her night-vision goggles she kept on the hook by her rifle. Logan grabbed her hand as she triple-checked her rifle rounds.

They turned to look at one another. He pulled her in tight. So tight she could feel his belt buckle cut into her skin, the one he earned for riding that bronc at the Marias County Fair last summer.

He inhaled her. "Have I ever told you how much I like that shampoo you use? What's in it—lavender, cedar, lemongrass? You're always coming up with those crazy concoctions."

Heather's gaze met his hazelnut eyes. She touched his lips with her fingers. Her mouth quivered with the silliness of his question. Logan always knew how to make her laugh, even when she was scared out of her ever-lovin' mind. His lips tasted of the teriyaki he used when he smoked the jerky; she inhaled his smoky scent greedily. If she could bottle that manly smell, she'd be a gazillionaire.

He grabbed both sides of her face and pulled her closer, smashing their mouths together. He knew this could be their last kiss, and he savored every last taste. His tongue was sweet and tangy; she bit at his lower lip. Her hands slid down his back and around the front of him.

BOOM! BOOM! BOOM!

The C4 blasts sent them reeling to the floor. Jumping up, Logan offered Heather a hand and grabbed his crossbow with the other. He pushed the cooler out from behind the bucket of sawdust they used as a toilet, and Heather blew out the hurricane lamp. It was time to hang the rotting meat on the outside of their shipping container. Deaders surrounded the compound; maybe they would shuffle past them, thinking they were nothing but dead and gone. This was their last line of defense.

24 HOURS EARLIER

"I wish we could have purchased that old missile silo instead of setting up these container cars, but we did the best we could do, sweetie." Heather gave an impish smile laced with an *I told you so* smirk to her mouth.

Logan checked the fuel level of the fire launchers. "I mean, seriously? We've been prepping for a nuclear EMP blast, solar flares or even the G.D. global economic collapse, but instead, the CDC was right. It had to be the damn zombies coming to get us. They knew it! No wonder the government has been buying up all the bullets."

Heather dipped their remaining blocks of cheese into red wax. "We should have known when NOAA purchased all that ammo that something was up. Why would scientists who study the ocean have a need for hundreds of thousand-round munition cartridges? The government has known about this for a long time."

"Right! I just wonder whose military science experiment got loose and created this deader outbreak." Logan closed the gas valve on the generator and checked the loads in the Gatlin gun. "This'll mow 'em down until we run out of bullets."

"I think we ought to talk about a Plan C." Heather touched his hand and bit her lip.

"Plan C? But we already have a plan B in place, Babe. What more could you want? We've got the boat prepped and ready for bug-out."

"What if they get through? There's a helluva lot more of them than there are us, and we have no way to get underground. It may only be a matter of time. We need to figure out what we're gonna do if this happens to us."

"What? Are you freakin' nuts? Are you saying you want us to kill each other before we ever fight? Give up already?"

"No, not at all. That's Plan D. We have provisions to last us for months, a year maybe, but we have no idea how long this will last. And worse yet, we have no idea if there will be other humans wanting to take what we have."

"By the look of those deaders out there, other humans ain't what we ought to be afraid of. Dead ones, yeah… but I get what yer sayin'. Whaddya suggest?"

"Well, the way I see it, we were going to take an oath for better or for worse, right? This is undeniably worse. Till death do us part." Logan nodded at Heather. "But why do we have to part in death? Look at them—they're alive somehow. They seem to have some sort of communication between them."

"What in blazes are you suggestin'?"

"Just hear me out, okay?" Heather calmed Logan down with her hands. Logan swallowed hard and crossed his arms over his chest. She went on. "If either one of us gets bitten or scratched or whatever and not eaten alive, then I think for the sake of our love, we should make another oath to change the other so we can stay together."

Logan blinked at her for a few moments, then checked the gas gauge for the generator again. He turned around and fixed his hand on his hip. "Are you f'n nuts, woman? Are you saying you want to live as one of those... *things*... eating other people? Of all the idiotic, pig-headed stunts to pull. You want to turn deader?"

"No, of course I don't, but I do want to be with you. What if this is just some sort of temporary virus thing and it goes away after thirty days or something? If we kill ourselves, then we'll never know that we could have had a chance to make it if things get reversed. I love you and I want to stay with you forever." Heather quieted her voice. "Even if I have to be something else."

"I'm listening. Just need a while to think about it."

Heather gave him a weak smile. "Okay, fair enough. Of course, this would have to be the Custer's last stand kinda situation. The last act of defiance, us against the man sort of thing, ya know? I have lots of faith in what we have done to prepare ourselves against this end-of-the-world apocalypse crap. Truthfully, I wish it could have been a volcano erupting or pandemic of sorts. We're prepared for all that."

Logan pulled out his old chewing tobacco can and stuffed an extra hunk of beef jerky into his lower lip. "Yeah, for all we know we should have made wooden stakes. If there are zombies, what else is out there? Something has to hunt them. Zombies can't be at the top of the food chain." Logan shook his head and frowned. "I can smell fire." He looked around. "Look at the smoke across the horizon. People are killing those deaders with fire. If we don't get any deaders here tonight, it'll be one helluva sunset." Logan smacked Heather on the ass. "Let's go check our fuel reserves; we may need to move barrels up here and next to each flame thrower."

Heather chewed at her nails. "I'm not trying to be a worry wart, but there are only two of us. What if they get over that fence? How can we keep them from getting to us? What if we are cut off from being able to get back into the bunker?"

"You've got a point. Maybe we need to relocate everything to our strongest wall of defense and cage ourselves in somehow."

They spent the next few hours hauling guns, ammunition, food, blankets, even a sawdust toilet over to their container compound. Later on, Heather scrolled through the radio stations, anxious to hear anything.

"Anything on the radio?"

She scratched at her head. "No, the signal went dead about an hour ago. Do we have any batteries left?"

"Not here, I took most of the batteries down to the boat." Logan took a deep breath and sat on the chair beside her.

"Should we go fire up the generator and crank on the HAM radio? It's been a few days since we've gotten anything over the airways. I can take the first watch." She twirled little patterns on his hand with her pinky finger. "Flannery said we've got a nasty storm heading this way. Thunderstorms. It might even hail."

"Yeah, might be a good idea just to hear if this thing is bigger than what we think." He squeezed her hand and kissed her on the cheek.

Logan stood up, but Heather stayed firm to his grip. "Please don't stay too long. I honestly wish we could have moved the generator in here. And yes, I know that it needs ventilation."

He kissed her hand and decided to take one last look out through his telescope before leaving for the barn. "Holy Jesus, Mary and Joseph, would you look at that?" Logan spoke without leaving his eyepiece. "Look, under the fence. In the red plaid."

Heather looked. She saw something moving. A piece of plaid fabric, worming its way across the compound.

Heather let go of the telescope and grabbed her binoculars for a better look. "What the… What the hell? No way… Oh yuck… That is disgusting! Is that a hand crawling?"

Logan took over the scope once again. "Well, that's something I've never seen before. Just 'cause it ain't attached to the body don't mean it still doesn't want food."

"Yeah, but the hand itself can't eat anything. Can it?"

"Dunno. I once read this funny little story about this ghoulie named Robbie. He said that until you kill the brain, the body keeps moving. They keep trying to feed the mouth, even though it ain't attached." Heather scrunched up her face while she watched the creepy horror movie scenario come to life. She shivered off the heebie-jeebies, thinking about the old urban legends of a hand with a claw and unfortunate campers somewhere. Slowly, the hand inched its way across the rain-soaked mud and barnyard muck.

Logan checked the rest of the lookouts before opening the container door. "Okay, I'm going. Cover me, but don't waste your bullets on the hand, okay? It can't get up here. It doesn't have feet to climb. I'll be back in thirty minutes." In unison, they set their watches. "Ready, set, go!"

Heather wondered how he knew she was going to shoot the hand. She hollered out to him, "Hey, when you come back from the HAM, please bring the other rifle scope, will ya?"

"Ooh baby, I love it when you talk dirty to me. Gets me all doped up."

She shook her head as she watched him climb into the far container and out towards the barn. Sighting in her rifle, Heather felt a little better about the hand not being able to climb. Not crazy about the silence or being alone, she talked to herself in the darkening tin can.

Twenty-eight minutes went by. A cow bellowed in the distance. Logan opened the creaky door to the container.

"Listen, I got 'ole man Flannery on the HAM. It sounds like there are deaders heading our way. Quite a few of them. We should be able to take them down. Let's get ready."

*

BOOM!

Heather searched in desperation for what blew up the outer rim barricades. "Looks like we don't have any time, they're already here!" Both of them grabbed their binoculars and started the drill they had rehearsed a hundred times.

"There! One o'clock—southeast. They're coming down the ditch road from old man Flannery's ranch."

"Maybe we still have time to get to the bug-out location. What does it look like coming from the lake?"

"Oh no! No, *NO!* Baby… they're coming from the lake too. We're gonna be surrounded. We aren't gonna be able to make it to the boat. There are too many of them! Plan B just got royally screwed."

Logan tried to stay calm. He ran through the drill exercises in his mind.

1. *Guns loaded. Check.*
2. *Flame throwers lit. Check.*
3. *Hang the meat.*

"We need to get the meat hung on the outside of the container." They grabbed the Igloo containers of dead meat and skin from prior deader attacks. Several decomposing bodies were stashed outside to help ward off any rogue hungries. "Grab your mask, this is gonna be real bad, babe." Opening the Igloo, Logan about lost his MRE.

Heather gagged at the pungent, putrid odor, but was used to it from working in the hospital night shift. Once you smell dead, it never leaves you. They draped the skins on welded hooks by the doors and the peep holes to keep the deaders away. After the last skinned body was in place, Logan finally tossed his cookies.

"C'mon, babe, let's get back inside before they get any closer." Heather kicked the Igloos away from the door as they crawled inside, barricading themselves in. They washed the stench off of their hands as best they could and waited to see how the zombie shuffle would react to their decoy. Logan prayed that somewhere else someone would fire gunshots to attract their attention, but they kept coming in from all directions. Like fireflies to a campstove light.

BOOM! BOOM!

Heather's body shook uncontrollably. Logan placed his hands on her shoulders and drilled deep into her azure bloodshot eyes. "Take a deep breath. It's okay. It's time to fry a few of these suckers, just like we've been practicing. I need you to run and crank on the generator, while I start the rest of the flames."

Without another squeamish thought, Heather hugged him fast around the neck. "I'll be right back. Love you! Cover me."

"You know it, babe. Okay, slow down, just like we've rehearsed. Open the door, look everywhere. Run like hell and close yourself in. Don't leave the door open. Run into the barn and push the button."

Heather breathed in slow and tried to clear her mind.

BOOM! BOOM!

"Go, babe!"

Heather opened the door and ran outside. Not a deader in sight, but the gnashing sound of their moaning mantra was more than she could handle. Darting into the next container, she got the door closed behind her. The generator cranked over in three pulls and she clicked her flashlight in quick succession—on and off—to indicate her success.

"Excellent. That's my girl." Logan spoke under his breath. He hooked up two cable wires, and the screeching sound of electrified barbed zombie was on the menu. He flashed his light three times back at her, before she cautiously opened the door. Running back to the open door, she slipped in cow manure and fell face first into the mud and barnyard slime. Hail pelted the roof with clanging, deafening sounds.

"Here, babe. You did a terrific job." Logan handed her a towel and a bottle of water when she got back inside.

Heather shook from the cold and wind as well as the deaders. Logan cranked up the juice on the fence and the smell of electrified flesh filled the pregnant, muggy air.

"Careful, don't use too much of our juice. We don't want to run out."

He turned and disconnected the cables. The stunned zombies began their forward momentum towards the compound once again. "Guess they don't feel pain."

"Looks like we barbequed a couple of them, though." Heather continued to scrape off the muck. She undressed down to her bra and panties. "Maybe electric fences don't kill them."

"Well, the fence was built to keep out cows and humans, but not dead humans."

"Look, time is running out. Have you thought anymore about my proposition? Plan C?"

Logan grimaced. "I have. I don't particularly like the idea of becoming a deader."

"Neither do I, but what would you do if I become one?"

"I don't want to lose you, Heather. You're my everything, ya know? The head on my beer, the jelly in my donut, kinda thing." He couldn't resist her; with her hair all muddied up, smelling like cow crap, she gushed beauty from every dirty pore. He grabbed another bottle of water and doused her neck, nibbling as he went. She smiled at him. Logan never was one for romance, so this was probably as good as it would get.

An alarm sounded, announcing more deaders had arrived. They were inside the preliminary barriers. "Logan, we've got to finish lighting the flame torches. It looks like the south end fence collapsed at the edge of the field."

"Holy shit. Look at 'em go!" He marveled. "They aren't slowing at all. Damn things might be able to outrun us."

Heather grabbed her rifle and shot the deaders at the knees, dropping them before they could get any closer.

"Hit 'em in the head! We need to bust out their brains so they don't keep coming after us. Have you seen where that hand went?"

Heather looked down at the bloody scrape on her ankle. She took another deep breath, and shined the red dot laser at the frontal lobe of a woman who looked vaguely like Mrs. Orcettar, the lunch room lady at the junior high school. Heather mumbled under her breath, "Never did like that woman, always charging me more for extra crackers and salad dressing." *BANG!* Down she went. "Damned teacher assistants do all the hard work, the pain-in-the-ass jobs, we shouldn't be overcharged by lunch room Nazis." Scorching hot flames filled the barnyard; haystacks lit up with flaming dead bodies walking into anything in their paths.

"Keep shooting them, babe. It doesn't look like the fire kills them, just slows them down."

Heather did as instructed, plinking off more exploding heads than she ever imagined she would.

Hours later it seemed as if hundreds of scorched bodies were scattered over the barnyard compound. They grabbed their pistols and silencers to finish off the remaining live ones.

Heather tripped over a branch and fell to her knee, but it wasn't a branch. The crawling hand grabbed her and cut a gash with its thumbnail deep into her ankle. She slapped at the zombie hand, but it kept coming at her. She picked it up and threw it over into the burning pile of deaders.

"Logan! The damn hand—it scratched me! It got me!"

"No, Logan, stop! Please don't! Keep me in the shed if you have to, but please don't kill me. This might all go away in a month." Without a second thought, Logan shoved the pistol at her head, scared for his own survival now. She pleaded with him. The rain continued to come down, hiding her tears as she begged for her life. "You can keep me until you run out of food or run out of time. Then we can be together. Our Plan C. Wait until you run out of bullets and you have no other options left."

Logan gave in, moved forward and cradled her in his arms while huddling in the rain. He cried along with her, screaming into the night.

"Make love to me while we still can. We don't know how long I have."

"Let's get to the showers, babe."

Months passed. Logan visited Heather daily in the freezer room. She steadily decayed in her cold room; he considered her well-preserved, for the most part. Heather had a few teeth missing, though, and her skin peeled a bit. Every day Logan would sit and talk to her. Sometimes he even thought she answered his questions.

"Babe, it's getting pretty serious out there. Every day it's the same thing. Our fuel is almost gone and it's the fire that slows them down enough for me to shoot them dead." Heather groaned at him. Her chains to the container wall kept him from harm, but she genuinely hated the rash under the shackles. She grinned up at him and moaned.

"I brought you a present today." Dismissing the thought that she might still be conscious and trying to talk to him, he changed the topic. "It's one of our last ones, but I thought you might enjoy it." Logan brought in their nanny goat. Heather's body went into spasms, eagerly anticipating the live flesh offering. Logan scooted the goat over to Heather and ran out of the room, listening to the wailing BAHHHS of the goat until it was silenced.

More months passed. Winter was coming. Days, weeks without hearing from another human soul on the HAM radio had finally taken its toll. When Logan managed to grab onto a signal, it was too far away and difficult to understand. He studied his survival manual, trying to understand Morse Code, but the transmission codes never aired. No one sent out SOS or emergency broadcasts any longer.

Driving into town and nearby farms proved to be a fruitless search as well—no humans were around except dead ones. He scavenged food and clothing anywhere he could find it, but most of it had already been consumed or filched by other survivors. At this point, he wasn't sure what he would do if he came across another survivor. Would he be able to trust them? What if they found out about Heather? Would they kill her too? He couldn't take that chance and ventured out less and less away from the farm.

After another long day of scrounging for anything left in their small town, Logan had to tell Heather his decision. He opened the door to find her sitting on the floor. Excited by his presence, she started her feeding frenzy dance. Arms outstretched, mouth open, moaning something that haunted his thoughts constantly, Plan C. Now it sounded more like a garbled spewing of vowels, but the singsong of the moan always stayed the same. He knew she still had to be in there, desperately trying to communicate.

Logan's grip on reality began a slow decline. He pulled the chair from the corner and turned on the light above his head. The yellow cast from the bulb illuminated a circle around him on the floor.

"Hey, babe. How ya doing?"

She warbled at him.

"Tough day, huh? I had a pretty rough one myself. I came to tell you I've made a decision." Heather dropped her arms long enough for silence to fill the room. "I have decided that I need to make a run into Great Falls in order to see if there are any humans left up here. Conrad is empty of people. Not a soul to be found up here. No traffic on the interstate, just deaders walking all over the place."

She moaned again and sank down to her knees, her arms extended. Logan wrung his hat between his hands. "I'm gonna go tomorrow morning at first light. Thing is, I don't know if I'll ever make it back, and I'm worried about leaving you in here. I was thinking about moving you outside into one of the pens. Give you a chance to free yourself. I just don't know what to do."

She sat down onto her legs as if she could understand his plight. She continued to moan that singsong of 'Plan C' over and over.

"Yeah, I've been thinking about your Plan C. I hear you." He got up, clicked off the light and said, "I'll see you tomorrow, babe."

Several days later, Logan pulled safely back into the farm with his truck, loaded with enough food and fuel to last him for the winter. He opened the door to her darkened freezer room to find her slumped over, not moving. Logan shook her, but got no response. He could hear her labored breathing. She needed to feed.

"Wait right here, sweetie, let me get you something." A couple of minutes later, Logan brought in a live chicken, feathers and all. Heather's eyes opened. She lunged for the beast as Logan tossed it in the air towards her. A cascade of white feathers flew around the room as he explained his plan to her. "So here's what I found, babe. I didn't see anyone down there. Most of everything has been pilfered, but I was lucky enough to find the chicken from a house not too far away from the military base. The Air Force base was abandoned and no one was at the airport. No one at the police station. I'm beginning to think we are all that's left of this world." The squawking of the chicken finally died down as Heather bit into its neck, tearing out the throat, drinking the warm-blooded animal for every ounce it had. Logan swallowed hard and averted his eyes once again. "Yeah... anyway... I think I've found enough food for the winter if we ration it."

Day in, day out, the same thing. Alarms cried out, booby traps sprung, the smell of dead decay blanketed everything. Winter was harsh, and spending additional resources to light a fire during the day was not a consideration they could afford. Logan never wanted to take a chance of anyone knowing he and Heather were surviving on the farm. Many days he sat huddled under hay bales and mounds of covers reading books. Any books he could get his hands on, just to pass the time until spring.

When spring arrived, the ground began its muddy thaw. Three days after he had eaten the last of the food he had scrounged from town, he decided it was time to get her. Logan grabbed Heather by the throat with a dog pole and unlocked her from the chains in the freezer room. Walking outside, her zombie eyes squinted at the gleaming sunlight coming up over the horizon. It was one of those fiery red mornings where the sky looked as if it was on fire. In the corral, he tied her to a fence post, much like he had done with his horses before they were consumed.

She garbled the same singsong to him as he grabbed a piece of paper from his pocket and held it in front of her eyes. On it, he had written "Plan C" in solid red letters.

"You see, Heather, I figure I've kept you alive all this time and you haven't given up on me… so," Logan kicked at the thawing dirt clods, "I'm not gonna give up on you. There's nothing left here. Nothing for anyone to live through alone." He pulled out a tin of real chewing tobacco, a score he found at a liquor store. Saving it for when this day arrived. He hit the can against his boot a couple times to pack the tobacco and grabbed a hefty wad of it. He stuck it into his cheek and let loose the rope.

Heather lunged at him and bit him deep in his neck. Logan managed to pull her back and tie her tight to his side, facing away from him. It was only a matter a matter of time now.

"Can you hear me, Logan? Logan, sweetie, can you hear me. Are you in there? Wake up!" Logan looked through hazed eyes, he heard Heather's voice. Was he imagining her talking to him? Did she eat him? Was he dead?

"Thank you for believing in me, sweetie. Plan C—I knew you could do it. I love you." Heather garbled her words, but her thoughts were as clear as the Montana sky.

Logan looked at her as she held out a hand towards him. She helped him up. Once he got his footing, he smiled as best he could. He groaned "Plan C" as they walked off into the Montana horizon.

AN UNDYING LOVE
By John Edward Betancourt

A beautiful evening called for beautiful roses.

But these roses went above and beyond the call of duty. With petals so full and colors so vibrant, they appeared to be artificial. A quick whiff of their magnificent scent, however, confirmed that they would be the centerpiece of the night. With a smile on his face, he approached the counter and laid down some cash.

"Oh thank you, Miss Havisham," he said with a smile. "Christine is going to flip over roses so beautiful. One of these days you will absolutely have to tell me your secret!" Miss Havisham returned the toothy grin but said nothing. "Well, thanks again! Make sure you tell your husband I said hello."

With a wave, he stepped out into the gorgeous day. Oh, how summer brought joy to his senses. The lush green grass, the magnificent blue sky full of gentle sunlight left him in near ecstasy. For today was the most special of days. Not only was it the six-month anniversary for him and Christine since their reunion; tonight he would ask her to become Mrs. Morty Meeks.

The thought of his high school sweetheart answering an emphatic 'yes' to a lifetime of love left Morty soaring as he walked down Main Street toward Jack's Jewelry. Once more he ran through the plan. There would be the candlelight dinner, beginning with a fresh garden salad. That would be followed by a fantastic beef stew and wrapped up with cheesecake. Their favorite band would be playing on his iPod, and when their song arrived at last, he would drop to one knee and ask for her hand.

He chuckled as he pushed open the door to the jewelry store. There was no need to be ashamed; Morty had spent a lifetime waiting for this night. Besides, with the way his luck had turned around over the last six months, anyone close to him would have expected nothing less than jubilation.

"Afternoon, Jack! Today's the day!" Morty said as he walked up to the counter. "Here you are; the last two hundred dollars for the ring. This is it, man! Tonight Christine and I start our lifelong voyage!" He slapped a wad of bills onto the counter, but much to his dismay Jack appeared unmoved. After a moment or two of awkward silence, Morty noticed the tiny, neatly wrapped package atop the counter.

"Oh Jack, you're the best. You even wrapped it in her favorite color!"

Morty scooped up the ring, gently placing it in his pocket. "Thanks, Jack! Wish me luck!"

He waved once more, surprised at the silence coming from Jack as he bathed in the fine summer day again. All worry for his friend slipped away as the thought of Christine, the absolute love of his life, weeping as she told him she wanted nothing more than to be his forever. Morty reached into his pocket and smiled as he held the ring gently, whistling a tune all the way home.

The brilliant glimmer of the afternoon sun disappeared as menacing thunderclouds rolled across the sky. They churned as the wind steadily grew, pushing forth the might of nature as searing flashes of lightning arrived, sending forth tremors that would blanket any mortal soul with raw terror. Nature's wrath fell upon deaf ears as Morty continued home, barely conscious of the powerful storm brewing before him. He whistled until he arrived in front of his lovely home, taking a moment to inhale with pride at the sight of his newly acquired digs before jogging toward the front door. As he fumbled for his keys, his heart began to race. Anyone within earshot would be able to hear the slamming in his chest. As he slid the key into the door, he did his best to steady himself.

After all, she would say yes.

It made little sense for her not to, not with the world in its current state of destruction; their reunion after so many years only solidified the possibility. He recalled that fateful night, the United States left in tatters, civilization collapsing around him—and she was there, standing on his front lawn, aimlessly afraid until their eyes met through the window. She moved with such fluid motion that Morty figured he must be dreaming. For there was the visage of an angel at the window, begging for him to be her white knight, to take her in and clothe her, feed her, love her. He did not refuse her, for she was everything he ever dreamed of. In the midst of what some were calling judgment day, their love was at last a reality.

His fear subsided as logic prevailed.

She was inside the house, waiting for him, waiting for this moment with the same excitement that flowed through Morty's veins. This was destiny. With that, he turned the key, slid open the door and stepped inside.

There were eyes upon him the instant he closed the door, allowing the joyful butterflies in his stomach to consume him. To feel the adoration and desire washing over him from something as simple as a look kept his spirit soaring. This was a love that only a handful of men would ever know, that every lonesome soul searched for with endless resolve.

He truly was the luckiest man on earth. Their gazes were now locked upon one another, and the tension building between them from this simple act left the air in the room heavy with anticipation.

"Hey, gorgeous," Morty said with a smile.

She sat at the dining room table, wearing a red dress that brilliantly complimented the radiant glow of her ivory flesh. Her blond hair draped down over to frame her perfect cheekbones and enchanting eyes. She was as beautiful as the day he met her so many years ago.

There was no reply, just the desire in her eyes as he approached her. Her gaze remained locked upon him, the need for Morty pouring out with every step that drew him closer to her. "I missed you, too. Did you have a good day?" he asked as his fingers ran through her hair. A few strands remained attached to his palm; he carelessly tossed them to the ground. She moved with his touch, her face gently nuzzling his forearm. Yet she still did not speak one word.

"I hope you are hungry, my love. I planned a fantastic feast for tonight. I was thinking something simple yet delicious, and we can enjoy some music by candlelight while we eat. Doesn't that sound wonderful?"

She continued to press against him, sending shivers down his spine with every brush of her lips. He pulled his hand away, amazed at her need for contact as she strained to once more place her mouth against his skin. "Plenty of time for that later, my angel. You must be starving; I know I am. Let me go get dinner ready first and I can hear all about your day. I have some amazing stories to tell you. You have no idea the crazy things Tom did last night. I swear that man never left college!" He chuckled. "When you hear this story your sides are gonna split!"

She pushed forward once more, nearly falling out of her chair as her look of desire turned to panic. Had it not been for the chains restraining her, she surely would have fallen to the ground face-first.

"Baby! Relax before you hurt yourself. I missed you too and I promise there will be plenty of quiet cuddle time on the couch later, but for now, we need to eat!" She leaned back, the anxiety leaving her as she settled into her seat.

Morty flashed her a weak smile as he began to move toward the kitchen. That unfortunate moment reminded him of the difficulty their love would forever face, bringing tears to his eyes. While there would never be a cure for her handicap, there was, at the very least, hope. When she came to him she was confused, hurting, and much of the basic fundamentals of her humanity seemed lost. But their need for one another was equal from the moment he saw her on that fateful night. Their love had grown quickly and with every day that passed, his gentle care nursed her back from the abyss.

The golden rule that love endured all things rang true, but his frustration at being unable to reverse her condition would haunt him always. Despite their unspoken bond, Christine was, and would forever be, dead.

A sigh escaped Morty's lips. Regardless of the advancement in his culinary skills, this beef stew would never be as exquisite as the one they made downtown. This slop came from a can.

Morty tasted it once more. A few more minutes atop the stove would bring forth perfection, he decided, tapping his spoon clean as he smiled. Perhaps looking at the end of mankind was truly a matter of perspective. While so many saw this 'event' as Armageddon, to Morty it was nothing more than justice. Granted, those first few days were as frightening for him as anyone else. After all, the dead were returning to life, and they craved warm human flesh. There was panic in the streets, even in this tiny, insignificant town where the first member of the living dead did not appear until one week after the news was revealed to the blubbering masses. Of course, with the arrival of the first creature came the birth of two, then four, and then it was utter disaster. They were everywhere.

Morty merely watched the carnage from his living room window with a detached glee. While it was indeed awful to see so many innocent lives end and begin again under such a horrific circumstance, it was all too fitting. What goes around comes around. Those words echoed in his mind even now in regard to the town that had spent so many years shunning him, mocking him. Yes, in the end it was Morty who survived. Good old Morty Meeks, whom everyone referred to as 'Super Geek Who Totally Reeks'.

His fists clenched with rage at that unfortunate memory. However, the fire within did not last. His fingers relaxed, comfortable in the fact that every last one of those bastards not only suffered before they died, but that they answered for their sins. For when the fires had burned themselves out and the dawn had come at last on the most terrifying night in this town, when the dead had grown to numbers completely uncontrollable and ravaged the town, tearing into every man, woman and child they could find, there was only Morty left standing.

One by one he faced off with the most unsavory human beings from his past. Those who once tormented him now shuffled about, their eyes listless, their bodies broken and ripped asunder. They were weak and pathetic; Morty was more than happy to place a bullet in their barely functioning brains. One by one they fell at Morty's hands, and one by one he placed those he hated most in positions of servitude where their corpses would accommodate him until their bones turned to dust.

Justice was a beautiful lady indeed.

It was nice to be the big man on campus for a change. Hell, he was mayor of this town now. Maybe even governor of this great state, by the way things were going. Why, he might even be the president of the United States of America for all he knew.

Those possibilities made him smile. At this rate he would need new business cards with the title of *'King of Everything'*. Of course, a King would need a Queen, and the woman fortunate enough to soon hold that title was waiting just beyond the door.

With that, he filled a tray with two delicious salads and two steaming bowls of beef stew before venturing back out to the dining room.

"My, my, you truly are stunning, you know," Morty said to the creature sitting across from him. He shook his head; it was difficult to look at her at a moment such as this, with black sludge slipping from her lips. But love knew no bounds; he would take the good with the bad.

Of course that was easier said than done, and she in no way made it easy. So far his best efforts to wean her off of human flesh had failed miserably. Tonight was no different. When he removed her mouthpiece she merely moaned and drooled, choosing to play with the meal before her, turning it into an accessory for her lovely dress as she splashed and spilled food everywhere, a look of dreary boredom upon her lifeless face. Morty watched with morbid wonder, gulping down wine as he searched for a way to return the mood to romance.

"Darling, am I truly that bad of a cook?" he said, laughing aloud. Her head tilted to one side as he spoke, reminding him of the beagle he'd owned as a child. Morty smiled, gulping down more wine as he stared into her milky white pupils. They had once been an enchanting blue. "It's all right. You know me, my love; if it doesn't come from a can, then I'll either burn it or make someone sick!" He chuckled again. She held her ghostly stare.

"I... I'm not very good at what I am about to say, Christine. So, I'll say it outright. I love you. I loved you from the moment I saw you in Mr. Blackard's English class so many years ago. I loved you every minute of every day." He paused, the tears welling up in his eyes. "You were so perfect and pretty, and you never bothered to be mean to me like everyone else. I never told you how much I appreciated it the day you told James Warner to stop picking on me.

"I know we both had big plans following graduation. I know we both failed miserably at them. I'm sorry you ended up marrying that bastard James, that you ended up working in that shitty waitressing job. And I'm sorry I never went to college. I hated every minute working in that video store, but seeing you come in with your idiot husband every Friday gave me a hope you will never understand. It reminded me that there are truly beautiful things in this world, and you represent every last one of them. I would be lying if I told you the only reason I came into that greasy spoon of a diner was the food. It was you. Just to see you! It left me soaring when I walked out of there. I need you, and I've always needed you.

"When all of this went down I wondered, no, prayed that you were okay, even though there was nothing that I could do. So imagine my surprise when I saw you standing outside my mother's home, and you didn't make me your dinner!" He laughed again; this time with such force that he thought his belly might shake the table enough to knock over the wine. When he finished wiping the tears from his eyes he rose and moved to her, dropping down to one knee. "I see it all now, Christine. We were meant to be, we were born to be together. I know this isn't exactly the way either of us planned it, but I know we can be happy together. I promise you, I will do everything in my power to make you feel like a queen, if you'll do me this one thing…" He reached into his pocket, removed the lovely ring and opened the case, allowing her a good look at the magnificent diamond. "Will you be my wife?"

Morty's lip quivered, and the tremor moved to his body as he held the ring high, close to her now wide and wild eyes, doing his best to hold back the rush of emotion flowing through him. This was the magnificent moment he dreamed of night after night for so many years; this was the splendor and beauty of true love.

It took but a moment for that wonder and majesty to come crashing down. She lunged forward, her rotten maw clamping down hard upon the soft and supple skin of his left hand. The pain blinded him as her teeth sliced him open, grabbing hold of the tissue beneath, grinding and twisting, tearing muscle and ligament with every ravenous movement.

He howled and tried to pull his hand away. But his effort merely made things worse; he heard the nauseating sound of his own flesh ripping between her jaws. At last the meat gave way. He fell back upon the floor, the lovely ring joining him atop the carpet, sparkling ruby red from his own blood.

Morty gripped his hand, looking down at the wound as it continued to ooze precious crimson. He might very well bleed to death. He rose to his feet and ran into the restroom, crying out again as he cleansed the ragged wound with icy water. How many passes it took before the bleeding stopped, he did not know, but the searing pulses of agony dissolved coherent thought from Morty's mind. He merely stood there in a now-bloodstained bathroom, stunned at the events of the evening. His efforts to fix her, to remove those horrible primal instincts and replace them with devotion, now seemed to be in vain. Her lack of gratitude left him surging with anger. He had half a mind to go back out there and knock that corpse on its ass and bash its barely functional brain in with a frying pan.

But his fury quickly turned to sorrow and heartbreak. Morty sat on the toilet, bandaging his still-aching wound, tears streaming down his face over a love that never was and never could be. He wanted to punish her, he truly did, but instead he swallowed a handful of pain relievers, went to bed and cried himself to sleep.

The storm unleashed its fury shortly after midnight. Lightning brought forth thunder that rumbled through the darkness, followed by a rain heavy enough to rattle the shingles of the rooftop.

Morty slept soundly, snoring as he dreamt and mumbling to no one in particular until he at last shifted beneath his sheets and pinned his injured hand beneath his massive body. A yelp escaped his lips as he sat upright, his good hand cradling the wounded one while he rocked his body back and forth, waiting for the throb to subside. The relief did not last; the pain evolved, moving from agonizing hurt just below a knuckle to a deep-rooted ache now buried in the center of his heart. His whimpering elicited a response from his roommate downstairs. Her moans reminded him of the true problem at hand, and the tears came fresh once more.

It had been an eternity since feelings such as this found their way into his life. Not since the divorce of his parents. Not since his father blamed them both for his life troubles and walked out when his mother refused to sign the papers. Morty Meeks was lost once again, without hope or direction, and it left him paralyzed in his bed, staring beyond the ceiling.

All the while Christine moaned downstairs, the hunger inside her taking over. She had a renewed taste for human flesh and knew full well a fine meal was within her reach. The scent of him only aggravated her further, and her cries grew louder.

"Shut up, Christine," Morty said at last, her mottled howl grating against his nerves. It was a request that went unanswered. The only place to find peace was in the solace of a warm shower.

The water felt good as it poured over his skin and the steady sound delivered the solitude he so desired, but that would end as soon as the hot water ran out. Staying indoors would only make matters worse. He should take a walk, get away and simply think. He dressed his body and his wound before heading down the stairs, being careful to make as little noise as possible when opening the door. She was agitated enough. Morty stood in the doorway, staring at her with fascination and terror at once before shutting the door and starting toward town. There was still a great desire for her raging through his veins, leaving him unsure that last night's event could do anything to shake their love. Rough patches were a part of any relationship; this could be nothing more than just that, a tiny pothole on the long road of happiness. The greater problem he faced was that the stability of their connection stemmed from one simple obstacle: her living death. It was clear now that regardless of how much love he bestowed upon Christine, this part of her would never falter. The pain in his hand was a reminder that neither would her hunger.

Even with the world coming to its end, few things had changed. Morty Meeks and Christine Wagner were still of two different worlds.

He would never overcome such an obstacle. Suddenly the air was sucked from his lungs as the endgame to this mess presented itself, forcing his stumbling legs to halt and deposit him atop a bench. As he struggled to reclaim precious oxygen, a powerful image played in his mind: she was chained to her special chair in the dining room, golden hair flowing as her head moved about ever so gently, those sunken and hollow eyes darting about the room, trying desperately to find the warm and bountiful meal that her dulled senses had alerted her to. He was behind her, the gun trembling in his hands as he moved the muzzle ever so slowly toward the back of her skull.

Morty slapped himself for thinking such awful thoughts. The refreshing sting removed the disgusting image from his mind, but not the possibility. He smacked himself once more. She was the one, everything he ever needed; ending her second life was purely out of the question.

Yet she had not hesitated to end his first.

Looking down at the bandage over his knuckle Morty saw the blood soaking through. The wound was in no way mending. In his panic and concern over her commitment to this union he had overlooked one important issue: no one survived a bite inflicted by the living dead. Soon the symptoms that would lead him to a slow and painful death would come. And the end would culminate in resurrection.

His head sunk as the reality settled into his soul. He was damned, one way or another, and it seemed only fitting. For in this life whenever opportunity arose to tease him with a shred of happiness, the door would promptly shut in his face. This was nothing new. He was foolish to believe that he was master of his domain. In the end the world was against him. Those he despised from the past were certainly mocking him now, reveling through hollowed sockets at his final screw-up.

Some part of him wondered if what happened last night was planned all along. That before the end, James and the others made sure she would end up at his doorstep, knowing of his need for her, knowing that she would be his undoing.

The last shred of hope left Morty with the realization that all those who had done him wrong, all those he hated so strongly, would garner the last laugh.

They had finally got the best of him.

Or had they?

A thought washed over Morty's mind. There was still a chance at happiness. There was a way out of his mess indeed, one that he had completely missed. There was little time to waste. He jumped to his feet and ran home to his love, and to his future.

The timing could not have been better. The midday sun poured through the skylights in the dining room, bathing Christine in its warmth. The fine strands of her blond hair shimmered as Morty entered the room, shrouding her in waves of amber as she turned her head to see him.

"Oh baby. I'm so sorry I left without telling you. I needed to work some things out. I was too stupid to see everything, but I get it now. I really do. You weren't trying to hurt me. You were only trying to love me." He stepped behind her as he spoke. She growled and spat, but there was no fear this time, just understanding. Destiny had a way of removing terror from one's soul.

"Opportunity like this comes once in a lifetime. We're a tale as old as the earth itself, Christine. Two lovers, meant to be together, but separated by circumstance beyond our control. But it doesn't have to be that way anymore. The stars have aligned, my love. All the obstacles that have kept us apart are gone. They wanted us to fail, get it? But they're dead now. I've seen to that. Even your worthless ex-husband. All that's left alive in this world is you and me. The only thing that can keep us from being truly happy is your condition, but we can solve that too. You need me. I need you. So I will give you what you want. I will be a part of you and you will be a part of me. I love you, Christine. Be my wife?" A single tear ran down his cheek as he unlocked her chains, letting them slip to the floor.

Her response was quick. She rose to her feet, turning to face Morty. She grabbed him tight, teeth bared and ready. He was happy to receive her and slowly turned his neck toward her, grunting with surprise as her slightly blood-stained whites sank into the tender flesh. "She said yes."

They would be Morty's last words. After he spoke them, Christine pulled back, taking a chunk of him with her before comforting him in a blanket of his own blood. He had beaten the odds at last. In a few moments he would slip into the darkness of sleep. When he awakened she would still be there; she would be his wife. No one could keep them apart anymore. No one could hurt them anymore. They would be the last true lovers on the face of the earth, left to wander through their magical kingdom as King and Queen, until the end of time.

I'VE GOT YOU UNDER MY SKIN

By Anthony J. Rapino and Monique Snyman

From: Crazy Jane Smith <crazyjane666@live.co.uk>
To: Jimmy "Jug" Walters <JUGgernaut37@yahoo.com>
Date: Tuesday, Dec 11, 2012 at 10:32 AM
Subject: Waiting on the apocalypse… so far nothing!

Hey Jimmy baby!

Here we are, it's the Mayans' D-Day and so far nothing has happened, not even a minor earthquake or a neighbor trying to eat my face off. Frankly I've been more than a little underwhelmed by the whole situation. I thought I'd go out in an interesting way, you know, so I can at least show off when I get to the Pearly Gates and all that jazz, but no such luck for me. It's still early in the morning, though, maybe we'll get lucky and later tonight the cool stuff will start happening.

I can already see you pulling your face, but it's so much fun to make you question my sanity sometimes.

Other than that, I hope to be with you again sooner rather than later. I just need to get this contractual work done, but then I'm on a plane back to you… (Just remind me not to take Egypt Air, those birds fall out of the sky for nothing. Believe me; that's one of the wrecks I'm currently investigating, and so far the main culprit is none other than bird shit against the window.)

I love you, Jim-Jim

Jane <3

From: Jimmy "Jug" Walters <JUGgernaut37@yahoo.com>
To: Crazy Jane Smith <crazyjane666@live.co.uk>
Date: Wednesday, Dec 12, 2012 at 02:47 AM
Subject: Re: Waiting on the apocalypse… so far nothing!

No shit, was that tonight? Ha! Hell, baby I got so blasted I wouldn't have even known if a comet hit me on my head. Guess none did though, huh? However, that face-eating thing sounds okay to me. There were some punks at the bar I wouldn't have minded going all cannibal on.

Who knows, though, there's still time for this world to get fucked, and hell, I'd love to be the one doing the fucking. Haha. Yeah, well, that's the booze. I better sleep. Everything was spinning more than usual on the way home.

Before I go, let me tell you about this guy. This one guy I saw. Hell, I'm drunk. But this one guy had me laughing. I passed him on the sidewalk, and he was walking all tilted forward like he was about to bust into a run, but never did. Like he was falling forward, but always just catching himself before going nose to pavement! Yeah, anyway. Looked funny. Damn funny.

Get finished with that work, baby. Get finished soon.

Love you,

Jug.

From: Crazy Jane Smith <crazyjane666@live.co.uk>
To: Jimmy "Jug" Walters <JUGgernaut37@yahoo.com>
Date: Wednesday, Dec 12, 2012 at 08:55 AM
Subject: RE: Waiting on the apocalypse… so far nothing!

Whoops, that's me for you, always making mistakes with the date. I think it's actually the 21st that the shit is supposed to hit the fan, which means there's still hope for the whole "eat my face off ye darn zombies." I'm getting too British for my own liking.

And Mr. Walters, you better not think of getting too happy with me not being there. The whole "I slipped and landed on top of her naked" routine may have worked with your ex, but not with me. Get a grip on yourself, all right?

That guy sounds like he would have made some brain stew from you if you gave him the chance. Granted, things have been a little strange on this side of the pond too… people have been acting weird lately. Ugh, I hate people. Just give me some proper metal to puzzle together and I'm happy, which brings me to the other weird things which have been going on.

I don't know if you heard over the news, but last night two more birds came down. I've been reassigned to that wreck, but the only information I've been given in regards to it is that the pilot went a bit crazy…

I've been thinking that maybe you should come over and be with me? I miss you.

Love you babes,

Jane <3

From: Jimmy "Jug" Walters <JUGgernaut37@yahoo.com>
To: Crazy Jane Smith <crazyjane666@live.co.uk>
Date: Wednesday, Dec 12, 2012 at 13:11 PM
Subject: Sorry baby.

My damn head is killing me. Sorry about that last e-mail. Oofa! I know I shouldn't be out drinking like that during the week, but clients, ya know? Seems the easy sales are always the ones that require some booze and (sorry, sorry, sorry) strippers.

Oh, shit. You know that guy!? The one I mentioned? He musta been pretty messed up or something, but early this morning sirens woke me up. I stumbled out onto the sidewalk and saw that "I'm about to bust into a run" dude. Turns out he did eventually topple over. He toppled over right in front of a car.

Poor bugger (how's that for British? Haha).

That's some crazy shit about the planes going down. And what do you mean about the pilots? Were they drunk or something? I hope this doesn't mean you'll be gone longer. I wish I could come see you, travel with you. I know it was always the plan, but the job, Janey. I can't up and leave. You know that. Not yet anyway. Soon though.

I promise.

-Jug

From: Crazy Jane Smith <crazyjane666@live.co.uk>
To: Jimmy "Jug" Walters <JUGgernaut37@yahoo.com>
Date: Thursday, Dec 13, 2012 at 1:12 AM
Subject: RE: Sorry baby.

    Sorry I couldn't get to the computer earlier, Jim-Jim, there's been some supernatural nonsense going on here. You know how I told you about the planes and the pilots and stuff? Apparently there was a message on the black box (that thing that basically records the flight and whatnot? I told you about those things once, remember?) and the message was:

    "Forgive me father for doubting in you. I'll do as you ask."

    Suddenly you just hear the co-pilot screaming and the plane losing control, before BOOM! I tell you, baby, it was some scary-ass stuff that makes no sense. Worst of all, these pilots get screened regularly for mental fitness.

    I don't know how long I'll be here anymore. There are some other people on their way to make sure I didn't miss anything, but who knows how long they'll take to arrive.

    As for the guy you passed by… that's such a shame, darling, but even drinking and walking is dangerous these days. I'm just happy it wasn't you that stumbled into the street and got hit by a car. I tell you, babes, this world is turning to shit at a rapid pace. Just stay safe and don't go doing something I wouldn't do (scratch that. Don't do something that'll get you into too much trouble).

    How's work by the way? Is the boss still giving you crap?

    I love you, baby. So much. Be good and be safe for me…

    Kisses

    Jane <3

From: Jimmy "Jug" Walters <JUGgernaut37@yahoo.com>
To: Crazy Jane Smith <crazyjane666@live.co.uk>
Date: Thursday, Dec 13, 2012 at 18:31 PM
Subject: Nutjobs and maggots and plane crashes, oh my.

    Janey,

    Holy hell! That sounds like some serious crazy talk coming from the pilots. It can't be terrorists, right? I mean, it's the first thing I thought of, but god knows I'm not too bright about these things. I hope you've got the support you need to puzzle this thing out. Jesus, all those people dead at the whim of some nutjob pilot? What could he have meant, you think? It sounds religious to me, but, oh hell. I don't know.

And speaking of the world turning to shit, you ain't kidding. On the way to work there was a huge pileup. Ambulances and cops as far as the eye could see (and you know how the sight of cops gives me the shivers). People had to be dead. I was stuck in traffic for two hours! I'll have to check the news tonight.

Oh, one other thing. You know more about this stuff than me, but how long does it take for maggots to show up? It's just, you know yesterday afternoon, after I sent the last e-mail, I went out for some grub (boss gave me the day off after that bender, he's been okay lately), and there were some CDC people poking around where the drunk guy got hit. Now I *know* CDC don't normally clean up crime scenes, but there they were picking up these little squirmy things that were slithering around in the blood. Too soon for maggots, right? And wouldn't they normally be in the body or something?

I dunno, just thought I'd ask. Gave me the creeps, though. I was itching all the way to the store and lost my appetite anyway.

Jane, be careful out there. I don't want any raving pilots taking you hostage or anything like that.

-Jug

From: Crazy Jane Smith <crazyjane666@live.co.uk>
To: Jimmy "Jug" Walters <JUGgernaut37@yahoo.com>
Date: Friday, Dec 14, 2012 at 09:03 AM
Subject: Hack, slash, and dash…

Jug,

I want you to stay at home, don't go anywhere. Stock up on food and any other essentials today, tomorrow… just don't leave the house. You've seen the news, right?

Things aren't normal anymore, baby, it's all over the world. It's almost like a rapture… People are disappearing! I mean, Jim, there are like ten people unaccounted for from the plane wreck. There's not a single sign of them ever being on that plane! As for the maggots, I got to work this morning and the wreck was covered in maggots. Billions of fat, slimy worms… *shudders* That's not normal. Maggots don't act that way.

Pile-ups, plane crashes, ships sinking, the whole world is turning to crud. Jesus, baby… you need to see the chaos around here. It's actually safer for me to be at the hanger than at the flat I'm renting. I've decided (after I've cleaned up this mess with the maggots) to make up a bed in the locker room for me.

Just stay inside. Don't open the door for anyone you don't know and check in with me regularly, please?

If this is the rapture, then I'm fucked anyways… you know about my past and yeah… I know you're just as screwed as I am, but it would have been better if we could go out with a proper bang together. Go out like Bonnie and Clyde did. Unfortunately, that's not going to happen, so you and I will have to keep safe until this crap blows over. When it does, I'll be with you soon.

Stay safe, Jim. Love,

Jane. <3

P.S. The gun is hidden in the kitchen. Underneath the sink is a canister, hidden in the back of everything. If you need it, use it.

From: Jimmy "Jug" Walters <JUGgernaut37@yahoo.com>
To: Crazy Jane Smith <crazyjane666@live.co.uk>
Date: Friday, Dec 14, 2012 at 11:00 AM
Subject: RE: Hack, slash and dash…

I woke up to screaming on the street. The screams, they sounded like people were being burnt alive. That sound of hysterical insanity. Like animals. Howls of finality.

And it was right outside my window. Felt too close for comfort, made me think about bad, bad things. Yeah, if this is the rapture, well. Shit.

I went outside. I had to. There's nothing here, and if this is it, I wanted to be ready. I took the gun, and, baby, I always knew where it was. Have a couple of my own even. Sometimes, when I told you I was going off for a game of poker with the guys, really we were at the shooting range. Old habits die hard and all that.

But it's a good thing. A good thing I had guns. When I got outside, it wasn't long before… Things are bad, maybe worse than even you thought.

I killed someone. I had to. They weren't normal… They went crazy. I think those things, no, no they ain't maggots at all, are they? No. They were inside him. His skin, I could see it moving, like the worms were slithering around. He came at me. I panicked. I didn't want those things near me. Didn't want them *in* me. I shot him right in the face. Bugs came oozing out instead of blood.

I made it to the store okay, got supplies, food, gas, water, ammo. No more killing was needed.

When I got back though, the the man I shot was all worms. Just a pile of white, squirming, evil lying there on the sidewalk.

Is that what we're gonna be, Janey? Is that what happens to the ones left? You may have that crazy story for the Pearly Gates after all.

I wish you'd come home. Can't you just come home?

-Jug

From: Crazy Jane Smith <crazyjane666@live.co.uk>
To: Jimmy "Jug" Walters <JUGgernaut37@yahoo.com>
Date: Friday, Dec 14, 2012 at 18:23 PM
Subject: Dirty Harry

Oh my god, baby! That is horrible! Are you okay? Are you safe?

I DON'T LIKE THIS. Jim, I'm scared, I don't know what's going on… I don't want to turn to worms… but I don't want to disappear either. I just want to be in your arms, baby. I need it. It feels like I'm going insane and I don't know what to do anymore.

After my previous email, things got worse. I was outside real quick, taking a smoke break and suddenly I heard the wailing. It was horrid… Like you said, howls of finality. I was fortunate enough to be alone in the hanger at that point, and I locked up, made sure I was all right. But yeah, I wish I had a gun. How can I even think about being angry with you for killing someone if you were in danger? I'd have done, and probably will do, the same to survive.

Some way or another I'll get to you. There's an airplane here. It's small, but it might be okay. If things get too much I'll put those flying lessons to good use.

I don't want to die alone. I know we've had our ups and downs, but I'd rather be with you or die trying to get to you than just give up and die alone.

I'm so scared, Jimmy...

Love you always and forever

YOUR Janey <3

From: Jimmy "Jug" Walters <JUGgernaut37@yahoo.com>
To: Crazy Jane Smith <crazyjane666@live.co.uk>
Date: Saturday, Dec 15, 2012 at 07:00 AM
Subject: RE: Dirty Harry

I hope you're living up to your nickname, Crazy Jane. You'll have to be crazy to avoid going insane. Haha.

Do you have anyone there with you? Anyone to back you up if you need help? And weapons, anything you could use to bash someone's head in?

This plane idea makes me nervous. You say it's small? Does it hold enough fuel to get you here? And where would you land? Hell, I'm not trying to talk you out of it. I'm just worried.

The news is all over the place about the whole thing. Fox is saying it's the rapture (but you can just see the desperation on those pious fucks' faces that they didn't disappear off this rock yet). CNN is saying it's some kind of disease or else an infestation, which doesn't exactly explain the loads of people pulling a Houdini act. But hey, it's a bit easier to swallow I guess.

What are they saying over there? Anything? If this gets much worse, I'm predicting a media blackout, so says the great Nostradamus.

Well, now for the good news. I didn't have to go to work today. Pretty sweet, eh? Seriously though, things have gotten quiet. Haven't heard too many screams this morning, and I've got plenty of supplies here to ride this out for a while. Now don't you go making any snap decisions and come flying over here all half cocked. Things might calm down.

Who knows, maybe tomorrow the sun will rise and everything will be back to normal.

Be safe, speak soon.

-Jug

From: Crazy Jane Smith <crazyjane666@live.co.uk>
To: Jimmy "Jug" Walters <JUGgernaut37@yahoo.com>
Date: Saturday, Dec 15, 2012 at 13:00 PM
Subject: RE: Dirty Harry

You know me, Jim, if anything those fuckers should know better than to try anything with me. I have plenty of weapons here. Well they are makeshift weapons and all, but I can take care of myself. As for the rest, I'm alone, but that's good. I don't have to get emotionally involved with anyone and try to save anyone other than myself. It may sound selfish, but fuck it.

Yeah, as for the plane… that idea failed miserably. Firstly, I don't have enough fuel to get there, and secondly, there's a reason the thing was here in the first place, it's got a broken turbine. Don't worry though, I was just being desperate yesterday. I was scared.

You're asking me about the news? Dear, I'm stuck in a hanger. I don't have a T.V. here. All I have are the computers, and it's just the same thing over and over. I don't hear much. Disappearances, people dying, the worms, it's all the same… I do know that there's been scientists trying to figure out what caused it all, but I tell you, this is nothing more than a Biblical prophecy coming to life. At some point or another, those fucking monsters from Revelations will show face and then we're fucked. There's nothing we can do about it.

Reply soon.
Kisses
Jane

From: Jimmy "Jug" Walters <JUGgernaut37@yahoo.com>
To: Crazy Jane Smith <crazyjane666@live.co.uk>
Date: Sunday, Dec 16, 2012 at 11:01 AM
Subject: Time is running out

Jane,

I can't stay here much longer.

The situation has changed, and it's bad. Fucking awful if you want to know the truth.

The reason I didn't e-mail yesterday is because I noticed something strange happening out on the street. Remember how I said the guy I shot was all worms when I got back? Well, they stayed there all clumped together like that for a while. And you *know* those CDC assholes haven't been back around to clean up the mess this time. I figure they have a lot more on their minds at the moment.

Anyway, there were other people dead out there, from shootings, or just keeling over and dying. After a while they were all worms too. But that's not the bad part. The bad part is those maggots or whatever the hell they are, they started moving. Spreading out. Crawling along. It got so bad that the whole street looked like a mass of pulsating white.

It gets worse.

They've started climbing up the buildings. I don't know how long I have before they reach my floor, but I was never so happy to live sixteen stories up. The only silver lining here is that with all the maggots slithering up the buildings, there aren't many left on the ground.

I don't know if they can get in, not for sure, but my only chance might be to pack some gear and try to get to someplace safe. Only thing is, I haven't the foggiest idea of where that might be.

The TV hasn't been any help. The networks are all on the same news cycles now, claiming this is a "swarming phase" sort of like with locusts, and that they have some kind of insecticide they're going to spray. But come on, if this is all over the world they're gonna poison us right along with the bugs. And that doesn't even *begin* to explain the other strange shit that's going on.

The Guerrilla News website has some videos of people exploding with maggots. It's everywhere! Paris, Korea, the fucking Mojave and they're also reporting that what we're hearing on regular networks is pure bullshit. Do you think the people who "vanished" really just got eaten up by the bugs? Ugh, gives me the friggin' creeps.

So that's where I stand, baby. I'm not going yet. I'm still trying to puzzle this thing out before doing something supremely idiotic. But I don't have much time. Not much time at all.

I hope you're having a better time of it than me. Please, please, stay safe.

-Jug

From: Crazy Jane Smith <crazyjane666@live.co.uk>
To: Jimmy "Jug" Walters <JUGgernaut37@yahoo.com>
Date: Sunday, Dec 16, 2012 at 17:32 PM
Subject: RE: Time is running out

Jug,

I don't feel well…

It feels like my insides are being turned upside down and inside out, constantly. I'm stuck in the hanger's locker room. I had to seal myself shut in here and I can't get any medical assistance, believe me, I've tried. I rolled up some towels at the doors and windows to make sure nothing crawls inside, but I don't know how long it will hold. The odd one makes its way through every now and then… I've tried to make it as safe as possible, but I could only do so much. It's so cold here. This winter is so cold, Jim. It's a blizzard outside, but the maggots won't die! They keep on coming.

The food isn't inside the locker room either. I had to run and forgot the food. I forgot the food. How could I forget the food?

I sleep the whole day… What day is it today? I don't remember. Damn it I don't care! All I want to do is crawl up in a ball and disappear. Baby, disappear with me? Just put your arms around me and let's go away? Somewhere warm… Mauritius sounds so lovely right now. Will you disappear with me to Mauritius, baby? I think I have a new bathing suit waiting at home for me. I'll model it for you.

sigh

We had so many plans, Jimmy… marriage, a family, the white picket fence and a dog named Toby… I worry about why we took so long now. Why did we take so long? Why were we the way we were? We could have had it all, but we didn't. Why?

I don't feel well, angel. I think I should go to bed. Stay safe. Please.

Love you

Jane

From: Jimmy "Jug" Walters <JUGgernaut37@yahoo.com>
To: Crazy Jane Smith <crazyjane666@live.co.uk>
Date: Tuesday, Dec 18, 2012 at 04:07 AM
Subject: RE: Time is running out

    Jane, this is very, very important. Did any of the bugs get near you? Is it possible when you were sleeping that they crawled inside the room?

    Listen, if the cold isn't killing them, maybe heat will. If you have any source of fire, a lighter and an aerosol can, or gasoline, then use them, okay? Anything that you can burn a path through the bugs and get out, get anywhere but there. A secure room with some supplies, but it has to be airtight. No cracks or openings. I'm thinking of trying bank vaults, or hospital wards, or, shit, I don't know, maybe a medical lab or something?

    It's dark here, still early morning, but the noise woke me up. The sound of the bugs squirming up the building is driving me crazy. You ever get a tick on you? After you find one on you, you feel like they're all over you. You keep checking your clothes, sure you'll find one of those tiny bloodsuckers trying to burrow under your skin. You get all itchy and fidgety, and you can't get comfortable. That's how it is now, with those things out there. I feel like they're crawling all over me. I have to get out of here, and soon. Before sundown they were about a quarter of the way up. They'll probably be nearing the halfway point by dawn. If the ground is clear, I have to make a run. It's either try that or die here, waiting.

    E-mail me back as soon as possible. I'll take the laptop with me, but there's no telling what the power situation will be.

    Please be okay, Jane. And fight. You're Crazy Jane for Christ's sake!

Fight!

Jug.

From: Jimmy "Jug" Walters <JUGgernaut37@yahoo.com>
To: Crazy Jane Smith <crazyjane666@live.co.uk>
Date: Tuesday, Dec 18, 2012 at 07:15 AM
Subject: Where are you?

    Jane, I really hoped to hear from you by now. I messed up. I overslept and when I looked outside, the bugs were much farther up than I thought they'd be. They're only two stories away.

    I have to go.

    Where are you?

From: Jimmy "Jug" Walters <JUGgernaut37@yahoo.com>
To: Crazy Jane Smith <crazyjane666@live.co.uk>
Date: Tuesday, Dec 18, 2012 at 12:12 PM
Subject: Where are you?

    I'm in an alleyway a few blocks from the apartment. The maggots had been slithering their way into the building the whole time they were climbing up, so by the time I went to leave, the hallways and stairwells were filled with them. I had a lighter and spray can, cleared a path as best I could.

    I think I made it out okay. I think I'm good. I still felt all itchy like they were all over me, but it was all in my head. I think I'm fine. Funny thing is there are maggots out here on the street, but they aren't bothering with me. I got past fine. I just ducked into an alleyway to check the e-mail.

    Nothing from you though. I'll check in again soon.

    Jug

From: Jimmy "Jug" Walters <JUGgernaut37@yahoo.com>
To: Crazy Jane Smith <crazyjane666@live.co.uk>
Date: Tuesday, Dec 18, 2012 at 19:21 PM
Subject: Where are you?

    They're in me. I can feel the tin yfucks under mty skin. hurts. bursn like fire in my veins. I dont think ill know myself by morining and i guess youre in the same bpat baby, because you never repluied. ill always love you. always always awlwasy always.

God I messed everyting up. Always was you, should have done right by you, should hae been better.

maybe we'll see eachoteher soon. i hope so.

i really hope so.

your jug

From: Crazy Jane Smith <crazyjane666@live.co.uk>
To: Jimmy "Jug" Walters <JUGgernaut37@yahoo.com>
Date: Thursday, Dec 20, 2012 at 10:02 AM
Subject: RE: Where are you?

No, Jim, no! I'm on my way! Where are you? Baby, it was just a virus, please, I'm on my way. Hold on for me, Jim. Don't go without me, be strong. I'M ON MY WAY! I got a lift from one of the pilots that had been notified of my whereabouts, one of the other inspectors had told him where I was and what I was working on and he was sent by the government to take me back home, to safety... Baby, I'm coming home, just hold on for me, please?

I can't lose you. I'm sorry I was sick; I was knocked out by the virus, barely conscious. Please, Jim, for me, PLEASE be alright...

I love you so much.

Jane

From: Crazy Jane Smith <crazyjane666@live.co.uk>
To: Jimmy "Jug" Walters <JUGgernaut37@yahoo.com>
Date: Friday, Dec 21, 2012 at 12:02 PM
Subject: I can't find you!

Jug,

Let me know where you are, please? Just tell me where you are, I'll come get you. Please, Jimmy baby, don't do this to me. I've been home, and things are all right there, there aren't any maggots. The spray is working, it's killing all the bugs. It was nothing more than a well thought out terrorist attack... or that's what they say. Some of the people that went "missing" have come out of hiding. It doesn't explain the disappearances on the flight though, but their bodies could have easily been burned to a crisp in the initial explosion or eaten up by the bugs.

Come home, please, Jug. You need to come home for me now; you need to be all right for me. Please, please be all right.

I'm so worried…

Love you

Jane

From: Crazy Jane Smith <crazyjane666@live.co.uk>
To: Jimmy "Jug" Walters <JUGgernaut37@yahoo.com>
Date: Monday, Dec 24, 2012 at 21:44 PM
Subject: I'll be home soon baby…

My dearest Jim,

I cannot find you… I've searched high and low and you're gone. I found your cellphone a few blocks away, but no Jimmy. So now I'm writing you this letter… I know what happened; I know you're gone… I just… I don't know what I'm trying to achieve with this.

I look around the apartment and it's so empty. I keep turning around to see you walking through the door, shouting out: "Surprise! I made you worry, see." But it never happens. For days I've been waiting. Last night as I was falling asleep with your shirt clutched in my hands, just to smell you again, I could have sworn I heard your voice. I could have sworn I heard you say you love me and, Jimmy, it broke me apart because I know where you are. I can't be surrounded with all of you and not have you here. It's impossible.

I'm coming home, baby. I'm coming home to you now. I don't want to live alone when you were my world. You and your twisted sense of humor were my existence… you and your love were my reason for everything.

I've been drinking plenty of wine, but it's because I need strength and stupidity to do this now. A simple cut to the wrist and a little while later I'll be in your arms again. Don't worry, I'm making sure that I don't do it wrong. There's going to be a lot of painkillers involved.

You said you'd be alright, you weren't. I wasn't strong enough, but now I will be. I'm coming home to you, Jim Walters. We won't be apart again. Never ever again…

I love you with every part of my being, for all of eternity.
Your Jane <3

Editor Biography

MONIQUE SNYMAN lives in Pretoria, South Africa with an adorable Chihuahua that keeps her company, and a bloodthirsty lawyer who keeps her sane. She is a full-time author, part-time editor, and in-between reviewer of all things entertaining. Her short fiction has been published in a number of anthologies and the first two books in her fantasy series will be available through Rainstorm Press later this year. Visit www.charmingincantations.com/blog.

Author Biographies

JOHN EDWARD BETANCOURT was born and raised in Colorado. He decided he could no longer ignore the call of writing, and plunged into the craft feet first. In addition to writing short stories, John blogs regularly at www.girlsofgeek12.com, writes webisode scripts for *Denver Comic Con* and *StarFest*, is putting the finishing touches on his debut novel and recently had his first motion picture screenplay optioned by a film production company. In his spare time, John enjoys a quiet night at home with his beagle and his lovely girlfriend, Michelle.

JOSHUA BROWN grew up in the Midwest, and enjoyed the inspirations of his mother and father along with a wide range of books, films, and music. He has written stories for many years, including a fantasy-adventure series in the works to become e-books, as well as poems, songs, and other short stories. Josh is a film producer and director, focusing on both comedy and horror, with works including *Right in the Cloaca!* and *Escape from the Dead*.

KATIE CORD is a writer/publisher by day, nurse by night. She is the proud mother of three dogs and a precious cat, owner of Evil Girlfriend Media, and lover of all things zombie. Katie would not have made it through junior high without authors like Ira Levin, Stephen King, Ray Bradbury, and others. She currently lives in Washington State. Read more about Katie at www.katiecord.com.

PATRICK D'ORAZIO resides in southwestern Ohio with his wife, Michele, children Alexandra and Zachary, and two spastic dogs. He has dipped his toes into a variety of genres. His apocalyptic series dubbed The *Dark Trilogy* has been re-released with substantial new content by Permuted Press. Patrick is presently working on the fourth book in this saga, and plans on finishing the series with a fifth and final book. You can see what Patrick is up to via his website at www.patrickdorazio.com.

KRISCINDA LEE EVERITT is a writer with work published by Permuted Press and Postscripts to Darkness. She is also an editor currently working for Nightscape Press. She lives with her husband in Butler, Pa, along with one black cat, and two plush Spooks. Check out her blog at: www.kriscindaleeeveritt.wordpress.com.

KRIS FREESTONE is a native of Las Vegas with fantastical plans to take over Antarctica. She appreciates fine wine and dancing with her penguin. She can be found with some secret plans online at www.vikingessa.wordpress.com.

RANDY HENDERSON'S fiction has been spotted frolicking in places like Escape Pod, Realms of Fantasy, Every Day Fiction, and anthologies. He is a Clarion West graduate, a relapsed sarcasm addict, and a milkshake connoisseur who transmits suspiciously delicious words into the ether from his secret lair in Kingston, Washington. Blog: www.randy-henderson.com.

PAUL S. HUGGINS hails from the United Kingdom within the witchcraft rich county of Suffolk, and resides there with his wife, two daughters, and a familiar called 'George'. His introduction to the genre derived from being scared to death at an early age by a movie called *Dawn of the Dead*. It changed his whole opinion on the apocalypse, and now he thinks, when, not if! With numerous short stories published and a self-published novel *Beyond Isaiah*, Paul would say zombies are in his blood.

KATIE JONES lives in Australia and spends her working days caring for people with disabilities. She also enjoys writing and reading whenever possible. Facebook.com/MissKate.

MICHELLE KILMER is a writer and designer living in Seattle, WA. She is the author of *When the Dead*, and co-author of *The Spread: A Zombie Short Story Collection*, which she wrote with her twin sister. She enjoys playing video games, designing websites, singing and playing guitar, sewing, or dressing up in "full gore" to attend zombie events. Michelle lives with her husband, an attack hamster, and a fear of the dark. Facebook.com/whenthedead.

KEN MACGREGOR's stories have appeared in several speculative fiction anthologies, including *A Quick Bite of Flesh*, *The Dead Sea*, *Horrific History*, *Slaughter House: The Serial Killer Edition, vol. 3* and *Barnyard Horror*. His work has also appeared in magazines and podcasts. Ken is a member in good standing of The Great Lakes Association of Horror Writers. He lives in Ypsilanti, Michigan with his wife, Liz and their children Gabriel and Maggie. Facebook.com/Ken MacGregor - Author.

ANTHONY J. RAPINO is a horror writer with work published in *Black Ink Horror, On Spec, Arcane,* as well as a multitude of other publications. His first novel, *Soundtrack to the End of the World,* is available via Bad Moon Books in paperback and eBook formats. On weekends, he plants platitudes in sandy soil.

MICHELE ROGER is a horror author and harpist living in Detroit. When she isn't harvesting the fears of her readership, you can find her cooking for her children, drinking wine with her good friends and when all else fails, entertaining the darker side of the city. For more on Michele: www.micheleroger.com.

MR. AND MRS. KILLION SLADE are a married writing team who met in Second Life and virtually enjoy everything. Killion's anthology short stories are found at Rainstorm Press, Draconian Publishing, The Danse Macabre, Static Movement, and Sirens Call Publications. Mrs. Slade was honored as 2012 Wicked Women Writer for the *Children of Angels* short story podcast. Killion has found a new love of turning the written word into a podcast auralgasm. For current projects visit www.killionslade.com.

JAY WILBURN writes horror and speculative fiction from his home on the sunny coast of South Carolina. He appears in *Best Horror of the Year volume 5* with editor Ellen Datlow. Follow his many dark thoughts at www.JayWilburn.com.

DANA WRIGHT is a long time book fiend who used to hide in her room as a child to write odd stories and read Anne Rice novels. Her love of monsters began when she found Halloween cutouts of Dracula and his bride, and much to the worry of her parents, left them up on her bedroom wall year around. Dana writes short horror stories and is working on her two YA novels. She lives with several children of the furry variety and her husband in Texas. She is a contributing author to the *Siren's Call*

Magazine: Women in Horror edition, *Shifters*, and *Wonderstruck* anthologies. Blog: www.danasdarkside.blogspot.com

TOM D. WRIGHT lives in the Seattle area with his wife and a small pack of dogs. He primarily writes Sci-Fi tales that range from the near future to distant times and places. To support his obsessive writing habit, he works for a technology company in Seattle (not Microsoft) in communications technology. With an MA degree in Psychology, when someone calls to say their phone or video system isn't working, he can genuinely say, "Yes, I understand, and how does that make you feel?" Tom is currently putting the finishing touches on two novels.

MATT YOUNGMARK and **DAWN MARIE PARES** live in Seattle, in a neighborhood that has a church, a bar and/or a coffee shop every twenty feet. They enjoy board games, books and beer. Matt is working on his third book, and Dawn Marie has written hundreds of stories featuring sweet makeouts. "What I Was There For" is their first collaboration. For more adventures of Magnifica and the Liberty Patrol (in choose-your-own-adventure format!) see *Thrusts of Justice* from Chooseomatic Books.

EVIL GIRLFRIEND MEDIA

WWW.EVILGIRLFRIENDMEDIA.COM

Look for the big red heart to find new favorites in the Sci-Fi, Fantasy and Horror genres!

AVAILABLE NOW IN EBOOK AND PRINT:

The Heart-Shaped Emblor
by Alaina Ewing

Witches, Stitches & Bitches
A Three Little Words anthology

COMING SOON:

Stamps, Vamps & Tramps
A Three Little Words anthology
JANUARY 3, 2014

Made in the USA
Charleston, SC
23 February 2014